ONE EYE OPEN

Paul Finch

ORION

First published in Great Britain in 2020 by Orion Fiction,
an imprint of The Orion Publishing Group Ltd.,
Carmelite House, 50 Victoria Embankment
London EC4Y 0DZ

An Hachette UK Company

1 3 5 7 9 10 8 6 4 2

Copyright © Paul Finch 2020

A CIP catalogue record for this book is
available from the British Library.

ISBN (Paperback) 978 1 4091 8401 0
ISBN (eBook) 978 1 4091 8402 7

Typeset at The Spartan Press Ltd,
Lymington, Hants

Printed and bound in Great Britain by Clays Ltd,
Elcograf S.p.A.

MIX
Paper from
responsible sources
FSC® C104740

www.orionbooks.co.uk

For my wife, Catherine, and my children,
Eleanor (and her husband Sam), and Harry,
who make life so much more fun

Part One

I

6 January (Monday)

Blood.

Blood everywhere.

A virtual explosion of it. Bits of hair in it, bits of glass. The vile stuff thick and clotting, sticky rather than runny but spattered in every direction.

It was the very last thing Alan had anticipated when he'd set out that morning, despite his depressed state. He doubted there was any part of the calendar more drab or colourless than the first few days following Christmas and New Year. As he walked Angus across the meadow towards the line of leafless woods, the yellowed grass beneath his boots was crunchy with frost, the sky a lid of concrete. The dog was happy enough, of course. A springer spaniel, four years old but heavier set than he ought to be, he romped ahead, stopping every few yards to sniff, his tail wafting so hard that his bottom wagged in sync with it.

Alan didn't get to see enough of Angus. But that was the way of it when you were away at university. That was also the reason for Angus's weight gain. It wasn't unsightly as such, not yet. But each time Alan came home for the holidays, the dog was bigger around the belly and backside. It was unavoidable, he supposed, with only his mum to take the little fella out. Crippled by arthritis, the best she could manage these days was to let him out through the back door.

Perhaps that was another reason why Alan ought to kick uni.

He sighed, scrubbing at his hair. Ahead of him, the outer line of trees was less than fifty yards off. In the milky morning light, they were dank, skeletal.

He wasn't enjoying the course, plus he was sharing a flat with someone who, when he'd interacted with him in the students' bar, had been one of the good guys, but who once you got up close and personal with was an irritating oaf.

But he could have lived even with that, he supposed, if it hadn't been for the cash issue. Alan had his student loan and his student grant, so his fees and his rent were taken care of, but for everything else, for the fun stuff, he had nothing in the kitty. Christ, he was sick of being broke.

His head snapped up. It suddenly struck him that Angus wasn't here anymore.

He looked around. The meadow was empty. Which left the woods some twenty yards to his right. Ordinarily, this wouldn't be a problem. What gallivanting pooch could resist snuffling around in the trees? What harm could it do? Not much, except that not too far back in the woods was the A12, the high-speed dual carriageway connecting Ipswich to Colchester.

'Angus!' Alan shouted. 'Where are you, boy?'

No friendly yelp echoed in response.

'*Angus!*'

Throughout the holidays, Alan had walked Angus across this meadow and along the edge of the woods, and though the dog had ducked in and out of the trees, he'd never once shown an inclination to go deeper than that. But even if he had, it still wasn't worth panicking; yes, the A12 was accessible – there was no fence – but the high-speed road sat atop a steep embankment, which itself was deep in dead but thickly enmeshed vegetation. Most likely, the dog wouldn't even try to get up there.

But wherever he was, he wasn't *here*.

'Angus?' Alan ventured into the trees. The undergrowth was knee-deep, but dead and brittle. It crackled and crunched as he waded through it. 'Angus?' He tried to keep the unease from his voice, but where was the damn brute? *'Angus!'*

He moved quicker now, veering towards the A12, which at last was becoming visible, its bracken-clad slope materialising through the trees like a distant rampart. Alan heard again his late father's warning words.

'He's a lively one. So keep him on the lead when you walk him across the fields … that road's closer than you think.'

Without warning, the dog scuttled out from the foliage.

As always, he seemed hugely pleased with himself. His big, slobbery maw had curved into a canine grin as he tried to hang onto the latest treasure he'd found.

Alan slid to a halt, laughing with relief.

And then had to look closer.

The spaniel was dabbled with mud and hung with thorns, leaves and fragments of twig. Nothing unusual about that. It was the treasure he was carrying.

Alan had initially considered it 'treasure' because that was how the dog would regard it. Whatever it was – a knobbly branch, a lost tennis ball or discarded toy – they'd all proved so priceless to Angus in the past that he'd energetically ducked and dived to resist Alan's efforts to wrest them loose; there was no game he liked better.

The big difference this time was that it *was* treasure.

'Okay ... sit, yeah?' Alan said. '*Sit!*'

He hunkered down, enforcing the command with stern body language.

Angus obeyed, flopping onto his belly, eyes bright, offering only token resistance when Alan tried to work the object free from his jaws.

Alan hadn't been mistaken, and he was stunned. He glanced up, wondering which way Angus had come from, locking on a mass of holly to his left. Venturing forward, he pushed the spikey boughs apart. Eager to take point, Angus shoved his way past. Alan wasn't sure what he'd expected to find on the other side. Perhaps a half-dug pit that someone had given up on. Maybe a burst-open hessian sack.

But not this.

Not in the middle of the woods.

Not a vehicle ... even if it was mangled, twisted and wedged against a tree trunk, the force of which impact had caused the tree to splinter across the middle and sag part-way over.

Alan didn't think he'd ever seen a car as comprehensively smashed: concertinaed bodywork, an imploded windscreen, a crumpled bonnet from beneath which the engine had all but disgorged itself, its vital fluids leaking from a spaghetti-like tangle of melted, hissing tubes.

Finally, he took in the bodies.

Two, he thought dazedly. One on either side. Each hanging upside down from its respective doorway.

And blood. *That* blood, which seemed to be literally everywhere.

2

6 January (Monday)

Lynda understood why her kids were less than motivated that first morning of the spring term. It was 7.30 when the alarm went off, but the meagre light penetrating the bedroom was so dull that she could only locate the clock on the dresser because of its glowing digits. The central heating had been on half an hour, but the room was still chilly.

Don mumbled something, a motionless hump in the dimness.

'Coming down for breakfast?' Lynda asked, pulling a dressing gown over her nightie.

He didn't reply, which was the usual. She checked the radiator with her fingertips before heading out and trekking along the landing, banging first on Daniella's bedroom door. 'Come on, miss... back to school. Start getting ready.'

A muffled groan responded.

Charlie's door was already open. Glancing in across the pile of new Christmas toys, Lynda found her diminutive six-year-old already sitting up in bed, his blond hair ruffled. He regarded her with a bleak expression. And coughed. Three times in a row.

'The holiday TV's over, Charlie,' Lynda said. 'What're you going to do all day, sit watching quiz shows?'

'I might learn something.' His voice was feeble, purposely

pained. 'Grandpa Jack says you can learn things from quiz shows.'

'You'll learn everything you need to at school.'

Downstairs, Lynda hit the lights and pulled the curtains open in the living room. Outside, a pale, bloodless dawn was filtering across the estate. She used the remote to switch the satellite on, jumping to *Nicktoons*. On the way through the dining room to the kitchen, she gazed despairingly at the dining table, which was buried under a deluge of notebooks, scribbled paperwork and mugs of half-drunk coffee. In the midst of the mess, Don's laptop was still plugged in, despite her having raised repeated concerns about his habit of leaving gadgets on to charge up overnight.

She flipped the kettle on, threw some bread into the toaster and, digging the iPhone from her dressing gown pocket, checked her messages. Some twelve minutes later, having drunk her coffee and eaten her toast, Lynda stumped back to the bottom of the stairs and called Daniella and Charlie again.

'I have to go to work,' she added loudly. 'And you know your dad's too busy to take you. If you don't come down now, you'll have to walk ... and it's miserable as sin out there.'

She was preparing two bowls of cereal when Daniella appeared, looking as uncomfortable as possible to be back in her school uniform. Charlie entered the lounge a short time after, seeming groggy, still attempting to affect ill health.

'You shouldn't say things like that,' Daniella said, eyes locked on the TV screen as she munched her flakes. 'That we'll have to walk to school. It's not even light outside yet.'

'It's light enough,' Lynda replied.

'You know it wouldn't be safe for us. You're a police lady.

You should know that better than anyone. And it's cold too. We might not just get murdered. We might freeze.'

Before Lynda could respond, a text buzzed in her dressing gown pocket. She saw that it was from Clive Atkins.

Call me when you're up. It's important.

She headed for the hall. 'Eat up, you two. And then brush your hair and make sure you've got everything you need.' On her way upstairs, she phoned Clive.

'It's after eight,' she said. 'Why would you think I wouldn't be up? I've got two kids to get ready for school.'

'Yeah, sorry,' he replied. Muffled traffic hummed in the background. 'Holidays are over, aren't they?'

She entered the bedroom. 'When did I last have a lie-in, anyway?'

Her young DC could be annoyingly priggish. It wasn't that he was deliberately offensive, but he was so precise and correct in his behaviour at work that he sometimes took it as read that no one else ever was.

'Sorry about that ... Look, don't come to the office.'

'Why not?' she asked, seeing that Don was now seated upright in bed, his hair a mop as he rubbed at the back of his neck.

'We've copped for a job. And it's a big one.'

Lynda put him on speaker, and propped the phone on the dresser, as she slung her gown and nightie onto the bed and grabbed some underwear from the drawers. 'Tell me.'

'There was a smash on the A12 last night. Only one vehicle involved as far as we can tell, but unusual circs. Rachel wants us over there straight away.'

'Are we talking critical incident?'

'Not yet.'

'Not *yet*?'

'We've got two seriously injured, male and female. Alive at present, though unconscious. It could still turn into a double-fatal.'

Lynda had already climbed into her jeans. She pulled on a T-shirt and sweater and groped around in the half-light for her lace-up boots. 'Where is it?'

'Four miles north of the A120, southbound. You won't be able to miss it.'

'You there now?'

'Almost. I've got you a radio and signed you on.'

'Okay. Just hold the fort. I'll be with you in twenty.'

'Wilco.' He cut the call at his end.

'So, *I* don't get a lie-in this morning, either?' Don grunted.

Lynda tied her laces, before standing up and moving to the wardrobe. 'Do you need one?'

There was no immediate response. She glanced around as she put her anorak on.

'What I need is a break.' He didn't bother looking round as he padded naked into the en suite.

Despite his forty years, he was still tall, lean and in relatively good shape, his bare bottom tight and round. It might have been an erotic sight in any other circumstance, but he'd only taken to going to bed nude recently because he sweated so much when he was asleep. It had reached a stage where he was getting through several pairs of shorts a night. The reason, the doctor said, was stress. But then that was always the reason with Don. It had been the same during his final months with Major Investigations. The problem had subsided a little after he'd accepted the medical retirement package. But now, two years on, he was still unable to sell *Nick 'Em*, his warts-and-all exposé of life at the sharp end of British policing, and his presence in society was fast receding from view (in Don's mind, at least).

'You go, it's all right.' He stood in front of the sink, gazing at his unshaved reflection. 'I'll drop them off.'

Lynda checked that her gloves were in her anorak pockets, before moving to the bathroom door. 'It'll happen, Don.'

'In that case, everything'll be fine, won't it?' he said.

He didn't bother looking round at her.

3

6 January (Monday)

Lynda had turned thirty-six two months ago, but didn't think the years, or her two pregnancies, had been cruel. Her shoulder-length brown hair was still thick and lush, she hadn't wrinkled up very much yet, and if she wasn't naturally slim anymore, she was at least trim – the result of punishing sessions in the gym whenever she could find the time.

She'd been an officer with Essex Police for sixteen years now. The first two she'd spent in uniform, before joining CID in 2005, where she'd met and been swept off her feet by the handsome, debonair Detective Sergeant Don Hagen. Once they'd become involved, they'd moved to separate subdivisions so as not to let their feelings for each other get in the way of work. It had been a good plan, their courtship and 2006 marriage passing off without a hitch. In 2007, when Lynda returned from maternity leave, having given birth to Daniella, she'd remained a detective – in fact she was now a detective sergeant herself – but had accepted reassignment to the Essex Roads Policing Division, in other words 'Traffic', specifically the SCIU, or Serious Collision Investigation Unit, so that she could work nine-till-five, Monday-to-Friday.

Her phone rang, interrupting her thoughts.

'It's me,' Clive said via the hands-free, HGVs rumbling past him. He had to shout to be heard. 'How are you doing?'

'I'm stuck in a jam on a backroad between Lawford and Dedham,' Lynda said. 'Presumably this is because you've closed off the A12 southbound?'

'Correct. There's a diversion along the B1029.'

Lynda was more than a little irritated, but she supposed that even had he warned her there'd be traffic chaos all the way in, there was no easy route around it, even by activating the blues and twos wired into her Qashqai's exterior lighting system, which she'd already done.

'Listen, Clive … we can't close the A12 all day.'

'I agree. Especially as I'm here now, and it doesn't look as if there was any obvious collision on the road itself.'

That puzzled her. 'So, what exactly have we got?'

'Beige Ford Mondeo, 2-litre. Looks as if it came off the dual carriageway at high speed – *extraordinary* speed, I reckon. The side barrier's been flattened like cardboard. Then it went down the slope into the woods on the east side of the road. No trace of any other vehicle involved. Not yet. The sooner we get Aziz on the plot, the better.'

Aziz Khan, an ex-Traffic man of thirty years' experience in his own right, was now their resident Forensic Collision Investigator and an expert in vehicular accident reconstruction. He ought to be arriving soon, though doubtless he too was stuck in the gridlock of cars.

'What about the two casualties?' Lynda asked.

'Male and female,' Clive said. 'Both in their mid-thirties, I'd say. Unidentified so far. Both removed to Colchester General with severe head injuries. They were out cold when the ambulance arrived and remained that way even when the paramedics were carting them up the slope – and that was a job and a half, I'll tell you.'

'What do you mean unidentified?'

'Well ... they were lacking any documentation. No wallets or purses containing credit cards, driving licences or whatever. No handbag. Didn't even have mobile phones on them, except for a throwaway cheapie.'

'That's a bit odd, isn't it?'

'There's odder stuff, but ...' He was distracted by someone talking to him. 'Yeah, I'll come in a sec,' he said. 'You still there, Lynda?'

'What about the vehicle registration? Can't you ID them that way?'

'Like I say, there's odd stuff here. I'll bring you up to speed when you arrive. How long do you think you'll be?'

Lynda glanced at the clock on her dash. 'ETA ten.'

Even on a dreary January morning, Detective Constable Clive Atkins managed to look smart. He was ten years younger than Lynda, and a tall guy of mixed-race origin, handsome, and always clean-shaven. His suits and ties hung well on him even with a heavy, hi-vis POLICE jacket worn over the top.

Lynda pulled on her own jacket as she approached along the blacktop. Navigating the standing jams of traffic on the country lanes between here and Manningtree had taken forty minutes when it should have taken ten, even with her lightshow activated. When she'd reached the A12, she'd cut north along the southbound carriageway, this section now empty, of course, parking beyond the incident tape, next to Clive Atkins' grey Peugeot 308, just short of the designated control vehicle, a Traffic Range Rover. This was unmanned but still occupied the middle of the two-lane carriageway, its beacon swirling.

'There're going to be a lot of upset commuters,' Lynda said, accepting a radio and pulling on her gloves. The sun was aloft, but no more than a dim radiance amid clouds the colour of dishwater. The frost along the verges had melted, but the air was piercingly cold.

'Rachel's been on to Chief Superintendent Templeton,' Clive replied, falling into step alongside her. 'We've got till twelve noon. After that, he wants to review.'

'No pressure then. Who's Road Scene Manager?'

'Gina Tubbs. She was first on the scene and recommended the case for investigation.'

Lynda nodded. Traffic Sergeant Gina Tubbs was usually on the money with these things.

They walked north along the southbound. Beyond the central barrier, northbound vehicles moved freely, though cars slowed as they passed. This section of the A12 passed through open countryside. It was also elevated at this point, with low-lying fields, meadows and woodland on either side of it.

'Like I say, no obvious sign there was a collision on the road,' Clive said.

A point came up on their right where a portion of the roadside barrier, perhaps thirty feet or so, had vanished, and now was replaced by a taut line of incident tape. Gina Tubbs stood to one side, huddled under her hi-vis slicker, her white TRAFFIC hat tilted down as she scribbled on a pad. Beyond the missing barrier, Lynda saw a tangle of splintered shrubs and saplings.

'The accident seems to have occurred last night,' Clive

added. 'Which I presume is why no one reported it until this morning.'

'Who *did* report it?' Lynda asked.

'Some local guy. He was walking his dog.'

'What time was that?'

'Not long after seven.'

'Only two people on board the Mondeo?'

'Yeah. The bloke was driving, the girl riding.'

'Both still unconscious?'

'That's the last word from the hospital. Being prepped for surgery as we speak.'

'Did the paramedics give any indication how bad they were?'

'Sounds like the female's got a severe skull trauma. We could be close to losing her. The male ...?' Clive shrugged.

Lynda turned, checking back across the whole breadth of the road. Normally, even if there'd been only a minor collision, its surface would be scattered with fragments of glass and splintered alloy. But there was nothing obvious. She turned back to the Road Scene Manager. 'Morning, Gina.'

'Lynda,' Tubbs replied.

'Your lot are going to have a busy day, I think.'

'Tell me about it. We've already got queues on B-roads that most people didn't even know existed till this morning.'

Lynda approached the tape. Two strips of the grass verge underneath the barrier had been churned to black pulp. Snapped struts were all that remained of the barrier itself. The undergrowth behind had been pulverised: smaller trees smashed and bushes uprooted. She leaned forward to gaze down a sloping trail of such destruction, which was further defined by strips of fluttering incident tape tied between the trees on either side.

'That's Little Crickledon Wood, down there,' Clive said. 'It's only a coppice really. Runs along the bottom of the embankment for a couple of miles.'

At the far end of the damage trail, perhaps twenty feet below their position, but a good thirty yards from the foot of the embankment, Lynda could just about distinguish the battered wreck of a beige vehicle glinting through the devastated foliage.

She glanced back at the road. 'Am I right in thinking there's a distinct absence of skid marks here?'

'That struck me too,' Clive replied.

'And me,' Tubbs said.

'So, they didn't try to brake?' Lynda asked.

Clive shrugged again.

'Checked for traces of oil on the road?' she wondered.

'No sign of it from a cursory exam.'

'Ice?'

'It got down to minus three last night,' Tubbs said. 'But even if they hit black ice, you'd still think they'd have tried to brake.'

Lynda walked the length of the shattered barrier. Clive followed. Behind them, Tubbs resumed her writing.

'Attempted suicide?' Lynda suggested.

Clive was non-committal. 'We've seen it before, but … it'd be quite a way to go, with no certainty you'd go quickly or even at all. Plus, it's difficult to imagine *two* of them wanting to give it a whirl.'

She mused. 'Maybe it was only the driver who wanted to end it. And the poor passenger got taken along for the ride.'

Clive grimaced.

They straddled the barrier on the right side of the tape, and commenced clambering downhill, keeping clear of the path of destruction, but blundering from tree to tree just to stay upright.

'What's this other thing you wanted to tell me, anyway?' Lynda said, as they arrived on the flat. 'Concerning the IDs, or lack thereof.'

'Oh,' Clive replied, 'the car was running on dummy plates.'

She glanced back at him. 'Come again?'

He checked his pocket book. 'That index, Oscar-Sierra-nine-six-one-Hotel-Uniform-Bravo, is a professionally made duplicate. I ran it straight away. Belongs to an identical vehicle currently in the ownership of Mr Harold Ball in Bournemouth.'

'This Mondeo is a clone?'

'Seems like it.'

Lynda pushed through a few tangles of desiccated undergrowth. The wreck lay in front of them, encircled by an extra cordon of tape. The car had been scrunched out of shape by the front-end impact on a mature sycamore, which had split crosswise and half toppled onto the Mondeo's roof, compressing it downward. The engine hung out in pieces from under the bonnet. Every window had gone, and what she could see of the interior was crammed with shattered branches. All four doors hung buckled and twisted, having burst open on impact. The closest of the front two was the driver's door; congealed blood was much in evidence, streaking the door inside and out, spattering what she could see of the car's interior.

Another Traffic officer, Tim Philbin, a burly guy in his early thirties, with a dense brown beard and thick, horn-rimmed glasses, stood close by with a clipboard. He nodded to them, made a note on his log and offered it for them to sign. They both complied, before pulling their woollen gloves off and replacing them with latex disposables. Lynda walked around the cordon's exterior.

'This is definitely *not* Harold Ball's car?' she asked.

'Definitely not,' Clive confirmed. 'He's a retired gent and his car's currently sitting in his garage. He was good enough to show the local divisional lad who went around to check.'

On the other side of the car, the passenger door was equally stained with dried blood, as was the dashboard when Lynda leaned over the tape.

'We haven't gone over it in close-up yet,' Clive said. 'But I'd like to bet the ID number's been changed.'

Lynda nodded. 'So, we're talking chop–shop ... or something similar?'

'Seems possible.'

'How intriguing.'

'There's also *this*.' Clive signalled to Philbin, who approached and offered something to Lynda. It was a transparent plastic evidence sack containing what looked like a bundle of £20 notes bound with elastic bands. 'This was found in the vicinity of the wreck,' Clive added.

'Specifically, where?'

'We don't know. The guy who was walking his dog...' Clive checked his notes again. 'Name's Alan Langton. His dog found it. The dog was already running around with the money in its mouth when Langton got here.'

'I assume we've not counted it?'

'Thought I'd leave that to Forensics. But if they're all twenties, I reckon there's at least a thousand quid there.'

Lynda pondered that as she wandered around outside the cordon, eyes glued to the ground. She followed the outer circumference of the taped–off area, starting on the north side, then the east, then the south, and then back again, each time moving three or four yards further out, covering a wider and wider arc of woodland. Clive followed her.

Briefly, her eyes were drawn to a scattering of white, flaky material at the foot of a silver birch. But it turned out to be a few fragments of torn wood and tree bark.

'A grand just lying here,' she mused. 'A car that doesn't exist, which swerves off the road at high speed for no obvious reason. No immediate sign that another car was involved ... at least there was no impact to cause the swerve. And then the driver doesn't even brake.'

'Told you it was odd.'

'You did.' They climbed back up the slope. 'What's this guy Langton like?'

'Gina Tubbs interviewed him. No statement yet, though.'

At the top of the slope, Tubbs was still engaged in paperwork.

'What's the story with Langton?' Lynda asked.

'He was back at his house when I went to see him,' Tubbs said. 'In a bit of a state.'

'Define "a bit of a state"?'

'Shaking, pale. Drinking coffee like there was no tomorrow. Didn't think I'd have much joy getting a coherent statement off him. Not yet anyway. He's not going back to uni till tomorrow. I'm calling back later on.'

Lynda wandered a few yards north. 'Something I want you to do for me, Clive.'

He walked up behind her. 'No probs.'

'Find out how many Ford Mondeos have been reported stolen and never recovered in the Essex Police Force area. Go back five years. Not just beige, of course. Any colour.'

He nodded. 'CCTV?'

'I'll start that ball rolling.' She advanced again because

something else had caught her attention. 'Do that in a minute. What do you think of this?' She walked more quickly. 'And *this*?'

Clive hurried to catch up. Some fifty yards north of the flattened barrier, a lengthy smear of rubber arced across the blacktop. Twenty yards further on, Lynda stopped next to another; this one zigzagged in a different direction. There was yet another one close behind that, though thus far there was no rhyme or reason to the pattern.

Clive shrugged. 'Could be relevant.'

'The sooner the lab rats get here, the better,' Lynda said. 'These marks lead up to *our* incident, but we need to know if they're connected.'

They walked on several hundred yards, encountering further such smears and smudges on both lanes, all of which indicated abrupt braking, swerving and skidding. Even though Photographic were en route, no doubt mired in the traffic like everyone else, Lynda took several pictures on her mobile. Half a mile from the crash site, the central barrier displayed what looked like recent damage, the white-painted metal gashed and scraped.

Lynda photographed this too, and then dug some tweezers from her pocket. Picking one or two flakes of metallic beige paint from the gouge marks, she slipped them into an evidence envelope and held them to the light.

'Bits of glass on the road surface here too,' Clive said.

'Bag them,' she replied.

The glass in itself told them nothing. There was broken glass the length of Britain's highways, but quite clearly something had been happening here.

'Our guy was all over the road, wasn't he?' she observed.

Clive glanced back. 'And over quite a distance. I hope Aziz

Khan's got his whole team with him. If we've only got till lunchtime, they'll have to go up and down this carriageway on their hands and knees in double-quick time.'

'We're going to need an extension on that,' Lynda replied. Again, she scanned the repeating crisscross of melted rubber stripes. 'You know, I've seen this kind of thing before.'

'Yeah?'

'2013 ... RTA on the A414 near Harlow. No other vehicles involved, but the couple in the car were fighting.'

'Fighting?'

'Physically. The driver lost control, clipped the kerb, rolled his Porsche over four lanes.'

'We don't *know* there's no other vehicle involved in this one yet.'

'That's true. Compelling case to kick off the New Year, eh?'

Clive didn't seem enamoured by the prospect, which was not atypical. In complement to his smart appearance and conscientious attitude, he was a worker bee. You could always rely on Clive to get a job done. But he didn't like complications.

'What's up?' She nudged him. 'You don't like a challenge now and then?'

'Gives us something to get our teeth into, I suppose.'

4

6 January (Monday)

'You've got the southbound carriageway till five, Lynda,' Rachel Hollindrake said. 'Your team has to wrap up by then.'

Lynda clamped her phone to her ear as she paced the Neurological Intensive Care Unit waiting room in the Neurosciences Building at Colchester General Hospital.

'Rachel, if we reopen that road to ordinary traffic, all the forensics will have gone.'

There was no immediate response, and Lynda knew why. You didn't close a major highway like the A12 lightly. DI Rachel Hollindrake was head of the Serious Collision Investigation Unit, and as an official detective and trained investigator, was recognised as having a particular and rare expertise. But she was still answerable to the higher echelons of the Essex Roads Policing Division, and its overarching boss, Chief Superintendent Templeton, would already be leaning on her hard.

'Can't you clear it one lane at a time?' Hollindrake asked.

'From my last conversation with Aziz Khan, we can give you the inside lane in the next half-hour.'

'Well, that's not going to work. If I go back to Mr Templeton with that, he'll blow his top. How you doing with the CCTV? Surely that'll tell us if there was another car involved?'

'We're still collecting footage, but we haven't got too many cameras along there.'

Hollindrake sighed. 'How are the casualties doing?'

'Incommunicado at present. Both suffered severe head traumas.' Lynda moved to the shatterproof glass door serving as the NICU's internal entrance. Though the angle was awkward, she could just about see into the room where the woman from the accident was being treated. From here, she was virtually invisible, just a hump under blankets with life-support equipment on either side. NICU nurses moved briskly around her. 'The female's out of surgery now. Seems they had to elevate a depressed skull fracture. She's in a medically induced coma, to try and aid recovery. She's seriously ill, Rachel ... we could still lose her.'

'How about the male?'

'He's in NICU too. He's not been operated on, but he's had a scan and is currently under sedation. He's suffered what's called a minor basal skull fracture. That's not considered to be life-threatening. But he's out for the count at present. In a nutshell, neither of them can be interviewed yet, and probably won't be available for some time.'

'And that's all we've got?'

'There are a couple of oddities ...'

'You mean like why we haven't been able to put names to their faces?'

'Well ... the car's untraceable and neither of them had any ID.'

'There was nothing else inside the car? No paperwork of any sort?'

'Nothing. Clean as a whistle. Like it had just been valeted.'

'Fingerprints?'

'I've not been able to run the female's yet ... she's been

out of reach all day. I've arranged for Gina Tubbs to come in later and try again. In the meantime, I've run the male's but there's no match.'

'He hasn't got a record?'

'It would appear that way.'

The DI was quiet again. She might be frustrated at how slowly things were moving, but the detective in her was fascinated. A car that shouldn't exist, and yet which had looked as if it had just been driven out of a showroom, and by the original John and Jane Doe. 'When are you thinking of going public on this?' she asked.

'Thought we'd leave it until tomorrow,' Lynda said. 'Give concerned friends and relatives a chance to report them missing.'

Hollindrake pondered again. 'What are these oddities you mentioned?'

'Oh … yeah. Well, the woman has a mouth injury dating from a couple of days prior to the accident. There's a mild trauma to the upper lip, which hasn't yet repaired. The doctor who examined her said that he can't be absolutely sure, but that it's consistent with her having been punched in the face.'

'And you think that may be pertinent?'

'Could be. At the same time, the male has three parallel gouge marks on his left cheek, running diagonally from the lobe of his ear to the side of his nose. They're relatively recent and about half a millimetre deep.'

'They couldn't have been caused by woodland debris inundating the car through the windscreen?'

'The doctor doesn't think they're *that* recent. Plus, he said they look like scratch marks. You know, from fingernails.'

'And in your mind, this adds up to …?'

'I'm entertaining the possibility that she and the driver were having some kind of altercation.'

Hollindrake was surprised. 'You mean while he was at the wheel?'

'Well, if they'd had one a few days earlier, they could have been having another.'

'So, this is what we think happened if there *wasn't* another car involved? That the driver and his passenger were fighting?'

'It's only a theory, I admit.'

'Seriously, Lynda?' The DI sounded irritable again. 'After nearly a whole day's investigation, this is what we've got? A load of supposition and nothing solid?'

'We are where we are, ma'am. And if we lose some forensics, it could be even worse.'

There was another long silence. 'Okay,' Hollindrake said, 'I'll call Templeton. But he won't be happy. And in the meantime, you get back in touch with your FCI. Tell him they still might say *no* ... this isn't a murder case, after all.'

Not yet, Lynda thought, though she didn't say it aloud.

As she crossed the car park towards her Qashqai, her phone rang again. She climbed in, and switched the engine on. The call was redirected through Bluetooth.

'Detective Sergeant Hagen,' she said, pulling out of the car park.

'Oh, hello, Mrs Hagen ... this is Mrs Campbell.' The voice had a distinct West Indian lilt. 'We've met a couple of times. I'm deputy head at St John's.'

Lynda found Charlie sitting in the deputy head's office, working away with a box of crayons. Mrs Campbell, a huge,

26

mumsy figure, beamed when Lynda entered the office. Charlie grinned too.

'What happened?' he asked, excited and intrigued by this change to his routine.

'I'm so sorry, Mrs Campbell,' Lynda said, trying not to look as flustered as she felt.

'We rang your husband's number a few times,' Mrs Campbell said, standing. 'But couldn't get through.'

'Terribly sorry. Complete mix-up in Don and my communications.'

'Not to worry. Everything's fine.'

'Was Daddy too busy to come and get me again?' Charlie asked.

'No, no ... that won't have been the case.' Lynda refused to meet the deputy head's eye as she grabbed Charlie's coat and baggage from the spare chair. 'Come on.'

When they arrived back at their home avenue, Westcombe Close, the weather had deteriorated, gusts of razor wind driving sleety flakes across the houses and gardens. At number sixteen, Don's beaten-up BMW 3 sat on the drive, but the front of the building was mostly dark. Glancing through the window, Lynda saw that light only spilled into the lounge from the dining room. She opened the front door and ushered Charlie inside.

'Go up and get changed,' she said, switching on the stair light. 'Put your uniform away neatly.'

As Charlie trudged upstairs, she went through into the lounge, and then the dining room. As expected, Don was slumped in his usual place, surrounded by a mess of paperwork and open books. He wore tracksuit pants and a coffee-stained T-shirt as he scribbled in a pad. On top of his dog-eared 2006 copy of the *Crime Investigator's Manual* was balanced an empty Pot Noodle carton with a fork in it.

She didn't bother looking past him into the kitchen, because as usual, the dishwasher would not have been loaded, nor the scrapings of breakfast disposed of in the bin.

'Hi,' he said, without looking around. He hadn't bothered shaving or even combing his hair.

'What happened?' she asked.

'The usual,' he muttered.

'You've not been reachable this afternoon,' she said.

'Been on the phone to Abby.'

Abby, aka Abigail Cartwright, was his literary agent. London-based and well connected, she'd promised so much when he'd first contacted her, seeming blown away that an ex-Major Investigation Team DI had wanted to join her list, though so far she hadn't been able to get him a sniff of a publishing deal.

'This bigshot editor in London. You know what he said? Abby sent him the first four chapters of *Nick 'Em*. He got back to her, having expressed serious interest when she first approached him about it, to say he hadn't bothered reading past the first one. Said he found it "non-authentic". I mean, non-authentic, for fuck's sake! Did I do the fucking job, or what?'

'Don ...' Lynda shook her head. 'I mean what happened about you picking Charlie up?'

At first, Don looked puzzled. And then the penny dropped, and he jumped to his feet in panic. '*Shit!*'

'Don't worry. *I've* brought him. He's gone upstairs. But he can still probably hear us. So, you can tone down the effing and jeffing if you don't mind.'

'Christ ...' Don leaned forward, shoulders sagging. 'I ... I just... it totally slipped my mind.' He shook his head, as shocked as he was remorseful. He glanced up again. 'You say *you* brought him home?'

'Yes, but only by knocking off early.'

'Hey.' His voice tightened again now that Charlie was safe. 'I've explained what happened, okay? I'm sorry.'

'Yeah, you really sound it.'

'Jesus, Lynda! Get over yourself, eh? I've just told you I'm having a crap day. And it affects both of us if you actually give it some thought.'

'It doesn't affect both of us as much as it would if I end up losing *my* job. This is the third time I've had to do this. And today I'm up to my eyes in a difficult investigation.'

He snorted, grabbing his Pot Noodle carton and lumbering into the kitchen. 'Difficult investigation?' His tone was scathing. '*Traffic?* Give me a bloody break!'

'Don...'

'I've said I'm sorry.' He threw his fork into the sink and walked back into the dining room. 'I'll go up and apologise to him right now. I'll play with him on his castle for a bit. Christ knows, I can't get any more work done today.'

Lynda followed him through the lounge.

That had been quite a blow to him, she supposed; the publisher who he'd thought was interested in his book to say 'no' without even reading it. But it was hardly likely to impact on their lives the way Don imagined.

'You knew it was going to be hard,' she said up the stairs after him. 'Especially as you'd never even thought about writing until...'

Don looked back down. 'Until I became society's spare part?'

Well, you took the medical retirement, she thought. *You didn't have to. You could have gone back into uniform, taken an inside job.*

But again, she didn't say any of that. Sometimes, she was too patient with him for her own good, let alone his.

Don plodded on up the stairs. 'I'll go and play with him for a bit.'

Lynda nodded. That was something Don was good at, and Charlie would love it. She could soon hear their muffled laughter overhead; it made her smile, but that smile faded when she saw what passed for Don's writing career strewn in front of her again.

He'd never asked permission to use the dining table as a desk, even though it meant that the rest of them would have to eat their dinners with plates balanced on their knees. But getting angry wouldn't help – every counsellor she'd spoken to had advised that understanding was the best way forward. She had no clue how *she* would react to being taken hostage by a maniac gunman and driven over a hundred miles, being told all the way that it was her final day on Earth.

She took her anorak off, hung it in the closet and started to get the tea ready. But a few things were bugging her.

Obvious questions remained concerning the anonymous status of the A12 casualties – who the hell were they, and why no one had reported them missing, and the fact they were in a stolen car that had never been reported stolen (as far as the police were aware) – but there was also the not insignificant matter of the money.

For some reason, that wad of twenty-pound notes was niggling her. A full count had now confirmed that it was £1,000 exactly. In itself that wasn't too suspicious, but couple it with the other curiosities surrounding the crash and you had to wonder about that as well. Lynda slipped her phone from her jeans pocket and called Clive Atkins.

'Sorry I left you with it earlier,' she said.

'No problem.' By the sounds of it, he was back in the office. 'Get everything sorted?'

'Yeah, it's okay now. Listen, Clive ... that bundle of cash the dog found. A single neat bundle of twenties totalling a grand and fastened with elastic? I've been trying to work out what was bugging me about it, and now I think I know. Isn't that the sort of thing you see when there are larger sums involved? When there are several such bundles in fact?'

He considered this. 'Maybe, but we both saw the crash scene for ourselves. There was no more money lying around, and there was none inside the Mondeo. Aziz Khan's team would've found it. Why, what're you thinking?'

'I don't know.' She flipped the kettle on. 'It's just another piece of the puzzle, and every piece we've got so far suggests those two casualties were up to no good.'

'Well, it's not helpful to that hypothesis, but the cash is all legit.'

'That's been confirmed, has it?'

'Just in. All the notes were issued at different times and have been in circulation for quite a while.'

'Okay, fair enough ...' If the cash was legit, there wasn't much more they could learn from it. It wouldn't even be traceable. 'Sorry again about today. I'll be in extra early tomorrow.'

She chucked teabags into a couple of mugs. As she did, her phone rang again. This call was from Gina Tubbs.

Lynda put it on speaker. 'Hope you've got something good for me, Gina?'

'Think I may have,' Tubbs replied. 'I managed to run the woman's prints. And we've got a hit.'

'Yeah?'

'Name is Jill Brooks. Londoner. Thirty-four years old. Only one offence, but it's an eye-opener.'

'Go on?'

'GBH. It was back in 2008, when she was twenty-two. She put a stiletto heel through some guy's cheek.'

'Ouch.'

'She pleaded guilty at Westminster Magistrates Court, where she drew a five-month suspended sentence on the basis that it was her first offence.'

Lynda mulled this over as she poured boiling water on the teabags.

'So, what're you thinking?' Tubbs wondered.

'I'm thinking there are two kinds of girls in this world, Gina. Those who wear their heels to look pretty. And those who have a wide range of other uses for them.'

5

14 December (Saturday)
– 23 days earlier

It was a frigid night, glacial stars scattering a clear black sky.

As long as it stayed clear, that was fine by Elliot. The neon barometer on the dash of his BMW Sport read minus two. If it rained now, it would fall as snow, but while that wouldn't be a problem on the main roads, here in the backcountry he was less certain. Since leaving the A1071, he'd worked his way through a network of farm lanes so little used that in many cases they didn't even figure on his sat nav. He'd been given directions which he'd written down and tried to memorise, so he was sure he'd be okay – so long as the weather held.

At nine o'clock, he halted at a T-junction and a moss-covered fingerpost. Elliot didn't remember this from the instructions, which he now checked again. As there were no clues there, he opted to go left. He wasn't sure why, apart from some vague memory in which Jim Naboth had said that if he got lost it was best to keep bearing south. That wasn't hugely helpful, but there was one landmark he was supposed to look out for: a derelict silage tower standing left of the road. After that, he'd been instructed to go straight on for half a mile, before taking his next right and then his second left. He had his mobile with him, so he could always ring ahead and tell them he'd got lost. But he was loath to do that. The whole purpose of this evening was to demonstrate his professionalism. If he finished up floundering before he even got there, how would it look?

Not for the first time, Elliot wondered about the wisdom of this venture.

It had been a relief to be asked. In this game, you only earned for as long as your reputation lasted, and reputations could diminish quickly if you laid low for too long, and yet lying low wasn't always your choice. So, getting an invitation wasn't just an ego trip. It meant that you hadn't been forgotten, not yet, and that your skills were still prized.

Assuming you hadn't lost your edge in the meantime.

Elliot was sure he hadn't, but then he hadn't tested himself much recently, and it wasn't always the best idea presenting yourself for duty with the Naboths when you weren't prepped. Jim was the affable face of the firm, the 'Hail fellow, well met' guy, the seeming good egg. But then there was Jo as well, and that was much darker territory. Before he could ponder more, a distinct shape caught his attention, approaching on the left. At first it was a tall silhouette which slid into the corner of his vision as he rounded a bend on the narrow lane. But the closer he drew, the more it materialised until soon there was no mistake.

It was the vertical, dome-topped outline of a silage tower.

Elliot followed the turn-off for about thirty yards, wheels jolting on the rutted, frozen surface, until he came to a tall iron gate. From a decayed, shack-like structure behind the gate on the right, a figure emerged in grey jeans and hoodie top with the hood pulled down over his face. Elliot flashed his high beams four times. There was a dull clatter as a bolt was disengaged, the figure lugging the gate open.

Elliot drove through, entering a parking area at the back of a building, the purpose of which was unrecognisable in the darkness. The redbrick wall in front of him had a single door in the middle, covered in flaking green paint. A couple of other vehicles were parked about forty yards to the right, but at that distance they were indistinguishable. There was no other sign of life. He turned his engine off, pulled on his fleece and gloves, and climbed out. It was so dark that he had to grope hand–over–hand along his Sport towards the building. As he did, the green door opened, and he could sense a figure standing there.

'Where the fuck do you think you're going?' a voice asked. It was low, with a northern accent. It sounded amused.

Elliot stopped half a yard from the entrance, puzzled. He'd assumed he'd be recognised. At six foot two and well built, with a collar-length shock of sandy hair and 'patrician' good looks, which included a square jaw, firm mouth, straight nose and blue/grey eyes, he wasn't easy to misidentify. 'I'm ... I'm expected.'

'Yeah?' A gloved hand at the end of a bare arm reached out, planted itself on his chest and pushed him backward. 'Who by?'

Elliot had no option but to retreat a couple of feet. The guy from the door stepped outside. Elliot's eyes were adjusting to the moonlight, and he saw a solid, stocky figure; about five foot ten in height, with an unruly mass of dark hair, plus a dark beard and moustache. As well as his black gloves, he wore a black vest. His bare arms were thick with muscle.

'I said – who by?'

'What's it got to do with you?' Elliot retorted.

A crescent of white teeth split the untidy facial hair. 'That's the right answer.'

The guy spread his arms, indicating that Elliot should do the same.

Elliot complied, and the guy frisked him. Not just checking his pockets, but along his arms, under his cuffs, under his collar, down either leg of his jeans, and around the tops of his training shoes. Up close, he was somewhere in his late thirties, with cold, pale eyes and a hooked nose. The scruffy fuzz of beard gave him a loopy, piratical air. He continued to smile, but there was nothing congenial about it; it was crooked, scornful – especially when he yanked down the zip on Elliot's fleece, exposing the patterned silk shirt underneath.

'Who are you, Austin fucking Powers?'

Chuckling more than the joke merited, he unbuttoned the shirt, not just working his rough leather gloves across Elliot's chest, but under his armpits and around his waist again. Most likely, he was looking for a wire rather than a weapon. When he'd finished, he turned and walked back inside, leaving the door open so that Elliot could follow. Elliot found himself stumbling in darkness across a floor littered with broken glass and loose planking.

'I could've saved you all that trouble if you'd just asked my name,' he said. 'I'm ...'

'I know who you are,' the guy interrupted. Definitely northern, possibly Manchester. 'You've got a big rep to live up to. Hope you don't disappoint us.'

They followed a few dank brick passages, before emerging into a hangar of some sort, a vast open area some seventy yards in length by forty wide, with a beaten dirt floor and bare electric bulbs suspended by cables from the steel girders underpinning the roof. In the middle stood a row of about eight cars, each one covered by a green canvas sheet.

'You still shacked up with that hot blonde piece?' the guy asked, turning to face him.

'What?' Elliot was fleetingly tongue-tied. 'You know Harri?'

'Harri, eh?' The guy grinned. 'Don't know her personally. Last time I saw her, you wouldn't believe what she was wearing...'

'Elliot Wade!' a Cockney voice called out.

They turned. Two men had emerged from a door on the far side of the vast chamber and were now walking past the row of vehicles. Both wore gloves and blue overalls, but while one was older, tubbier and white-haired, the other was younger, in his late thirties, tall and lean, with slick black hair and a wolfish smile. It was this latter, Jim Naboth, who'd called out.

'Mr Naboth,' Elliot said.

The white-haired older guy waited by the cars, but Jim Naboth approached Elliot and shook hands with him. 'You two've met, then?' he said.

'We've met.' Elliot glanced at the Beard. 'We've not been introduced.'

'Allow me,' Jim said. 'Elliot, meet Ray Lonnegan.'

'Ray,' Elliot said, assessing the Beard properly now that they were in the light.

He might not be as tall as Elliot or Jim, but he was thickset with muscle, his torso wedge-shaped as if he worked out. He too wore blue overalls, but they were pulled down and tied around his waist. His brawny left shoulder was marked with a single tattoo: spread wings and an upright dagger, which, Elliot suspected, indicated Airborne Forces. Lonnegan's smile had now hardened into something callous and cruel; he didn't bother returning Elliot's greeting.

'Ray needs to be impressed before he gets friendly,' Jim

explained, placing a hand on Elliot's back and steering him towards the cars. 'His distrustful attitude is something we all have to live with, but it's worth it. You know what tonight's about?'

'I've got half an idea,' Elliot replied.

'That's the most you ever have about anything, eh?' Lonnegan said, walking behind.

Elliot swung back. 'Hey!' With Jim Naboth now present, it felt safer to say what he thought. 'I've come here to do a job, okay? Now, I don't expect to be treated like royalty, but a bit of mutual respect couldn't hurt. Otherwise, I can just walk out the door again.'

'You can walk out the door any fucking time. You think we can't do better than you?'

'All right, Ray,' Jim cut in. 'Enough. We're at least going to put Elliot through his paces and find him wanting before we give him the heave-ho, yeah?'

Lonnegan shrugged, as if it didn't matter to him either way.

Jim continued to the line of cars, steering Elliot alongside him again. 'Don't worry, you've got the skills to get on the right side of him. I see you're gloved up. That's good. Just don't take 'em off while you're here.'

As Elliot had already seen, the cars were draped with green canvas, but the white-haired older guy now whipped the cover off the one at the far end, revealing a sleek Mercedes-AMG in gleaming metallic maroon.

'What do you think?' Jim asked.

'Beautiful,' Elliot said.

'Come around the back. I want to show you something.'

Elliot followed. The older guy was waiting at the car's rear;

he opened the boot. Inside, it had been loaded with four paving stones, two on the left, two on the right.

'These slabs weigh fifty kilograms each, so that's an extra two hundred kilos in this little beauty's backside,' Jim said. 'What do you reckon, Elliot?'

'Tough to handle at high speed, that's for sure.'

Jim nodded. 'Which is what tonight's all about.' He glanced at the older guy, who plodded away across the chamber to the facing wall, where Elliot now noticed there was a large pair of wooden sliding doors. With a heavy clanking, a chain was removed, and the doors were pushed open along their tracks, one after the other.

Jim slammed the boot. 'Fancy taking her for a spin?'

'Sounds like fun,' Elliot replied.

He opened the driver's door, seeing a key waiting in the ignition. To his surprise, Jim then climbed into the front passenger seat, Ray Lonnegan into the rear.

'If you want a proper test drive,' Elliot said, 'I can't guarantee anyone's safety.'

'That's okay,' Lonnegan replied. 'At no stage can we guarantee yours. So it all pans out.'

Elliot glanced at Jim, who arched a laconic eyebrow.

They drove forward, trundling through the doorway and down a shallow ramp into a gritty siding, where Elliot braked, fascinated by what he was seeing outside of the car.

Three electric floodlights on tall steel poles had been switched on about forty yards to his right, and now cast their silver radiance over what looked like a disused racing circuit. The hangar behind them had obviously been a repair and garage facility, while to the left of that was the boarded-up structure of an old clubhouse or pavilion, complete with an upper balcony. On the other side of that stood a row of decayed, wooden scaffold-like structures. Tiered seating, he realised; bleachers. The track itself swung away from them both to the left and right. As its central area was little more than strewn rubbish, rusty cars and broken-down buildings, it was visible almost in its entirety. It wasn't a circle, more of a rectangle, but with curved, steeply banked corners, covering maybe a mile and a half's circumference.

Elliot marvelled. 'Is this the old Tunwood Raceway?'

'Should've known an ex-Formula One guy like you would recognise it,' Jim replied.

'Didn't realise it was still here, let alone intact enough to use.'

'It's not very intact, as you're about to find out,' Lonnegan said.

'Did you buy this, Mr Naboth?' Elliot asked.

'Let's just say a friend of a friend owed us a favour.'

'Fantastic.'

'You see, Ray?' Jim glanced around. 'This guy's a purist as well as a pro. Knows quality when he sees it.'

Lonnegan snorted.

Elliot was still impressed. Tunwood, though now buried deep in the Essex countryside, and forgotten by near enough everyone, had once been a legendary venue. Opened around 1908, initially for the UK's burgeoning auto industry to test its new products at continuous high speeds, within five years it had begun hosting competitive motor racing. At least two or three land speed records were attempted here. He thought that it had closed sometime around 1938. Talk about old and venerable.

'Shall we get cracking?' Jim said.

Elliot checked the gauge, seeing that the Merc had a full tank. 'How many laps?'

'Just take her out. Let's see what you can do.'

Elliot fastened his seatbelt before proceeding forward, turning the Mercedes right and joining the racetrack. In width, it was about a hundred feet across so there was plenty of room, but its uncoated concrete surface, so long out of use, was broken, cracked and filled with weed. As such, it was a rough ride straight away, the car bouncing and jerking. It was possible that large sections of the track might also be damp, so ice could be a problem. But then, an easy and straightforward trial run would prove nothing.

Elliot accelerated, working up through the gears. With a *click*, Jim snicked his seatbelt into place. There was no such sound from the rear, which wasn't sensible. This was a genuine 1920s raceway, which meant there'd be no point even looking for safety zones or shock-absorption barriers, just rickety wooden fences with rotted concrete posts located every dozen or so yards.

'You want to belt up, Mr Lonnegan?' Elliot said. 'You might not care about getting hurt yourself, but if we hit anything, I don't want you flying into the back of me at a hundred miles an hour, okay?'

'A hundred,' Lonnegan sneered. 'I'll believe that when I see it.'

That comment made Elliot's mind up. They were already running at thirty plus, and he was fast becoming aware of the extras in the boot. The Merc swayed like a boat, but he tromped the gas harder. As they entered the first curve, they passed forty and the car's rear end swung out of line even with the steep banking. Elliot hung a sharp right against the turn, tyres shrieking, to bring it back under control, sending them rocketing uphill, but then swung a left and hit the gas, gunning them down onto the next straight.

'Nice,' Jim commented.

Lonnegan said nothing. But it was satisfying to hear his belt *click*.

Tiered rows of bleachers flickered by on their right, but they were close on fifty when they reached the next real obstruction. The track banked again, shallower this time, when from some dark place above and to the right, a hidden party shoved a wheelbarrow down into their path. It was heaped with house bricks, which scattered as it rocked and juddered.

Elliot spun the wheel right and then left again, swerving past the obstacle without losing speed. In the boot, the heavy paving stones clattered. Elliot checked the rear-view mirror. Lonnegan's gaze was fixed back on him, narrow and cool. Elliot glanced sideways at Jim, whose tall, well-cut form sat braced, though his expression was relaxed. It took more than a quick drive around a crumbling old circuit to make men like this jumpy, but Elliot had more to give them yet.

At the next bend he was pushing sixty. Along the centre of old-fashioned banked raceways like this, a dotted line would once have been marked in black paint. That was the 'Fifty Foot Line'. If drivers stuck to it, even at high speed, they supposedly wouldn't need to steer around the corners. Needless to say, the Fifty Foot Line had long faded, so now it was about personal judgement.

Elliot commenced a long, slow turn before he'd entered the bend, but already the back of the car was swinging like a pendulum. As he'd feared, there was black ice too – and in consequence he lost traction, the Merc spinning out of control like a top, turning round and round, wheels screaming, shocks bouncing, the windscreen an ever-changing array of track and bleacher. Jim swore, but on the third revolution, Elliot drove them out of it, ramming back up through the gears, flooring the pedal and blasting them forward. They'd lost speed – they were down to fifty again – but he rapidly re-ascended to sixty and then seventy.

On this next stretch, three corroded wrecks had been abandoned in the middle of the track, one in front of the other, with perhaps fifty yards between each one. It was a classic slalom, but Elliot veered through it, tight on seventy-five, barely braking, though in every case steering well clear of the jagged, rusted metal. Even nicking the Merc's paint-work would go against him, as that might render it useless for whichever job was in the offing.

A hundred yards after the wrecks, a wall had been con-structed across the track. It wouldn't be mortared, just house bricks piled on top of each other. But it stood a good seven feet tall, and there was no apparent gap. Elliot bore at it full speed. He knew it would be an optical illusion. The needle rode past eighty, the wall looming at them until it filled their entire world. Jim was as tense as coiled steel. Elliot even heard the sucked-in breath of Ray Lonnegan. And then he saw it.

The way through.

The wall had been constructed in two halves, one thirty yards in front of the next, both overlapping each other by a few feet. Only when you were right upon it did the per-spective change, and you spotted the space between them.

With half a second to spare, Elliot spun them into a handbrake turn, the Merc swinging around again with that weight in the back, and then floored the accelerator, screech-ing forward, before swinging again, the other way this time, to get around the second wall.

Beyond the chicane, they spun 360 degrees – another patch of black ice – but Elliot didn't lose control and gunned them forward again. The needle dropped back to seventy, but they were already approaching the next bend, and he hammered them through it, the car ascending the steep bank with frightening velocity – they shared a vision of the Merc taking off, smashing the wooden fence and lofting high, before exploding down through the skeletal framework of the bleachers – but Elliot held the curving track right the way around, a foot of clearance between himself and the fencing, and when he brought them down onto the flat again they were travelling at just under 100 mph, the world whipping by in a blur.

'You wanted a ton, Mr Lonnegan, you've got it!' Elliot shouted.

The cement mixer in front of them had materialised from nowhere.

Elliot yanked the wheel right and left again, slewing sideways at mind-boggling speed, and when they hit more ice, spinning right the way around again. He kept his nerve, tromping the accelerator to drag them out of it.

The home straight now lay ahead.

The boarded-up clubhouse zoomed up on their right, and then the hangar and beyond that, the towering floodlights. The old guy with white hair stood in the sidings, hands stuffed into his overalls pockets. Elliot didn't need to ask them if they thought they'd seen enough. He braked, and the rugged running surface became an issue again, the Merc jolting and rocking. But he could detect the relief filling the car's interior.

'We can go around again if you want,' he said, easing down past thirty.

Jim stared dead ahead. 'What do you reckon, Ray?'

There was no reply from the back.

Elliot nodded and smiled.

6

7 January (Tuesday)

Lynda swivelled the chair around from her desk. 'So ... we've got no medical records for this Jill Brooks? None at all?'

'Apparently not.' Clive sat at the other side of the cubby-hole-sized section of the SCIU they called their office.

'Which is a bit weird,' Lynda said.

'According to her sheet, she was a stripper and a prozzy. So she probably used walk-in centres.'

'And the only home address we had for her has now been demolished?'

He shrugged. 'That's London for you.'

'And we've got no known associates or next of kin?'

'Not on record.'

Lynda sighed. 'What about this club where she worked?'

'It's called the Pink Elephant. Still in operation. The Met's Clubs & Vice Unit are going to have a word on our behalf, but the staff tend to be transient and it was eleven years ago, so they advise we don't hold our breath.'

Lynda gazed at the printed-out image of a pretty girl with pale, mascara-stained cheeks and a 'bedhead' of messy black hair. 'Some lead this is, considering it's our only one.'

Thus far, the day wasn't going well. She'd come in that morning to a message from the Stolen Vehicle Section of the Force Intelligence Bureau to the effect that they'd never be able to trace the original owners of the Ford Mondeo. It seemed that every scrap of identification had been erased. When Lynda had rung up to say that she'd thought they had all kinds of new techniques, chemical analysis, thermal etching and so on, it had been explained to her that where all the car's stamps, serial numbers and other identifying marks were once located, whole sections of chassis and bodywork had been removed and new blank sections welded into place. It was real chop-shop stuff. Ultra-professional.

Which also hinted that what they were looking into here was far more than an average RTC.

Around them, the walls of the small room were glazed, but coated in photographs, reports and diagrams depicting the stretch of the A12 above Little Crickledon Wood. Lynda stood up and examined a couple.

'Well, Brooks is still critical,' Clive said, 'and the bloke's improved a little, but they're both still incommunicado. They'll wake up at some point, though. Shouldn't we just sideline it until then? There are other jobs piling up.'

'What if they're not able to talk when they wake up?' she replied. 'What if they *won't* talk? This stolen car they were riding in gets more mysterious by the minute.'

'Okay.' He didn't put up any resistance. He knew that Lynda liked a puzzle, and was aware that his desire for clean, orderly cases got her back up. 'What do you want me to do?'

'Crack on with the CCTV.'

'You know there's no footage covering the actual point of the accident?'

'I know that, but like we discussed before, we need to check several miles of road leading up to it. See if you can spot the Mondeo. If you succeed, see if you can locate the point where it came onto the A12. If you're successful with that, we can maybe run a camera trail back along the side roads to its point of origin.'

Clive nodded.

'Failing that, just make a note of any other vehicles on the A12 in the vicinity of the crash site. If nothing else, that might give us some extra witnesses.'

'Will do.'

She grabbed her bag and the anorak from the back of her chair.

'Where are *you* off to?' he asked.

'Little Crickledon. To speak to Alan Langton.'

'Didn't Gina Tubbs do that?'

'Yep. Now it's my turn.'

She headed out, only to be hailed from the far end of the main corridor. 'You got a moment, Lynda?' DI Hollindrake was approaching. She was a tall, stern-looking woman who favoured a short haircut and severe, dark-coloured suits.

'I've got a mo,' Lynda said, 'but I'm off to speak to someone.'

'You've seen the report from Force Intelligence?' Hollindrake said.

'I have, yeah.'

The DI appraised her. 'This case is getting heavier by the minute.'

'All the more reason for us to stick with it as a priority, I think.'

'All the more reason for us to go to press and see if the public can help.'

'I'm hesitant to do that, Rachel, when we haven't been able to contact next of kin.'

Lynda didn't mention that to do this would also flood her office with unhelpful interest from dozens of tragic

individuals looking for lost loved ones who had no connection with this incident, all of which would still need to
be addressed.

'The accident was a good thirty-six hours ago,' Hollindrake
replied. 'Don't you think next of kin, if there are any, would
have contacted us by now?'

Lynda couldn't deny that.

'I note you've sent bulletins out nationwide to that effect,'
Hollindrake said. 'Nothing back thus far?'

'Not yet.'

'In which case, it seems to me that you've done everything in your power to try and ID these two, so why not
go public with it?'

'I'll be doing that tomorrow,' Lynda said. 'Whether we
hear from relatives or not.'

'What about this Jill Brooks? Anything new on her?'

'Not yet. We're still trying to work out exactly who she is.'

'The sooner the better, okay? We need to know what was
going on.'

Lynda shrugged. 'I'm hoping that our main witness can
still help with that.'

Hollindrake frowned. 'Langton, you mean? Haven't we
already spoken to him?'

'I'm not totally happy with his statement.'

'Well, whatever that means, do yourself a favour and get
something useful from it.' Hollindrake backed away. 'We need
progress, Lynda. Fast.'

Sandycroft Way was a cul-de-sac on the furthermost edge
of Little Crickledon village, its turning circle only separated
from a broad meadow by a low, slatted fence with a stile
in the middle. The houses here were mostly semis, with

small front gardens now bedraggled from the winter. Before approaching No. 22, Lynda parked against the fence, got out of her Qashqai and climbed through the stile into the meadow, which rolled away towards a distant line of naked trees. The rumble of vehicles she could hear indicated the presence of the A12.

She wondered why she was here. The money find had been odd, there was no question about that, but even though it looked for all the world as if it had been part of a larger consignment, there was nothing in Alan Langton's statement that seemed unlikely to be true. It was perfectly reasonable that he had come this way with his dog for an early morning stroll.

But then, Gina Tubbs had said that he'd seemed nervous in the presence of the police. That wasn't unusual. But as SIO on the case, Lynda felt obligated to make her own assessment.

She strode forward a few yards. Clearly, she could walk all the way from here to the crash site, though there was no need. The wreck had been removed, but the place where it had come to rest would still be taped off, with a few of Aziz Khan's Tyvek-clad kids mopping up the few last clues. There'd be nothing she could add.

She turned back, and just to the side of the footpath, a clump of briars caught her attention. They were brown and desiccated from the winter cold, but with rags and tags of vegetation still clinging to them.

Along with something else...

The woman who answered the door was in late middle-age and leaning on a stick.

'Morning,' Lynda said. 'Detective Sergeant Hagen. Serious Collision Investigation Unit.'

The woman didn't smile. She had short but thinning wire-grey hair, lean, pale features and metal-rimmed spectacles. Her build was waif-thin, and she wore a flower-patterned pinafore over trousers and slippers. The hand with which she clutched her walking stick was knotty with rheumatism.

'Mrs Langton, is it?' Lynda asked.

'That's right.' The woman spoke quietly. 'Erm … Maureen.'

'Alan's mother?'

'How can I help you?' The woman seemed uneasy, as if a police officer coming to her house after her son had reported a serious road accident was somehow unexpected.

'I need to speak to Alan about the car he found in the woods yesterday,' Lynda said.

'He's not in at the moment. He had to nip into Colchester.'

'That's okay,' Lynda replied. 'Perhaps you and I can have a quick chat, eh?'

For half a second, Lynda thought she was going to be refused. But then the woman nodded, somewhat resignedly, and led the way inside.

They entered a living room, which had just enough space for a sofa, an armchair and a television. A gas fire glowed on the hearth, and in the corner, a plump brown-and-white springer spaniel was curled up in its basket, though watching her with keen interest.

Mrs Langton directed her to the armchair, but, despite her disability, remained standing.

'Can I get you some tea?' she offered.

'No, thanks,' Lynda replied. 'Tell the truth, Mrs Langton, I'm a bit surprised Alan's here at all. I understand he's a student at Goldsmiths, University of London.'

'That's correct.' The woman looked puzzled.

'And he's not due back yet? I mean, it's January 7 – Christmas is over.'

'He *is* due back around now. But he'll go when he's ready.'

'When he's ready?'

'Excuse me, but is this relevant to anything?'

'I don't know.' Lynda leaned forward. 'You see, Alan provided us with a signed witness statement. And when you sign a witness statement for the police it becomes a legal document, and it may be produced in court as part of a prosecution case.'

Mrs Langton made no reply.

'So, if all this happens,' Lynda added, 'and that statement turns out to be untrue, it constitutes perjury. And that, Maureen, is a criminal offence. Which could ruin a promising young graduate's future.'

The woman paled. 'I'm sure Alan would never...'

Further words seemed to fail her.

'Sure that Alan would never what?' Lynda asked.

'He came running home... he was in a state. He told me what had happened. I'm his mother and I believed him. Do you not?'

'Let me ask you a different question.' Lynda sat back. 'How's it going for Alan at Goldsmiths?'

'Well...' The woman seemed unsure how much to divulge. 'Well... he's not happy there.'

'Oh.' Lynda made herself sound sorry. 'Any particular reason?'

'He doesn't think he suits student life, and he hates having no money. He had to sell his motorbike before he left, just so that he'd have something to spend, which he was very upset about.' Mrs Langton looked upset, herself. 'He talks about students coming out of college with huge debt. He says that he might as well begin his working life now as leave it another year. His father was the same.' She shook her head. 'He never felt like a man unless he had a wallet full of notes in his jacket...'

They were interrupted by a thunderous rumble from outside. Mrs Langton seemed as mystified as her guest. They crossed to the window together.

On the drive stood a large Triumph Trident motorcycle. It was likely second-hand, but by the shimmer on its British racing green livery, was in showroom condition. There was also a shine on the black and green leathers worn by its rider. Clearly, they were brand new, as was the black, full-visor circuit helmet that he was in the process of removing.

'How you doing, Alan?' Lynda said, going outside to meet him, flipping open her warrant card. 'DS Hagen. Shall we chat about this bike?'

7

14 December (Saturday)

Elliot Wade was only thirty-four, but there were times when he felt much older. Though he'd seen and done a lot in his short time on Earth, the years were weighing on him. Not because of this wide experience, but because he felt that all his many escapades, though they'd doubtless be the stuff of dreams to schoolboys, had ultimately brought him nothing.

Trundling along these isolated back lanes and yet still nervous in case someone saw him, it was difficult to believe that in 2008 he finished second in the Turkish Grand Prix and was hailed as one of the most exciting young drivers in Formula One. Another kind of payday was looming now, of course. But as his headmaster father had been fond of saying, 'What shall it profit a man, if he gain the whole world and lose his soul?'

Elliot didn't believe in souls anymore. An inner voice told him that this was because he didn't dare. But he would always refute that with the argument that this was a world where the innocent suffered most and the wicked prospered. If God and the Devil were real, the latter was doing the better job of the two. Of course, it was easy to be flippant about that kind of stuff when you were driving back from a meeting with Jim Naboth. At times like this, you didn't *want* to believe that some celestial bean counter was keeping a narrowed eye on you.

It was discomforting how such thoughts only ever seemed to occur to him *after* he'd signed on the dotted line. But what was that popular phrase these days?

They were where they were.

He had to face facts. He wasn't racing now. There was no legit prize money in the offing, no lucrative contract. He was another non-entity heading home among legions of anonymous others with Christmas just around the corner and no idea how to pay for it.

Until tonight.

That was the upside of it. That payday again.

Sometimes, having a conscience was an expensive luxury.

Elliot saw Harri as soon as he sauntered into the pub.

She was working at the 'front door' end of the bar, which was decked with festive lights and loops of evergreen. The Three Pigeons uniform of black jeans and a white T-shirt with the pub's logo on the front suited her better than anyone else here – at thirty-four, she still possessed the buxom figure that had first drawn his eyes to her all those years ago – but she looked flustered, her long fair hair tied in a ponytail and hanging unkempt after so many hours on duty.

She signalled that she'd be five minutes. Elliot nodded and found one of the few tables unoccupied. Business was good, the pub raucous with booming, beer-soaked laughter and the good-natured gabble of East Anglian voices. At the bar, Harri had placed four frothing pints of real ale on the counter and was now adding four double measures of Jack Daniels to the order. The guy paying Harri for it, a short, squat, white-haired fella, old enough to be her father, made some quip – no doubt rude – which caused her to laugh.

Elliot couldn't help feeling sour.

Harri had been his partner for nine years and his wife for seven, and just to look at her, she was a fabulous catch, but there were downsides too. She was so used to her own overt sexiness that it was never a problem for her. She didn't feel cheapened or objectified when men ogled her because she was so used to it. As she'd once said to him: 'Being a glamour puss has done me lots of favours. Why should I be ashamed of it?' He'd struggled to answer, mumbling something about him not expecting her to be ashamed of it, about him not being ashamed of it either ...

But then uncouth specimens like Ray Lonnegan came along.

You still shacked up with that hot blonde piece?

Elliot saw again that brutish, bearded face with the crooked, leery mouth, the hooked nose, the eyes like broken glass.

'Earth to Elliot,' someone said.

He glanced up, and was surprised to see Harri there with an anorak folded over her arm.

He stood and grabbed his fleece. 'Sorry, thought you were going to be five minutes.'

'I've been ten,' she replied.

He shook his head as they walked out. 'I was off in Disneyland.'

They were outside before either spoke again.

'You been out somewhere?' Harri asked.

Elliot unlocked the car. 'Not especially. Why?'

She indicated the Sport's nearside flank, which was spattered all the way along with drying mud.

'Oh ... just went for a drive.'

They hit the road network, which at this time on a Saturday evening was empty.

Harri gazed frontward. 'Any particular reason you went out for this drive?'

Elliot sighed. 'Look, does it matter?'

'So you weren't going to tell me you went out for a drive. And now you won't tell me where you drove to?'

'Look, everything's fine.'

'You expect me to believe that?'

He shrugged, feigning disinterest. 'It doesn't matter what you believe.'

She shook her head, which riled him.

'Let me ask you something, Harri. How do you want to spend Christmas? Trapped indoors by sleet with a few tins of lager and the crappiest TV schedule in history? Or roasting yourself on a Caribbean beach, sipping chilled champagne?'

'And will you be on that beach with me, Elliot?' she wondered. 'Or will you be in jail?'

8

7 January (Tuesday)

'Admittedly, it was only a couple of twenties that I found hanging in those thorns on the meadow,' Lynda said. 'But it obviously meant Langton had brought more money back than he'd admitted to.'

'Even so – £34,460!' Though he was far away at the other end of the phoneline, Clive sounded stunned. 'No wonder it was falling out of his pockets.'

'Taking into account the £2,500 he's just spent on a second-hand motorbike,' Lynda said, 'and the money retrieved by his dog, this means the original amount left lying around that wrecked Mondeo was £38,460.'

'That's pretty amazing.'

'And you didn't even see it spilling out of the spare pillowcase in Langton's bedroom,' she said. 'Some of it was in £1,000 bundles, some of it loose. Said he just grabbed it while he had the chance.'

'So, you've charged him with theft?'

'No real option. But they'll go easy on him. He's got no form and he cooperated fully once I laid it on the line.'

'Are you still at Colchester nick?'

'I'm on my way home,' she said. 'But I thought I'd pop in to the hospital first. Not that it's proving fruitful. It's been twenty minutes and they still haven't let me in.'

'There was no change when I rang earlier.'

'Didn't expect there'd be any, to be honest... Hang on.'

The door buzzed open and the Neurological Intensive Care sister came out into the waiting area in her scrubs, anointing her hands with sanitiser from one of the wall dispensers.

'We have action,' Lynda said, cutting the call.

'Yes, sergeant?' the sister said brusquely.

The name on her plastic tag was Carolyn Margoyle, and she was a young Irish woman, with long copper-red hair, a strand of which she continually and irritably flicked out of her face with her left forefinger. She was sallow-featured, and like Lynda, had probably had a busy shift.

'Just calling in to check...'

'As they were, I'm afraid,' Margoyle interrupted. 'The woman's still critical.'

Lynda attempted to glance past her through the glazed entrance door and the sliver of open doorway connecting with the treatment room in which the female patient was being held.

'Come through if you like.' Margoyle stepped aside. 'But neither of them can talk to you yet.'

Lynda went through with her. 'Is there still a possibility we could lose either of them?' she asked.

Margoyle shrugged. 'It's hard to say. But the woman's suffered a brain injury, so even if she pulls through, we're not sure how much of the original personality will remain. The whole thing's up in the air at present.'

Lynda gazed down at Jill Brooks, if that was indeed who she was. She'd known all along that there'd be no possibility of comparing the patient with the custody mugshot back at the office. All her hair had been shaved, and she'd suffered extensive facial injuries, but at present even these were concealed by a mask of bandaging and gauze, not to mention a web of tubes and pipes feeding the motionless form with nutrients, medication and oxygen. The woman's eyes were visible but deeply bruised and swollen closed. Their lids didn't so much as twitch.

'What about the male?' Lynda asked.

'He's receiving special care too,' Margoyle said.

They went together into the next room.

John Doe also lay inert amid a variety of bleeping machinery. He wasn't so heavily bandaged, but he still appeared to be unconscious.

'Is this normal?' Lynda asked. 'It's been a couple of days and I thought he wasn't as bad?'

'We've noted a leakage of cerebrospinal fluid from his left ear,' the sister replied, 'so observation and complete bed rest are the only real response.'

And that was it. Nothing further was volunteered, and there were no additional questions that Lynda felt qualified to ask. When she headed home, she was forty-five minutes late, having learned nothing new.

Of course, the problem wasn't really that she was late. It wasn't yet seven o'clock. But knowing Don, he wouldn't have got the tea on or even have washed up from breakfast.

Something else was bothering her too.

She parked on the drive and climbed out. The air was icy cold, the temperature having dropped again. It wasn't encouraging to see the living room in full darkness.

Clinical depression was a real thing, and her husband was suffering from it. But even though she understood that, it didn't make her feel any easier about his recent unpredictable moods. She wasn't going to admit to any kind of worry that she'd come home one evening and find that he'd done something silly, but his endless struggles were starting to get the better of him.

She walked up the drive, produced her key and stepped inside.

The hall was pitch-dark, which was unusual.

She went first into the lounge. The lights were switched off in there too, a single streak of moonlight slanting across the room. No light shone from Don's workstation in the dining room. Two empty beer cans stood next to his closed laptop.

'Don ...?' she said, nerves tightening.

'*BOOOM!*' came a muffled voice overhead.

Lynda hastened upstairs.

The landing was also in darkness, but a shaft of light spilled out from under Charlie's bedroom door. Inside it, Daniella, still in her school uniform, was seated on the bed, absorbed in her tablet, while Don and Charlie hunched together on the floor as they advanced legions of miniature soldiers towards the toy castle they'd bought Charlie for Christmas to try and wean him off computer games.

'*BOOM!*' Don shouted again, a whole swath of soldiers taken down in the latest artillery strike, which Charlie found rib-ticklingly funny.

'Isn't this cosy?' Lynda said, out of breath.

'Hi, Mum,' Daniella muttered, preoccupied.

Don glanced up and grinned. 'World War Three in here, I'll tell you.'

'It's noisy enough for that,' Daniella added.

'I was wondering where you all were,' Lynda said. 'There isn't a single light on downstairs.'

'Sorry,' Don replied. 'Really got into it, didn't we, Charlie?'

'Yeah.' Charlie nodded, as he picked the soldiers up and reorganised their battle formation.

'It was light when we started,' Don said. 'But you know what it's like at this time of year.'

Lynda assessed her husband's body language. He was clad in the usual tracksuit, slippers and T-shirt. Even with his good shape, such a sloppy outfit didn't suit him. His hair was tousled as well and there were reddish patches on his cheeks and nose, which, now that he was in his forties, indicated that he'd had a drink.

She didn't want to spoil the happy atmosphere by querying why the tea wasn't on, but no one gained if questionable behaviour wasn't at least questioned.

'Have we had a party downstairs?' she asked.

Don glanced up again. Surprisingly, he didn't look annoyed. 'I take it you mean the empties ... sorry about that. But we've got something to celebrate.' He lumbered to his feet. 'Back in a mo, Charlie, okay?'

Charlie nodded, absorbed in his game.

Lynda backed onto the landing and headed downstairs, turning lights on as she went. Don followed her.

'I've had another long chat with Abby today,' he said. 'Seems one of the new editors at Fortress Books is interested in *Nick 'Em*.'

'Okay ...?' She was hesitant to sound enthusiastic. He'd had interest before. Given who he'd been and what had happened to him, his agent had found no shortage of editors who were interested. The problems arose when they saw his writing.

'I know what you're thinking,' he said from the dining room, cramming the empties into the bin. 'The difference this time is this lad, Barry Harvey. They've brought him in to open a new "true crime" line. He reckons this is the perfect time for a book like *Nick 'Em*. And what's more,' he couldn't resist a boyish smile, 'he's already had a look at it...'

'He has?'

'Yeah, and he likes it. Says the writing's a bit rough round the edges, but it's not far off. The main thing is that he thinks I've got an amazing story to tell, and if I'm prepared to work with him on it, the chances are that he'll take it.'

Lynda was so used to coming home and finding him in the blackest of moods that she didn't quite know how to take this. The fact that he was now whirling around the lounge, tidying, left her wondering if she'd slipped through a wormhole.

'I mean, what've we ever been apart from coppers, Lynda?' he asked. 'I learned to write by producing crime reports. It's a whole new world for me, this. But this lad, Barry... he reckons I've got a unique experience. He says I've got stories to tell that no non-ex-copper could get anywhere close to.'

'Don...' she ventured, not wanting to bring him back to Earth too hard. 'Don't you think you should be cautious at this stage?'

'Yeah, yeah, I know. I'm not getting too carried away. Could be that when I sit down with him, he decides I'm a hopeless case. But it's better than nothing, isn't it?'

'Yes, it's better than nothing,' she agreed.

'So, do we keep celebrating, or what? We don't often get the chance, do we?'

Lynda glanced around the room. The kitchen was still a mess, and it was almost quarter past seven. Even if she started cooking now, they'd be eating at eight at the earliest.

'What do you want to do?' she asked.

He shrugged. 'I was thinking... Texas Tony's?'

'Hell,' she said. 'I don't see why not.'

'Yaaay!' Charlie and Daniella yelled in unison, as they charged into the lounge, having both been waiting at the bottom of the stairs until they heard what their mum had to say.

9

14 December (Saturday)

Elliot and Harri drove in sulky silence. Only the occasional minicab flitted by. Elliot raised his beams to full, the leafless hedgerows sparkling with frost.

'You had to start asking questions, didn't you?' he finally said. 'You had to get nosy.'

'Yeah, course. It's my fault. For asking a question.'

'But what you didn't know wouldn't have hurt you.'

'Until it goes wrong.'

'It hasn't gone wrong yet.'

'There's a first time for everything.' Harri looked round at him. 'I mean, does that not worry you? Never mind the fact that it's morally wrong, does it not at least bother you that this whole thing – whatever it is, I know you'll never tell me – could go belly up?'

They swung onto the single-track lane connecting with Ravenwood Cottage.

'You know, Harri ... at Abu Dhabi in 2010, I crashed at 199 mph. I broke my collar bone and five ribs.'

'I know about that,' she said. 'So?'

'So I was lucky. Think about it. 199 mph. Roland Ratzenberger died at 195. Ayrton Senna at 191. Riccardo Paletti at 110.'

'What are you trying to say?'

He shrugged. 'I'm saying that danger's always been part of it. Compared to getting burned alive on a racetrack, getting arrested seems like a minor risk. Any sentence I have to serve, even if it's a big 'un, would be made a lot easier for me because I know the right people.'

'Tough guys!' she snorted. 'Christ, I am so sick of tough guys. Do you ever consider anyone but yourselves? What about me? Left here on my own? Maybe getting roped into it?'

'You won't get roped into it because as you yourself said, I won't tell you anything.'

'But you can see it would be a bit of an inconvenience for me?'

He shrugged.

'So, why've you agreed to be part of it, Elliot? After everything we said last time?'

A second passed, and he shrugged again. 'It's what I do.'

She shook her head, as if this was too silly to respond to.

Ravenwood Cottage slid into view ahead. It might have sounded luxurious, a typical rural pad that all townies dream of retreating to each weekend, and at first glance it appeared to satisfy that expectation, built from whitewashed stone, with smallish mullioned windows, and a rich mantle of ivy cladding its front wall. However, upon closer inspection, the steep roof comprised rotted, rain-damaged slates, the iron gutters were rusty, and the gravel on the drive was worn away. It had once possessed a broad garden to the north-east, but it was now invisible, overgrown with thorns and bracken so dense that it merged with the surrounding woodland.

It was the same indoors – the living room carpet thread-bare, the sofa and armchair covers frayed. All that said, it was pretty enough on a frosty night in December; Harri had hung fairy lights in the downstairs windows, and with the glow of the Christmas tree in the corner and the ruddy embers in the hearth, the room at least looked cosy.

While Harri went into the kitchen, Elliot moved to the drinks cabinet and poured himself three fingers of Glenmorangie.

'What would you say if I was to tell you that we stand to make quite a bit from this job?' he called through after her. 'And all of it tax-free. Should I turn my back on that?'

Harri returned with a dish of ice cubes. She didn't answer, just dropped a couple into his glass, and then poured herself a Southern Comfort.

'You're asking *me*?' She plonked herself on the sofa, kicking off her heels and sliding her feet into the worn, fluffy slippers that lived under the coffee table. 'Seriously?'

'Like you say, you're part of this.'

'I don't think you'll want to know my opinion, Elliot.'

'You might be surprised.'

'I've spent my entire adult life around spivs, pimps and other kinds of lowlifes,' she said.

That threw him a little.

'I'm not saying you're in that category, Elliot, but you *are* a criminal. And seeing as you're asking me, I can't help admitting that I've often wondered what it would be like to have a guy in my life who's simply got a job. You know, makes an honest living.'

'Stacking shelves in a supermarket, maybe? Working in a call centre?'

She remote-clicked through the channels. 'Are those jobs below you then?'

'Of course they are.'

'Why?' She turned the TV off and stood up. 'Because God put you on this Earth to be a daredevil, and doing nine-till-five is not fulfilling that destiny?'

He felt himself grow flustered. 'I ... *what*?'

'Don't worry ...' She got up again, grabbed some towels from the radiator, and headed to the stairs, stopping to pat his cheek on the way. 'I wasn't being serious.'

'Yeah? Because I think you hit the nail on the head.' She'd now gone up, so he raised his voice. 'I mean, fast driving ... Shit, Harri, that's the only thing I've ever been good at.' He stared at his glass of malt. 'Apart from blowing my cash on this stuff.'

That night, he nuzzled up to Harri as she lay with her back turned. 'You awake?'

'Mmm ...' she half responded.

He put a hand on her bare shoulder. 'I know you don't like this sort of thing.'

'So?' By her mumbled tone, she wasn't fully awake.

'It's odd that you seem so peeved about it. You weren't last time.'

'Because I didn't know about it till afterwards. Either way, it's called stealing, Elliot, and it's wrong.'

'I *do* wonder if all this should be below me, you know. Call it pride, vanity, but I increasingly wonder if maybe I should be better than this.'

'For God's sake, go to sleep.' She was still mumbling, still sounded sleepy. 'Stop navel-gazing.'

'Harri, I'm serious.'

'So am I.' She shook his arm off. 'Things always seem worse at night. Tomorrow, it'll be a whole different thing.'

She had that right, he supposed, as he lay back under the quilt. Tomorrow, he'd receive info about the next meeting, which meant that wheels would then be in motion – which meant there'd be no turning back.

10

8 January (Wednesday)

'The good news is we've located the Mondeo on a roadside camera,' Lynda said as she and Rachel Hollindrake left the canteen, which, as it was still breakfast time, was bustling. She wafted a fistful of printed-out image-grabs as they ascended the stairs back to SCIU. 'The camera in question – let's call it Camera X – belongs to the Highways Agency. It's purely for traffic management purposes and is not equipped with Automatic Number Plate Recognition. It's located on the A14, near Ipswich Park & Ride, which is fourteen miles north of the crash site. The image was captured at 8.39 p.m., so we've got to assume the accident happened within the next hour or so.'

'You haven't been able to trace the Mondeo further back to other cameras?' the DI said.

Lynda shook her head. 'The next camera north of there is a SpeedSpike at Sproughton. That one *is* equipped with ANPR, but there's no trace of the Mondeo on there – and we went back through three hours of footage. The problem is, between the SpeedSpike and Camera X, there are several points of access to the A14, but these are all minor roads that aren't covered by any camera at all.'

'So, we've found them, and then we've lost them again – straight away?'

'I'm afraid so,' Lynda confirmed. 'And the frustration doesn't end there. In the time zone we're looking at, aside from our Mondeo, we've been able to identify and trace twenty-eight other vehicles passing through Camera X. Fourteen went south onto the A12. All the vehicle owners have now been spoken to, and none remember seeing any-thing unusual, let alone an accident. With one exception.'

The DI waited.

'There's one vehicle we haven't been able to identify.' Lynda pulled out a dark, grainy image. A set of digits in its top-right corner revealed that the picture had been snapped at 20.40 on the night in question, but the vehicle itself was hard to distinguish. 'This one passed through Camera X, heading south, half a minute after our Mondeo did. It's the next car behind it. We think it's a Corsa, but as you can see, the VRN is so dirty that it's unreadable.'

Hollindrake gazed at the vehicle in question, but the central section of its rear registration plate was blotted out.

'Tried enhancing it?' she asked.

'I've enquired but I'm informed that no tech we possess would be good enough. That VRN's unreadable because it's covered in mud, I think.'

Hollindrake eyed her. 'You *think*?'

'Well … it's always possible that it's been deliberately ren-dered illegible. But you know, it's January, we've had terrible weather. There're piles of slushy, snowy muck everywhere. We can't automatically assume that this is suspicious.'

Hollindrake handed the image back as she led the way into Lynda's office, where Clive Atkins spun around from his desk.

'Have you guys actually got any good news for me?' the DI asked.

'I don't know,' Lynda replied. 'Clive?'

Clive waved a bunch of documents. 'We've got the preliminary Forensics report.'

'Oh ...' Even Lynda was surprised by that. 'Good.'

'Not quite.' He leafed in a few pages. 'Aziz Khan concludes that, as far as is provable, our Mondeo, though it did strike the central barrier several times in the run up to the RTC, had no detectable contact with any other vehicle during or immediately before the accident.'

'So there was no other vehicle involved?' Hollindrake said.

'Apparently not.' Clive grabbed another wad of paper. 'We also have the final mechanical report, ma'am. The Mondeo was in good nick. Its airbags had been disabled for some reason, but it didn't leave the road because of a mechanical fault.'

Hollindrake mused. 'So, in a nutshell, there might not be any road traffic offences here at all? Jill Brooks and John Doe could have hit a patch of ice?'

'They were in a stolen car,' Lynda reminded her.

'Yes,' Hollindrake countered, 'which has never even been reported stolen.'

'Rachel, come on ...' Lynda couldn't conceal her frustration. 'You're not thinking of downgrading this? I inspected that road surface myself. There were lots of indications that these two were going through some kind of crisis when approaching the crash point.'

Hollindrake folded her arms. 'You still working on the basis there was a fight?'

'The vehicle was being driven erratically. And we know there was something dodgy going on because it was a professionally made clone. Look, Jill Brooks is critically injured. I spoke to the hospital again first thing this morning. It's touch and go. Rachel, don't put us on something else till we've bottomed this one. I have an instinct there's a lot more to this than meets the eye.'

Hollindrake looked at Clive. 'What do *you* think?'

'I understand that we've put the official press statement out?' he said.

'That's correct. One hour ago.'

'Might be worth hanging on, ma'am, just to see if the public can offer any help.' He sat back in his chair. 'I *do* agree with Lynda – for two or three miles leading up to the point where the Mondeo crashed, there's good evidence that it was all over the road. That needs looking into, especially given the severity of Jill Brooks' injuries.'

'You think the driver was beating her up at the time?'

He shrugged. 'Her main injuries are consistent with the accident, but it's clear she'd suffered violence in the days before then.'

Hollindrake sighed. 'How close is John Doe to being fit for interview?'

'Hospital told me to call back later,' Lynda said. 'But if he's involved with something iffy, he won't necessarily talk.'

Hollindrake rubbed a hand through her short, dark hair. 'Okay. Let's at least see what the public can tell us. But there are other jobs coming in, Lynda. You've got one more day.'

'One day?' Lynda said.

'Tomorrow morning.' Hollindrake edged into the corridor. 'If there's nothing new by then, we de-prioritise until we're able to get statements off those two in the hospital.'

And she was gone, striding back to her office.

Lynda slumped into her chair. 'Fat lot of good one day's going to do.'

'What's the big deal?' Clive asked. 'If they'd been DOA, I

could understand. But the chances are the guy will recover, at least. Where's the urgency?'

She couldn't answer – in truth because she wasn't quite sure, herself.

'I hope this is not what I think it is,' he said, handing over the newly arrived files.

Lynda had taken possession of them before she realised what he'd said. She glanced up. 'What's that supposed to mean?'

'Nothing.' Clive sat back. 'I don't want to speak out of turn.'

'Hang on. If you've got something on your mind, let's hear it.'

He looked sheepish. 'Look, Lynda, we're not the big time.'

'Excuse me?'

'Us – in here.' He was already floundering (something to do with the piercing stare she'd fixed on him). 'This place sounds like a cool unit, but the truth is we're a low-level conveyor belt. A vehicle gets pranged, someone gets knocked about, and *we* work out who's culpable. It usually takes half a day. The most serious thing I've charged someone with in the last two years is causing death by dangerous driving. The suspect got two years and served eight months.'

'I know what we do here. What are you driving at?'

Clive was saved by the ringing of the office landline. He snatched it up. 'Serious Collision Investigation Unit, DC Atkins. Okay … yeah? … *yeah!*'

Lynda watched him sternly but noted his growing excitement, especially when he grabbed a pen and started scribbling. It was a couple of minutes before he said, 'Yeah, no problem,' hung up and looked around at her. 'DC Kareena Chopra … Metropolitan Police Clubs & Vice Unit.'

Lynda sat forward. 'She was the one making further enquiries at Jill Brooks' former place of employment. She got something for us?'

'Nothing on Jill Brooks. However, she's learned that Brooks had a close friend at this Pink Elephant place.' He glanced at his notebook. 'Polish girl called Anja Moskwa. Fellow stripper. Seems they both quit the Pink Elephant at roughly the same time. Only difference is, Anja left a forwarding address. Pussycat Bar ring a bell?'

'Felixstowe?' she said.

Felixstowe was covered by Suffolk Constabulary. It wasn't on their patch, but it was only fifty-six miles from where they sat now, and cross-force cooperation was a regular occurrence. Perhaps, it wasn't too surprising that the name was familiar.

'That's Anja's latest gig,' Clive said.

Lynda jumped up and grabbed her anorak.

Clive stood too. 'Can't think what Naomi'd say if she knew I was rushing off to a strip-club.'

'I know. And it's not even lunchtime yet.'

18 December (Wednesday)

It was a week to Christmas and Ipswich was looking the part. The glowing, thatch-roofed stalls of St Peter's street market sold all manner of seasonal crafts and festive food. The towering Christmas tree twinkled at the crowded heart of Cornhill. Elliot ignored all that, parking in a backstreet near Portman Road, and walking northward. His breath smoked, a thin layer of snow crunching under his feet. At the end of a row of workshops, he turned into a dark alleyway and reached a barred gate that admitted him into a narrow passage. Halfway down it stood a steel door with a slat at eye-level. Elliot knocked. It was a coded knock: three rapid raps, a delay of two seconds, and four more.

Feet clumped down a staircase, the slat grated to one side, and although it was difficult to tell in the dimness who was there, he could sense the hostility of the gaze boring into him.

'Didn't think you were bothering,' Ray Lonnegan said.

'I'm not late,' Elliot replied. 'I was told to get here for eight-sharp, and that's the time now.'

'You want to know the problem with you? You think that giving smartarse answers makes you the fucking man.'

'I'm not trying to be a smartarse, Ray,' Elliot said. 'I'm just here because I've been asked to attend. Now look, you may not like me because you think I'm a posh git...'

'I don't think, I *know*.'

'But frankly, you don't matter. We both work for the same fella, and that fella *does* like me – or at least he likes my driving. Now, do you want to cut the crap and open the door?'

'You'd better not have been followed.'

'I'm pretty sure I haven't. I've been all over town before coming here. I've even done some Christmas shopping.'

'Bought that saucy missus of yours a pair of sexy Christmas knickers, did you?'

'Just open the fucking door, eh?'

Lonnegan smirked but slid the slat back into place.

With a loud *clunking*, several locks were disengaged, and the door swung inward. 'Up there,' Lonnegan said.

To their left, a wooden staircase ascended, the dull glow of an electric light just about discernible at the top. Elliot made his way up and entered a long, narrow room occupied by men who he mostly didn't know. They were a rugged crowd; some were scarred and nicked, others simply looked mean as sin. And yet all had one strange but common feature: prominently displayed on each one of them, either on a jacket lapel or sweatshirt front, was a large coloured sticker depicting the head of, in each case, a different animal. At first glance alone, Elliot saw a lion, a rat, a goat, a beetle, a gorilla. Lonnegan came into the room behind him. Up close, he too wore a sticker on his vest. It depicted a wolf.

'Okay, that's all of us – good,' came a voice from the far end.

Elliot turned and saw Jim and Jo Naboth standing one to each side of a large VDU mounted on a desk, with another upright object on their left, draped with a sheet.

As always, it was difficult to believe that they were actual brother and sister.

While Jim, who'd just spoken, was a tall, lean, thirty-something with good looks and a shock of dark hair, Jo was somewhere in her mid to late forties, and clearly had once been voluptuous, though much of that had run to fat. She had long hair bleached so blonde that it was almost white, wore heavy make-up and despite her business-like pinstriped skirt-suit, was adorned with jewellery: multiple necklaccs, pendulous earrings, rings on every finger, so many bracelets and bangles that they clattered when she moved her arms.

It was a trashy look, though no one would have said that to her face. Her grey eyes were small and beady, her mouth fixed in a permanent tight line.

'I was just saying,' Jim added, coming down the central aisle, 'none of you are going to be told each other's names. So, we're all wearing animal badges.' He nodded to someone in a chair on Elliot's left.

That someone, who wore the rat sticker on his jumper, got to his feet. Aside from Lonnegan and the Naboths, he was the only person in the room Elliot recognised because they'd worked together before. He looked eighteen or nineteen. In reality, he was in his late twenties, but he had a lithe, gangly frame, a mop of black curls and a cheery, schoolboy face that was very deceptive. He was the Naboths' cousin, but Elliot knew him only by his nickname, Iago, and if that implied villainy, it was well chosen because he was a regular drug user, crack and PCP, often both at the same time, which, if necessary, meant that he could also be relied on to perform acts of extreme, crazy violence.

At present, though, he grinned and nodded at Elliot, before reaching into a shoebox and taking out a sealed brown envelope made thick by hefty paperwork inside and with another sticker attached to it by paperclip. He handed the envelope to Elliot, but first detached the sticker, which depicted a raven with spread wings, peeling the back off it and then spreading it, adhesive face down, on the left panel of Elliot's jacket.

'Perfect for our lead flyboy,' Jim Naboth chuckled. 'All right, as I say, that's everyone.' He strode back down the room. 'Okay, listen up! The majority of you lads don't know each other. Even if you do, behave as if you don't. That means, from this point on, you only refer to each other by your animal alter-egos. You with us, Toadie?'

'With you,' a guy wearing a toad sticker said.

Jim turned around. 'This is a safety precaution for all our sakes. The fewer names you all know, the fewer people get pinched if it goes wrong. Everyone here knows me and Jo, of course. And we know every one of you, but where me and Jo are concerned, well, that's a different ballgame, isn't it? You know your secrets will always be safe with us.' His smile hardened. 'And there are all kinds of reasons why ours should be safe with you. Of course, on the day of the job, just in case that slips any minds in the stress of the moment, I too will be an animal.'

It didn't surprise Elliot that Jim only referred to himself in this regard, as Jo would not be coming on the job with them. This wasn't a reflection of her gender – the Naboths had always been equal opportunity gangsters – but because as head of the firm, she had many other duties. Hence her pinstripes, which, in contrast to her brother's jeans and sweater, indicated that earlier in the day she'd been taking care of legitimate business.

Jim, meanwhile, yanked the sheet off the upright object,

unveiling a display stand bearing a flipchart, on the front of which was what looked like a complex diagram, but which, on closer inspection, was a street map with certain roads marked in red. He picked up his laptop and hit a couple of buttons. The VDU came to life, and a PowerPoint presentation commenced, a succession of images flickering onto the screen: multiple photographs of streets, buildings, vehicles, the entrance to what looked like an industrial park somewhere. All the while, Jim gave a running commentary.

'Christmas Eve this year, as you may be aware, falls on a Tuesday. As you're also aware, all our local banks close for business on Christmas Eve afternoon. Technically, they re-open the following Friday, December 27. But as that's only two days before they close again until Monday December 30, and then close again on Wednesday, January 1, there is a certain money-holding facility in Harwich that will be taking this opportunity to remain closed throughout the holiday to enable vital renovations to its basement area, which, among other things, holds a high-security vault. These renovations will necessitate the temporary clearing out of said vault and the removal of all the safety-deposit boxes contained therein to a short-term home on an industrial estate just outside of town.'

He paused to sip from a bottle of water. The spectators remained rapt.

Jim continued: 'Now, according to our man inside, who, very fortuitously for us, is charged with organising this transfer, these security boxes contain all kinds of valuables, everything from jewellery to gold bars to bonds to cash. There'll be stolen items in there too, and stashes of narcotics with significant street value, which is more grist for our mill because these are the sorts of goodies that are unlikely to be reported missing.'

This was greeted by chuckles of approval.

Jim leaned on the back of the chair in front of him. 'We're in the world of estimates rather than certainties, but our man on the spot has made an educated guess that the total haul could be five hundred grand's worth. Maybe more. Maybe a lot more.'

Silence followed as he allowed that to sink in.

It was a good ballpark figure, Elliot realised. Anything a lot higher than that – in the tens of millions, for example – would provoke a massive police response and an enquiry that would run forever. This, on the other hand, especially as much of the loot would be illegitimate in its own right and therefore wouldn't be reported, would instigate a more finite investigation, and yet there'd still be plenty to go around.

'The transfer commences late on Christmas Eve afternoon,' Jim said. 'Around three-thirty, with one armoured security truck to make the delivery.' He pointed across the room to the street map on the flipchart. 'You can have a closer look at this in a sec, but you've all got the same info in your personal packs anyway. As you'll see, it's a busy route, but it's not by any means foolproof, and me and Jo have already identified the perfect spot for an intercept, which I'll be elaborating on shortly. Any questions so far?'

'Yeah,' a guy wearing a bear sticker spoke up. 'Christmas Eve afternoon at three-thirty. Won't be much daylight left.'

Jim shrugged. 'Christmas Eve afternoon works for us in various ways. Like you say, it'll be getting dark, and we rarely hit cash-in-transit in the dark. But that's because it's rarely being transferred in the dark, not because it's not a decent option. Think about it, gents. The British army would always rather fight its battles at night. Ain't that right, Wolfie?'

'Totally,' Lonnegan called back.

'All the best commando raids happen in the dark,' Jim said. 'Darkness is our friend.'

'What if this cold snap continues?' Toad chirped up. 'What if we have heavy snow or something?'

Jim mused. 'Well, the longer-range forecasters, who by their own admission, are not the most reliable, think the cold snap will continue, but none are forecasting snow. If it *does* happen, again it ought to work to our advantage in that it'll cause chaos. Only a severe snowstorm would work to our disadvantage, and let's be honest, how many of those do we get on Christmas Eve in the South-East? How many have we had in our lifetimes – two, three …?'

There were mumbles of agreement.

'What's the other way, then?' Bear asked.

'What's that?' Jim said.

'You said the timing of it, Christmas Eve, would help us in various ways.'

'Well …' Jim grinned. 'And I must admit, I like *this*. Christmas Eve, as always, will be a lively time in the pubs and clubs. It'll end up being a busy night for the law. Even so, Jo and I know a few people who can make it even busier. You see, certain reprobates of our acquaintance will be celebrating the season in various watering holes in Harwich … from about three-thirty onward, and they're going to be causing a right royal ruckus wherever and whenever they can. There'll be extra police on duty because of the date – trust me, they're gonna need them.'

The chuckles were louder than before.

As always, Elliot noted, the Naboths had covered every base.

Each time he'd worked for them, it had been planned meticulously. It wouldn't be a case of leaving nothing to chance. With a blag, there was no way you could do that. But they always loaded the dice in their favour. He looked at the thick envelope in his hands. Glancing round the room, he saw that everyone had one – their 'personal packs' as Jim had called them. Each one would contain documentation relating to the job, but personalised to the individual who held it, outlining exactly what he'd be required to do, including timings, locations, clothing they'd need to wear, weapons they'd need to bring, precautions to take; nothing relevant to their unique role would be left out.

Jim continued to talk, detailing the plan. Meanwhile, Jo Naboth stood in stony silence. It wasn't so much a 'good cop/bad cop thing' with these two, it was more the case that Jo, unlike her brother, was the iron fist *minus* the velvet glove. Her pinpoint eyes roved across them, scanning for the slightest twitch or nervous tic that might mark someone out as potentially untrustworthy. Of course, if anyone was to back out at this stage, – *without* having participated in the job – they'd become a very real threat to the firm, and who knew what would happen then.

12

8 January (Wednesday)

'The seaside isn't what it used to be,' Clive said.

Felixstowe was quaint enough along the promenade. It had its pier, fun park and beach, and its row of ornate sea-facing buildings, all whitewashed and with pan-tiled roofs. But there was nobody around. The sea was flat and still and so grey that somewhere out towards the horizon it merged seamlessly with the sky.

'To be fair, you're not seeing it at the best time of year,' Lynda said, glancing at the sat nav as Clive drove.

They turned inland, entering a shopping district, and then a part of town where nightclubs and fast-food outlets were located, most of them standing closed. Here, the sat nav led them into a snow-lined backstreet. Part way down it, a neon sign, currently switched off, read Pussycat Bar. All around it, images of sexy female cats cavorted in leotards and stockings. Underneath this, a steel grille had been pulled down and fastened over a double-sized entrance door, to the left of which, a poster depicted real women in lingerie. There was also a bell-push.

Lynda stuck her finger on it until an intercom crackled to life, and a harsh female voice demanded: 'Who is it? We don't open till four.'

'Police officers,' Lynda said. 'We won't take much of your time.'

A thudding and grinding sounded as the steel grille powered up. On the other side of it, standing in the porch, was a short, dumpy woman dressed in overalls and a tatty yellow cardigan, holding a broom. She was about sixty and wore wire-framed glasses and an auburn wig. The cigarette that drooped from her lips was mostly ash.

'Well,' she sneered, 'is this the best our cut-price fuzz can do these days? Hire a bunch of do-gooding leftie students?'

'Sorry?' Clive said, surprised.

'You two wouldn't scare a mouse,' the woman cackled, 'let alone some of the bloody animals I get in here on Friday and Saturday nights. Fortunately, we use *real* muscle. What do you want, anyway? And make it quick, we've got a show to put on.'

Unfazed by the hostile attitude, Lynda flashed her ID and explained who they were.

'Collision investigation?' The woman's belligerence faded. She looked concerned. 'Has someone had an accident then?'

'I'm afraid they have,' Clive said. 'Any chance we can speak to the proprietor?'

The woman ignored the question. 'Isn't any of our staff, is it?'

'I don't know,' Lynda replied. 'You don't happen to know a girl called Jill Brooks?'

The woman looked relieved. 'No, I know all our girls. That name doesn't ring a bell.'

'We still need to speak to the proprietor,' Clive chipped in.

The woman deigned to glance at him. 'That would be *me*, darling. Mandy Crawford. I'm the owner.'

'How about Anja Moskwa?' Lynda asked. 'She wasn't in the accident, but she might know someone who was.'

The woman blew out rancid smoke, flicking her dog-end away. 'Like as not. Every lowlife in the port knows Anja. Still, I don't care what she does with the rest of her life, long as she's here on time for work and looks good enough to eat.'

'So, where can we find her?'

'Applewood Road, seventeen, down towards the Point. On the Kaywood Estate.' The woman laughed. It was a hard, crow-like sound. 'Spanking seafront property, that.'

'Thanks for your help.' Lynda turned away.

'Hey, darling!' Crawford called after them.

Lynda glanced back.

'You ever get bored beating up Brexit supporters or chasing people for asserting their right to free speech, give me a call.'

Lynda frowned. 'Excuse me?'

'That girl-next-door thing really does it for my regulars.' Crawford laughed again. 'Piles of cash wouldn't be the only tips you'd get.'

'Piss off, you pathetic old tom!' Lynda turned and walked on, Clive hurrying alongside her. Behind them, the raucous, cawing laughter echoed down the side-street.

Inevitably, that spanking seafront property was not as described, comprising a few parallel rows of two-up/two-down maisonettes, many boarded, their front gardens carpeted with days-old frozen snow, clumps of black weed, old cans and bits of broken toys poking up through it. When they came to number seventeen, it abutted onto a rusted fence, in the middle of which a kissing gate led through into a leafless, litter-strewn park.

'Bit of a mess, isn't it?' Clive said.

Lynda unclipped her belt. 'She's a stripper, not a stock-broker. What did you expect?'

They opened a timber gate so rotted and rickety that it almost fell from its hinges and walked up a bare earth path. The green paint on number seventeen was faded and flak-ing, and covered with graffiti. It had no doorbell, so Lynda knocked. Clive stepped back, glancing around, perhaps a little unnerved by the deep quiet in the cold, empty street.

She knocked again, and again. Still there was no reply.

Disgruntled, they were about to turn away when the door to number fifteen burst open, and a squat, heavyset man, wearing a fuzzy brown dressing gown, which flapped open revealing a hairy potbelly and stained yellow underpants, came flying out. He had matted, longish hair and a thick, red-grey beard, his sallow cheeks pinpointed red.

'The fuck's all this racket?' he raged. 'She's not fucking in – can't you tell?'

'Who would that be?' Lynda replied coolly.

'Whaaa?' He rubbed his bleary eyes as he peered at her. 'You come here at the crack of fucking dawn, and you don't even know …'

'It's midday, mate.' Clive flicked open his wallet. 'And we're police officers, so I advise you to keep a civil tongue in your head.'

The guy gave Clive's warrant card a long, penetrating stare, determined to be unimpressed.

Lynda glanced past him into a dim, dingy downstairs, which smelled of stale beer and boiled cabbage. 'Who are you?' she asked.

'Jordan Crabtree,' he replied. 'I fucking live here, if you'd bothered to check.'

'I said cool it,' Clive warned him.

'And who lives at seventeen?' Lynda asked. 'You evidently know.'

'Anja.'

'What's her full name?'

'No fucking clue.'

'What does she look like?'

Crabtree mused. 'Polish bird, I think. Mid-thirties, red hair, big tits on her.' He smirked. 'Not that I'd go there. Fucking death sentence, that'd be.'

'What do you mean?' Lynda asked.

'What do you think?' He bent his left arm and feigned a hypodermic injection.

'You're saying she's ill?'

'I don't know. Could be. I wouldn't take the chance, I'll tell you that.'

'Bet that'd upset her,' Clive said.

Crabtree scowled at him but looked back at Lynda. 'Isn't this why you're locking her up – for possession?' A second thought then occurred to him, and he leaned forward, checking that the street was deserted. 'You didn't get that from me, okay? If it gets back to her that I've said anything... you know, she's got mates...'

'Just tell us where she is,' Lynda said.

He shook his head. 'Bollocks! Enough's enough.'

He backed into his cave-like premises and tried to slam the door. Clive stepped forward, jammed a foot in the way and clamped the door with his left hand. Frustrated, Crabtree opened it again.

'She's just a user, as far as I know,' he protested. 'You don't get time for that these days, do you?'

'Depends what it is,' Lynda replied. 'If it's smack, that's pretty serious.'

'That's also serious for those who are aiding and abetting the offence,' Clive said.

'Aiding and abetting?' Crabtree retorted. 'Give it a rest!'

'You're refusing to tell us where she is, Jordan,' Lynda told him. 'That's not just aiding and abetting, that's obstructing an enquiry, also known as perverting the course of justice.'

'Oh, *come on!*' The householder's voice rose in panic.

'But it's easily sorted,' Lynda added. 'Just tell us where she is, and it all goes away.'

When he spoke next, it was from the side of his mouth. 'The park. That's where she always goes around lunchtime. That's where she gets hooked up.'

'How will we recognise her?' Clive asked.

'She'll have a hoodie on. Grey thing. Always has the hood up when she's buying.'

'Cheers.' Lynda backed off. 'That's all we needed.'

The shabby front door banged closed as they filed through the kissing gate.

'Everyone we meet today's bringing the worst out of us,' Clive complained.

'Thought you did pretty well back there. Don would've been proud of you.'

'Don would've kicked that info out of him.'

'Must admit,' Lynda said, scanning the drab parkland ahead of them. 'It's starting to feel like *that* kind of case.'

13

24 December (Tuesday)

It was a hobo encampment, or at least that was its appearance.

It sat on a barren patch of ground under a flyover section of the A120, on the eastern outskirts of Harwich. It had been specifically chosen because three little-used roads led away from it in different directions. If that wasn't enough, it wouldn't attract any undue attention because there'd been a genuine hobo encampment here before, which had only emptied recently, the colder weather driving its handful of squatters into the town to look for shelter. They'd taken with them the few belongings they possessed, including their makeshift tents. Though now, a whole new range of such flimsy structures had been erected, much larger and sturdier, their frameworks draped with canvas sheets.

Across the rest of the camp, greasy flames flickered where rubbish had been piled up in impromptu campfires, and ragged figures loitered. A couple sat by the fires; a third leaned against the great concrete stanchion at the heart of the camp; a fourth limped around, muttering to himself. The fifth and final one, who, at first glance – thanks to his grubby overcoat and full-head balaclava – you wouldn't realise was former Formula One ace, Elliot Wade, lingered by the kerb. The impression this last figure gave was of dazed or drunken incomprehension. In reality, he was waiting tensely, eyes fixed on the slip road leading down from the A120, which shot by overhead. In reality, the rest of the tattered figures were equally on tenterhooks. In reality, their tent-like structures concealed three untraceable, high-performance cars. The Mercedes-AMG that Elliot had driven at Tunwood was one of them.

On waking up that morning, he'd found his BMW Sport missing, and a note and car key posted through his letterbox. The key was for the AMG, the note explaining which close-at-hand layby he could collect it from. As per his written instructions, in late morning he donned a shabby outfit designed to look like 'homeless' rags, and then walked across fields to the layby in question, locating the AMG and driving it here.

Though he was protected by the car's innocent status all the way to Harwich, to avoid any vapour trail of CCTV leading back to the vicinity of his cottage, he took a circuitous, little-known route, which included lots of country lanes along which there were no cameras. Arriving here at noon, a team was waiting for him. They too were dressed as deadbeats, but they'd quickly taken charge of the vehicle, disguising it alongside the four other cars among the tent-like structures, before departing in a nondescript van. He recognised most of them from the meeting a couple of weeks ago, but he hadn't conversed with any of them.

If you talked, even about nothing, you got to know each other a little better, and in this line of work that was never a good thing.

Elliot fumbled with his grubby sleeve to check his watch underneath. It was just after three, which meant they had another hour to wait. He was shivering. Even now, at mid-afternoon, it was well below zero. Overhead, spears of ice dangled from the underside of the rumbling concrete bridge. But that was the worst of it; there hadn't been a significant snowfall for several days, and all the roads were clear. The cloudless sky was dimming from blue to lilac.

For so many, it would be the perfect Christmas Eve: cold, crisp, blazing with stars.

He turned and remembered to affect a careworn stoop as he walked back to the fire.

Just after 3.30 p.m. that afternoon, a sole security van left the HarCorp Safe Deposit Centre on Main Road in Harwich. Immediately, there was heavy traffic to negotiate, the majority of the town's workforce, having finished early, clogging both carriageways in slow-moving rivers of headlights. But it wasn't too much of a problem. The security van had a police car escort, an Essex Police Volvo V70, navy blue but marked with Battenberg flashes down either flank, riding just in front. Whenever things snarled up too much, it briefly activated its blues and twos, and other vehicles moved aside.

'So, what you getting up to?' the van driver, Len Hargreaves, wondered.

Lewis Wright, his co-pilot, glanced around. 'Over the holidays?'

'Yep.'

Lewis focused on the back of the police car again. 'Janey's grandma's flying in from St Kitts. Should be on the train as we speak. Janey'll be heading over there soon to pick her up.'

'St Kitts, eh?' Len sounded impressed. 'Think it'll be cold enough for her?'

'She won't mind. Said she wanted to see a white Christmas. This'll be her first ever.'

'It's whiteish, I suppose.'

Lewis chuckled. 'We've still got snow in the garden. That'll do for her, seeing as she's never seen any before. How about you, anyway?'

Len pondered. 'Won't be a quiet Christmas for us either. You've got the grandma coming, we've got the grandkids. That's on Boxing Day, mind. It's just me and Freda till then.' He smiled, yellowing teeth showing through his wiry beard and moustache. 'Which is the way we like it.'

'What time do you reckon we'll be done today?'

Len glanced at the clock on the dash, which was just about visible despite the tinsel and baubles. 'We're on schedule so far. Be there in the next fifteen. Another twenty to unload, assuming they've got some beefy lads at the depot. After that, well ...' and he went into an out-of-tune 'It's the most wonderful time of the year ...'

'Leave it out, man,' Lewis groaned. Before sniggering.

The pair might have been less jovial had they known that the two police officers riding in front were listening to increasingly alarming exchanges on the force radio. First off, a mysterious fire at a furniture warehouse near the docks, which had been reported half an hour ago and despite the attendance of several fire engines, was already blazing out of control and endangering nearby residential properties, which meant that a mini-evacuation was in progress. Secondly, though it was only late afternoon, repeated incidents of violence were being reported from pubs and bars around town. By all accounts, a pub doorman had been beaten unconscious with a bottle, while the interior of a McDonald's diner had been trashed by a whirlwind of a brawl. In the McDonald's incident, a policewoman had suffered a broken nose.

The two officers in the escort vehicle had been assigned

to chaperone the security van all the way to its final destination at Unit 71, a nondescript but secure holding facility belonging to one of the shipping firms that used the port, located on the Ringwood Trading Estate just outside of town, and they weren't supposed to diverge from that. But when members of their own shift were being assaulted and hospitalised, their loyalties were torn.

The Three Pigeons was rammed full, the tables crowded with noisy drinkers, more punters clustered along the bar, waving money and having to shout their orders to be heard over the festive hits pumping out of the sound system. Harri and her fellow bar staff worked flat out to keep up with demand, but it wasn't as if they hadn't entered into the spirit of it. They were clad in elf outfits, each one comprising a green doublet with gold buttons, a black buckled belt, tight red shorts and green turned-up slippers, while Harri had gone one stage further, wearing her hair up with a coronet of tinsel twined around it.

Of course, none of this distracted her from the more serious aspects of the day.

She had no option but to keep smiling, but every so often would sidle through into the back room to check the local news feeds on her phone, though she wasn't sure what she was looking for. Elliot never revealed to her the exact nature of this mysterious 'work' he would sometimes do, though on the two previous occasions it had been easy enough to guess just from looking at the newspapers the next day.

The difference this time was that she knew something was happening in advance, so she couldn't help but keep checking the newswire. She wouldn't even have known it was today had she not wandered into the spare bedroom first thing that morning and instead of seeing Elliot sitting at the desktop computer, as she'd expected, found him rooting through a cardboard box filled with all kinds of ragged, Skid Row-type clothing. He'd looked guilty and tried to be evasive, insisting that these were just some bits and bobs he'd got together in anticipation of a fancy-dress party he'd had mentioned to him. It was obviously a lie, and there was further evidence later, when, instead of giving her a lift to the Three Pigeons for her day shift, he'd informed her that they didn't have use of the car and on this one occasion she'd need to get a taxi.

They'd rowed; Harri upset mainly because, having heard nothing about this job since 14 December, she'd hoped against hope that perhaps it had been cancelled for some reason, Elliot responding by repeating over and over that she shouldn't get involved and that this included asking questions. When she'd begged him to think twice, he'd told her that it wasn't an option. He'd seemed firm about that, and yet his whole demeanour was off that morning; he'd looked tense and nervous. This affected her too, the terrifying thought striking her as she waited for the taxi that she might never see him again. When she'd put this to him, he'd told her not to be ridiculous and that it wasn't that kind of job and that no one would get hurt.

During the taxi ride to work, she'd fought hard not to cry. This was Christmas Eve and the last thing the punters wanted to see was someone blubbering. Besides, she didn't know what kinds of questions were going to be asked in the future. Might a weepy barmaid even have looked a little suspicious?

Thus far at least everything seemed to be quiet out there. Until the third time she went into the back room to check and learned that a large warehouse fire had started in Harwich. The grainy footage the website carried was unclear, depicting a chaos of moving bodies, a large angular structure behind them framed against a night sky fast turning red.

She headed stiffly back into the bar.

Fire.

Apparently, nearby houses were having to be emptied. Families, youngsters – and on Christmas Eve.

She shook the idea from her mind as she took an order for three lagers, two bitters and five bags of crisps. Surely Elliot wouldn't have got himself embroiled in something that led to that? It was probably an accident, an unpleasant coincidence. But was it? By all accounts – and though she'd only glimpsed the news item – the blaze was reportedly so fierce that emergency services were being pulled in from towns all over Essex and Suffolk.

'Jesus, Elliot,' she said under her breath. 'Sweet Jesus!'

14

8 January (Wednesday)

'One thing that puzzles me,' Clive said. 'How can this girl be a stripper *and* a junkie? Do needle tracks turn blokes on these days?'

'The way I hear it,' Lynda replied, 'a lot of them inject between their toes.'

He grimaced as they strolled along the park path, which now followed a broad curve. About fifty yards ahead, it brought into view a bench on which a figure in a grey hoodie top was sitting alone, the hood pulled up.

'Excellent,' Clive said. He made to walk forward, but Lynda halted him. 'What're we waiting for?'

'Leverage. Real leverage, this time.' She nodded. 'And *here* it comes.'

They ducked behind some skeletal bushes, watching as a spindly character sauntered from the other end of the path towards the seated figure. He'd come from a battered white van, which waited, exhaust billowing, at a distant gate. He was about sixteen or seventeen, wearing skinny jeans, a black puffer jacket and blue baseball cap. His fluorescent green and orange trainers somehow exacerbated the spider thinness of his legs.

'Can't be long out of school, that one,' Clive muttered.

'County Lines shithead,' Lynda said under her breath.

The kid stopped at the bench. There was an exchange of words, and then he passed something to the seated girl, she passed something back, and it was over. He strolled back towards the van, the girl pocketing her purchase and standing up.

'Let's move,' Lynda said.

They sidled out onto the path. At first the girl didn't notice. Even though she was coming in their direction, her hands were in her pockets, her head down. But then, sensing their presence, she glanced up – in response to which Clive made a critical error. He stepped out and away from Lynda, expanding their line in the standard police way when approaching a suspect, though of course in this instance it clearly indicated to the subject who and what they were.

She ran, veering left onto the grass, heading towards a distant hedge, on the other side of which lay the nearest road. Lynda veered the same way, trying to cut her off. Clive sprinted down the path to try and prevent her doubling back.

'Anja, we're police officers!' Lynda shouted. 'Stay where you are!'

But the girl turned and cut sharply back the way she'd come.

'Clive!' Lynda yelled, as she turned to give chase.

She was briefly distracted by the kid at the far end of the path. He'd twirled around, spotted the police activity and now leapt into the van, which screeched away. Looking back, she saw the diminishing shape of the girl haring towards the far side of the park. In the foreground, Clive climbed to his feet, swearing at the mud streaked down the side of his trousers.

'Clive!' Lynda complained.

'She's a dancer!' he protested. 'She's nimble on her toes!'

Lynda ran past him. 'She's also an addict.'

They galloped in pursuit, but it wasn't easy going, clumps of snow alternating with frosty patches, beneath which there was broken, slushy ground. Ahead, their target raced across a football kickabout area and into a belt of fir trees.

'What's through there?' Lynda grunted.

'Dunno.'

They slipped and slid across the kickabout area, and then were into the evergreens. They wove through with difficulty, now feeling a faint sea breeze in their faces. On the other side, a rusty wire-mesh fence marked the park's perimeter, but beyond that lay what appeared to be a derelict caravan park. Lynda swore volubly.

'Isn't this Suffolk Summer Camp?' Clive panted. 'Been disused for ages.'

Lynda lifted a flap of wire mesh. 'There's only the sea after this. We'll find her.'

'Why don't we just come back later? She has to come home at some stage.'

'Yeah,' Lynda said. 'But that'll mean contacting Suffolk officially and setting up an obbo on their patch.'

'So?'

'So, I want her *now*, Clivey! This case is dragging on as it is.'

'Okay, fine, but you know we left the car on that crappy estate?'

Lynda's thoughts raced, but she had to concede his point. Like her Qashqai, Clive's Peugeot was authorised for use on police duty. It was therefore a police vehicle, and at present was sitting unprotected on a street of dubious character.

'Okay.' She swooped under the mesh. 'Go and get it. Just don't be long.'

He nodded, before turning and hurrying off.

Lynda headed downhill, and a few seconds later was amidst the caravans.

The place clearly hadn't been used in several years. The caravans themselves sat in orderly rows with narrow shingle passages between them. But they were static structures on crooked legs rather than wheels, their paintwork drab and scaling off, their windows grimy and cracked. Lynda moved from one junction to the next, but there was no sign of anyone flitting about.

'Damn!' she breathed.

After she'd been wandering like this for several minutes, she dug her phone out.

'I'm bringing the car round now,' Clive said, breathless. 'According to the sat nav, there's an entrance to that old park on View Point Road.'

'Park *across* the entrance, yeah? Then come in on foot.'

'Will do,' he said.

Not that this felt as if it would help. Assuming the Polish girl was still here, there were any number of spots where she could get out. Irritated, Lynda went left and then right, taking turns at random.

And heard a dull *thud*. She halted. A distant wind hissed over the nearby sea. But there was nothing else. She couldn't even hear the rumble of traffic.

She pivoted around, trying to work out which direction the noise had come from, settling on a passage, which as far as she could tell, ran roughly north. She ventured along it. The temptation was to shout out and explain her purpose here, but that probably wouldn't yield a result; junkies caught in possession tended not to trust the word of any copper.

Of course, this created a potential additional problem.

If the girl was bent on evading custody, and she had a couple of syringes with her, these could quickly be turned into weapons. And if they'd already been used…

Another *thud*. This time from behind her.

Lynda spun around.

The caravan looming at her rear was indistinct from most of the others; once white or cream-coloured, now a yukky brown, moss crabbing its few bits of tarnished metalwork. The inside of the window facing her was so thick with dust that it was virtually opaque. A faint shaft of light was just visible inside, presumably from a skylight, the lumpy shadow of some heavy, shapeless bit of furniture framed against it.

A skylight in the roof…

Lynda's eyes strayed to the caravan's upper parapet, as if she expected to find a figure crouching there, about to leap down on her.

But there was no one.

Thinking about those syringes had spooked her, she realised. She glanced at the window again before heading away.

And saw that the shadow was no longer there.

Lynda stood rigid. Before jolting to life and scrambling around the caravan's exterior, looking for the door. It was on the far side, still closed, though fragments of moss that had once covered the join between the door and the jamb now hung loose.

She called Clive again.

'I'm just parking up,' he said. 'Where are you?'

Absurdly, she realised that she couldn't tell him. She'd

come a considerable distance into the caravan park, but it wasn't like she could give him directions.

'Just make your way in, and fast,' Lynda said. 'Keep your ears pinned back.'

She cut the call and listened again, hearing nothing from the interior.

Fitting her gloved fingers around the door's edge, she held her breath and yanked it open. 'Anja?' she said.

There was no response from the dim, dank interior.

'I'm Detective Sergeant Hagen from Essex Police. I know you think you're in trouble, but you're not. I just want to speak to you about someone you may know.'

The silence lingered. A very complete and profound silence, as if there was no one there.

Lynda stepped up into the doorframe, glancing left and right.

Inside, it smelled of mildew and was cluttered with decrepit junk: old clothes, old furniture, old boxes, everything dense with dust and cobwebs. Crooked passages led left and right. Overhead, there was indeed a skylight, though only weak light leaked through thanks to its coat of dirt.

'I repeat,' she said aloud, 'all I need to do is speak to you.'

Nothing stirred.

She peered left, her eyes drawn to what appeared to be a shadowy, upright form. She approached it slowly, the breath tight in her chest. As she did, it resolved itself into a person standing with their back turned. A long oilskin coat covered most of the figure, while what looked like a broad-brimmed wedding hat sat on the head. The backs of two boots were visible below.

'Anja, we need to talk.' The figure didn't move. 'We need to talk – about Jill Brooks.'

Again, nothing.

'Look, Anja, you're not in trouble.' Lynda was now within touching distance. She reached out. 'But I'm not playing this childish game ...' Gently, she tapped the figure's shoulder.

It rocked. The coat fell off, revealing a coat stand.

Lynda stared at it, pink-cheeked, before turning around too quickly, tripping on a divot torn in the rotted carpet and falling backward against the stand, which toppled over. With a furious *BANG*, a door flew open a few yards back along the caravan – the door to the lavatory – and a figure, a real one this time, came out in a blur of speed, dashing outside.

Lynda leapt up and flung herself out as well. Just in time to see the hooded shape of the Polish girl going left. However, she didn't get past the next junction, before Clive jumped out and caught her by the collar, swung her around and threw her to the ground.

'Careful, Clive,' Lynda said, hurrying up. 'She might be carrying sharps.'

Clive nodded but held his ground.

The girl had already partly got up, limbs coiled like springs, but Lynda had arrived too, and she was hemmed in. Her hood fell back, and long, flame-red hair, damp with sweat, unravelled. She gazed at them with wide, haunted eyes, her ample chest rising and falling.

'Take it easy, okay?' Lynda said. 'I know we saw you buying drugs, but you are *not* in trouble. Do you understand, Anja? Not yet anyway ... so, it's up to you how you want this to go.'

The girl remained crouched, her green-eyed gaze sullen. 'I know nothing, I say nothing.'

Lynda shrugged. 'Truth is, you can say anything you want. We haven't cautioned you yet. Maybe we won't need to.'

'I say nothing.'

'We're here about a friend of yours.'

The girl's expression tightened. She no longer looked nervous; now she looked frightened.

'That bothers you?' Lynda asked.

'I know nothing.'

'You know nothing about who? Jill Brooks?'

Anja swallowed.

'That name really worries you, eh?'

A short, tight shake of the head. 'I know nothing.'

'Why does the name Jill Brooks bug you, Anja?' Lynda asked.

The girl clamped her mouth shut.

'We *know* you know her,' Clive said. 'One of your ex-employers told us she was your best mate at the Pink Elephant club in Knightsbridge. That you were so close you used to do routines together on stage.'

Anja looked as if she was about to comment on that, but then thought better of it.

'Look, Anja,' Lynda said, taking out her handcuffs. 'I don't want to arrest you. But you're going to leave me no choice. And that could be a big problem for you. Because possession of heroin is not a small offence, especially if it's not your first. And deportation has to be a possibility – I'm sure you're aware of that.'

'If it helps, Jill Brooks isn't in trouble,' Clive said. 'Not the kind you're thinking about.'

The girl looked bewildered by that, glancing from one to the other. But Lynda wasn't going to tell her any more than she needed to.

'Where does Jill live?' she asked. 'Where can we contact her family?'

Anja regarded the cuffs dangling from Lynda's hand.

'It's not much to ask in exchange for cutting you loose without charge,' Lynda said. 'You seriously think you'll get a better deal today?'

Reluctantly, rather quietly, the Polish girl said: 'She no live anywhere.'

'What does that mean?' Clive asked.

'She get married.'

'Married?' Lynda replied, surprised by such a mundane explanation. 'You mean she's not Jill Brooks anymore? What's her married name? Where does she live?'

The girl struggled with this, torn between loyalty to her friend and a concern that something might have happened to her.

'It's not a lot to ask,' Lynda said. 'Give us that basic info and we can go our separate ways.'

'All that to clear up an RTC,' Clive said, as he drove back into Felixstowe.

'We haven't cleared it up yet,' Lynda replied.

Clive glanced at the open notebook on her lap. 'Harriet Wade? Explains why the old bitch at the Pussycat Bar didn't know her.'

'Hmmm.' Lynda was only half listening.

'Married to Elliot Wade. Either of those names mean anything to you?'

Lynda shook her head.

'Least we've got an address,' he said.

Lynda glanced back through the Peugeot's rear window. 'Did Anja seem inordinately frightened to you?'

'Like you say, she's worried about getting deported.'

'I don't know.' Lynda looked front again. 'They run that risk all the time. But hell, I thought she seemed terrified.'

15

24 December (Tuesday)

The police escort saw Len and Lewis onto the Ringwood Trading Estate, some two hundred acres of new commercial property enclosed by high net-fencing and accessible by a single entrance/exit, which connected with a slip road to the A120. However, after that, the cops peeled away and headed back into town. The security guards had already been advised of this via radio. It seemed that there was a serious problem down at the docks; a major fire had broken out in a warehouse and was in danger of spreading to adjoining homes. But on top of that, there'd been disturbances in a number of town centre bars, and the police, though they had extra manpower on for Christmas Eve, were already at full stretch.

'We'll be there in five minutes,' Len said as he drove along the estate's main drag, a broad but unmarked roadway passing between open lawn areas and the towering, corrugated box-like structures that were the units. 'We'll be fine.'

It was late afternoon, and in normal circumstances wouldn't yet be the end of the working day, but given the date, cars flitted past them as estate staff headed for the exit. Many lights were now switched off, most of the warehouses featureless outlines on the silk-black sky. Here and there, a reception lobby was still lit up, as were a couple of front offices, but few people were moving around. Several car parks were already empty.

Though he'd been five years in the Royal Anglians, Lewis was less easy about it than Len. He'd never ridden cash-in-transit when it had been hit, but back in 2006 he'd been part of a five-vehicle convoy in the Sangin District when they'd fallen foul of a Taliban ambush. Despite being heavily armed, the troops had suffered serious losses, three British soldiers and one Afghan interpreter killed, six others wounded. If three Apache attack helicopters hadn't showed up ten minutes into the firefight, they might all have bitten the Afghan dust.

On this occasion, they weren't even armed, of course.

Lewis glanced into the side-mirror to ensure there was no vehicle behind them. They swung a sharp right. The road ahead ran between more formal buildings, low-rise office blocks, all of them shrouded in darkness, particularly the side lanes dividing them.

'What are all these places?' he asked. He'd never made a delivery to the Ringwood before, so it was unfamiliar to him, though he was becoming aware of its expansive, labyrinthine layout.

'Centrica, Electrolux, Virgin Media,' Len replied. 'All sorts. Large, small, you name it.'

They swung a left, passing some kind of depot with numerous vehicles arrayed in straight lines on its forecourt, their windscreens and roofs encrusted with frost. After that, they were back among taller outlines again. Recognisable names flitted by in their headlights: O2, Network-i, GlaxoSmithKline. Several minutes had passed since they'd seen another moving car or any light that wasn't a motion-sensitive security light.

'Relax,' Len said, surprised that someone with the look

and aura of Idris Elba should be so uptight. 'We're almost there. Next left, a couple of hundred yards and the job's a good 'un.'

'Fine.' Lewis glanced into his side mirror again.

It looked dark and empty back there, but without night vision you couldn't be sure there was nothing happening.

They veered right onto another straight but much narrower passage running between the backs of buildings that were more like old-fashioned warehouses, all redbrick, rusty pipework and dumpster-type bins. It spooled ahead a considerable distance, way more than a couple of hundred yards.

'Down there?' Lewis said. 'Len, hold up. Wait.' Len eased to a halt. They were about forty yards in, their headlights showing nothing but cracked tarmac and gutters clumped with frozen snow. 'This is a shortcut?'

'This is the way to Unit 71.'

'Looks a bit ... I don't know, basic?'

Len shrugged. 'Unit 71's high-security storage. There is no front. It's just breezeblocks and steel-slat fencing all the way around. The only gate's down the far end, here, and you can't even tell it's a gate if you look at it casually. Come on!' He nudged Lewis's shoulder. 'Tough ex-squaddie like you. Surely you can see the advantage of secret passages and hidden doors?'

'Suppose so,' Lewis conceded.

'Problem?' a muffled voice sounded from the rear.

It was Ted Cox, the third guy on the transport. He was locked into the back of the van.

'Nah, we're good,' Len shouted, putting the vehicle back in gear, easing forward again.

They passed several rear doors on either side, all closed and padlocked. Several were double-sized and set into recesses, clearly entrances to garages. There were windows too, all black. It was reassuringly ordinary and utilitarian, and Lewis found himself relaxing again.

Fifty yards further on, it didn't strike him as odd when they passed a series of three spacious parking bays on the right, two empty, but with a high-sided van bearing nondescript company logos and cardboard covering its windscreen, occupying the third one. Not that he would have had much time to think about it, because just ahead of them now, a huge pair of headlights sprang dazzlingly to life.

They were on high beam and filled the entire alley with a blinding glare.

Len shouted, slamming his brake to the metal, the van screeching such a distance that it almost front-ended the obstacle. When they halted, they were so close that, even in the dark, they were able to see what it was: an HGV of some sort, which had just veered out from its parking space, and only then had bothered to switch its lamps on. It didn't look like an artic, but it had a tall cargo compartment at the back, like a removals wagon.

Len gazed up at it dazedly. Lewis was shocked into momentary paralysis, but then heard an engine revving behind them and, glancing into the side mirror, saw that the high-sided van, now minus the cardboard on its windscreen, had pulled up behind and braked, blocking them in. What was more, its back doors had already been flung open, because shadowy figures were leaping out and gambolling forward along either side of it.

Lewis got onto the radio. 'Mike Sierra Three ... under attack. I repeat, we're under attack ... on the Ringwood Estate, we're under attack ...'

With a CRUNCH, the window alongside his face

splintered. Lewis slammed down the Perspex visor on his helmet. The window didn't shatter – it was supposedly shatterproof, but it must have been struck with monumental force to react the way it did.

Now he saw why.

Someone had come out of the lorry, an enormous guy wearing grey hooded overalls and gloves and – Lewis goggled at the sight – a gorilla mask. He was wielding a sledgehammer and had just delivered it full-swing to the glass. A second blow followed, and a third. The glass was punched inward but remained intact. It would come out of its frame before it broke properly, and was in the process of doing just that.

'Oh, Jesus … Jesus help us …' Len whimpered, his prayers turning to squawks of terror as his own window was hit by the roaring teeth of a chainsaw. Churning flakes of safety glass spurted in. Len screamed again as he caught them in the face.

'Get your visor down!' Lewis shouted, his attention torn between colleague and radio.

He grunted in shock as the fourth blow from the sledge punched the windowpane clean through, slamming it into the side of his helmet. Several different arms thrust their way in, all clad in overalls and heavy-duty gloves, and grappled at him, ripping the device from his hand, ripping at his harness and Kevlar vest, ripping at his visor. He kicked and struggled, before bracing his knees against the dash and his back into the seat, trying to wedge himself in place, at the same time knocking hands away from the seatbelt to stop them releasing it and dragging him out through the window. At which point, his visor flirted up, and the cold muzzle of a pistol jammed into his cheek.

'Wanna throw your life away for someone else's stuff?' came a calm voice. With a *click*, the firearm was cocked. 'Your fucking call, pal!'

Lewis went rigid, sweat beading his brow, the heart hammering his ribs. This was the moment those on any kind of front-line duty dreaded: where there was nothing else to be done, where you'd lost control of the situation and your life was in someone else's hands – someone who couldn't give a toss about it.

'Open the door. *Fucking do it!*'

Before Lewis could comply, Len did it for him. He hadn't had a chance to pull his visor down and his ashen face was riddled with cuts, but his window had been smashed too, the chainsaw having sliced through and chewed several inches into the armoured door. At which point a second pistol had found its way to Len's right temple.

The doors were lugged open and the twosome hauled out, the helmets torn off their heads, and their hands secured behind their backs with zip-ties. From here on, from Lewis's perspective at least, it was nothing but fleeting glimpses in the glare of the HGV headlights. All their assailants – he couldn't tell how many there were – wore animal faces under their hoods. The one holding the gun to his cheek was a toad, while Len was in the grip of a wolf. Lewis only saw two pistols – a Glock and a Beretta 9000 – but there were truncheons on show too, pipes, coshes and the like.

The guy with the chainsaw wore a rat face. As Len was hustled around the front of the van, the Rat handed the chainsaw to someone else and jumped in behind the steering wheel. The ignition was still on, but the clutch ground and the vehicle juddered as he banged it into reverse.

'Out the fucking way!' the Wolf snarled, pushing Len

across to the far side of the alley, but because Len was hyperventilating with fear, he stumbled and half fell, and the Wolf growled, hitting him twice with the Glock. Blood shot from the older guard's nostrils as the second blow visibly broke his nose.

'Wolf, chill the fuck out!' came a commanding voice. 'Deadweights are harder to move.'

Lewis turned his head as he too was hustled across the alley to the other side and made to stand against the wall, alongside a closed yellow door. The voice had come from a tall blagger who'd emerged around the side of the HGV. He wore a tiger mask, carried a sawn-off pistol-grip shotgun, and had a pack slung on his back from which a wire connected to an earpiece.

That latter would be a police scanner, Lewis realised.

The team bustled, the high-sided van that had brought them here reversing twenty yards, before driving forward again and swerving into the same parking bay it had occupied before, its rear doors swinging. Rat, in the driver's seat of the security van, copied the manoeuvre, sliding into the next bay and parking. The HGV moved last, but not before Lewis and Len were pushed hard against the wall, allowing it to rumble past, the guy with the scanner walking next to it. When it had cleared the other two vehicles, it braked. Lewis saw that its rear door, a roll-up shutter, was already open, revealing a cavernous interior.

Alongside him, Len moaned aloud. His white face was slathered with blood and sweat. He sagged where he stood.

'You all right, mate?' Lewis asked.

Len mumbled something, his legs buckled, and he half toppled. The Gorilla had to grab him to hold him upright.

'Stupid bastard,' Lewis said to the Wolf, his voice almost breaking. 'Look what you've done!'

The Wolf rammed his Glock between Lewis's eyes, pinning his head against the brickwork. 'You got something to fucking say?'

'No ... I'm sorry,' Lewis stammered. 'Look, man ... I've got a wife, a kid.'

'I give a fuck?' The two eyes blazing at Lewis seemed perfectly suited for the wolf mask that encircled them. They were livid with rage.

'Wolf!' came that warning voice again. 'Bring 'em over here.'

Wolf continued to glare at Lewis from point-blank range, his finger still tight on the trigger, the Glock's muzzle boring into the front of his skull. Then, with a subdued curse, the gun was withdrawn. Lewis was grabbed by the harness of his vest and hurried across the alley. The other gunman did the same with Len, the older guy stumbling and tottering.

The HGV waited in a cloud of exhaust, engine chugging, its interior still empty. But the rest of the robbers were at the back of the security van, weapons hefted. The Tiger stepped forward.

'Seems you two are taking all the shit,' he said – his accent was Cockney, Lewis realised – 'while your dumb fucking mate inside tries to be a hero.'

'We can't open that door ...' Lewis stammered. 'Even if we had keys, it's on a timer.'

A sickening blow from the barrel of the Glock dug into his lower right side. He doubled, choking in pain. Len sagged down as well, as if the mere sight of this was too much for him. This time, they let the older guy drop to the tarmac, where he lay in a shuddering heap.

'Don't bullshit us,' Wolf hissed into Lewis's ear. 'We know your mate in there can bypass the timer.'

Lewis shook his head. The pain carving through his body was so intense that at first, he couldn't speak.

'Fuck this!' Wolf, who sounded Mancunian, shoved the Glock into his hip pocket and pulled something else out.

It was concealed in his gloved fist, but a plastic stem protruded between his fingers. The blagger raised it, and a jet of transparent fluid hit Lewis in the eyes. Initially, he only smelled the ammonia. But then he felt its deep, burning sting. He issued a strangled but prolonged cry.

'Hear that?' Tiger shouted through the door. 'Your mate's being tortured. And it's all on you.' He turned. 'The other one too.'

Wolf stepped over to Len, who though he still lay prone, squawked and tried to wriggle away. His squawks became yowls as Wolf hunkered down, taking careful aim with his jet nozzle. Before he could do more, there was a *clunk*, and a motorised *whirring* sound, and the back door opened. They spun as one, pushing forward, yanking the doors open and pulling the terrified third guard out. They threw him down face-first, landing on him with their knees as they wrenched his helmet off and zip-tied his hands in the small of his back.

'Get their personals,' Tiger instructed.

The men groaned and whimpered as the robbers ransacked their pockets and pouches, locating their wallets, which were waved in front of them. Lewis watched through eyes blurred by hellish, fiery fog, but he understood the significance.

'We're keeping these,' Tiger said. 'And you know what that means. It means we know who you three jokers are. When this thing's over, you'll never see us again — assuming you give the coppers the biggest cock-and-bull story they've ever fucking heard. You tell them anything that leads to our door, you'll be looking over your shoulders for the rest of your fucking lives ...'

Wolf added emphasis with a hard kick to Ted Cox's ribs.

As he did, Tiger cocked his head sideways, receiving a message through his earpiece, then rounded on the rest of the gang. 'Emergency call acknowledged! Move it! Three minutes!'

Two of them went into the security van armed with bolt cutters. The rest formed a human-chain, linking the back of the van to the back of the HGV. In a less high-tech era it would have been quicker and easier just to steal the van, but such inconvenient gadgets as trackers had put paid to all that.

'Two minutes, forty-five seconds!' Tiger shouted, shotgun levelled as he pivoted around, scanning the alley in both directions.

One by one, the steel, tray-shaped security boxes were handed out of the van and passed along the chain, at the end of which they were hurled into the HGV, their shockproof status protecting both them and their contents from damage.

Lewis blinked away peppery tears, but he felt he owed it to whatever investigation would follow to try and take in as much as possible. Only one man now stood over them: Wolf, his pistol drawn. But one was all the bastards would need, especially this one.

'Two minutes!' Tiger shouted.

The rest of the gang worked at phenomenal speed, a mountain of boxes building up inside the HGV's rear compartment. Given that these came from the high-value vault, it would already be a sizeable haul.

'One minute,' Tiger shouted, filching a mobile from his

overalls, hitting a number on speed-dial, and shouting a simple order: 'Deploy stingers.'

Agonised and nauseated as he was, Lewis observed their captors' clockwork efficiency. This whole thing was well organised and well rehearsed.

'Twenty seconds ... *time!*'

The gang abandoned the human chain, half of them scuttling to the rear of the high-sided van, throwing their weapons and tools inside it, and clambering in themselves, the others making for the HGV and doing the same. The doors on the high-sided van slammed closed, and it reversed out of the parking bay, spinning around in a rapid three-point turn. Tiger, meanwhile, leapt up onto the ledge of the loading platform at the rear of the HGV and pulled down the shutter. When he'd jumped off again and secured it, he slapped the side of the lorry, and with a crunch of gears, it accelerated away along the alley.

Wolf, meanwhile, grabbed the back of Lewis's vest and hauled him to his feet. Gorilla did the same with Ted and Len, dragging them upright one after the other. Lewis flinched as the cold steel of Wolf's muzzle pressed the side of his neck.

'Back into your truck,' Wolf hissed. 'Through the back door ...'

'*Oy!*' a sudden beery voice interjected. '*What the bleeding hell ...?*'

They whipped around.

Some fifteen yards away, the yellow door in the wall where the guards had been held at gunpoint had opened, and a tottery figure stood there, a balding, overweight character, his huge belly sagging down over the front of his trousers, his tie hanging loose over a white, beer-stained shirt. Behind him,

PAUL FINCH

they saw disco lights, heard voices, laughter and Christmas pop songs. The guy stood stunned, one hand still clutching his open flies.

There was a fleeting, frigid silence, before Wolf swung to face him, turning Lewis around in front of him. Though the party guy was unarmed, some deep-ingrained instinct had provoked a military response. Lewis was a human shield, he realised.

The Glock appeared to the right of his head, aimed over his shoulder.

Two rapid shots were fired, the double detonation almost deafening him.

The first slug tore through the guy's left hip; Lewis could tell that from the way his pelvis spun around before the rest of him could follow. The second hit him in the right shoulder, which spun him the other way, before throwing him back and through the open doorway, a slimy trail of blood left on the yellow door as he slid down it.

'*Move it!*' Tiger shouted, his pump-action levelled in both hands.

Wolf and Gorilla hustled Ted, Len and Lewis towards the open back doors of their own security van, where Ted and Len's legs were kicked from beneath them as they were thrust inside. Lewis craned his neck around to see what was happening.

Tiger stood facing the open yellow door. The bottom half of the fella they'd downed was still sticking out over the step. Other partygoers crowded into the space behind him, wanting to see what had happened. Tiger fired once, the lower half of the yellow door exploding.

'Stick to the plan!' he shouted over his shoulder as he ratcheted another shell into the breach.

'They saw everything,' Wolf protested.

Oh God, no ... please no, Lewis thought. *Janey, I love you, girl ... I so love you.*

'Whatever it takes,' Tiger said.

'Get in!' Wolf snarled, seeing that Lewis was hanging back.

A foot landed on the guard's backside and he was propelled forward, falling on his knees into the rear of the van, which was a chaos of hanging chains and spilled, broken cagework. Ted and Len already lay face down amidst it, both of them wailing in terror.

'I said get the fuck in!'

Another kick hit Lewis in the back, sending him sprawling on top of them.

'Didn't you fucking hear me!' Wolf shouted as he climbed inside behind them.

I love you, Janey ...

Lewis heard the impact on the back of his skull before he felt it.

16

8 January (Wednesday)

'So, you can't find it?' Clive said as he crossed the hospital car park.

'I'll find it ... it's just a tad off the beaten track,' Lynda replied. 'Hinge Lane. Sounds like an everyday place, doesn't it? In actual fact, it's well out in the sticks. How are *you* doing, anyway?'

'We've got some movement down here,' Clive said. 'I took the new info to Neuro IC, so they can dig up the medical records. Seems Elliot Wade has now been moved to the Billington Ward, which is one of the recovery units. Sounds like he's doing well.'

They were referring to the male patient as Elliot Wade, even though there was no proof yet that he was one and the same. It seemed likely though, given that now they had an address, they'd managed to find him in the phonebook but had got no response despite repeated calls – which was why Lynda had headed straight over there.

'See if you can have a word with him,' she said.

'Doing exactly that.'

'Just a bedside chat, Clive. No caution yet. Don't start discussing the stolen car aspect.'

'No probs.'

'Good. Least one of us is getting somewhere.' Lynda cut the call.

When Clive reached the correct entrance, it led into a waiting area for several different recovery wards, the Billington just one of them. It was late afternoon, not visiting hours, but there was a man waiting, a well-groomed chap in his thirties with neat blond hair, wearing a blazer and tie, reading a copy of the *Telegraph*. Clive went past him onto the ward. There were two staff on duty at the nursing station: Nurse Zara Abimbola and Nurse Adam Reynolds.

'I'm afraid he's still not recovered sufficiently to talk,' the former said.

'I see,' Clive replied, looking frustrated.

'No harm in checking again,' Reynolds said. He entered the ward, beckoning Clive to follow.

There were eight beds in there, four ranged down either side. Men of various ages lay reading or listening to music. The first bed on the right contained Elliot Wade, or John Doe or whoever he was. His face was puffy and bruised, the back of his head shaved and padded with gauze and plasters, his neck fixed in a soft brace. But a drip was plugged into his left wrist, and he appeared to be out for the count.

'They sleep a lot,' Reynolds said. 'Even though a basal skull fracture's not technically a serious condition, he'll still suffer headaches, nausea, extreme lethargy. His body needs to rest. Better if you come back later.'

'No problem.'

As they departed the ward, neither of them noticed how the patient's left eye, though swollen and purple, cracked open to watch.

★

As Clive headed back out, Nurse Abimbola called after him.

'Excuse me, detective,' she said. 'Now that I think, there was a gentleman here earlier. Asked if he could see the driver from the accident on the A12. Said he was a close friend.'

Clive turned back to her. 'He actually said "the driver from the accident"?'

'Yes, specifically.'

'Did he leave a name?'

'Just said he was called Nick. Nice-looking man. Quite smart. Blond hair, blazer and tie.'

Clive pointed towards the waiting room. 'The guy who was sitting out there?'

Abimbola nodded. 'He was out there earlier. He came on to the ward at one point. But I had to shoo him out again.'

Clive hurried through to the waiting room. But it was empty.

17

24 December (Tuesday)

It was only five o'clock but Harri felt as if she'd been on duty for ages. The party atmosphere had intensified, the Three Pigeons bulging at the seams. The fact that there was still nothing out of the ordinary on the news, apart from the conflagration at the docks in Harwich, was an issue for concern rather than comfort. Had something gone wrong? Had the job been nipped in the bud, so that none of the newshounds even knew about it?

Each time, she tortured herself with these fears, always fighting hard to regain control.

She didn't know anything about the job so there was no point trying to guess at its outcome.

Unless it's been cancelled, she thought again. *Unless there was an unforeseen problem, which has put the kibosh on the whole thing.*

As she pulled more pints, she glanced towards the pub door, always wondering if Elliot was about to saunter in, back in his ordinary clothing, twirling his car keys.

And then she heard the newscaster on one of the eight large flat-screen TVs that adorned the pub's interior.

'Some breaking news. We're hearing about a shooting incident on an industrial estate just outside Harwich in Essex. No details yet, but we have unsubstantiated reports that a number of shots have been fired and that there are several casualties. More on that story as soon as we get it.'

Harri stood frozen, paying no attention to the punter offering her a wad of fivers.

A number of shots fired. Several casualties.

'Hello ...?' the punter said. 'You all right, gorgeous?' He grinned. 'Or are you giving the booze away in honour of the season?'

'What ... oh, sorry.' Harri snapped back to it. She took his money and dashed to the till so that she could hurry back to the bar and the TV screen.

'A bit more on that story from earlier,' the newscaster said, 'concerning the possible shootings in Essex.'

Possible? Her heart soared with hope. Perhaps they'd got it wrong?

'Still no details on the casualties, but according to an initial police statement, the incident is not thought to be connected to terrorism. It may, in fact, be an armed robbery.'

Harri's world crashed, and with it, the tower of empties that one of the glass collectors had just pushed across the bar towards her.

Elliot wasn't sure what unnerved him more: the police siren that he heard on the overpass, or the fact that it hadn't yet dwindled into the distance when a pair of headlights hurtled around the bend in one of the country roads adjoining the junction. Judging from the massive, angular shape behind them, it was the HGV, and it was travelling at such reckless speed that it crossed the central line, nearly ploughing into the barbed-wire fencing on the other side and the frozen meadow beyond.

Everyone loitering there came to life, Elliot joining the

other drivers in rushing across the waste ground to their vehicles. He tore down the canvas rags concealing the Mercedes-AMG and opened the boot, before reaching under his tatty old coat, dragging out his raven mask and pulling it over his head. All around him, the others were doing the same. Lion had reappeared, along with Bear. The two who were not drivers, Goat and Beetle, had produced pump-action shotguns, and now took up sentry positions watching the other approach roads.

With a thundering crash, the HGV bounced up onto the waste ground, its driver braking so hard that it turned on its axis, slithering sideways, its glaring headlights flooding the pillar and the underside of the bridge. Its front doors burst open, and the driver, Cobra, leapt out, racing around to the rear where the others had congregated. The shutter went up with a rattle and the two guys inside, Pig and Eagle, were already handing down safety-deposit boxes. A sharp screech drew Elliot's attention back to the road. He saw the high-sided van hurtling forward. That too jolted over the kerb, braked and slid to a crazy halt, Jim Naboth, Ray Lonnegan and Iago, all masked, scrambling out while it was still in motion.

Its front windscreen was spider-webbed with cracks.

Elliot pushed his mask up to look properly. 'What happened?'

Iago pushed his rat mask up too, exposing a white, sweat-soaked face. 'Fucking party-goers. Just as we were pulling away, one of them whizzed a bleeding gin bottle at us!'

'Shift your arses!' Jim bellowed in the background.

'Stingers took out the first two cop cars coming onto the estate,' Iago added, 'but we got into some shit on Brentwood too.'

Elliot listened, numbed. On paper, the getaway plan had sounded foolproof, the lorry and the high-sided van speeding away from the ambush point by following a carefully plotted route across the estate, exiting it through a panel in its boundary steel-mesh fence, which had already been sawn through and merely propped up, and then taking a residential road called Brentwood Avenue. With the first-responding police units' tyres in shreds, there'd have been no immediate pursuit, and the team should have got clean away.

'More Christmas parties, innit?' Iago complained. 'All double-parked.'

'Christmas parties,' Elliot said, unable to believe the simple oversight.

'Anyway, we had to slow down. Even then, the wagon ripped off some cars' wings trying to get through. Brings the owners out, shouting, dunnit. Then they see *us*. Fucking windscreen gone, so they suss something's up and call the cops. One little twat even snaps us on his phone … so now they've got the van's reg.'

'This is all fact?' Elliot asked.

'According to the fucking scanner. Main thing is … they know which way we've come, so they'll be right fucking on us!'

'Move it!' Jim urged them again. 'All of you!'

The doors at the back of the van had opened, disgorging the rest of the team. A total of thirteen men were now present, enough to form two human chains connecting the back of the HGV to the three waiting getaway cars, though this time it wasn't quite as simple. Even though the cars had all been chosen for their extensive storage space at the back, not an inch could be wasted, or it would cost them money. So, in each case, the driver of the car in question had to stand close by and supervise, slotting the boxes in neatly.

Because his AMG wasn't among the first two cars, Elliot, his mask back in place, had to stand in line with all the others. They'd rehearsed this, and previously it had seemed a sensible, efficient procedure, but now, as he humped one heavy steel box after another, it was laborious and tiresome. He tensed when he heard another police siren go howling over the concrete gantry above. But clearly the authorities' response was still in chaos. Whatever vehicle it was, it carried on towards Harwich, ignoring the slip road down to the junction.

'We've got three minutes and then we're going!' Jim shouted.

Three minutes didn't feel to Elliot as if it would be long enough, but the procedure continued in well-oiled fashion. The first escape car's boot was now loaded and closed. Its driver, Lion, leapt behind the wheel and revved it to life. Gorilla, Toad and Pig climbed on board and it sped away, bucking over the rubble, before joining the road network.

'Come on, lads!' Jim urged the rest of them. 'Halfway there.'

Sweat boiled inside Elliot's rubber mask as he worked. The boxes came at a rate of knots and were heavy and awkward. It was a relief to see the second car fishtail away, driven by Bear, carrying Goat, Beetle, Eagle and Cobra. The problem was that each time there were fewer men to do the work, so it got heavier and slower. At last, with two full minutes elapsed, only Elliot's AMG remained. He waited by the boot while Jim and Lonnegan scarpered back and forth in relays, each hefting two deposit boxes at a time. Iago couldn't help because he'd opened a crate and was stuffing several bottles with rags.

'Come on, come on!' Jim cajoled them.

He was still listening to the scanner, and by the increased tension in his voice, wasn't liking what he was hearing. Almost certainly, those few local officers who'd managed to muster in the immediate wake of the attack had now been supplemented by reinforcements from off-division. They'd probably be performing a basic pattern search in the area. That wouldn't happen quickly given the network of country lanes between here and the Ringwood, but they'd get here at some point, especially if they'd managed to put spotters on the main roads, who'd now have reported back that there'd been no sign of the villains leaving the district.

From somewhere in the near distance, another police siren sounded.

Iago glanced up. 'Fuck! Hear that?'

The others stopped what they were doing and looked around. The youngster was right to be alarmed. This one wasn't rocketing by overhead but was growing steadily louder.

'We're on thirty seconds,' Jim said. 'How many boxes left?'

Lonnegan ran to the HGV. 'Three!'

'One each ... *Move it!*'

Elliot dashed over there too. With grunting efforts, they each grabbed a box and stumbled back to the AMG. One by one, they inserted them into the remaining boot space.

There was a searing flash and an accompanying *BOOM*.

Elliot jumped in shock, before realising what it was.

Iago had thrown one of his Molotov cocktails into the back of the high-sided van, and it had gone off with a blast. Jim slammed the AMG's boot closed, unslung the haversack containing the scanner, dumped it into the front passenger footwell and threw himself onto the seat. Lonnegan piled into the rear, Elliot climbing behind the wheel, gunning the ignition and glancing into his rear-view mirror, watching Iago throw more bottles into the HGV.

'Move it, ratboy!' Lonnegan roared as the kid fled back towards the car.

A pair of headlights and a spinning blue beacon had swerved around the corner on the nearest approach road. Iago leapt into the back seat, and Elliot hit the gas.

18

8 January (Wednesday)

Lynda adjusted her scarf and pulled on her gloves and a woolly hat as she assessed Ravenwood Cottage.

With a bit of work, it could be turned into something idyllic, but at present the ivy was unkempt; moss and abandoned birds' nests choked its gutters, clearly signs of long-term neglect. But now she noticed something else: a holly wreath hanging on the front door – even though today was 8 January, a Wednesday, and last Monday had been the final day on which Christmas decorations were supposed to be left up.

She glanced through the windows but it was dark inside and no one moved around. She raised the heavy knocker and banged it three times. As expected, there was no response. She tried again. Nothing.

It struck her how quiet it was here. At which point her eyes were drawn to the woods on the left. For half a second, she fancied she'd spied movement. She squinted, but the stony cloud-cover cast the trees in shadow. It was impossible to see very far into them.

She turned back to the door and knocked again. The heavy impacts resounded through the still, silent interior. No one responded.

They were pretty certain that the man in the hospital

was Elliot Wade, so she hadn't expected him to answer. But maybe there might have been other friends and family on the premises?

Not so, it seemed.

She would have headed back there and then had her gaze not fallen upon the ramshackle building standing just to the north-west. An old barn of some sort, perhaps used to house a vehicle.

Lynda walked towards it, but before she got there, came to a slatted gate, which opened into a narrow, paved passage. At the end of it, she emerged at the back of the property, where there was a small patio with a couple of wheelie bins and some garden furniture. Beyond that lay another lawn, though, as at the front of the house, everything here had the air of dilapidation. She looked at the house again, only for a crackle of splintering woodwork to swing her back around. Her gaze swept the empty garden. Nothing moved, and the silence of the woods returned.

But now there was something else. A deeper, eerier stillness, as if whatever had made the noise had stopped and was listening to her.

Lynda's eyes narrowed as she tried to penetrate the deeper tracts of foliage encircling the garden, but it remained motionlessness. Her attention switched back to the barn. It was a sight, its roof sagging, its brick walls eroded. But the noise must have come from inside it. She wanted to call out, to announce who she was and what she was doing there. But an inner voice forbade it. If someone was present, they already knew she was here, and they were hiding from her.

Back at the front, she moved towards the barn's heavy wooden doors. They stood ajar by a foot or so. She glanced through, but the day's greyness shrouded the interior. She took out her torch but hesitated before going further. There were questions here about her actual powers. The obvious fall-back was that oldest resource, Section 17 of the Police and Criminal Evidence Act, which allowed her to force entry to any premises if she felt that life or limb was endangered.

'I heard the sound of something breaking,' she pictured herself saying in court. 'I imagined a loft ladder collapsing. I imagined someone falling...'

There was a prolonged creak from inside, and another clatter of woodwork.

Before she could harbour further reservations, Lynda stepped inside and shone the torch left and right.

There was nothing; no person lying injured, no vehicle.

As her eyes adjusted to the gloom, she noted a door some distance to her right, standing open on a dim corridor. Closer, in a nearby corner, she saw a mattress stuffed with straw. When she ventured over to check, there was a dint in it, indicating that someone had lain there recently. She glanced overhead, seeing several apertures in the actual roof, through which milky daylight intruded.

She switched her torch off before turning to the other doorway. And the breath caught in her throat.

Someone was standing there. A dark, featureless someone, rendered that way by the deep gloom, but male from his outline, wearing a heavy jacket with its hood pulled up.

She blinked, and the figure was gone.

It hadn't backed away or turned and run. It had popped out of existence.

Lynda was seeing things. There was no other explanation.

But she advanced anyway, peering down the dim corridor. Still, she saw no one. However, as her vision attuned, she could now see it wasn't a corridor but an open space. There was a central passage of sorts, but with animal stalls on either side of it.

A stable, she realised. That made sense, as the closed door at the far end was unusually tall.

From what she could see of the stalls, there were five on either side, the woodwork between them coming to about chest-height. Which meant, that if she walked all the way down there, she'd pass several points on either side where someone could be lying in wait. 'I'm a police officer,' she said aloud, though her voice quavered, hardly impressive to anyone, let alone a hardened criminal. 'Detective Sergeant Hagen. I'm here to speak to someone who knows either Elliot or Harriet Wade. Are you able to help with that?'

There was no reply.

Lynda proceeded, one step at a time. Again, she took her torch from her pocket, but now for reassurance; it was a weighty item.

She saw that there was nothing in the first two stalls, just flattened straw. It was the same with the next two. And the next two. When she passed the fourth pair, the stall on the right appeared to be stacked with wormy old furniture. There was a similar stack in the next and final stall as well. It was certainly the case that no one was hiding, and the exit door hadn't opened and closed.

She couldn't help wondering if the figure she'd seen had been an illusion brought on by her heightened state and the gloomy half-light.

There was no one here. And then there was another clatter of woodwork.

Directly left of her.

Lynda twirled around, torch ready to use as a truncheon. It was that first stack of thrown-away furniture, loose fragments of broken slate still working their way down through the middle of it. Bewildered, Lynda glanced up to where a hefty hole gaped in the underside of the roof. A face peered through.

Small, furry, with buck teeth and bunched cheeks.

'You can't be bloody serious!' Lynda exclaimed.

Shaking her head, she exited the building the way she'd come in. She didn't bother looking at the house again, just followed the drive around to her Qashqai and headed back along the dirt road.

19

24 December (Tuesday)

'Two of them,' Lonnegan said, peering through the back window. 'Look like fast-pursuit cars.'

'Can you shake them off?' Jim asked.

Elliot nodded.

'Do it soon. We'll have the chopper here in no time.'

Elliot said nothing. Ahead of them, the narrow rural lane ran on. It was twists and turns all the way, but Elliot kept his foot to the floor, pushing seventy then eighty plus, holding the knife-blade bends despite the terrible weight in the boot with a strength and skill that defied the police-trained drivers at his rear. They regularly fell back out of sight, though the ongoing blare of sirens and the flickering blue lights never faded completely.

Lonnegan had already suggested that they slow down so that he could lean from the window and take out the pursuing vehicles with gunfire.

'None of that,' Jim had replied.

'Do their lights, do their tyres – what's not to fucking love?' Lonnegan had argued.

'I know you,' was all Jim had said, and that had been the end of it.

Elliot was relieved. Despite his current focus on the borehole of light through which they virtually flew, he was still concerned about things he'd overheard while unloading the HGV. The blag hadn't gone to plan. Some bystander had intervened, and the Wolf had 'put him down'. Even now Elliot wasn't sure what that had meant. Knocked him to the canvas, or something more permanent? It was evident at least that Jim Naboth didn't want to make things worse, but it was noticeable that his pump-action was still on view, resting by his left leg, his left hand clamped around its barrel.

Down to you then, Elliot told himself. *Get us the fuck out of here!*

The route was pre-planned, and he'd driven it several times in different vehicles. That was a key part of the getaway strategy. Because the police could put observers in the air quickly these days, you couldn't just rely on outrunning them on the ground. You needed to be clever as well. Before you could do that, however, you had to elude any immediate pursuit, and in the process do your damnedest not to attract more attention than was necessary. It wasn't always easy. Now, for example, they were bulleting through Little Scalding, a village of perhaps seven houses, where the speed limit was a strict 20 mph. Though it was Christmas Eve, it still wasn't late, and people would be around. Elliot hoped and prayed that none of them got in his way because he wouldn't be slowing down; he couldn't afford to.

At first it seemed okay, but in the village centre they came to a red light, where a Nissan Micra was waiting. In his efforts to swerve around it, travelling seventy plus, Elliot hit a series of ice-filled potholes and lost traction. The car skidded through the crossing, the heavy cargo in the boot thumping sideways, spinning it 360 degrees, another vehicle screeching past, horn wailing, before Elliot slammed his foot to the floor, kicking them out of it and hurtling on. In heavier traffic, they'd now be enmeshed in mangled metal and broken bodies. But again, the road ahead was empty. They accelerated.

'Let the bells ring out for Christmas!' Lonnegan hooted, laughing.

'Fuck me!' Iago yelled. 'That was intense.'

Elliot glanced into his rear-view mirror. Behind them, the diminishing forms of the two police cars were hampered by the vehicle the AMG had almost hit. He tromped the gas harder, the needle surging up from seventy to eighty to ninety. The trees and hedgerows sped by in an indiscernible blur. In what looked like a speeded-up outtake from an old movie, a flatbed truck in front raced back towards them. Elliot veered past it by inches. They were on a tight curve, so he couldn't see clearly ahead, but it was a chance he had to take. Beyond that was another crossroads, this one unmarked.

'Yes,' Jim said under his breath.

They'd planned to have shaken off their police pursuers before reaching this point. They took the second left to Great Oakley but long before they got there, swung right onto a single-track lane, which they could burn along at limitless speed, assuming they didn't meet something coming the other way.

Lonnegan wound his window down and leaned out.

'Watch your head!' Elliot shouted. 'This road's narrow.'

'Shut up!' Lonnegan replied. 'I hear rotor blades.'

Elliot felt Jim tense up alongside him.

'How far away?' the gang boss asked.

'I don't know. Impossible to tell.'

'Elliot, get your fucking foot down.'

Elliot didn't bother replying that they were already doing ninety.

'And search the sky.' Jim glanced over his shoulder. 'Find the bastard before he finds us.'

'Five minutes and the chopper's not a problem,' Elliot said, though in truth he wasn't as calm as he sounded. His gloved hands clenched the steering wheel to the point where the tendons in his fists hurt. But focus was everything at this speed and on roads like these.

'That's still five fucking minutes,' Jim replied. 'They can direct a lot of ground forces onto us in that time.'

The truth was that the police helicopter wouldn't have to be physically close to spot them. With its heat-seeking and night-vision cameras, any blip of light travelling at reckless speed on the black panorama of the night-time countryside would attract their attention.

'Anything on the scanner?' Lonnegan asked.

Jim adjusted his earpiece but shook his head. 'Just chaos. They haven't caught anyone yet, but they're getting more bodies in to search. Wait ...' He listened, then nodded. 'The chopper's defo in this quadrant. Those bastards we left at the crossroads have called it in.'

Elliot hit the gas harder, rocketing past a left-hand turn at such speed that if the Ford Focus about to pull out hadn't braked of its own accord, they'd have smashed clean into it.

'Fuck's he doing in the middle of nowhere?' Iago wondered.

As they swung around a tight bend, he had his answer.

Several hundred yards ahead, a cluster of lights denoted cars parked or parking in a line on the right side of the road, but as there was no pavement there, that side of the road was also milling with people. Further back among the trees stood the spot lit upright structure of a bell-tower.

'It's Christmas Eve,' Elliot said. 'And they're all going to church.'

To make things worse, *because* it was Christmas Eve, there were lots more parishioners than there would be normally. He saw lights in the field on the left as well. It was being used as an overspill car park. His own headlights picked out multiple figures crossing the road on foot, some leading children.

'Christ!' He braked as hard as he could, throwing the AMG into a protracted, screeching skid that lasted maybe eighty yards.

Which was all it took to draw the attention of the previously unnoticed police vehicle heading the other way. It had slowed down to allow the pedestrians to cross, but now its blues and twos came alive and its siren began to whirl.

Elliot had no choice.

He swung the AMG left in a furious handbrake-turn and then jammed the gas back on, battering-ramming through a closed farm gate, which thankfully was only made of timber, though even then it was fortunate that Jim's back-up team, having anticipated a rough ride, had disabled the AMG's airbags. The wood flew apart, and despite the most monstrous jolt, which threw all four of them against their seatbelts with rib-cracking force, they were now jerking and bouncing across rough, tussocky pasture. Elliot looked right. The field being used as the overspill was a paddock enclosed by stone walls, which at least meant that no civvies would be straying into their path over here. He looked front again.

Only one headlight remained to show them the way across the field, but that was adequate under the circumstances. It revealed a ground that was frozen hard, which of course was to their advantage, though the winter grass was also slick with frost.

He accelerated to sixty again, and then up to seventy, but it was perilous. The tyres had no grip, slipping constantly. If Elliot so much as touched his brake on here, they'd lose control, be sent spiralling, and if they landed front-on at this speed, the engine could explode. Not that it would matter. Because the cargo in the back, God knew how many hundreds of kilograms of edged steel, would have travelled clean through the interior long before then. So, he kept on at full throttle.

In the rear-view mirror meanwhile, a spinning blue beacon showed him the cop car turning into the field.

'Fuck me!' Jim snapped, seeing the same thing.

'You think that's bad,' Lonnegan interjected, hefting his Glock. 'I can see the chopper. Its light, at least. It's a couple of miles off, but it's coming this way.'

'It's clocked us, for fuck's sake,' Jim snarled, listening to the scanner. He grabbed his shotgun and pumped a shell into the breach.

Elliot rammed his pedal to the floor again. When they struck a hidden dip, the AMG launched into the air. On crashing down again, the metal underpinning the driver's seat struck Elliot like a sledgehammer, the top of his skull hitting the padded ceiling.

'*Fuck!*' Iago shouted.

They proceeded at the same speed, but the car had suffered, its undercarriage creaking, the exhaust howling as a portion of pipe rolled away in the fog of frost filling their taillights. Beyond that, the police car wasn't gaining. But now Elliot could also see the copter, a blazing point of light high in the sky.

'Where the fuck are we going?' Jim said through clenched teeth.

'Same way as we planned,' Elliot replied. 'We'll be there in no time.'

Again, he sounded calmer than he felt. Once they'd passed the church, which they'd all assumed would be closed and in darkness, the plan had been to turn left at the next T-junction. The little-used road, no more than a farm track, would take them three miles south-east to Hamford Ness, a one-time Cold War radar station now standing in hollowed-out ruins. If they made it that far, everything would be okay, they knew – they'd checked it enough times. They were still headed in the right direction now, it couldn't be more than a mile ahead, but they were currently on agricultural land, which was almost certainly enclosed. Elliot had no clue how they were going to rejoin the road network.

A deafening crunch sounded behind them. He glanced at his rear-view mirror. The pursuing police car had hit the same dip or ditch but had landed side-on. It didn't surprise him. But the copter was much closer; pretty soon the orb of its searchlight would be chasing them across the meadow.

'You sure we're still heading east?' Jim said.

This was an important question. Hamford Ness lay to the east. In every other direction lay who knew what, though Hamford Water wasn't far to the south, a vast spread of reed-beds, creeks and mudflats – it wouldn't do to go blundering into that. Elliot couldn't answer. But then he spotted the approaching beam of the police chopper, and swung them left, his tyres eating through frozen grass and subsoil, throwing great clods behind them. They rose past eighty again, were almost up to ninety.

'Flying pigs have got a bead on us for sure,' Lonnegan said, twisting in his seat so as to try and push his upper body out through the passenger window. 'At least let me put some shots across their bows. Make 'em back off a little.'

'Won't make any difference,' Jim replied. 'They can see us from anywhere.'

Elliot drove them relentlessly forward, the car rising and falling, cresting humps and ridges – at which point he saw something which for all their misfortune so far, he couldn't believe. The ground ahead commenced a sudden, rapid descent. It wasn't a steep gradient, but it was continuous for a couple of hundred yards, and at the bottom of it, he saw the reason why: a belt of frozen rushes and reeds fringed the flat, white surface of a river, completely bisecting the course they were following.

'Shit!' He remembered now that the route they'd planned had taken them over this minor inlet of the sea by a narrow bridge. But there was no bridge here, and the inlet didn't look minor anymore.

He swerved left, the car lopsided on the lower slope as he followed the course of the waterway.

'Can't we just drive over it?' Iago said. 'It's frozen.'

'Where do you think we are, fucking Alaska?' Jim responded. 'This thing'll go through like it's soggy paper.'

'Must be something,' Elliot chunnered. 'Must be.'

He checked the rear-view mirror. He'd lost sight of the chopper, but then spotted it again, running parallel to them. Perhaps quarter of a mile away.

'Fuck this!' he hissed. 'There *must* be something!'

And there was…

At first, he passed without registering it. But half a second later, he veered left, taking them back uphill, the heavy-laden boot swinging them like a pendulum, pulling them right the way around, the tyres ripping deep into the turf, bringing them almost to a standstill.

'*The fuck!*' Lonnegan barked.

'Shut up,' Elliot replied calmly. 'I know what I'm doing.'

He gunned the engine again, driving them back the way they'd come. Forty yards later, he spotted what he'd seen and braked hard. He hadn't been mistaken.

It was half a bridge. Not something intended for human use, more likely for cattle; it was built from old, desiccated timber. It wasn't particularly high, jutting up from the river-bank on this side at a shallow gradient and ending midway across, at which point the other part of it had collapsed.

'You can't be serious,' Jim said as they idled there.

'You got a better idea?' Elliot replied.

'You don't think we're too heavy?'

'The weight's an advantage if we get up enough speed.'

In the dim glow of the dash, Jim Naboth's handsome face was damp with sweat, his black hair hanging in lank wet strands. His posture tautened, and he clutched his shotgun with both hands. 'Do it,' he whispered.

Elliot turned the car again and gunned them up to the top of the grassy slope. All the way, he was aware of the copter hovering close by. He couldn't just hear it but could see the spot of its searchlight crossing the meadow. He also realised that the night was filled with police sirens.

There was no time to worry about it.

At the top of the slope, he turned the car again, so they were facing downhill. But it was as he swung them back down, changing up through the gears, that Lonnegan and Iago realised what he intended.

'Jesus wept!' the former shouted.

The latter laughed hysterically and howled like a wolf.

There was no guarantee the lower section of the bridge, the only part that was still intact, would hold them. But Elliot reasoned that the car would be travelling at such velocity that it would barely feel the weight. It was little more than a ramp, anyway, so they'd be over and beyond before it had time to collapse. Even so, when their front tyres struck the timbers, the crash was shudder-inducing, and when the back tyres got there, the splintering and snapping of disintegrating woodwork filled all their ears, but by then the car was already in the air.

It wasn't such a feat as Elliot had initially thought. The river was no more than a couple of car lengths' across, so they'd covered it before they started to descend. Even so, the wind whistled around them, the sensation of high-speed flight was dizzying. Thankfully, the excess weight in the boot acted as an anchor, bringing them down rear-first. Elliot had no clue what they were about to land on. It could have been a reedbed, in which case they'd be lodged in place and gradually sucked into the morass, ultimately relying on the coppers to haul them out and save their lives.

Or it could be rocks, in which case the entire vehicle might blow.

But in fact, it was the cattle track that he'd guessed the bridge connected with in the first place. It was grassless and beaten into ridges by innumerable passing hooves, but it was also frozen hard. They landed with a phenomenal *crump*. The car skated, fishtailed, threatened to overturn, but Elliot fought the wheel and brought them right.

And then they were among trees. The course narrowed, but he held it tightly, foot clamped on the accelerator. Ahead, the horizontal iron bars of a farm gate ghosted into view.

Elliot didn't panic – he knew where they were. Thirty

yards before the gate, the track was bisected by a road. A wooded, little-used road these days, its surface broken and weedy, no more than beaten earth.

Nevertheless, it was the road to Hamford Ness.

He spun them left as they reached it. The car careered across the icy surface. Again, he fought the wheel to bring them back in line, the broken bough of a smaller tree banging along their nearside flank, shattering both windows. But again, none of that mattered. Because now, directly ahead, stood the steel-mesh fence that blocked the entrance to the age-old radar station.

PRIVATE PROPERTY
KEEP OUT

proclaimed the luminous signpost suspended in the middle.

Elliot maintained full speed, the crew whooping like schoolboys. On previous visits, they'd used an oxyacetylene torch to sever the fence's strongest joints. It was only upright now because it had been propped up, and it fell flat beneath their tyres as they blistered past.

Before Hamford Ness became an MOD listening post in the 1960s, it was an atomic weapons research establishment during the 1950s. Hence the secrecy and high security that had once surrounded it; hence also its impressive size and ultra-austere appearance.

On a sunny spring day, you might glimpse it through the budding woods on the eastern shore of the inlet and wonder at the immense concrete structure, which, when you looked closer, were actually several structures, all similarly bleak and faceless. Most likely, you'd think it an abandoned power station or something similar.

Very few would experience this, though, because Hamford Ness was now owned by the National Trust, which considered it unsafe to open to the public, plus it was only accessible along a private road that ran through farmland. As such, when the gang crossed its broken-down threshold that cold Christmas Eve, and skidded to a halt in the rubble-strewn courtyard concealed between the gaunt, gutted buildings, they were certain there'd be no one here to see them. The eye-in-the-sky would still be following, still attempting to direct ground forces onto them. But they were shortly to take care of that problem too.

Slower now, Elliot navigated the heaps of masonry and fallen pipework that littered the central yard, turning sharp right and entering the largest building through a pair of double doors that had long rotted from their hinges. After several hundred yards along a bare passage, the AMG turned a corner and was faced with three options: sets of double doors located to the left, the right and in front.

They looked like blast doors, all made from heavy steel, and at first glance, all sealed – except for the one on the right. The inch gap running down the middle of this one had allowed access to the horizontal steel bar on the other side, and the oxyacetylene torch had come in handy again.

Elliot braked, while Lonnegan and Iago leapt out, and pushed one door backward each. When the AMG slid through into the darkness beyond, the doors were closed behind it, and a new steel bar laid across. The duo climbed back on board, and Elliot drove on, descending a concrete ramp, at the foot of which he joined the labyrinth of old bunkers and air-raid tunnels that ran for miles along the coast, connecting countless other airfields and research and listening installations that had once been so essential to this most vulnerable corner of England.

'Like to see the bastards find us now,' Iago chuckled.

But Elliot wasn't taking any chances. He put his foot down again, accelerating along the arched brick passage, the dust of ages flurrying behind them. He'd memorised the route, so when the turns came, he made them easily: left, right, right again, right again, left, left again. After fifteen minutes, they pulled into an underground hangar now serving as their impromptu parking space. Three vehicles waited there; one of them was Elliot's Sport. The other two were a metallic-red Jaguar XF and a silver-grey Ford Escape.

He pulled the AMG up twenty yards short and applied the handbrake.

A brief appreciative silence followed.

Then Jim nodded. 'Outstanding, Mr Wade. Out-fucking-standing.' He glanced back at the twosome in the rear. 'What do you think, gentlemen?'

'Out-fucking-standing,' Iago agreed, also nodding.

Lonnegan gave a surly shrug.

'Let's get to it.' Jim opened his door and climbed out.

They reckoned they'd bought themselves about forty minutes before the police located this place, so they still had to work quickly. Again, it was a matter of unloading the safety deposit boxes from one vehicle and reloading them into the Jaguar and the Escape. Elliot, as a hired hand rather than a full member of the firm, would not be trusted to take the goods further, though he was still expected to assist. There were thirty-five boxes in total, and they were all packed away within ten minutes. After that, the men stripped to their underwear, Elliot ripping off his 'homeless' rags, the others removing their overalls. They bundled them into the back of the AMG, along with their shoes, masks and gloves, before taking grab bags from their respective vehicles and dressing again in clean, everyday casuals.

Jim slung his police scanner into the backseat of the Jag and approached Elliot.

'I may as well tell you,' he said. 'I'm impressed. Very. You did what we wanted, and more. So, you're getting the full rate, as agreed, but on top of that, you're getting a bonus. Okay?'

Elliot shrugged. 'Anything extra's always good.'

'We'll talk about that soon. In the meantime, you get yourself home – give that lovely missus of yours a Christmas kiss, yeah?'

Each now got into their respective cars, the keys awaiting them inside. Before jumping in with Jim, Iago took a petrol canister out of the Jag's boot, and splashed it all over the AMG, ensuring to pour plenty through its broken windows, soaking the heaps of clothing in the back. When done, he backed away and flung a match.

It didn't matter because though it was a powerful car, it was another of the Naboth crew's chop-shop clones. Stolen, with its VIN professionally altered and plates that were either duplicates of those worn by a legit AMG somewhere else in the country, or real ones removed from an identical model that had recently been written off. Normally such creations would be sold under false paperwork, but though the Naboth crew did this too, there were others they kept for occasions just like this.

Elliot was already en route when the AMG went up, the glaring flash of light filling his rear-view mirror. He ignored it, driving down the hangar's access passage and found the wooden doors at the end open, as promised. He passed through into another corridor, though this one was dappled with moonlight from gaps in its roof. He followed it for fifty yards before turning left and pulling out from under a railway arch.

He was on an industrial estate on the outskirts of Frinton-on-Sea. It was a thirty-mile drive home from here. The temptation again was to hammer the gas. But he resisted. He hadn't done anything wrong, he reminded himself. He was an ordinary guy on his way home for Christmas.

Part Two

20

31 December (Tuesday)

'Harri!' Elliot said to the en-suite door. 'We can't afford to be too late, okay?'

'It's New Year's Eve,' came a mumbled response. 'You think anyone cares what time we turn up?'

'Come on, love, please – don't be like this.'

'Go without me if it's so important to you.'

'What do you mean "go without you"? You don't think that'll look a bit weird?'

'In that case, you'll have to wait.'

He walked around the bedroom, still wearing his Gucci leather jacket over his patterned silk shirt, occasionally checking his watch and seeing that it was now after eight. She'd frozen him out most of the last week, only speaking to him if she needed to. He'd hoped, however, that it would have run its course by now.

'You know,' he said, 'you *knew* what all this was about. I'm not sure where all this high moral ground crap's coming from.'

The door opened and Harri stepped out.

She'd fixed her make-up, pinned up her hair, and had donned a tight, black minidress, which did her buxom figure proud, and a simple set of pearls. She sat on the bed and slipped on a pair of black stiletto slingbacks. He wasn't surprised that she looked so desirable – that was Harri's stock-in-trade – but was taken aback at the effort she'd made. Earlier that evening, when she'd finally succumbed to his persistent requests that they accept the Naboths' invitation, she'd only done so grudgingly.

'You assured me that no one would get hurt,' she said.

'I *hoped* they wouldn't,' he replied, somewhat lamely. 'No one got hurt the last time.'

That part was true, at least. The two previous jobs he'd done for the Naboths – in 2015, when he'd driven away from the back of a jeweller's in Cambridge, carrying Jim Naboth and one other bandit, and over thirty items of jewellery worth £500,000, and in 2017, when he'd driven one of three getaway vehicles after a Security Express break-in at a depot in North London, which had netted the gang just under £1,000,000 – had seen no one so much as scratched.

'It's the way you just accepted it,' Harri said, donning her wrap and grabbing her clutch. 'There we were, sitting with the Christmas presents we'd given each other while it was all over the radio.'

'What else could I do?' He followed her downstairs. 'I wasn't involved in that part of the job.'

'You obviously knew something like that had happened. You didn't look shocked.'

'I knew something had gone wrong,' he admitted, tapping in the alarm code. 'But that was all.'

'Gone wrong? Good God, Elliot… those men were almost killed.'

They walked outside, Elliot locking the door behind them. 'I didn't know it was going to happen like that, okay? It wasn't supposed to.' They climbed into the car. 'I presume the shots were fired because the guy took them by surprise.'

Harri fastened her seatbelt. 'And what about the security guards who had their heads beaten in while their hands were tied behind their backs?'

Elliot shrugged as he drove. 'Like I say, I don't know. I wasn't there.'

'My God. And these are the people we're seeing the new year in with.'

'I've received an invitation. What am I supposed to do, say no?'

'I thought you didn't want me involved?'

'The Naboths are a family firm. They don't know I keep you out of the loop. If I'd ever told them that, they'd think it was because you aren't trustworthy.'

'You could've made something up.'

'It doesn't work like that.'

'Not when you're a poodle, no.'

'For Christ's sake, Harri...'

'You realise a load of houses got burned down?'

'I don't know anything about that either. Look...' His own patience was wearing thin, but he couldn't deny that since the gruesome details of the robbery had made the news, he'd felt a smaller, lesser person. 'All I did was drive. You understand that? All I *ever* do is drive...'

'There are professional drivers all over the world who haven't just gone through the Christmas we've gone through, Elliot.'

'Yeah. They deliver bread. Or drive rag-and-bone carts. Look, if it's any consolation, we're going to get a chunk.'

'It isn't.'

'Really?' he said, as they joined the A14. 'Well, that's new. You never had a problem spending the money before.'

To her credit, Harri didn't attempt to deny this, but continued to gaze out front.

'Are they going to force you to do another of these jobs?' she asked.

'No one gets forced.' He said that airily, as though unconcerned. But it was impossible to hide the reality. 'The problem is, when you've done a few, it means you know stuff.'

'And let me guess, because of that, if you're not involved any more, you become a security risk?'

He shrugged. 'Well... maybe, yeah.'

They didn't speak again for ten minutes, following the A14 around Ipswich's southern perimeter, before joining the A12 and heading north again, entering a leafy and secluded corner of Woodbridge.

'Jesus,' Harri said, as houses that looked more like giant wedding cakes glided past, their exteriors glimmering with Christmas neon. 'This is where they live?'

'This is where Jo lives.'

'Who says crime doesn't pay? And that's an observation, by the way. Not a vote of approval.'

'Don't be too impressed,' Elliot said. 'Hoodlums that make it to this level are one in every fifty thousand. Most wind up in halfway houses, mental hospitals, or on Skid Row.'

'That's where Susan always said *I'd* finish up,' Harri replied.

Elliot snorted. Susan was Harri's older sister by eight years. He'd never met her, but according to Harri, she was strait-laced to the point where she creaked when she walked. Inevitably, she'd disapproved of Harri's lifestyle. It was no surprise that they rarely communicated any more.

He braked in front of another impressive house. It was electronically gated, with a huge front garden behind a high wall. The gates were wide open, however, and a number of cars were parked on the drive and on the road. The house was clad with ivy, but of the trim, pruned variety, not the wild, straggling mass that grew all over Ravenwood Cottage. It had been cut back to expose six tall upstairs windows, and downstairs two enormous panoramic bay-windows. Its huge front door was made from white-painted wood, with gold lettering to denote its number: 12.

'Talk about beggars at the banquet,' Harri said.

They pressed a button that chimed inside like a church bell. The front door swung open and Jim Naboth stood there, wearing a slim-fit Ralph Lauren suit, which fitted his tall, trim form like a glove, though his collar was already open, and his tie hung loose. He had a cocktail in his hand; a green thing with an olive hanging out of it on a stick.

'Well, well,' he said, grinning. 'All the best for the season.'

His eyes lingered on Harri, but that was often the case when Elliot introduced her to men she hadn't met before. What didn't usually happen was that Harri returned his appraisal.

'I'm Jim,' Jim said, offering a hand. Harri shook it demurely. 'Come, come.' He remembered himself and stepped back. 'Join the party.'

They entered and handed their coats to a girl dressed in a maid outfit.

The house was just as impressive on the inside as on the outside. Its central feature was a grand staircase sweeping up through the middle of the building, while downstairs was a succession of large, ornate rooms, all filled with sumptuous furniture and expensive artworks, and adorned with festive evergreens. Elliot couldn't help wondering if Jo Naboth, the gangland daughter turned gangland matriarch, appreciated all this good taste, or if it was just for show on occasions like this.

There were certainly a lot of well-heeled people present. Elliot wasn't sure what kind of guests he'd expected. The Naboths were an old East End outfit; the father, Les, had been one of London's top heist men until he was killed by an unknown assassin after the Tonbridge Securitas robbery in 2006. Jo had taken over the firm and moved them out to this part of the world to avoid knocking heads with the incoming Eastern European mobs but also to gentrify them. They were still involved in crime, but they didn't want to be on the run all the time. Hence, they ran legit companies too and presented this façade of respectability. It clearly paid dividends. Everyone here was presentable, the men wearing the slickest suits, the women glammed up, both sexes dripping with gold. And though among the men, Elliot caught the occasional shifty expression, the odd razor-scarred cheek or nasty jailhouse tat, the majority seemed like upstanding characters: businessmen, local landowners.

There was no one else who'd participated in the job, with the exception of Lonnegan, who was also in a suit – and looked good thanks to his athletic shape – and Iago, who was in a suit as well, though it looked small and tight on him, and his scruffy baseball cap didn't exactly set it off. Even Jo Naboth was absent. It seemed to be Jim who was playing mine host, talking animatedly, laughing aloud, and steering Harri and Elliot through into an expansive kitchen, where the worktops groaned beneath the weight of food trays, wine bottles and cold boxes filled with beer cans.

Elliot opted for lager, Harri a glass of wine. She then said that she'd be back in a minute as she needed to freshen up.

'Thought it'd be nothing but champers for an F1 champ like you,' Jim commented.

'I won the British Open Kart Championship in '99,' Elliot replied. 'I never reached that dizzy height in Formula One.'

'You still do all right for yourself.' Jim watched Harri as she wove out of the room.

'Suppose I was a romantic figure once,' Elliot agreed.

'Pity you can't brag about your current achievements. That was some driving, mate.'

Elliot nodded in grateful acknowledgement but didn't respond.

'Something wrong?' Jim asked.

'I just …' Elliot wasn't sure whether he was talking out of turn now, but he seemed to have credit in the bank here. At least with Jim. 'I didn't realise it was going to get so brutal.'

Jim shrugged. 'That wasn't the plan, but anything can happen once you're out there. Sometimes it works in your favour, though. Who'd have expected that blaze on the docks?'

'That wasn't us?'

'Was it bloody hell! What do you take us for, a bunch of nutters? The main thing is the job, on the whole, went well.'

'On the whole?' Elliot lowered his voice. 'Was the take not what you expected?'

Jim glanced around. 'The take was good. A lot of jewellery, most of which we've already fenced. Six hundred grand's worth. Bit more actually.' He gave a sly smile. 'And that's significantly down to you as wheelman. So, like I say, you're getting a bit more than we offered. In fact, there'll be something nice waiting for you when you get home.'

That news gave Elliot a warm feeling, but it was evident

that some problem had arisen that he wasn't going to be told about.

'Should make the January sales go with a bang,' Jim added. 'Just don't overdo it. And have a good time tonight.'

He moved away, shouting a greeting to another guest. Harri reappeared and Elliot handed her the wine.

'Something wrong?' she asked. 'You look a bit pale.'

'No, it's all good.' He kept his tone neutral.

It proved to be easier socialising with people they hadn't met before than Elliot had expected. Most guests were pleasant and talkative. The seasonably cold weather they'd had over Christmas was one subject of conversation, along with the fact that another year had passed already and everyone was hoping for better things. Inevitably, one or two of the bigger nobs present proved garrulous when discussing themselves, eagerly filling Elliot and Harri in on who they were and how many acres they owned.

The wine flowed, music thumped, the food, which was brought around by catering staff, was gourmet standard, and the clock ticked on towards midnight. But it was well before then, around eleven, when Elliot and Harri found themselves separated; Elliot listening to a local farmer bemoan the illegality of proper fox hunting, Harri entertaining a couple of older ladies with stories from her modelling days and the creepy hands-on characters she'd had to fend off.

And then Iago appeared.

'How you doing, Evel?' He wrapped an arm around Elliot's shoulders, his breath befouled by whiskey.

'I'm doing good,' Elliot replied, bemused. 'What do you mean, "Evel"?'

'Evel, you know ...'

Elliot steered the youngster out into the hall where there were fewer guests.

'No, I don't know,' he said. 'What do you mean, "Evel"?'

'The racing driver,' Iago slurred.

'Evel Knievel was a biker, you pillock. A stunt rider.'

Iago frowned. 'Was he?' His pimply visage split into a brown-toothed grin. 'Yeah, course. Getting my supermen mixed up.'

'Listen ...' Elliot lowered his voice. 'Is there something going on I need to know about?'

Iago looked confused. 'I'm not following.'

He really was toasted, his eyes glazed. His breath reeked, but Elliot had no option but to lean close.

'Jim seemed a bit, I don't know ... put out?'

'Oh, well, yeah,' Iago replied. 'You know what that is, don't you?'

'No, that's why I'm asking.'

'Fuck me!' Iago said loudly.

Elliot glanced around uneasily. A couple of reproachful glances were aimed in their direction from various open doorways.

'It's a bit of a shitter really,' Iago said, even louder.

'Okay, easy on the language,' Elliot muttered.

'What? Oh, yeah, well ...' Now even Iago lowered his voice. 'One of them boxes we lifted. Them safety-deposit things. Turns out it belongs to the fucking Corporation ...'

'The what?'

'You know ... the Corporation.'

'*What the fuck are you playing at!*' a voice hissed behind them.

They spun around together. Neither had heard Ray Lonnegan approaching.

'Ray?' Iago chuckled. 'Where you been, man?'

'Never mind where I've fucking been!'

Lonnegan grabbed the kid by the lapels and hauled him several feet across the hall. Elliot watched, startled. Given Iago's reputation for violence, he expected an immediate response. But that never came. Perhaps even Iago knew better than to raise a hand to Ray Lonnegan.

'The fuck are you babbling about?' Lonnegan demanded. 'You realise we don't fucking know this guy?'

Iago goggled with confusion. 'Course we know him. It's Evel.'

'You fucking dim bulb. Just what we need. A druggie like you on the payroll.'

'Look...' Elliot interceded. 'I don't know what this is, but I *can* be trusted, you know.'

Lonnegan rounded on him. 'No, I don't know it. No disrespect to you... I mean I know you're a deadeye with the gearstick and all. But you're not part of the inner circle, okay? You're a hired hand... with a fucking tom for a bird.'

'All right, that's enough...' Elliot retorted, growing heated himself.

'Hey, hey...' Iago pushed himself between them. 'Evel got us out the shit...'

'Shut your mouth, junkhead!' Lonnegan snarled. 'Before someone shuts it for you.'

'What's going on?' a stern voice broke in.

Jim had reappeared, entering the hall from a door down at its far end.

Lonnegan pointed at Iago. 'It's this fucking moron again.'

'*You* weren't exactly cooling things,' Elliot fired in.

Lonnegan glared at him, but now that Jim was here, said nothing else.

'I said, what's going on?' Jim glanced from one to the other. 'Or am I going to have to take all three of you out-side?'

Suddenly, there was no trace of the affable personality. Jim was hunched, taut, dark-faced; he looked like an angry wolf.

'I've just caught *him* ...' Lonnegan nodded at Iago, 'telling *him* ...' he nodded at Elliot, 'about you know what.'

'It's my fault,' Elliot cut in. 'I asked. I could see there was something bugging you.'

Jim regarded him for several long moments. 'Should have left well alone, Elliot.' He turned and glanced at the curious onlookers in the various doorways. 'Sorry about that, people.' He laughed. 'Family issue that's now been sorted.' One by one, the onlookers turned away. Jim edged along the hall, beckoning to Elliot. 'Didn't I tell you just to enjoy the party?'

Elliot followed, aware that Lonnegan was behind him. 'Look, if something's gone wrong, my neck's on the chop-ping block too. Don't I have a right to know?'

'Should've left well enough alone, Elliot,' Jim said again. 'Should've quit while you were on top.'

21

8 January (Wednesday)

Lynda was so shaken by her experience in the cottage out-
house that at first she didn't recognise Clive's number on the
Qashqai's dashboard display.

'Sincerely hope you've got something good,' she greeted
him.

'Well...' He sounded unsure. 'There's good and bad.'

'Isn't there always. Give me the good stuff first.'

'Our guy in the Billington Ward.'

'Yeah?'

'Still incommunicado. I've got to go back later. But he's
got a friend. Name of Nick.'

'Nick what?'

'Good question. But I presume, whoever he is, he responded to the publicity notice we put out this morning
when our patient was still John Doe... because he was at
the hospital earlier, asking to see the driver from the A12
incident. Apparently, they're close mates.'

'Did he elaborate on that?'

'No. Nor did he hang around. I imagine he heard about
the smash, his mate hasn't checked in since Sunday, and so
he put two and two together. It could end up being nothing,
but with luck, he'll show up again.'

'Fingers crossed.'

'There's more,' Clive said. 'Medical records make it sound as if we've got the right fella in Elliot Wade. Six foot two inches tall, fourteen stone, fair-haired.'

'Sounds about right,' Lynda said.

'On that basis, I've been back in the office and I've done some digging. Does that name, Elliot Wade, still not sound familiar to you?'

She frowned. 'Not really.'

'How familiar does "Elliot Wade the racing driver" sound?'

Lynda pondered as she drove. Now that he mentioned it . . .

'Let me clue you in,' Clive said. 'Few years ago, he was one of the rising stars of Formula One.'

'Where'd you get *that*?'

'I googled the name.'

'You're sure it's the same guy?'

'I wondered about that too, but it soon came together. The backstory is that Wade fell from grace a few years ago.'

Lynda swung onto the A14, listening intently.

'He'd already had a successful rookie career when, in 2005, McLaren were so impressed with his test driving that they offered him a race contract. He was twenty years old and Britain's youngest-ever Formula One driver. Sounds like he had the world at his feet. Do you ever watch Formula One?'

'Not really.'

'He made his debut at San Marino in 2006. He was leading the field till his engine failed four laps from the finish. That same season, he finished fifth in the European Grand Prix and third in the Spanish Grand Prix. Seriously, he was only twenty-one years old.'

'I take it that's good?'

'I don't follow F1 either, but I'm informed it's pretty incredible.'

'So, what's happened since? I know you said he fell from grace, but I've just been to this Ravenwood Cottage and it doesn't strike me that anyone in the jet-set crowd has ever lived there.'

'You'll notice all this was over ten years ago?'

'Yeah.'

'Well, as I say, he was a young guy to be thrown into such a pressure cooker, and by all accounts he soon got onto the party circuit. Wine, women, you name it.' Paper rustled as Clive checked his notes. 'From about 2009 it was all down-hill. Nothing but problems. A year later, he was almost out of the game. Sounds like he performed poorly all that season. Left McLaren midway through, joined Brawn-Mercedes. But he crashed in a couple of races, and generally finished well behind the leaders. His father died in 2011 – that was his only surviving relative. Sounds like Wade spent the whole of that year drinking away his sorrows. Became a regular around the bars and nightclubs of West London. This was when he first met the lovely Harriet.'

'I was wondering when she was going to come into it.'

'There's not much on her,' Clive said. 'Generic glamorous girlfriend.'

'Doesn't say anything about her real name being Jill Brooks?'

'It's Google, isn't it. Just the basics. Anyway, they got mar-ried and lived in a flat in West Brompton, but in 2013 Wade had to sell it to pay off his debts. The two of them moved back into Wade's father's cottage. This Ravenwood place you checked out. Apparently he opened a bar in Ipswich, but that failed too.'

'Drank away his profits?'

'He's a party animal. Or *was*. But there are lots of reasons why businesses go tits-up, aren't there? And didn't the toxicology report clear him of drink-driving after the crash last Sunday?'

'Yeah.' Lynda had to concede that. There'd been no alcohol or drugs in Wade's bloodstream.

'One interesting cross-reference.' Pages rustled again. 'I've been on the database just to see if he's on there, and while he's got no form, there's a reference to him in an intel report prepared by the Major Investigation Team on the subject of organised crime in Ipswich. Seems Wade got in with some bad company when he was part of the clubland there.'

'When you say "got in"…?'

'No actual details, no suggestion of criminal activity on his part. It's a "known associates" type thing.'

'Known associates who've casually provided him with an untraceable car?'

'Maybe.'

'What about relatives and loved ones?' she asked.

'Remarkably few. His mother died from a brain haemorrhage in 2002, when he was seventeen. And like I say, his father passed with cancer in 2011. He had no brothers, sisters or other close relations.'

She mulled it over. 'So, what was the *bad* news?'

Clive sighed. 'Rachel's been in again.'

'Okay.'

'Half an hour ago there was a seven-car pile-up on the A131, just north of Halstead. She wants us on it.'

Lynda felt a stab of irritation. 'Both of us?'

'Yeah.'

'So, what happened to her giving us until tomorrow morning to clear up this other case?'

'Lynda, it's a seven-car pile-up. This is serious stuff.'

'And the A12 smash isn't? We've got two people at death's door.'

'That's the problem.' Clive tried to sound reasonable. 'Elliot Wade's not at death's door, not anymore. And this other job's a dog's breakfast, by the sounds of it. We've got multiple injuries, all kinds of potential offences that need looking into ...'

'And none of the others can take it?'

'Rachel says she's picked us because now that we know Elliot Wade's going to recover, his case can wait.'

'And if he associates with gangsters, what're the chances of him telling us anything?'

'Perhaps you should ask Rachel that, eh?'

'Well, yeah ... I'm going to have to, seeing as *you* clearly didn't.'

'Lynda!' he protested. 'I'm just a grunt. I don't have arguments with DIs.'

Again, this was vintage Clive Atkins. Give him a quiet life. No issues with other colleagues. No controversy. Nothing that might drag him out of his comfort zone.

'Are you on your way out there now?' she asked.

'I'm about to go.'

'Great. Just when we were making some progress.'

'Lynda, don't you think you're maybe attaching more importance to this case than it merits?'

'Clive, we've got a car that shouldn't exist, we've got an unexplained injury-RTA, a pile of unexplained money, and now we've got a guy whose name has cropped up in an anti-organised crime enquiry.'

'But that's not our field.'

'God, Clive, you are so bloody unambitious.'

'Lynda! This isn't Al Capone. It's a stolen car that's come off a road at high speed. How many incidents like that are recorded every single day?'

'There are other factors ...'

'But none that can't wait or can't be dealt with by someone more experienced. Look ...' He paused. 'Look, you've got to stop trying to compete with Don.'

A moment passed before that sank in. 'What?'

'Sorry,' he muttered awkwardly, 'but this is what I meant before. When I said I hoped this thing wasn't what I thought it was.'

'Compete with Don?'

'Come on, Lynda, that's what this is, isn't it? You only have to go back to the Christmas do, four weeks ago. You, Don, me and Naomi at the same table. I could see you were embarrassed, but there was something else too. You were angry, I mean livid. You didn't say anything at the time, but you were bristling, like you'd just been challenged ...'

He was referring to the Unit's last Christmas dinner. Not atypically, Don had got drunk and talked all night about his days in Major Investigations, when he and his close colleague, DS Terry Sullivan, had busted what he repeatedly referred to as 'real criminals'.

And yes, it had infuriated Lynda.

'Terry was built like a brick shithouse,' she recalled Don saying. 'Ex-guardsman, six foot six, shoulders like a bloody ox. We collared one druggie bastard who'd beaten up his partner's baby until every bone in its body was broken. We nabbed him at Tilbury. He was trying to leave the country. He went for Terry with a Stanley knife. Cut him twice on the neck... left this X-shaped wound. But that didn't help, I'll tell you. Terry hit him so hard I thought he'd cross the fucking Channel without paying a fare. Course, nothing came of it. Scrote pulled his blade first, and Terry had the blood to prove it.'

Lynda had understood why her husband was being such a bore that night. His insistence that dealing with dangerous criminals was the only kind of policework worthy of the name was a way to big himself up because, no longer a copper, he often felt out of place these days when attending police functions. Not that this excused his indirect belittling of the work they themselves did.

'I know it's aggravating,' Clive said. 'But it must be even worse for you. You must get it all the time. But you know, you can't just invent something to try and get one over on him.'

'Get one over on him?' She tried to refocus on the traffic. 'You think I'm jealous of my own husband?'

'No, I think you were embarrassed because he was being embarrassing. But I also think you believe that, if you get a decent score, that might put him back in his box.'

She said nothing.

'Look,' he said, 'I'm sorry if I've overstepped the mark.'

'You've not overstepped the mark, Clive.' That wasn't true, but it didn't matter, because now, suddenly, she was distracted by something else. 'All you've done is give me your honest opinion. It's up to me to either take it on board or dismiss it as the self-justification of a nine-till-fiver who's always got one eye on the clock.'

'Come on, that's not fair...'

'En route to the A131, swing by the hospital again.'

'Did you not hear what I just...?'

'Until Rachel says otherwise, the A12 is still our case. You told me the hospital said to go back later. It's now later, so go back. And if you still can't speak to Elliot Wade, at least get them to tell you when we *can* ... which is something you should have done last time.'

She cut the call before he could answer.

Not because she was being sulky with him, but because she'd just driven through Camera X, which meant that she was fourteen miles north of the point on the A12 where the Wades' accident had occurred, and it had tripped off a sequence of rather incredible thoughts, thanks in no small way to the activities of a mischievous rooftop rodent.

22

31 December (Tuesday)

Elliot thought of it as being an 'orange room'. That was because its prevailing colour was orange, though he soon realised that, in actual fact, it was a conservatory, a small glazed annexe to the main house, with plush orange curtains, orange carpet-tiles, and a portable electric fire in the corner. The fire rendered the room hot and stuffy, which wasn't helped by its smoke-rich atmosphere.

Jo Naboth was in there, seated at a circular table, the dog-end of a cigarette hanging between her fingers as she pondered a hand of cards. There were several other players at the table, all men – heavy-set slabs of meat with scarred faces and beringed knuckles, and yet crammed into their Sunday best – also smoking, also brooding over closely guarded hands. A great pile of cash sat in the middle. A couple of other women – overdressed, overpainted floozies to Elliot's mind – sat in a corner.

Jo glanced up as Jim and Elliot came into the room. Lonnegan was close behind them. He closed the door, reducing the party's disco beat to a distant repetitive thud.

Brother and sister locked gazes for several seconds before Jo laid her cards face-down. 'Take a recess,' she said quietly.

Like her brother, her accent was solid East End.

The heavies at the table complied, laying their hands down

and standing. One by one, they dabbed their smokes out in an ashtray, and left the room with their women and drinks. When they'd gone and the door was closed, Jo stood and went to a drinks cabinet, where she poured malt over ice.

'Seems our resident Ben Hur has found out about the Red Book,' Jim said.

'What?' Elliot was confused. 'I don't know anything about any Red Book.'

Jo regarded him long and hard. There was no warmth there. For all Elliot's Christmas Eve heroics, the person who'd benefitted most from them seemed determined to remain unimpressed.

'How did that happen?' she asked, still dangerously quiet.

'Iago,' Jim said.

Jo nodded. 'Dumb little shit. Anyone else hear?'

Jim glanced at Lonnegan. 'Did they?'

Lonnegan shrugged. 'Don't think so.'

Jo nodded again. If the boss woman's smouldering personality wasn't intimidating enough, she was physically large, standing almost six feet tall in her heels, and massive across the chest and shoulders. She swilled more whiskey, blew more smoke.'

'How much do you know?' she asked.

Elliot shrugged. 'Only that during the blag we acquired some property belonging to a group called the Corporation.'

'You know who the Corporation are?'

'No, and by the sounds of it, I'm bloody glad.'

'Which shows how little he *does* know,' Lonnegan cut in. 'And ignorance is dangerous.'

'Leave it to us, Ray,' Jim retorted. '*You've* caused us problems in the last few days too.'

Lonnegan glowered but said nothing else.

'The Corporation are the big league,' Jo explained. 'The heavy mob.'

Silence followed, until Elliot realised that he was expected to say something in response. 'So, what's this Red Book business?'

Jo tugged on her cig. 'Tell him.'

'The Corporation is the UK's number one team,' Jim said. 'There isn't a crime league as such, but if there was, they'd be so far up it they'd need oxygen just to function.'

'I've never heard of them,' Elliot replied.

'You wouldn't have, would you?' Lonnegan snorted.

'Ray's right, you wouldn't have.' Jim also headed to the drinks cabinet. 'Who's the deadliest killer? The one who's never even been detected. What's the most dangerous animal? The one no one knows about. Here's the situation. There're too many foreign mobs in the UK at present.' He picked up a bottle of Jim Beam. 'Started with the Yardies in the Eighties, the Columbians in the Nineties. Now we've got Russians, Albanians.' He handed a drink each to Elliot and Lonnegan. 'It was getting out of hand basically. Till about twenty years ago, when a bunch of traditional old London firms decided enough was enough. They joined forces. Created an alliance so strong that they could see off almost any challenge.'

'And this is the Corporation?' Elliot asked.

'You won't find info about them online,' Jim said. 'You won't read about them in any "true crime" books. But they've got their mucky little fingers in near enough every pie. Racketeering, narcotics, human trafficking, you name it. Its board of directors comprises four men. They're known as the Four Horsemen...'

'Because they can rain down a fucking apocalypse on anyone they like,' Lonnegan interjected.

'Few outside the organisation know who these four are,' Jim said. 'But they're a bunch of total cut-throats. No one gets near them personally. They have layers of captains and soldiers to carry out their orders, run things day to day, kill and torture anyone they decide deserves it.'

Elliot felt sweat on his brow. 'And we've lifted something of *theirs*?'

'Don't get too jumpy.' Jo eased herself back onto her chair. 'We have some reputation, ourselves. But this thing needs to be handled with care.'

'One of their lieutenants is a lunatic called Jacques Marat,' Jim said. 'He's a French-Canadian. His nickname is Scissorman Jaq because, when making his mark on documents, instead of signing them, he stamps them like some medieval king. Uses crimson ink and a ring inscribed with a pair of expanded garden shears. Which are also, as it happens, his favourite killing tool.'

'He likes chopping people to death,' Lonnegan added. 'Usually finishes by slicing open their throat and snipping out their tongue.'

'Fucking great,' Elliot said.

'It gets better,' Jim added. 'Because one of the safety deposit boxes we took during the raid was being rented by *him*.'

Jo tossed something onto the table. A small notebook about the size and thickness of an office diary, bound in smooth red leather. Elliot peered fearfully down at it, though he didn't know why. Jo tossed something else: a strap of white, waxed card, perhaps one inch wide, eighteen to twenty in length.

'Have a gander,' she said, applying her lighter to a fresh cigarette.

He picked the two items up.

'That strap was fastened around the book like a seal,' Jim said. 'Check it out.'

Now that he'd been directed to it, Elliot noted that the upside of the white strap had been imprinted with the crude, blood-red image of a pair of expanded shears.

'Okay,' he said. 'I can see who the owner is.' He turned the book over. 'But it's just a book. Is it really so valuable?'

'That wasn't just on its own inside one of the safety deposit boxes,' Jim said. 'It was inside its own strongbox too. Couldn't even use acid on the thing, we had to torch it open.'

'Look inside,' Jo muttered.

Elliot flipped the book open and turned several pages. It was filled with handwriting, which had been scribbled in blotchy ballpoint. At first glance, it was unintelligible, but it had been applied in orderly fashion: five blocks of text per page, each one separated from the next by a line break. It was as though each block was a separate entry of some sort. However, reading it proved to be impossible. This wasn't just because the handwriting was poor; even the letters were unrecognisable. Only belatedly did it strike him that whoever had filled in this diary, or whatever it was, had been using a code.

He flipped more pages. It was the same front to back.

He replaced the book on the table carefully.

'No doubt, if we had the time and inclination,' Jo said, 'we could find some little nerd who'd be able to crack that encryption for us. But...'

She shrugged and blew more smoke, her cold, grey eyes fixed on Elliot.

'But you'd rather just give it back?' Elliot suggested.

For the first time Elliot had *ever* seen it, Jo Naboth smiled. And it wasn't endearing. It was amused, almost scornful. 'If only it was that simple.'

'The Corporation didn't get where they are by forgiving and forgetting,' Jim said. 'And that particularly applies to Scissorman Jaq. At present, they don't have a clue who stole their weird piece of merchandise. If we wanted to, we could hang onto it long term and see if we get away with it. But that would be a risk. Because the Corporation have ways of gathering intel the rozzers can't even dream of. And if they learn the truth in due course, they'll come after us with everything they've got. One alternative is to get on the blower right now and, as you say, offer it back. But if we do that, we'll be admitting responsibility for pinching it in the first place. And they'd likely still come for us, only a lot more quickly.'

'So, what we've been thinking,' Jo interrupted, 'is to make a truce with them. Anonymously of course. Not giving our identities away but arranging a meeting. A get-together on neutral ground ... a pow-wow between intermediaries.'

'Why go to all that trouble?' Elliot asked. 'Why not just find a drop-off point and mark their cards later, so they can collect it? They get their property back and our names never arise?'

Jo looked at him askance. 'You *are* joking, I trust? We put a lot of time into that job. We lifted this Red Book fair and square. So, we're not just giving it back. The Corporation are going to have to pay.'

Elliot was fascinated. 'Won't that make them even more furious?'

Jo shrugged. 'Yeah. But they still won't know who we are. Because, like I say, the negotiations will be handled by an intermediary.' She smiled again. 'And as you know all about it now, and as you're a presentable sort ... that intermediary may as well be *you*.'

New Year was close, when Harri found Elliot seated on the front doorstep, grasping a bottle of Jim Beam.

'Where've you been the last half-hour?' she asked.

Elliot took another swig. 'In the inner circle, apparently.'

'Am I supposed to know what that means?'

He shook his head. 'Knowledge is a dangerous thing in this company, my love.'

'So, you're not going to tell me?'

'Believe me, it's for your own good.'

'Is it? Or is it for *yours* – so I won't be able to grass you up?' She glared down at him. 'Because that's the world we're living in now, isn't it? Previously you were in and out of it, but this is the real thing. I mean now we're neck-deep ...'

'What do you want me to do?' he hissed. 'I've told you I can't just walk away from this!'

'Actually, you can.' She huddled into her wrap as she stood and surveyed him. 'You can walk away right now. In fact, why don't we?'

He glanced up at her, bemused.

'Why don't we just go down to the car, get in it and drive off home?' Her voice had become a plea. 'You never need to see these people again.'

For a millisecond he appeared to be half considering it. Then he fluttered a hand at her. '*You* do that.'

'What?'

'If you don't want to be part of this, there's no reason why you should.' He dug into his trouser pocket, pulled out the car key and tossed it towards her. 'Why don't you go *now*?'

She caught it. 'You really want me to? Think carefully about this, Elliot.'

'I've had enough grief without you piling in too. We're all better off if you go.'

'And you're not coming with me?'

'You can't have it both ways, I'm afraid.'

'God, you are such an idiot.' She backed down the drive, before turning on her heel. 'You'd better hope you can afford a taxi home.'

23

8 January (Wednesday)

The Forensics team had been and gone, the crash site no longer had a police guard, and the A12 was in full use again, vehicles hurtling back and forth behind Lynda as she stood next to the Accident Hotline placard on the shoulder, and gazed down the steep passageway torn through the frozen undergrowth. What remained of the Mondeo still rested in the SCIU examination bay at Chelmsford. But the route of its descent was marked by shattered saplings, broken branches and fluttering strips of incident tape. It was the same for the impact point at the bottom of the embankment, where the tape still hung in place.

She wasn't sure what she could find after Forensics had sifted the scene so thoroughly. Clive had annoyed her with his suggestion that she was competing with Don, but even if she resented the way her husband's swaggering tales of roughneck coppering disparaged what he clearly saw as her own paltry police efforts, she didn't think she would cling to this case purely on the chance it might hand her a big result.

That said, *any* result would do at present.

She was supposed to be head of an accident investigation unit, and yet in three days she'd only managed to name the two parties involved, and one of those was a 'probably'. She hadn't a clue what had caused the accident, or what offences it revealed, if any. Even so this would be one hell of a straw to grab at, so much so that she wondered if it would be another colossal waste of time. Before she could deliberate further, the phone trilled in her pocket.

She put it to her ear. 'DS Hagen.'

'Just the person,' a male voice said. 'Andy Kepler, detective super at NCG, Organised Crime Division.'

'Oh, hello, sir?'

'I understand you're making some enquiries about a certain Elliot Wade?'

'Wow, news travels fast.'

'Faster than thought these days, thanks to the internet.' He sounded amiable enough, with none of the cool, clipped, 'worship me or get out of my way' attitude affected by so many of the top brass. 'It's nothing sinister, sarge. It's just that someone in your office accessed an intelligence file concerning Wade prepared by Essex Major Investigation team ... and it's been flagged to come to our attention straight away if there was ever any interest.'

'Really?' This surprised her. 'Wade hasn't got any form.'

'No, but he's connected to certain people who have. Can you explain the situation?'

'The situation is that he's in hospital ... Well, we *think* it's him. We're pretty sure it's him. He was involved in an RTC last Sunday night on the A12.'

Kepler paused for thought. 'So, there are no sus circs?'

'I wish there weren't. But the car was a clone and there was an awful lot of money in Wade's possession, none of which has been explained yet.'

'What's *his* explanation?'

'Nothing. He's still incommunicado.'

'What actions are you initiating?'

'We're still investigating, sir. We haven't got any real leads yet … not until we speak to him.'

Another pause. 'Can you keep us copied in, sarge?'

'Sure,' she said. 'Anything I should know?'

'You'll know that as soon as I know it. Sorry to be vague.'

'That's okay, sir.'

'Thanks for your help. No doubt we'll speak again soon.'

And he cut the call.

'No doubt,' Lynda said. 'Shit.'

Now there was no option.

24

1 January (Wednesday)

A hand gripped Elliot's arm.

He screamed. And struggled. And kicked.

'For God's sake, Elliot!'

His eyes snapped open – and Harri was looking down at him. Before he could recollect anything about the hideous nightmare he'd just had, before he could even speak, a spike was pounded into his skull.

'Ohhh my Lord.' He fingered his temple.

'How come you're here?' she asked, standing up.

Elliot looked around, bleary-eyed, wondering why he was so cold, and why his bedroom smelled so stale and damp, before realising that he was still in the clothes he'd worn the night before and huddled on a dirty mattress.

'I said, how are you here?' Harri's voice was stern as she stood over him. Her hair was still up, and she was dressed only in a short bathrobe and fluffy slipper booties. A squarish brown parcel was tucked under her arm.

He struggled to explain, calling up some vague, hallucinatory memory of falling into the back of a car. 'I ... got a minicab. About three.'

'I bet that cost a bloody fortune on New Year's morning.'

'What else could I do? Couldn't invite myself to stay at Jo Naboth's, could I?'

Harri assisted him to his feet, but he was so dizzy that he couldn't cross the barn's derelict interior without leaning on her arm.

'Why didn't you come into the cottage?' she asked.

'You had the key.'

'Why didn't you knock?'

'I didn't think you'd let me in.'

'For God's sake, Elliot.'

Outside, the white light of a cold January morning all but blinded him.

'How did you know I was in the barn?' he asked.

'I didn't. When I got home last night, a slip had been put through the letterbox. A private courier had left a card saying the parcel was in there. I came out to get it this morning, and lo and behold, there *you* were.'

In the cottage, she lowered him onto the sofa, before getting him a glass of water and two paracetamol. She left the brown parcel on the coffee table.

'What's this, anyway?' he asked.

'I don't know. It's addressed to you.'

He fiddled with the package, his fingers making no headway on the thick taping. Harri brought scissors from the kitchen, though even then it took half a minute.

Once they'd opened it, they found fist-sized bundles of cash wrapped in cellophane. The notes were used and for the most part looked like twenties, each bundle held together with elastic bands. Assuming that each one contained a grand, and there were sixty-five of them in total, it was twenty grand more than Elliot had been promised.

He glanced up at Harri, who stood with arms folded, though her disapproval had given way to worry and uncertainty.

'So,' he said, 'do you want me to give this back?'

'Is that supposed to be some kind of test, Elliot? Because if it is, I don't appreciate it.'

'No, it isn't a test. I just want to make up for last night. Look, why don't we hit the sales, eh? I *earned* this money, whatever you think. It'd be nice to get something out of it.'

'Perhaps you should send it to the bedsides of the people who got injured?'

He gave her a frank stare. 'Do you think I should, Harriet? I mean, *really*? Life's about survival. It's not like we haven't got bills to pay, and on top of that it's dangerous. Word gets out that I've developed a conscience, and suddenly I become a problem.'

She sighed. 'And is this it? Is it over now? Can you give me your word?'

'I wish I could.'

There was a brief but lingering silence.

'Of course,' she then said. 'The thing you couldn't tell me about last night.'

He regarded her with a jaundiced eye. 'Why do you want to know about this stuff, Harri? You've never asked me about this side of my life previously.'

'Maybe I'm worried that it's suddenly getting serious. I mean you've been involved in stealing money before, Elliot. I know ... *I* spent it. But this time people got hurt. They nearly died, and maybe that's made me realise that you're now into something from which there might be no return.'

Elliot sat back. He was exhausted, his head still throbbing. 'You know, you *knowing* about things won't stop them happening ... for all the reasons I've already mentioned.'

'But two brains working on the problem are better than one. And you clearly need a solution. You got filthy drunk last night because you were unhappy or stressed – or both. So, maybe I can help?'

He pondered. In truth, there was probably no reason why he couldn't trust Harri.

They'd been together a decade and knew each other intimately. Okay, he'd never met her family, he didn't know her past intricately, but she'd put that behind her anyway. She was as stable as any ex-stripper could be. She was clean and had a steady and legit job. And she was more than just his wife; she was the closest thing he had to a best mate. It was true that he didn't want her to be part of this because he sought to protect her, though he wasn't sure that keeping her out of the loop would necessarily be security for her. If, for any reason, the Naboths decided she was a risk, they'd make that decision whether Harri knew about it or not.

It might even be more useful to her if she *did* know about it – or *some* of it. Then, at least, she'd see them coming.

So, he told her. Not everything, but quite a lot.

About the red leather book they'd inadvertently stolen during the robbery. About how they'd learned that it belonged to a major syndicate. About how a negotiating team was now being assembled to speak to these guys, and about how *he* was going with them.

'And what is this book?' Harri asked.

'It's like a list of entries,' he said. 'Four or five on each page. But it's unreadable, just gibberish.'

'Why don't they throw it back? Post it through a letterbox and run off?'

'Because it's clearly worth something.'

'Yeah, but if it's going to cause trouble ...'

'The fact that it's been nicked will already have caused trouble. The Naboths are in this heavy mob's sights as we speak. So, Jo reckons they might as well get something out of it.' Elliot shrugged. 'I know it's scary, but that's the way people like Jo and Jim think. They're gangsters too, Harri.'

'So ... let me get this straight. Your reward for Christmas Eve is to have to go and deal with this bigger mob?'

'I'm going as a driver mainly. There's a kind of logic to it. Doesn't mean I'm not scared shitless though. Who wouldn't be, having to drive a hard bargain with Scissorman Jaq Marat?'

If Elliot had been struggling less with his hangover, he'd have noticed the immediate and abrupt change in Harri's demeanour: from frustrated annoyance to sudden icy shock; and then to pale-cheeked fear. Only when she turned without a word and stumbled away towards the downstairs lavatory, did he perceive a problem.

He followed her curiously, hearing the sound of retching behind the closed door. It was several minutes before the toilet flushed and she came back out again, white-faced.

'So I wasn't the only one who drank too much last night?' he said. 'Good job you didn't get stopped on the way home, eh?'

She ignored that, shuffling to the foot of the staircase, where she halted by the newel post, fingers caressing her forehead.

Elliot came up behind her. 'Or is it something I just said?'

She started upstairs. 'It's nothing.'

'The hell it's nothing!' he shouted after her, though it set his head thumping. 'Harri, what the bloody hell's going on?'

Halfway up, she glanced back. Tears glimmered on her lashes. 'Elliot ... you didn't say it was the Corporation.'

Elliot was more than stunned. 'Harri, how do *you* know about the Corporation?'

'I can't...' She shook her head dumbly. 'Look, I'd rather not say.'

'Rather not say?' Elliot tried to work that out and decided that it didn't make sense. 'For God's sake, this is serious stuff. How do you know about...?'

'It's not just that, Elliot. It's ... it's *him*. Scissorman Jaq.'

'You know about *him* too. What's going on here?'

She hurried on upstairs. 'Sorry, I don't want to talk about it.'

'Harri...?' He stumbled up after her.

'Don't ask me again, okay?' The bedroom door slammed with an air of finality. 'Not now!' Her voice was muffled but intense. '*Not ever!*'

25

8 January (Wednesday)

At the foot of the embankment, pulped vegetation and broken, shredded branches lay in heaps on all sides. As Lynda took time to ponder the scene, a winter hush settled. Out among the trunks, wisps of white mist gathered. Dusk was approaching, so she couldn't afford to mess around. She headed away from the crash site, but walked slowly, scanning the ground, trying to work out exactly where it was that she'd seen the thing that now intrigued her.

On reflection, it was quite an indulgence, this. Especially when she was under orders to switch her attention to a different major incident. A seven-car pile-up, no less. It would take all her expertise to unravel the facts from so much carnage, but at the end of the day it would mostly be misadventure. In contrast, this was a stubborn mystery interwoven with strands of potentially serious criminality. Okay, Lynda had joined SCIU to work nine-till-five. But she was still a detective – unlike Clive, who, though he officially shared that role, was at heart a Traffic man. And when a case got juicy, detectives – *real* detectives – grew interested. (Especially when they felt a growing threat from bigger, better resourced departments like the Organised Crime Division.)

At which point she stopped dead.

She was about forty yards east of the taped-off area, next

to a sturdy silver birch, the base of which was sunk into a clump of frost-matted bracken. None of that was out of place, but what *was* – possibly – was the light scattering of wood flakes she'd spotted last Monday morning, and had dismissed as unimportant.

Lynda stepped away and craned her neck back. Some ten feet above, the silver birch forked. Both trunks continued to ascend to thirty feet at least, though far short of the top, they were bisected by the lower bough of a horse chestnut standing about fifteen yards away.

But as with the squirrel knocking noisy debris down through the roof of the stable at Ravenwood Cottage, something must have caused this minor mess. And when she shifted a couple of feet to the left, she saw that about twenty feet up, the right-hand trunk of the silver birch bore what looked like an enormous smash mark.

She glanced again at the flakes near her feet, then picked one up. Whatever had happened here, it was recent; the flake was green around its edges, where the sap hadn't drained out of it. It seemed unlikely that it could have anything to do with the A12 crash. She glanced back towards the taped area. Forty yards off. Okay, it had been a tremendous impact, and bits of scrap had no doubt flown in every direction, but it was still a long shot. Of course, she would only *know* if she got up there.

She stared upward again. With no helmet, no safety line, no spikes for her boots, and no one else here to assist, this could be a serious disciplinary offence. Even if that hadn't been the case, Lynda wasn't sure it was a risk that she was happy taking. She couldn't remember when she'd last climbed a tree. When she was eleven or twelve, a tomboy toughie trying to prove to the lads that she was as good as them? Even if she was an expert, the tree would be a challenge. It was a silver birch, so there were few branches low down. But she wasn't just walking away from this.

Her gaze settled on the horse-chestnut branch snaking between the twin uprights of the birch, about one foot above the point of damage. The horse-chestnut's trunk was massive, and there were numerous branches growing out from it, the lowest about four feet off the ground.

She walked over there, tugging her gloves off.

The climb, when it commenced, wasn't as bad as she'd feared. She clambered onto the first branch and was able to support herself against the trunk while standing and reaching for the next one overhead, swinging herself up onto that one too. She was already ten feet up, but now it got tougher. She used knots in the bark as footholds, gradually working her way around to the other side. Whereas the tree had leaned away from her before, now it leaned against her. At one point she glanced down, seeing a dizzying drop to the woodland floor. When she finally straddled the target branch, it was fibrous and resilient, and bowed downward the further across it she slithered. It soon sloped so far down that it brought Lynda face-to-face with the damage. This close, she saw that both trunks of the silver birch had been struck, not just one. The westernmost appeared to have been hit a glancing blow by something. But while this first trunk had only been clipped, the second one had taken its full force. The bark and virgin wood had blown out, leaving a gaping, shattered wound. More to the point, the two small objects responsible – shapeless nuggets of tarnished metal – were half buried in the pulp.

Lynda looked west towards the A12 – she was directly in line with the crash scene. She was also level with the road. The branch creaked, shifting up and down, but Lynda carefully pulled out her phone and placed a call.

Rachel Hollindrake answered on the second ring. 'Lynda, what's happening?'

'We've got a new lead,' Lynda said.

'A new lead?' The DI sounded confused. 'Are you at the A131?'

'That's negative. I'm still on the A12.'

'*Lynda!*'

'I know why that Mondeo left the road.'

'What're you talking about?'

'Someone was shooting at it.'

'Shooting?'

'I'm looking at the bullets right now.'

26

1 January (Wednesday)

On New Year's Day afternoon, Elliot and Harri drove down to London. There was no rail service, so they took the A12, parking at Newbury Park and catching the Central Line.

It was as crowded and chaotic as they'd expected, the West End pavements thronging, the department stores crammed. On top of that, they weren't talking.

Perhaps inevitably, their trip to the sales was as much about going through the motions as doing anything practical with their new-found wealth, watching others buy things they didn't need rather than indulging themselves. Not that it made them feel in any way superior; at least the money the hordes of eager shoppers was spending was lawfully theirs.

Elliot, as he repeatedly told himself, no longer believed in sin, and while crime was a bad thing – inasmuch as it might send you to prison – Jim Naboth had seemed to think they'd got away clean. In addition, of course, they'd lifted those valuables from dodgy characters; other criminals mostly. But then there was still the factor of the injured witness and security guards. Elliot wasn't comfortable pondering that.

That evening, at his terse suggestion, they looked for a West End restaurant, seeing no reason why they shouldn't treat themselves at least a little bit. However, most places they called at were full. In the end, they settled for a Big Mac and chips each, and headed home.

It was now dark, and the cold had intensified, threatening snow. Perhaps for this reason, there was minimal other traffic. On the southern stretch of the A12, the empty blacktop was lit only by the cone-shaped glow of their headlights. 'You know you're going to have to talk to me,' Elliot said. 'I don't know who you think you're showing loyalty to, but at present you're *my* wife, and I'm seeing these guys in a few days, and I could really do with knowing all about them.'

'Marat's a madman, Elliot,' Harri replied, gazing unseeing from the car. 'A murderer.'

'I've been told that much already. How do *you* know him?'

Again, Harri appeared reluctant to answer. Though now she seemed weary rather than afraid. 'You remember the club where me and you first met?'

'Hell, I don't know. The Pink Elephant, was it, Knightsbridge?'

'Yeah. The one before that was the Honeypot in Earl's Court.'

'The Honeypot?' Elliot had drunk his way around some of the sleaziest bars in the West End, but he didn't remember that place.

'It was more downmarket than anything you'd have been used to.' She risked a glance at him. 'I know it sounds gross, but that was the way it was back then.'

He shrugged, indicating that she should continue.

'There was this barman there, a sweet kid. Sean Maloney. Young Irish fella. Full of life, always good for a wind-up. At first I thought he was sweet on me because he was always joking around. But then it turned out he was gay. Not that it mattered…'

'How does this involve the Corporation?' Elliot interrupted.

'They killed him!'

There was a silence as Elliot absorbed this. He supposed it was only what he'd expected they'd be getting around to, but to hear it as bluntly as that was a shock.

'Sean was barman first and foremost,' Harri added. 'But he had another duty. Whenever the girls took customers up to the rooms, they'd sell drugs to them...'

'This place was a fucking brothel?'

She watched him worriedly. 'I told you it was seedy.'

'Shit.' Elliot hadn't known about this either.

'It was years ago, Elliot... and you knew I had a past.'

'All right... Christ.' He drove on doggedly. 'Just tell me what happened.'

She looked from the window again. 'Like I say, the girls kept drugs up there, packaged and ready to go. Mainly ecstasy and coke, but there were poppers, LSD, DMT. The girls didn't take the money themselves, of course. But they'd phone it down to Sean what each customer owed, and before the guys left, they paid their "bar bill".'

She hesitated to say more, clearly struggling with a memory that was sheer torment.

'Go on,' he grunted.

'I don't know what Sean was doing on top of that... I suppose there was ample opportunity for him to steal. And good God, what a mistake that was.'

'The Corporation owned the Honeypot, did they?'

'Or protected it. It was near enough the same thing.' A tear trickled down her cheek.

His eyes remained riveted on the road.

'Sean had had something going on with one of the other

girls,' she said. 'She'd pretend the customer had bought more drugs than he had. She'd then phone it down to Sean, who'd overcharge him, and pocket the extra drugs. He'd then take them and sell them in a few gay bars he used to frequent and split the proceeds with the girl. But I'm not sure that was what caused the problem because no girl got murdered. The *real* trouble started when Sean got caught in a police sting. I mean for selling gear. Suddenly, he's facing jail time. And he's just a wimpy young lad, you know. A party guy, an innocent. They'd have torn him apart inside.'

'So, let me guess,' Elliot said. 'The cops turned him into a grass?'

'They were trying to crack down on Corporation activities. And this was a good lead for them. Now they had an insider in one of the firm's clubs.'

'And the Corporation found out?'

'Somehow or other, yeah. So, they sent this guy they called the Scissorman. He turned up one night like any other punter. But he didn't choose a girl, he just sat there at the bar, sipping mineral water, but like a reptile, you know. His eyes never left Sean, who as usual was too giddy, having too much of a good time to even notice.' She sniffled. 'Until eventually this guy passed a note across the bar to him. I don't know what was on it, but Sean was interested. He told me he was on a promise after work.' She shook her head. 'The poor lad. He didn't know what kind of promise it was. When they found him the next day, oh my God, Elliot, it was awful.' Fresh tears glistened in Harri's eyes. 'When they found him, it was on a rubbish tip in Hornsey. There were deep wounds all over his body ... like pieces of it had just been sliced away. But according to the police, he'd only died when his throat had been slit open, his tongue yanked out through the hole and hacked off at the root…'

The tears ran freely down her cheeks.

Elliot's vision glazed as the road in front of him turned into a blur.

27

8 January (Wednesday)

Clive Atkins did indeed swing by the hospital en route to the A131, as Lynda had asked him to, though his loyalties were now at full stretch.

Lynda Hagen was normally great to work with. A thorough investigator, she led her enquiries by good example, efficiently working through the many uncertainties that fogged serious road accidents, making quick, straightforward cases against those culpable, effortlessly ironing out any complications. Which was just the way Clive liked it. He had a life outside the job, even more so now that he and Naomi were engaged.

But Lynda's home life was increasingly impacting on her professional life.

Ever since Don had taken his medical retirement, she'd become steadily more frustrated with their caseload. Not because there was too much, but, incredibly, because there was too little.

Or rather because it was all too uninteresting.

He was seeing this more and more: Lynda reacting to routine driving offences as if they were a boring nuisance, while probing other cases more deeply than was strictly necessary. Why did this particular individual try to run a red light when there was an HGV bearing down? Maybe the van driver who'd shed his load, causing three deaths, had been telling the truth when he'd insisted that it had been secure when he'd set out; could someone have loosened it?

And so often there was never an answer to these questions.

And then the company do last December had come along, and they'd been subjected to another three hours of the Don Hagen show.

Clive had never known Lynda's husband in any other capacity than that – as the guy she had on her arm at functions. But though he was pleasant enough when sober, his sobriety never lasted long at these events, and then the bombast emerged, and the demeaning of coppers who were straight bats commenced.

'Fuck me, we'd never let them get away with that in our day,' and so on.

Okay, it was a face-saving device for having crashed out early, but Jesus, it was annoying.

All that said, Clive wouldn't have wished what had happened to Don Hagen on anyone.

It had been three years ago now, when Hagen was a DI at Major Investigations. They'd been working a series of aggravated burglaries, lone farmhouses attacked by a solo raider whom the press had dubbed the 'Night Wolf'. Twelve householders had been tied up and tortured before the enquiry team received a tip that a certain Marcus Gray, a mechanic in Braintree, matched the e-fit. Hagen had visited the garage in question with a new DC called Chrissie Molyneux, only to spot Gray queuing at a chippie van outside. When the two detectives approached him, he pulled a gun and bundled them into a nearby car, forcing them to drive north through Cambridgeshire and into Lincolnshire, constantly threatening to kill them. When Molyneux, who was driving, panicked and attempted to cut across open fields to the busy A1, Gray shot her through the head. As the car slid to a halt, Hagen got out and ran. Gray followed, shooting at him repeatedly, missing each time, only to die himself when an undercover firearms unit that had been tracking the captives by their police radios opened up from behind.

It sounded bad enough when you discussed it, so the reality must have been worse. Little wonder it had left Don Hagen a total buffoon.

Of course, lots of people Clive met while doing his job had reasons for why they behaved badly. But that didn't make it okay. He sighed as he contemplated the problems in Lynda's life, and hoped to God that his own wouldn't go the same way.

At least the issue of wasting time at the hospital was solved. When he entered the Billington Ward, Elliot Wade was inert in his bed, still asleep, but this time Nurse Abimbola told him that the consultant in charge of the case, Mr Jaishankar, had visited that afternoon and left instructions that the patient needed complete rest and was not to be bothered by the police until the following afternoon at the earliest.

'At least he confirmed who he is,' the nurse said, as Clive headed out again. 'He was a bit more communicative than earlier. Told the doctor his name was Elliot Wade and asked about his wife.'

'What did you tell him?' Clive replied.

'The truth. It's not terrible news. Sounds like she's on the mend.'

Clive nodded, but as he stepped back out into the car park, his phone rang and he saw that the caller was Lynda.

'You up on the A131?' he asked.

'Forget that,' she said. 'Change of plan.'

'Oh?'

'There's been a major development, which I'm not going to elaborate on over the phone. Can you get back to the office ASAP?'

'What about the seven-car pile-up?'

'It's been reassigned.'

He couldn't help but feel suspicious. 'Has this come from Rachel?'

'No, from Donald Duck's brother-in-law. Just get your backside in, will you. We've got a pow-wow coming up.'

'I don't understand...'

'Move it, Clivey! Chop-chop! This is serious.'

Clive didn't notice that someone was watching from just inside the waiting area. It was Elliot Wade, wearing a hospital-issue dressing gown over his hospital-issue pyjamas, leaning on the drip that he'd wheeled alongside him.

Once the copper had departed, Wade lumbered back through the waiting area, but instead of re-entering the Billington Ward, went left, following a different passage. Working on memory, as he'd been brought via trolley along this route that very morning, he went left again and then right, and through a pair of double-doors into a staff-only zone. There was no one around and his luck continued to hold until he entered Neurological Intensive Care and found himself at Harriet's bed. He could hardly bear to look at her. As a former racing driver, he was well aware that facial injuries always tended to appear worse than they were. Bruised and beaten features could expand in all directions, which distorted a person's appearance horribly, even if they weren't too serious. It looked even worse, though, when the injured party was someone as beautiful as Harri. On top of that, the bandages and gauze swathing her shaven head, leaving only part of her face exposed, and the breathing tube extending from her nose, added an additional note of horror.

Elliot glanced at the monitors on either side, and the various cables connecting them to her semi-mummified form. He had no clue which ones provided life-support, of course, and it wasn't as if he could ask. But there was no option in the matter.

'I'm sorry, darling,' he said quietly. 'I am so, so sorry.'

28

2 January (Thursday)

Elliot stood in front of the full-length mirror and ran a fingertip down the line of his clean-shaven jaw. He was wearing his best Armani suit, his Prada tie and a brand-new shirt by Ralph Lauren. He had to look good, they'd said. Smart, professional. They didn't want the Corporation thinking it was dealing with some two-bit punks from the sticks. Even his feet sparkled, shod with his best Italian leather wingtips.

Reflected behind him, Harri wore her scruffy dressing gown and bootee slippers. Her blonde hair was piled in a tousled mess.

'Should I come with you?' she said.

'What would that achieve?' He flicked at more invisible dust motes.

'It'd give you company for one thing.'

'And when the Scissorman recognises you? From the Honeypot, I mean.'

His tone was brusque, partly to conceal his nervousness, but also because he still felt vaguely betrayed by her. Not only did she know this guy, Marat – this scumbag, this murdering pig – she'd met him in the brothel where she worked. Elliot had been just about okay that his wife was once a stripper. But a hooker too? He didn't know if he'd ever get over that revelation.

'I didn't look like this then,' she said tiredly.

'There's no point taking the chance. Besides, I'm worried enough about myself. The last thing I need is to be worried about you too.'

'This is the point where I'd normally say "don't flatter yourself",' she replied. 'That I've been around the track more times than you have, that I can take care of myself. But that would be a big lie in this situation. Elliot, for God's sake, surely you told them you don't think you're up to this!' She waited for an answer that she knew wasn't coming. 'You didn't, did you?'

'I've already explained – you can't do that.'

'Why? Because you're a gangster now? Elliot, you're not.'

'We've had *this* conversation too.' He swung to face her. 'Look, if I'm going to get out of this arrangement, I've got to do a couple of favours for Jim and Jo. Make sure I pay them back.'

'Pay them back? What did you do on Christmas Eve?'

'My job. This is something extra, a sign of good faith.'

'And the next time they need a sign of good faith from you? What will that involve?'

'Let's not keep going over it, eh?' He strode to the bedroom door. 'You want the truth? I'm scared of them. Of course I am. But if I do this, I can make the case that I've done enough. That I want out.'

Harri held her tongue as they went downstairs, recognising the thin logic, even if she wasn't convinced by it.

'Where's this meeting taking place?' she asked, as they stepped out into the freezing night air.

'I don't know. They sent me the postcode ... it's the one I

stuck on the fridge. I've written it here too.' He filched a slip of paper from his pocket. 'I don't know what it is, or where it is, except that it's somewhere in Dedham Vale.'

The Sport flashed and bleeped as he hit the fob.

'What was that TV show that used to be on when we were teenagers?' he wondered. 'That comedy about the spaceship?'

Harri looked puzzled. 'What're you talking about?'

'*Red Dwarf*, yeah?' He opened the driver's door. '"Fry me a kipper, I'll be back for breakfast."'

'Good God, Elliot, you're making jokes?'

What little courage he'd managed to screw down almost deserted him at that point.

What Harri had said earlier was true: she was the one who'd been around the track. Her hardscrabble upbringing as the daughter of a Romford taxi driver who most of the time couldn't do it because he was too drunk, and a mother addicted to prescription meds, had been way more deprived than his own. Elliot might be the ace wheelman, but Harri was the hardcase, the toughie who spoke her mind and didn't fear confrontation. To see *her* look frightened was a new, disconcerting experience.

'I'm going, okay?' He kissed her on the cheek.

She stood rigid, hugging her near-naked body against the cold.

'It'll be all right,' he said. 'We're just emissaries, delivering a message to this Jaq Marat and taking one back. Why would he cut up nasty with us?'

'Because he's insane, Elliot. Because he's a madman.'

'I've got my phone,' he replied. 'I'll give you a call when I'm on my way back.'

She didn't answer, just stood there, less than a foot from

the car. She didn't even move when he climbed in, hit the ignition and reversed out, which meant that he had to take extra care not to run over her toes. He programmed the postcode into the sat nav and swung the Sport around. In the rear-view mirror, Harri was silhouetted against the lights of the cottage, before he skirted a bend and she vanished.

If nothing else, at least he didn't have far to travel. He was already only fourteen miles from his destination. Once again, the roads were quiet. Some snow had fallen the previous night, but only lightly. During the day it had mostly melted.

Within what seemed like a very short time, he'd arrived – but was left bemused. It was a country pub called the Goose and Gander. It stood on the B1068, amid flat, extensive farmland, and was currently closed. Elliot pulled into the car park, where there was one other vehicle, a black Lexus GS with nobody inside. He parked next to it and switched off his engine. Immediately, a leather-gloved fist rapped on his window.

Elliot almost shouted.

'You going to sit there all night like some spare prick at a tart's wedding?' Ray Lonnegan asked through the glass.

Elliot climbed out and locked the Sport.

Lonnegan was also smartly suited, his beard and moustache trimmed, his dark tangle of locks washed, dried and hair-sprayed back so that he almost looked respectable.

'I didn't know what we were doing,' Elliot said.

'Don't suppose you could be expected to.'

It was a surprisingly conciliatory note from Lonnegan, who now walked to the Lexus's boot and took out an item of upper bodywear, a basic thing which appeared to fasten at the front and back with Velcro straps.

'Lightweight Kevlar,' Lonnegan said. 'Nothing but a

high-powered rifle can penetrate that. It's just a precaution but put it on anyway.'

'Now?'

'Easier than when we're in the car.'

Elliot took off his jacket, shirt and tie, and donned the protection, fastening it at the shoulders and under his arm-pits. 'This is hardly encouraging me,' he said.

'It's not supposed to encourage you; it's supposed to save your life.' Lonnegan closed the boot. He didn't wait for Elliot to finish buttoning up his shirt and adjusting his tie, just tossed the key to him and walked around to the Lexus's passenger side. 'Let's get to it.'

They climbed in together.

'Anything I need to know?' Elliot asked, unlocking the wheel and testing it. 'This thing armour-plated? We got a heavy weight in the back?'

'It's another of Jo and Jim's untraceable jobs, but that's all. As for cargo, tonight it's just me and you.' Lonnegan fastened his seatbelt. Again, by his softer tone, he was in a less adversarial mood than usual.

'Just out of interest,' he said, 'you carrying?'

Elliot had wondered if this would come up. 'No.'

Lonnegan handed something over. At first, Elliot had as-sumed that it would be a gun, but it was actually a fist-sized plastic tube and jet nozzle.

'What's this?' he asked.

'Ammonia. Same one I used during the blag.'

'So, my prints are now on a weapon used to GBH someone during an armed robbery?'

'Don't knock it. Someone gets too close, whack 'em in the eyes with that. They'll go down like a sack of shit.'

Elliot slid it into his pocket. 'Shouldn't we be carrying something heavier?'

'I am.' Lonnegan opened his jacket to reveal what looked like a machine pistol in a leather scabbard attached to a shoulder rig. 'Just in case it cuts up. But it's not going to. The agreement is we talk.'

Elliot turned the engine on. When the sat nav screen came to life, a coded destination had already been uploaded. The route unfolded before Elliot's eyes, leading them deeper into farming country. Soon after they'd set off, they found themselves on narrow, little-used lanes. As before, though, they approached their destination rapidly. Two minutes into the journey, it was less than three miles away.

'So,' Elliot said, 'does this Jaq Marat know we're only coming for a chat?'

'He's an underling,' Lonnegan said. 'Like you and me. He'll do as he's told.'

'I thought this Red Book thing belonged to him personally.'

'Even if it does, we haven't got it. So, what's the point him getting out of line? He does a number on us, he doesn't get it back, and he'll know that from the off.'

When Elliot had first met Harri, she was a performer at the Pink Elephant, which, while it was still a strip joint, was a tad classier than the norm, the girls sensational, the atmosphere glitzy. Prior to that job, things had been very different.

The Honeypot was a scummy fleapit where the air smelled of sweat, the carpets of vomit, and when you turned the lights on at the end, every bit of furniture was old and tatty. Harri had nursed a habit back then. That was how she'd got into the sex trade in the first place. She'd never injected, but she'd certainly been a cokehead, the solution to which, a boyfriend whose name she'd now forgotten had suggested, was to earn some real money by going to work in a club rather than selling herself online as a 'model'.

Being able to dance was one of Harri's natural abilities. She'd always had the moves. And it was this that had saved her long term. She was a good-looking girl; that too had been an attribute. But that alone would not have lifted her out of the Honeypot, where that scumbag boyfriend had taken her. The looks might have meant that Honeypot customers would pay more for her – not that she'd ever see much of it – but it was the dancing that caught the eye when she'd auditioned at the Pink Elephant.

Of course, the real catalyst – Harri reminded herself, as she sat rigid on the couch – had been the death of Sean Maloney. Without that, she'd never have galvanised herself to get clean and start auditioning at more upmarket venues.

Tears glazed her eyes as she remembered the young barman's inoffensive face. Pale skin, red freckles, a mop of even redder hair. Such a thin, delicate frame on him, always dancing behind the pumps, ever ready with a quip and a kind word if any of the girls were having a tough time of it – and there'd been no shortage of that in the Honeypot. And then, all along, that terrible risk he'd been taking. Not just stealing drugs but selling those drugs himself and pocketing the profits. And yet it wasn't even that that they'd eventually punished him for. Bloody coppers, forcing him to grass for them, trebling the danger he was facing. And poor naïve Sean, happy as Larry, pulling the pints with a smile on his face, cracking saucy jokes, singing his Irish ballads when he was down in the rat-infested basement.

It chilled her even now to think about *that* night. Sean

doing his happy-go-lucky thing, oblivious to that strange, silent figure across the counter, just waiting to cast his lure.

Harri remembered every detail.

He hadn't been a large man, but he'd stood out in that dissolute company because of his immaculate shirt and tie, his flash Italian suit, and his raincoat, which he hadn't taken off even though he was indoors. And then there was his eerie, reptilian aura. He'd been somewhere in his early forties, with jet-black hair slicked back, pale, aquiline features and most startling of all, the greenest, iciest eyes, which he'd fixed unblinkingly on Sean all through that evening.

Only later, when Sean's body was found wrapped in plastic on a refuse tip, had she been told who that man was and why he'd worn his overcoat indoors.

'It's not 'cause he was cold. How could it ever be colder than the blood that runs through a creature like him?' Brandy, one of the older girls had blubbed, red-eyed. 'It's 'cause of what he keeps under it. A pair of garden shears. Razor-sharp. That's his thing, his trademark – he uses garden shears on 'em.'

Jacques Marat – Scissorman Jaq – an enforcer for the Corporation.

'It's 'cause he was grassing,' Brandy had added, ill-advisedly. There were no customers in at the time, but she was drunk and loud. Harri had been uncomfortable just sharing a dressing-room with her. 'Skimming drugs is one thing. That would've been bad. But you can't go grassing too. That would've been the limit. That would've made them send their worst. And they did, didn't they?'

Harri glanced at the clock. Time had barely advanced since Elliot had left. This was going to be the longest night of both their lives.

She couldn't help wondering what they'd have done to young Sean if it had purely been a case of him stealing the drugs. Shot his kneecaps off? Beaten him till he was braindead? All of these sickening things she'd heard about. But to torture a guy for hours, to open his throat, dig out his tongue, slice it at the root. In their eyes, she supposed the punishment was appropriate for the crime ...

Harri stiffened where she sat.

Appropriate for the crime ...

A chain of deeply sinister thoughts followed, all connecting neatly.

Too neatly. Ridiculously neatly.

She was fooling herself, she realised. The secret to this terror could never be so simple.

Nevertheless, she stood and crossed the room. By the time she was ascending the stairs to the spare bedroom and their desktop computer, she was running.

'We almost there?' Elliot asked, the lane ahead weaving between ragged hawthorn hedgerows. They'd passed the destination programmed into the sat nav – an unmarked crossroads – and now Lonnegan was directing.

'Almost,' the enforcer said. 'Left here.'

'You're going to do all the talking when we get there, yeah?'

Lonnegan smirked. 'Scared, are you?'

'Fuck, no. You've given me a bulletproof vest. What's there to be scared of?'

'Been a bit of an arsehole with you, haven't I?'

'If you say so.'

'Didn't know you, that was all. But you *can* drive, Wade, I'll give you that. Next left again.' Despite their impending ordeal, Lonnegan seemed completely relaxed. 'And it wasn't your fault that pillhead Iago blabbed. Bet you're wishing he hadn't, though, aren't you?'

Elliot shrugged. 'If this is what it takes to prove I can be trusted, I'm in. Still wish there were more of us.'

'Bringing a whole team would've been a problem. The more we bring, the more *they'd* bring, and the more chance they recognise someone. And if they recognise someone, they don't need to make a deal. Next left again.'

Elliot turned onto another unlit lane.

'What do you see?' Lonnegan asked.

Elliot realised that he'd called someone on his phone.

'Three of them,' came a tinny voice. 'Waiting inside. No one else.'

'Outside?'

'No movement. Just the three of them, I reckon.'

'Deano, you're a star.' Lonnegan pocketed his phone.

'You never told me you already had eyes on this place,' Elliot said.

'What difference would it have made?'

'I'd have been less worried.'

'You should be more trusting.'

'Just tell me that whoever Deano is, he's got night vision?'

'You heard. He's cleared the surrounding fields. Now we know for *sure* that it's just us and them. Next left here. When you get through the gate, park. But give yourself plenty of space for one of those lightning-fast getaways you specialise in.'

Elliot saw that the turn coming up on the left was the entrance to a field, the withered vegetation on either side thinning out to reveal rusty metal fencing and a pair of stone gateposts. Only frozen earth lay beyond it.

Elliot eased the car through. Some sixty yards ahead, about forty to the right, there was a small building. He could vaguely distinguish its outline, though fiery light spilled from the front of it where a pair of double doors had been opened.

He turned them part-way around and braked, sliding the Lexus to a halt.

'What's this place?' he asked.

'Soaker's Farm,' Lonnegan replied, watching the distant structure. 'Don't worry, it's abandoned. That's just the barn … but that's the rendezvous. Let *me* take the lead, okay?'

For the first time, Elliot observed some tension in the guy. Lonnegan sat upright as he unhooked his seatbelt, his posture rigid. With a metallic *click*, he adjusted something under the left side of his jacket. Elliot realised that he'd just cocked his machine pistol.

'You got your tool?' Lonnegan asked.

Elliot patted his pocket. 'For what it's worth.'

But just as they climbed out, his phone started trilling.

'Don't answer that now,' Lonnegan hissed.

Elliot dug into his jacket, and thumbed a button, redirecting the caller to voicemail. He locked the car, and with a *ping*, received a text.

Lonnegan glared at him. 'What did I just say?'

'Suppose it's Jim or Jo?'

By the look on Lonnegan's face, he realised that he couldn't argue with that. But when Elliot slipped the phone out, the image on its screen was of Harri. Most likely, she was calling for an update, but then it struck him that the call had probably come from her too, and when he didn't answer that, she'd texted him – which meant that this might be important.

He opened the text and read it.

And then had to read it again to make sense of it.

I know what it is, the Red Book
They're London grasses
Call me

'Fuck me,' he breathed.

'Grasses?' Lonnegan said.

Elliot realised the guy was peering over his shoulder and jerked away.

Lonnegan looked bewildered. 'What's she talking about "grasses"? Informers? She saying the Red Book's a list of informers?'

Elliot couldn't speak, but it made a kind of sense. Every page in the Red Book had a list of coded entries on it. That could easily be names, addresses, contact details.

'Where's she got this shit from?' Lonnegan demanded.

'I don't know.'

'Hello, my friends!' The eerily musical voice floated across the frozen meadow. 'We're waiting for you.'

They glanced towards the barn, but neither of them moved.

'London grasses?' Lonnegan whispered.

'Hello? My friends. Are you out there?'

Lonnegan's expression changed, the steely mask of a man used to clandestine missions melting away into something more inscrutable, the mouth loose and wet, the gaze un-focused. For his own part, Elliot couldn't work out the immediate implications of this revelation, assuming it was true. Not when he was shaking to his bones on a frigid January night, the strange, taunting voice of Scissorman Jaq calling to him from close by.

'Doesn't matter,' Lonnegan said. 'We've got to see this through.'

'Shouldn't we abort?' Elliot whispered. 'Go and tell Jim and Jo?'

But they were already walking towards the entrance. Lonnegan shook his head.

'We are *wait-ing!*' That voice again.

'Where's the guy with the night vision?' Elliot asked.

'About half a mile away.'

'Couldn't he get any closer?'

'You mean so he can shoot these bastards? Two problems with that. First off, he doesn't have a rifle.'

'Fuck's sake!'

'What were you expecting? These guys are the under-world, not the SAS.'

This was the first time Elliot had heard Lonnegan refer to the Naboths' firm as 'these guys'; in other words, a group separate from himself.

'Second,' Lonnegan said, 'he's watching the interior of the barn through its open front door. So, even if he was a sniper, we'll be the ones in front of him.'

Elliot didn't respond. The yawning orange-lit entrance approached on their left.

'Man up, yeah!' Lonnegan gripped Elliot's elbow. 'This'll go okay, but one thing I don't need is a pile of fucking jelly standing next to me.'

29

8 January (Wednesday)

'The SCIs are extracting the bullets now?' Clive asked, as he and Lynda made their way along the corridor.

'As we speak.'

'You're sure they're bullets?'

'Clive, give me some bloody credit, will you.'

'But they've already gone over the car with a fine-tooth comb. Wouldn't there have been gunshot damage?'

'Not if the shots went straight through the windows.'

'So …' Clive still looked unsure. 'Rachel's prioritising this case now?'

'Sounds like it.'

'We going to get some extra bods to help?'

'Relax, Clive. We're going to get everything we need.'

She knocked on the DI's door.

'Come in,' came a shouted response.

They sidled in, to find Rachel Hollindrake behind her desk, and someone else, a bearded guy, standing by the window. He wore civvies but also a warrant card in a lanyard.

'Take a seat, guys.' Hollindrake shuffled some papers. 'Andy, this is the original SIO, DS Lynda Hagen. This is DC Clive Atkins.'

'The *original* SIO?' Lynda said.

Hollindrake nodded at the newcomer. 'Detective Superintendent Andy Kepler. Organised Crime.'

'Pleased to meet you, sir,' Clive said.

Lynda stared at him, baffled. 'Didn't we speak an hour and a half ago?'

'We did,' he agreed.

'And I was going to keep you informed?'

'You were. But things have moved on a little. Not just at our end, at your end too. This RTC is now attempted murder.'

Lynda shrugged. 'It would appear so, but I don't think it's anything that Scotland Yard need to get involved with...'

'Lynda,' Hollindrake interrupted. 'Organised Crime Division has a level of expertise in this field that we can only dream of.'

Lynda glanced around at her. 'So, *you* called them in?'

'Sit down.' The DI pointed at the empty chairs to the left of her desk. '*Sit!*'

Lynda slumped into the nearest one. More primly, Clive took the other.

'First of all,' Hollindrake said tersely, 'I didn't need to call them in. Organised Crime Division are part of the National Crime Group, and are automatically copied in on any investigation, no matter how seemingly insignificant, that may be connected to organised criminality. Secondly, Lynda, if I want to call expert assistance in, I will – okay? I don't need to run it by the lower ranks first.'

'Ma'am,' Lynda conceded.

The bearded guy stepped forward. 'DS Hagen? Or can I call you Lynda?'

'Lynda's fine, sir.'

He wasn't tall, about five foot nine, but had a stocky,

compact frame. His hair was short, dark and neat, his beard and moustache dark and trim. He had a pale complexion and blue eyes, and his demeanour was friendly. He spoke with a southern accent, but it was gentle, almost refined.

'Lynda,' he said, 'don't be put out. From what I've seen, you've done an excellent job.'

'Not excellent enough, apparently.'

Hollindrake huffed, but DSU Kepler shook his head and smiled.

'Okay, look,' he said. 'I'm going to be the new supervisor on this case, but I want you to view it as assistance rather than someone else taking over.'

'Whatever you say, sir.'

'*Lynda!*' Hollindrake cut in. 'Perhaps we can wait and see what Organised Crime Division are bringing to the party before we decide it's a damn imposition, yeah?'

Lynda glanced at Kepler again. 'Of course, sir. Sorry.'

'Don't sweat it,' he said. 'Just out of interest... Lynda *Hagen*? You're not by any chance related to DI Don Hagen?'

Lynda wasn't surprised by the question. This had happened before. 'I'm his wife.'

'Oh, right...'

'Don's not in the job anymore,' she said. 'He finished on a medical.'

'Oh?' Kepler's smile faded. 'Is he okay?'

'He's getting on with life. Know him, do you?'

'Not quite. A DS Terry Sullivan used to work under him. Big fella.'

'Yeah, I know Terry,' she said.

'Well, he's with us now.'

'I remember him transferring, yeah.'

Kepler chuckled. 'He's told us some tales … about working under DI Hagen.'

'You never know,' she replied, 'some of them might even be true.'

'You never know.'

'What undoubtedly is true,' Hollindrake interrupted, 'is that your concerns, Lynda, about Elliot Wade perhaps being involved with something iffy are well founded.'

'Allow me to explain,' Kepler said. 'During the enquiry thus far, you've pulled up some info that Wade has connections to a firm in Ipswich.'

'It's vague,' Lynda said. 'There wasn't anything we could work with.'

'Even so, you weren't wrong. Ever heard of the Naboths? Jim and Jo? You must've heard of Jo? The Ma Barker of the twenty-first century?'

Lynda considered. 'The surname rings a bell.'

'They're an ex-London firm who moved out here some time ago.'

He passed a couple of glossies around. They were custody mugshots, depicting two different people, a woman and a man. They were clearly related, though there was at least a decade between them. The older one, 'Josephine Naboth' according to the slip of paper attached to its corner, might have been handsome once, but in this picture at least, she had a thick neck and, minus make-up, the sort of brutish, hard-angled face that implied a tough upbringing. The younger one, Jim, was a more attractive specimen, his features leaner, sharper. He had dark eyes, slicked-back black hair and even though he'd been under arrest when this picture was taken, a roguish smile.

'If I was to say they're into everything,' Kepler said, 'it

would sound like a cliché. But it's true. They've got a lot of rackets going. Some of them are legit. I mean, that's the way these firms operate, you know. They hide their illicit activities behind legal stuff. Helps with the money-laundering too. They're not quite the force they were back in the smoke, but they're still players. And we still have a big interest in collaring the bastards. The trouble is, like all time-served villains, they don't leave many tracks. So, on the few occasions when their names crop up, we're inevitably interested.'

He paused while Lynda and Clive perused the images.

'Now,' Kepler said, 'what do you fellas know about Elliot Wade?'

'Ex-racing driver,' Lynda responded.

'Pretty good one, by all accounts,' Clive said.

'Certainly was,' Kepler agreed. 'His list of laurels was astonishing, even when he was still a kid.'

'Why did it go wrong for him?' Clive asked. 'We've got some basic intel that he was living the high life too much.'

Kepler nodded. 'When he left Renault, he was described by their press officer as an "undisciplined clown prince". He voluntarily withdrew from racing in 2011 and spent most of that year pissed. In 2013, skint, he moved to his father's home, Ravenwood Cottage, near Ipswich. Around the same time, he tried to open a bar in Ipswich itself, and made a bit of a go of it, though it wasn't a goldmine. It was sometime around then, as part of his involvement in the Ipswich club scene, that he met the Naboths...'

'We know that for a fact?' Clive asked.

'The Naboths bought Wade's bar,' Kepler said. 'We don't know what his relationship with them has been since. They could easily have gone their separate ways after that. But then suddenly Wade and his wife have a near-fatal accident because someone was shooting at them. Suggests things are ongoing, don't you think?'

'I'd say it was a possibility,' Lynda agreed.

'It wouldn't be the first time that a wild-living VIP has got involved with mobsters,' Kepler said. 'So many of them think it's a mark of their cool. But often it's been their downfall. Not that there's been many of them who've actually been shot at. Which rather implies to me that this Elliot Wade has got in too deep. But that creates an opportunity for us ... maybe, if we play this thing carefully.'

'So, just for clarity, sir,' Lynda said, 'you're going to be running this enquiry now?'

'If you'll have me.'

'And you're going to be based *here*?'

'If you can find room for me.'

'Well, there's no room in *our* office,' she replied. 'You can't swing a cat in there as it is.'

'Thankfully,' Hollindrake interjected, giving Lynda another warning glare, 'there's room in *here*.' She indicated a spare desk in the corner.

Kepler nodded gratefully. He turned back to Lynda. 'I understand that you only went public on this earlier today.'

'That's right, sir.'

'Any particular reason why you waited so long?'

'We didn't want to do anything that might be unseemly. For all we knew, the accident victims could have had relatives in the area. We didn't want them to find out about it through the internet.'

'Harriet Wade has a sister, I gather?'

'Initially we thought the female casualty was a striptease artist called Jill Brooks,' Clive said. 'When we found out that her real name was Harriet Wade, the hospital was able to dig up some medical records. Her next of kin is an older sister, Susan Clarkwell.'

'Lives in Colchester, but we've not managed to get in touch with her yet,' Lynda added. 'The fact she's not got in touch with us herself suggests they aren't close. However, we're still trying.'

Kepler pursed his lips. 'The point is, Lynda, your delay on announcing this may well have saved the Wades' lives.'

Lynda frowned. 'You mean if someone tried to hit them once, they'll try to hit them again?'

He shrugged, as if this ought to be obvious.

Lynda turned to Hollindrake. 'Perhaps we could use an armed guard at the hospital?'

'I've already made that call,' Kepler said. He looked at Clive. 'What condition are the casualties in?'

'Harriet Wade's still in a coma,' Clive said. 'But her husband's sleeping off a monumental headache. The last advice I had was to go back no sooner than noon tomorrow.'

'At the moment, don't go back at all.' Kepler's tone was firm. 'Before we speak to either of the casualties, I want to talk to some contacts of mine. It'll take a day or so, maybe a bit longer. In the meantime, speak to Harriet Wade's sister. Don't tell her anything she doesn't need to know. Just pass on the basic info.'

'She'll probably want to go down to the hospital herself,' Lynda said.

Kepler gave that brief thought. 'No reason why she can't. Harriet Wade's not the object of interest, really. We should put a guard on her room too, but if the sister's a grown-up, I'm sure she'll understand that it's for the best. The woman's comatose anyway, so no one'll be talking to her. I reiterate, though ... I want you both to stay away from Elliot Wade. At least until we know what we're dealing with here.'

A short time later, Lynda saw DI Hollindrake walk past the door to their office with her coat and scarf on, a handbag over one shoulder.

'Rachel!' Lynda called, hurrying out. 'Can we talk?'

'Lynda, I don't want any grief, okay?' The DI didn't look round as she walked. 'I've already explained that Organised Crime called us. We didn't call them. And you're not seriously saying that you'd want me to turn down assistance like that?'

Lynda fell into step alongside her. 'Elliot Wade's come round. We could talk to him tomorrow.'

'And achieve what? Put him on his guard? Ensure that whoever fired those bullets, he'll never, ever tell us?'

'He might do if he'd thinks he's under threat.'

'Lynda, we have no clue what's going on here. More specifically, *you* have no clue. This is high-level crime ... and you're a Traffic officer. Do you really think you could have handled it on your own?' She reached the door at the end of the corridor. 'Look, I'm sorry you feel your nose has been put out, but you've never dealt with anything like this before. I couldn't just leave you to sink or swim. Most likely you'd have sunk, and so would the reputation of this whole department.'

By her tone, she brooked no argument. When she headed downstairs, Lynda didn't bother following.

30

2 January (Thursday)

The barn was a long, narrow building, built from timber, with bits of farming rubbish scattered along its walls, and on the right a line of twenty rotted hay bales. A passage, lit by hanging oil lamps, ran ahead of them, forty yards on to a pair of double doors on the building's far side. Halfway along this, three figures stood in a row.

Elliot's heart hammered as he and Lonnegan advanced towards them, stopping about ten yards short.

Silence reigned as the two groups appraised each other.

The Corporation figure on the left was black and a virtual behemoth. He stood a hefty six foot seven with an ox-like chest and shoulders, and a head the size and shape of an anvil. His winter clothing – a heavy coat, thick khaki pants and steel-tipped boots – only added to his bulk. The figure on the right was even scarier. She was female and somewhere in her thirties. She wore jeans and a fleece, and had long dark hair, which hung fetchingly loose. Her smile might have been seductive, had the whole of the left side of her face not been grotesquely scarred, the eye nothing more than a white, sightless orb. She slid her left hand from her fleece pocket and flexed it. Its fingernails had grown into extended, eagle-like talons and were painted blood-red.

Jaq Marat himself, because it could only be him, was the one in the middle.

It struck Elliot immediately how closely he resembled Harri's description: the shortish stature, the slight frame, the pristine raincoat worn over a suit and tie, and then the pale face, the greased, jet-black hair, the green-eyed serpentine stare.

'Well, well … my villainous friends. Aren't we the bold ones?'

His voice suited the look of him perfectly; it was sugar-coated poison. Elliot couldn't help but wonder whereabouts under that raincoat the shears were concealed.

Marat indicated the black guy. 'May I introduce … Moose.'

'All right?' Moose said.

Next, he gestured to the woman. 'Ayita …'

'Never mind the fucking condoms,' Lonnegan interrupted. 'It's the dick we're interested in. And that would be *you*, I'm guessing. You're Marat, yeah?'

Marat's mocking smile remained. 'You need to guess? I'm disappointed.'

'I'll bet you are,' Lonnegan snorted. 'A frog having to dance to an Englishman's tune.'

Elliot glanced sidelong at him, shocked.

'I'm afraid you have the advantage of me,' Marat said.

'And I aim to keep it that way,' Lonnegan replied. 'So, no … I'm not giving you my fucking name. And I'm not giving you this fella's either.'

'Easy, eh?' Elliot muttered.

'This is how you negotiate?' Marat said. 'In such poor faith?'

'No,' Lonnegan retorted. 'But this is not a negotiation. I'm interested in hearing one thing from you, pal – how much you want that book of yours back. And don't give me some rambling, boring lecture involving your entire depressing life story. Just give me a number.'

The silence that followed this was pregnant. Marat's smile had faded.

'You think your anonymity will protect you so much?' he finally said.

'Anonymity isn't the only thing protecting us, trust me.'

'Oh, I think it is … but only for the moment. It will fail, for example, when the police catch you for this heinous robbery. You think you can hide from us then?'

'They won't catch us. You know why? Because they never have yet.'

Marat considered. 'Then perhaps *you* have a number in mind?'

That was a clever question, Elliot realised. Marat was trying to discover if they'd worked out what the Red Book contained by seeing if they knew how much it was worth. But Lonnegan, instead of being equally calculating, continued to be provocative.

'I'll give you a count of five, Scissorman. And then we walk out of here. And that'll be it. There'll be no more back channel messages. Your Red Book'll be gone for good.'

'You steal from us,' the girl called Ayita said, looking amused. She too spoke with a foreign accent, though hers was trickier to place. 'And you think you walk away?'

'Just watch us, darling.'

'Look, wait!' Elliot blurted. He hadn't meant to intervene, but this was getting out of hand. He'd known all along that Lonnegan was a blunt instrument, but he hadn't expected him to be as undiplomatic as this. 'We didn't know we were stealing from you.'

The trio eyed him for the first time.

'Well,' Marat said, 'when you put your hand in the till, my friend, you must know *someone* will be hurt. This time you were shit out of luck, uh?'

'We all were,' Elliot replied. 'You lost something valuable, we picked a fight we didn't want. But it's a simple mistake and easily fixed. First though, we need to establish some trust. If we can just accept that there was nothing personal in this. And that no disrespect was intended…' He half glanced at Lonnegan. But the enforcer seemed distracted. First, he looked to the left of them, and then behind.

'Okay,' Marat replied. 'So, we have your respect. We are all grateful. But you still have our book. And now this fellow says we must pay for the privilege of having it returned?'

'I'm sorry,' Elliot shrugged, 'but that's the way it is. The people we represent… they're fair, they know who you are, and they appreciate your status. As I say, no rudeness was intended. They don't intend it now, but they must be paid for the trouble they've taken.'

'Do you even know what that book is, bro?' Moose asked, venturing forward.

Again, Elliot looked to Lonnegan for assistance, but the guy was peering behind them.

'I'd like to know that too.' Marat also advanced. 'What is it you hold, uh?'

The questions spun without answers in Elliot's head. If he mentioned that they suspected the Red Book contained details of underworld informers, what would happen? Those names had been guarded and coded, so clearly, they were being kept secret – but now they might not be a secret anymore. So how vital was it that the Corporation repossessed this intel. More, or less? He simply didn't know.

'Okay, back off!' he said. 'Stay where you are. We have simple orders ... to check that you're willing to discuss numbers. Not the numbers themselves.'

Marat's pale face broke into a goblin's grin. 'Hey, you think ...?'

'We think fuck all!' Lonnegan roared, snatching the machine pistol from under his jacket and without slipping it from its rig, angling it up and pivoting left. In a burst of flame, he cross-stitched the barn wall, smashing out a line of plate-sized holes. '*Coming round the back of us!*'

Elliot was locked in place, senses scrambled. The crashing of gunfire filled his ears as Moose gambolled forward, his own hand clawing under his coat. Elliot tried to jerk away but tripped over his own feet.

Lonnegan meanwhile trained another burst through the open door behind, before spinning back and meeting Moose. There was a massive size difference, but Moose still hadn't pulled his firearm when Lonnegan's boot crunched into his groin. A flat-hand chop to the side of the throat followed, knocking the giant to his knees. His firearm, a big revolver, hit the dirt and Lonnegan kicked it away. His own machine pistol still hung by its strap as he twirled to face the other two, who hared across the barn, diving over the hay bales. Lonnegan fired a burst after them, a line of slugs ripping into the matted vegetation.

Elliot was now back on his feet. '*What the fuck are you doing?*'

'They were behind us, idiot!' Lonnegan retorted. 'It's a set-up!'

Elliot glanced around in time to see Moose back up and bearing down on him, throwing an enormous overarm punch. The blow caught his shoulder, the pile-driving force spearing down through his body. Elliot's knees hit the dirt, only for a huge hand to entangle in his hair and a heavy knee to slam into the side of his face. Senses spinning, he slumped onto his back. But then there was more gunfire – right over the top of him, flame spitting, and Moose flew backward, arms windmilling, legs askew.

'*Get up!*' Lonnegan shouted, grabbing Elliot by the collar and yanking him to his feet. Elliot swayed, his eyes fixing on the dust settling over Moose's prone form.

'Shit,' he breathed. 'Oh, bloody hell!'

Then there was a hand between his shoulders, propelling him. But not back the way they'd come; instead, it was down the barn towards the double doors at its farthest end.

'What the …?' he blurted.

'I told you – the fuckers are behind us,' Lonnegan snarled.

Elliot glanced back once, Lonnegan turning too, spraying another burst of slugs at the smoking hay bales.

As they stumbled outside, the sharp, flat crack of a single gunshot echoed behind them. Elliot felt a hammer blow in the upper-middle of his back; it half tipped him forward.

Incredulously, he realised that he'd been hit by a bullet.

'You can thank me for that Kevlar vest later,' Lonnegan grunted.

They blundered on over frozen, tussocky ground. A figure loomed out of the darkness on their left. With a twitch of his machine pistol, Lonnegan mowed it down.

'Christ's sake!' Elliot choked.

'It's them or us.'

Ahead, another structure materialised from the gloom. It looked like a house, but its windows and front doorway were black apertures. Lonnegan steered Elliot towards the entrance.

'How many were there?' Elliot gasped.

'I made eight or nine.'

'So much for that twat with the night vision!'

'Yeah, he's dead too when this is over...'

They scrambled over loose bricks and fallen guttering, and then were inside. Lonnegan shouldered the door closed, shoring it up with planks. Elliot pivoted around, trying to get his bearings.

Presumably this was the old farmhouse, but it was a gutted shell.

Another gunshot sounded, and one of the few windows with glass in it exploded.

Elliot spun around as a third gunshot punched a hole in the top of the door, firelight shafting through. Lonnegan threw himself to the nearest wall, replacing his machine pistol's magazine. Elliot also took cover but risked a glance through the nearest window. The firelit barn was less than a hundred yards off, but there were no figures on view. Instead, he heard an engine revving and spotted a pair of headlights moving on the far side of the barn.

'Why are they doing this?' he whispered. 'I thought they wanted a deal?'

'Who knows?' Lonnegan replied. 'You can't second-guess madmen.'

'Fuck's sake, Lonnegan! *You* said...'

'I know.' Lonnegan sounded calm as he moved from one window to the next. 'But even *I'm* not always right.'

He jammed his machine pistol through the window and unleashed another searing volley. Meanwhile, a hollow *plock* sounded from the other side of the building, as if a different window had just caved in.

'See what that is,' Lonnegan said, scanning the open ground out front.

Elliot stumbled across the room, but now that his adrenaline was ebbing, the upper-left side of his back throbbed, while his left shoulder was an abomination; he could barely lift his arm above the horizontal.

His eyes had adjusted to the dimness, however, and he saw a flight of rickety wooden stairs slanting up the facing wall to a trapdoor in the ceiling. If there'd ever been a banister, it was long gone now. At the foot of the stairs, a door stood ajar. Elliot pushed it open. An equally gutted room waited on the other side, its window hung with age-old drapes. There was another internal door on the left, this one closed. He leaned against it to listen, and hearing nothing, depressed the handle, shoving it open – to be assailed by heat and smoke.

It was ablaze in there.

Elliot backed off, coughing, wafting – and as he did, the window in that connecting room erupted inward as another Molotov cocktail was thrown, the drapes engulfed in a blinding sheet of flame, which quickly spread to the ceiling.

Elliot backtracked into the main room, where he lugged the door at the foot of the stairs closed. Lonnegan had seen what had happened and didn't need to be told. He stuck his weapon through the window again, firing another quick burst. Further shots sounded outside, more holes punched through the door, which now sagged on its hinges.

'Better get upstairs,' Lonnegan said.

'Upstairs? The bloody building's on fire!'

'Get onto the roof… it connects with a garage over the other side. From there it's about seven feet to the ground.'

'What do I do then?'

'Run the fuck away! Do I have to tell you everything?'

The staircase creaked, but Elliot reached the top without incident, climbing through the trapdoor. There he leaned back down to look — just in time for a shuddering BOOM to send the internal door below flying from its hinges, a ball of fire mushrooming through. Another Molotov had been hurled, and now the foot of the staircase was alight, the rotting wallpaper hanging around the doorframe catching as well.

'*Lonnegan!*' Elliot shouted.

Lonnegan, reloading again, turned and stared at the blaze enshrouding his escape route. The farmhouse's outer door then burst in and a colossal shape came through.

It could only be Moose, who also must have been wearing body armour, and now threw himself at Lonnegan with unfeasible speed. Lonnegan twirled to meet the threat, attempting to level his machine pistol, but Moose struck him full-on, and they hit the floor together, going crashing across the smog-bound room.

Elliot half descended the stairs but couldn't manage more than a few steps. Everything below him was burning, the stinking, scalding smoke pouring upward, swamping him.

He had no choice but to scramble back to the floor above, and then was staggering through a rabbit warren of dank, decaying corridors, smoke and heat rising through the naked floorboards. At last he turned into a passage that ended in a sash window made from frosted glass. It was open by an inch or so, and when he jammed his fingers underneath it and lifted, the panel slid upward. A few feet down, he saw a sloping slate roof. Panting, he clambered through, but straight away the rotted frame disintegrated. He fell onto the frosty tiles below, barrelling down them, turning over and over, knees and elbows barking on rugged slate. He grabbed out, but his palms and fingertips slithered on ice, and then he was over the roof's lower edge.

As Lonnegan had said, it was only seven feet or so, and his landing was cushioned by a thicket of dead, frozen vegetation. He clambered to his feet and reeled away. More grass led off in front. Perhaps fifty yards ahead, he saw a line of dark trees. Behind him, he sensed that the entire farmhouse was going up in flames. But before he'd got more than a few yards from it, he heard feet thudding and someone leapt onto him.

They were light, lithe, wiry with muscle, and they wrapped themselves around him like a cat, clamping his waist with strong athletic legs, one arm crushing his larynx. A claw-like hand tore into the left side of his mouth, yanking his head around, rending that whole side of his face.

Elliot tottered as he ran, ramming a punch backward but missing. His assailant hissed with glee as she – it was a *she*, he realised with horror – rent even deeper. He sprawled forward, slamming the ground, the wind whooshing out of him. His passenger was dislodged and went tumbling. Elliot jumped back onto all fours, gasping, the whole left side of his face raw and stinging.

He gawked at the sight of his attacker, who got back to her feet with incredible speed.

Ayita.

The woman with the single eye and the scarred face.

The woman with the blood-red claw.

She came at him again, screaming. He met her midriff with his shoulder, a solid rugby tackle. He was heavier than she was, and she went down beneath him, grunting as the earth struck her back, before slashing at his face again, going for his eyes.

Elliot ripped himself free and rolled away, clambering back to his feet. He tried to pull off his ragged jacket. He had some half-baked notion that he might wrap it around his arm like they did in films. But as he did, his hand came in contact with his right pocket – and he remembered something essential.

Ayita hurtled at him, an express train of primal rage.

Elliot let fly with the ammonia.

It struck her clean in her sole good eye. She lost all direction and balance, lurching sideways, screeching, before falling, pawing at her face.

Drenched with sweat and blood, Elliot continued running. The line of trees was just ahead.

31

8 January (Wednesday)

Susan Clarkwell's second address, 68 Woodfleet Row, was in a cul-de-sac lying between the backs of two rows of tall, gaunt buildings. Compared to the first address, a suburban townhouse, where no one had answered when Lynda had called, all the properties here were offices, workshops and mini warehouses, many of them 'To Let'.

Knotting her scarf, Lynda walked to the front door of the block. There was an intercom system on the left, with a row of buttons, each one connecting to a separate unit. She didn't know what Susan Clarkwell's business was, or the name of her company, but all she'd have to do was ring number 68, and she'd get an answer. However, before she could do this, she noticed that the door was open by an inch. There was no obvious reason why; no one was around and the lights inside the lobby were switched off, but Lynda sidled through anyway.

The lights, which evidently were motion-sensitive, came on.

It was one of those utilitarian entrance halls that you found in shared industrial premises. The walls were white-washed brick, the floor laid with grubby grey carpet tiles. The corridor appeared to run straight through the building to a plate-glass fire door on its far side. But before then, blue doors with bronze numerals opened off it, commencing at 40. As Lynda made her way along, she heard no noise behind any of them. At this hour, on a Wednesday, that seemed unusual.

Midway along the ground-floor passage, there was a steep metal stairway on the left. Suspecting that she'd find number 68 somewhere overhead, she ascended. Once she was near the top, another motion-sensitive light came on, but it was dimmer up here than below, a couple of the overhead panels buzzing and flickering.

She wandered to the left, again following the numbers, noting that her breath was visible. If there was any heating on in here, it was low. Surely a workforce would have a problem with that? But what workforce? Again, she was cocooned in silence.

Could it be that there was no one present? If so, why had the building been left open?

A footfall sounded to her rear. Lynda spun around, half expecting one of the doors to have opened. There was no one there, but as she turned, she spotted jerky movement down at the far end of the corridor. It looked as if one of the units was open, and that someone was moving around inside it. Glancing at the nearby numbers – she was already in the high fifties – that open door might be the unit she was looking for.

She strode on, when there came a *thud* from somewhere below, followed by a metallic *click*. Lynda glanced back.

Had that been the front door closing, and someone locking it?

She checked her watch, wondering if a caretaker could have accidentally shut her in. But it wasn't yet five o'clock.

She went to the top of the stairs and looked down, seeing nothing untoward. 'Hello?' she shouted.

No one replied.

It was tempting to go down and have a look, but she doubted it was what she feared. She hadn't heard an alarm being activated and all the lights were still on, plus she'd just seen someone on this first floor.

She walked back along the corridor, and heard a man laughing. It was only brief – a couple of harsh guffaws – but it was clearly from inside this building. There'd been nothing about it to make her uneasy, but it hadn't been a friendly laugh.

More movement flickered ahead.

Lynda was now close enough to see that the corridor, which was even dimmer at this end, turned at a right angle, but that there was a partly open door at the corner. The trouble was that there was no number on this door. It was still open, though, and there was a light on inside. She stuck her head through.

It was a closet with a sink and a kettle, and an unshaded bulb overhead. The movement she'd glimpsed came from a Venetian blind twitching against an open window.

Lynda backed out again. The corridor moved on to her left. She followed it, rounding a corner, where it ended at a frosted glass fire door.

The units to either side of it were numbered 67 and 69.

There was no number 68.

She'd just about had enough.

This monolithic old building was ridiculous by any standards, damp and cold, filled with work units, and yet with no one working in any of them. Except that, now she was looking, she noticed light fanning out from under the door to number 69.

She knocked on it.

The light was switched off.

'Oh, come on!' She knocked again, louder. 'Hello?'

There was no reply from inside.

'Can you come to the door, please?'

Still, there was no response.

'Look ... I'm a police officer on police business, and I know you're in there.'

Again, no sound.

She pressed her ear to the blue-painted wood. Nothing. She banged one more time, this time hard.

Presumably it was the vibration, but a yard to her left, another door – an unnumbered door made from bare wood, which she'd assumed led to a maintenance area – clicked open.

Lynda stared at it.

'Hello?' she said again.

No one replied, but the door remained invitingly ajar, even if the black recess behind it was less so. Lynda opened it, and saw timber stairs rising to about ten feet, at which point there was a small switchback landing and a faint glow from overhead. Her feet clunked as she ascended. When she turned at the landing, she saw that the light from above emerged around the edges of a door at the top of the next flight. It was painted blue and bore the bronze numerals: 68.

It stood ajar.

Lynda ascended to it and pushed.

It opened on a white room: white walls, a white ceiling, white floorboards.

There was a shelf to the left, heaped with paperwork,

and an arched entranceway on the right, leading to another room. Lynda edged over there and looked inside. The next room wasn't quite as bare. Again, it was white, almost sterile, but it was larger and there were some furnishings. However, it was the item in the middle that was most eye-catching.

Numbed, she found herself approaching what looked like a huge display board on a stand, perhaps seven feet high and seven feet wide; the sort of thing she'd seen in police major incident rooms, where crime-scene photos would be mounted.

But it wasn't crime-scene photos that had been mounted here.

It was vaginas.

Large, full-colour glossies depicting female sexual organs, spread open either by hand or by pieces of equipment. Six along the top, six underneath that, six underneath that, and on and on.

Thirty-six in total. Vaginas. Spread wide open.

Even as she stood transfixed, Lynda heard the booming trample of feet ascending the stairway behind her. They entered the antechamber loudly, the door banging closed, and came towards the arch. They were heavy, striking the floor with loud, awkward impacts. Heading straight towards this very room.

32

2/3 January (Thursday/Friday)

Beyond its first line of trees, the wood thinned out. This wasn't ideal from Elliot's perspective, but he ran on anyway, aware of shouting voices to his rear. How many there were, he couldn't be sure, but he kept on going, driving headlong into the darkness – and came to a barbed-wire fence.

He only saw it at the last moment, and so attempted to hurdle it. Though he made it to the other side, his trousers were caught and ripped. When he landed, it was bone-jarring, but he got up and stumbled on across open pasture, which tilted downhill at a shallow gradient. Risking a backward glance, he could still see the glow of the burning farmhouse on the far side of the skeletal trees. Whether there was anyone moving over there, it was impossible to say. The downhill slope now assisted his momentum. But when he looked back a second time, he was shocked to see two blobs of luminescence at the edge of the wood.

The bastards had brought torches.

Unsure whether or not they could see him – it looked as if they'd halted by the wire fence, which was a good eighty yards behind him now – he dived down and slithered towards a hump of ground, which he hoped would offer concealment.

He lay still. And listened.

He heard nothing save the thumping of his own heart. Several moments passed and there was no other sound. Elliot risked sticking his head up, and a gunshot blasted a wad of dirt and grass into his face. Fleetingly, he could do nothing but goggle into the eye of a torch as it approached downhill from maybe thirty yards away. The figure behind it was indistinguishable, but a second figure was silhouetted against the stars, rushing forward from a little further back.

Elliot ran like the wind. Another shot rang out, a slug zipping past his ear. He tried zigzagging and trod in a patch of cattle dung. His foot shot from under him and he fell into it. Dabbled with stinking slime, he jumped back up and blundered on. The ground began sloping uphill; against the sky at the top stood another line of trees. But when he was twenty yards away, he saw that it was a hedgerow, not a wood, probably consisting of briers and hawthorn. He could try and burrow through, but most likely he'd get caught in it. He halted, glancing back – the two orbs of light were about fifty yards behind.

Sobbing for breath, he stumbled on alongside the hedgerow until he reached a gap leading through to another field. This was broader and more level than the previous, and in one of its far corners, perhaps sixty yards to the left, he made out a cluster of box-like outbuildings.

With new heart, Elliot tottered towards them. Again, the darkened terrain was rough, tussocky, frozen hard. He tripped twice, landing heavily, but got up and hurried on, glancing over his shoulder, though torchlight was no longer visible. He supposed it was possible they'd switched their torches off, but they might also have given up; how long could they realistically follow him for?

He considered shouting for help. He didn't know what

these buildings ahead were; he saw no light as they drew close, so most likely none of them were occupied, but there might be a farmhouse just beyond them. Even so, he kept his mouth shut, which was just as well, because when he reached the buildings, they weren't even outhouses. It was a clutter of sheds and sties, mostly made from rough timber and corrugated metal. A putrid stench of manure gave away their purpose.

He threaded his way into the middle of the enclosure, where he halted, leaning against a coop. Though bone-weary, he felt he could run on, but to keep running blindly was no solution. Next up stood another belt of featureless trees, with no obvious path leading into them. Then he heard a footfall.

He glanced back down a narrow passage between the sheds. Icy mist lingered there. Beyond that, the open land was only vaguely visible.

Nothing moved, but he knew what he'd heard.

There was another sound. From somewhere to his right. A single metallic *clack*.

A pair of garden shears snapping together.

Elliot charged towards the treeline.

This time it wasn't an impenetrable hedgerow, but a proper stretch of woodland. But it plunged him into total darkness. He staggered on, hitting one obstacle after another, trunks, branches that whipped his face, clumpy bracken that snagged his feet. Only when he was several hundred yards in did he slow to a walk, and finally drop to all fours. He still wasn't physically drained – not completely, but he couldn't just keep forging on without at least knowing where he was going.

He stared around, eyes trying to pierce the arboreal shadow, ears straining.

Minutes passed as sounds came to him from all directions. Rustling undergrowth. A snapping twig. More distantly, another of those flat metallic *clacks*. Elliot hardly dared breathe, sweat streaming down his face. But the fact that he couldn't see a damn thing prevented him getting up and running again. If they were somewhere close by, they likely couldn't see any better than he and may not have located him yet. But if he did run, it could be a fatal giveaway.

Gradually his eyes attuned even to this much deeper darkness, but all he could identify were the black pillars of trees and bottomless tracts of latticework branches.

An immeasurable stretch of time seemed to follow. At one point, he thought he heard yet another metallic *clack*, closer than before. At another, he fancied two people were whispering. He insisted to himself that if these bastards knew where he was, there'd be no need for stealth: they'd simply move in on him. Loopy as they were, they couldn't afford to drag this thing out. But still he continued to imagine that things were happening out there: more furtive movement, more *clacking* steel blades.

But then, when he actually *did* hear something, it was the very last thing he expected.

A low rumble drew nearer on his right, before *swishing* by somewhere in close proximity.

A road? He was close to a road?

Elliot threw caution aside, jumped to his feet and ploughed thirty-odd yards through entwined vegetation, until sodium yellow streetlighting flickered into view. He checked himself one last time to listen.

There was no sound of pursuit, so he scrambled forward. As the trees opened up, he slid down into a ditch, his shoes breaking sheet ice, legs plunging to the knee in water so cold that it took his breath away. Kicking free, he blundered up another slope, scrambled over a dry-stone wall and found himself on the edge of a country lane.

And that wasn't all.

Forty yards to his right, Elliot spotted houses.

He hobbled towards them, and almost cried out with relief when a signpost came up on his right: HODDINGTON.

He knew the village well, and its location; it was only a mile or so from the B1068, where the Goose and Gander was located. Clearly, while fleeing across country, he'd been heading back in a north-westerly direction. He could make it to the car from here, but perhaps he wouldn't need to. Because it also happened that this village was home to an old schoolmate of his, one of the few he'd kept in touch with. Nick Scotzini had always been a whizz at maths, and in due course had made it pay. Though only thirty-four, he already held a major accountancy job with some top firm. Even though he'd divorced his wife several years ago, he could still afford the perk of an idyllic fifteenth-century house at the heart of this prosperous commercial village.

Not that Elliot considered himself home and dry just yet.

There was no sign of any more traffic, but he still hung close to the right. There were bushes and trees on that side, beyond which lay a tributary of the River Stour. Eighty yards past the signpost, the road became a humpback bridge as the waterway swung left underneath it. Beyond that, he was into the village proper, thatched and box-framed cottages arcing around an extensive green, along the far side of which stood a line of shops and the Sun and Moon pub. When he reached the pub, he ran the length of its car park, entering the network of lanes behind it. By the time he reached the foot of Hillcroft Drive, a secluded road ascending gently between some of the most luxurious residences in Dedham Vale, he was walking again, or rather limping, thanks to his many twists and sprains.

When he came to the gate at the front of 18 Hillcroft Drive, 'The Rookery' as a carved oaken plaque on the right gatepost proclaimed it, it was too high to climb over in his depleted state. However, he knew that there was a security camera on a branch about six feet above the left gatepost, and if he pressed the bell-push, the camera would activate. It was nearly two in the morning, but assuming that Nick had his laptop close to hand, or his iPad, Elliot would soon be inside, thawing his frigid body out with a slug of good brandy.

But even when he'd pushed the button several times, there was no response, and Elliot felt increasingly conspicuous and vulnerable. The house itself, some forty yards up the drive, was just visible as a grand, rambling outline. There was no sign of any lights.

Finally, inevitably, he retreated from the gate and trudged back into the village, where he turned south. It wasn't the end of the world, of course. He'd shortly be back at the B1068, and his car should still be waiting at the Goose and Gander. It was about a mile away in total, maybe a little less. No fun in his current condition, but at least he was alive.

Unlike Ray Lonnegan... possibly.

Elliot's thoughts strayed back to the farmhouse. Lonnegan had demonstrated to the boot-boys of the Corporation that there were others in this world as adept at violence as they. But in the end, inevitably, he'd succumbed. He *had* to have, the way the flames had raced through the decayed fabric of that old building. Elliot didn't want to think about it, but even that fate was minuscule compared to what Scissorman

Jaq and his compatriots would have inflicted had they taken him and Lonnegan alive.

Another troubling thought now struck him.

What was he going to tell the Naboths? Their guy with the night scope would have seen something at least. But from what Lonnegan had said, he was so positioned that once they'd emerged on the other side of the barn, they'd have been screened from him. That probably applied to the battle in the farmhouse as well. So, when Elliot got back to his paymasters, it'd only be his word that he'd had nothing to do with the truce going pear-shaped.

But then, did it matter? Really?

This predicament was now so hellish that he struggled to see any kind of exit from it.

That last mile or so was an interminable drag, and he swayed as he plodded along the verge towards the approaching outline of the Goose and Gander.

Only as a belated afterthought, did he slap at his pocket, thinking how ironic it would be if after all this, he'd lost his car keys somewhere. But they were still there. He might have offered a prayer of thanks had he believed in the Almighty. Though now, maybe, he was beginning to question that unbelief. There was certainly a force of evil in this world. He'd seen it for himself.

He turned into the car park. He was almost there, almost done with this worst night of his life. At which point, two headlights sprang to life, bathing him in their dazzling glow.

Elliot halted mid-stride.

The vehicle rolled forward, tyres crunching grit, stopping only a couple of feet away.

He sank to his knees, all strength leaving him, all hope departing.

What was it he'd just said? That he was done with this awful night.

Equally, it seemed, this night was done with him.

33

8 January (Wednesday)

'Jesus Christ!' the woman exclaimed. She dropped the heavy carton and books flew across the carpet tiles. 'You scared the life out of me!'

'I scared the life out of *you*?' Lynda replied.

'Who are you? What're you doing here?'

'Sorry... Hagen.' Lynda produced her warrant card. 'Detective Sergeant Hagen.'

'Detective...?' The woman's frown deepened.

She was somewhere in her early forties, trim and attractive, wearing a pale blue trouser suit and a black blouse. She had short fair hair and pretty, elfin features, but there was an aura about her too, an immediate hardness, as if she was used to issuing orders.

'Serious Collision Investigation Unit,' Lynda said.

'Okay...?'

'And you are?' Lynda asked.

'Susan Clarkwell.'

'Good.' Lynda put her ID away. 'You're the person I've come to see.' It was a relief that Susan Clarkwell seemed to be a normal citizen. Except that... Lynda couldn't resist glancing at the wall of explicit images behind her.

'*Doctor* Susan Clarkwell.' The woman pulled a cloth down over the display. 'I'm a sexual health specialist for ESNEFT...

that's East Suffolk and North Essex NHS Foundation Trust.'
She looked at the scattered books. 'I'm currently preparing
a lecture.'

'I see ...'

'This happens to be my private consulting room.'

'Oh.' Lynda felt awkward. 'We tried to contact you at
home, but ...'

'I'm not in very often.' The doctor moved around, scoop-
ing things up.

'And the only mobile number we had for you was dis-
continued some time ago.'

Doctor Clarkwell didn't respond. One by one, she stacked
the books on a desk.

'I'm sorry to have to tell you,' Lynda said, 'but last Sunday
night there was a road accident.'

The woman glanced around, though her expression remained neutral.

'No one's died, so you can put that worry out of your
mind.'

'But?' the doctor said.

'But there were a couple of casualties. And I'm afraid one
of them is your sister, Harriet.'

'Now there's a surprise.' The doctor busied herself picking
up the rest of the books.

Lynda watched her, bemused. 'I take it you and she don't
get on?'

'I haven't seen or heard from Harriet in years.'

Such indifference was disconcerting.

'You're not interested to know what happened?' Lynda
asked.

'You're here to tell me, so I suppose we'd better get it
over with.'

Lynda gave her bits of the story as they knew it, every-thing from the wrecked car at the foot of the embankment to the establishing of the two casualties' identities. She didn't mention the unexplained cash, the chop-shop nature of the car or the injured twosome's alleged links to organised crime.

'Harriet *Wade*?' Doctor Clarkwell said. 'She got married, did she?'

'She was calling herself Jill Brooks before then.'

'Brooks was our maiden name. Harriet's middle name is Gillian. She started calling herself "Jill" when she was ...' The doctor paused, as if the subject was just too unsavoury. 'You say she's in a coma?'

'That's correct. But it's medically induced.'

'Who's the consultant supervising?'

Lynda glanced at her notes. 'That's a Mr Jaishankar.'

'He's a good man. She'll be fine.'

'I don't suppose you can shed any light on what Harriet's been doing in recent years?'

'I've no idea, I'm afraid. And even less interest.'

'Things between you two are really *that* bad?'

The doctor looked thoughtful. 'Let me tell you about Harriet, sergeant. She was a sweet child ... when she was an actual child. But things went wrong when she got to middle school. And I mean *very* wrong. She became an arch-rebel. Aggressive, argumentative, assertive – take your pick.'

'Typical teenager then?'

'You say that as if it's normal and therefore acceptable. But I've often wondered if these *typical teenagers* have any idea just how much bad will they're storing up with their endless immature antics. We didn't have the happiest family anyway. Our father was an alcoholic, our mother a drug addict. So, as you can imagine, Harriet's juvenile narcissism only made things a lot worse.'

'Are your parents still with us?'

'No. My mother died in 2003, my father in 1997. Neither were much loss.'

No one seems to be much loss to this one, Lynda thought.

'At what point did you and Harriet lose contact?'

'Harriet was seventeen when Mother died. I'd just qualified as a junior doctor. So I was her official guardian for the last year of her childhood.' The doctor paused, her features tightening. 'There's only so much rejection you can take from a so-called loved one before you stop trying, especially when you're so young yourself. I was only twenty-five, which was probably too young to be parenting a wild child like Harri. And I suppose she was ... well, blooming would be one word. I don't know if you've noticed, but Harriet's rather beautiful.'

Not currently, Lynda thought.

'It was wonderful from Harriet's perspective, of course. Meant she could get whatever she wanted from people. Meant she could get a whole succession of boyfriends who were older than her, and in most cases completely inappropriate ... and then of course she turned eighteen, at which point there was nothing I could do.'

Lynda had encountered numerous parents who'd seemed to resent losing power over their offspring once they grew up. But she sympathised with many of them. It was always difficult to view your own children as adults, especially if they continued to behave like children.

'Gorgeous girls always think they're on top,' Doctor Clarkwell added. 'That they can wrap men round their fingers. But they attract predators too. In Harriet's case, it was a sleazebag who wanted to get her into glamour modelling. It's incredible that some piece of vermin could talk a young woman into that. But we live in a moral vacuum these days, so perhaps I shouldn't be too surprised. Anyway, they sent her photos to a website called Barely Legal. She *was* legal, but only just... and it showed. Naturally, the website loved her. So did lots of other websites. The whole thing was a sordid mess, but Harriet, now Jill of course, thought she was doing well because the money was coming in. But soon even that wasn't enough. Because now she was on drugs. The next stop was a backstreet club in London, which was a whole new world of high-risk awfulness. And of course, I couldn't dissuade her. I mean, what did I know... I was only a doctor.'

'You were also the straight player,' Lynda said, 'the one with experience...'

'And therefore the enemy. Oh, I understand the warped psychology of it. I understand that liberal society considers it wrong-headed of the old to try and school the young. But mine and Harriet's relationship was already rotten to the core. My constant disapproval did nothing but infuriate her.' Briefly, she looked saddened, which made Lynda wonder if the estrangement between them wasn't entirely by mutual consent. 'Officially, this awful place – the Honeypot, would you believe – was a lap-dancing bar. But then I found out that, for the right price, it offered interaction between the girls and the punters, which basically meant prostitution.'

She gave a wry smile and moved away to a sideboard, where she shuffled some paperwork.

'Her husband?' she eventually asked. 'Can he not tell you what you need to know?'

'I'm sure he will at some point, but...'

'But you don't know whether you'd trust him. Yes, that sounds like someone Harriet would marry.'

'I understand that Harriet's now thirty-four?'

'That would be about right.'

'And you haven't had any contact with her in the last few years?'

'We've had fleeting contact, but basically we've lived separate lives.' Doctor Clarkwell pulled on a coat and scarf. 'I suppose I'm going to have to come down to the hospital?'

'That would be helpful.'

The doctor led Lynda from the room, switching the lights off. They descended the narrow stairway. At the bottom, the doctor pushed the unmarked door closed and locked it.

'Any reason why your suite is separate from all the others?' Lynda asked.

'Just an extra layer of privacy. A requisite for a sexual health specialist.'

They walked along the dim, crooked corridor.

'Quite a building you work in,' Lynda said.

'Yes, and unfortunately it's mine.'

Lynda glanced sidelong at her.

'It was Gerald's originally. He's my ex-husband. He's a property developer and owns a few town-centre premises. I acquired this one as part of my divorce settlement. If only I'd known.'

They started down the main stairs together.

'Known what?' Lynda asked.

'It's riddled with damp, the roof needs repairing, the wiring's bad, there's no wi-fi.'

She spoke in abrupt, business-like fashion. It would have

been easy to conclude that this distant woman would have made her younger sister's rebellion a lot easier given that she seemed to lack any kind of warmth. But Lynda still didn't know the full circumstances here.

'It needs a complete refurb,' the doctor added. 'So, one by one, as the tenants' leases have ended, I've not renewed them. There are only one or two left now.'

'There seemed to be a few lights on when I arrived earlier,' Lynda said.

'They're on timers. It's a complicated arrangement, but they switch on and off all night.'

They stepped outside, the doctor ensuring that when she closed the door behind them, its locking mechanism connected.

'This thing needs fixing too,' she said. 'I presume that's how you got in?'

Lynda nodded.

'Well …' The doctor indicated an alley to one side. 'I go this way. My car's at the back. That's why we didn't run into each other earlier. I often use the fire door on the first floor when I'm bringing things in. I've had its alarm disabled. Sorry if that's a breach of regulations.'

Lynda didn't know whether it was or wasn't, so didn't comment. Instead, she said: 'If you're heading down to the hospital now, I'll follow you.'

'Do you need to?'

'Probably be easier for you if I do. Harriet's at the centre of an ongoing investigation. There may be other police officers there. It'll just be better if I'm with you.'

The doctor shrugged and walked away.

Lynda hadn't mentioned that any police officers on duty at Neurological Intensive Care were now likely to be armed.

It would be easier explaining that when they got there. But at the same time, she had her own motives. Accompanying the injured party's sister would give her just the excuse she needed to disobey DSU Kepler.

34

3 January (Friday)

'Oh my God,' Harri said with disbelief.

The BMW Sport stood rumbling as she staggered forward from it, barely able to comprehend the state her husband was in: blackened by smoke, smeared green with moss, and of course streaked and sticky with blood and cow faeces.

'Dear Lord ...' She hunkered down in her jeans and overcoat.

'What ... you doing here?' he stammered.

'What do you think I'm doing here? I've come looking for you.'

'How did you find ...?'

'It wasn't difficult, Elliot. You left the postcode on a Post-it note on the fridge, remember? I looked it up online and got a taxi to bring me here. What in God's name has happened?'

He tried to get to his feet, cringing in pain. 'Let's just get away. Quick as we can.'

She helped him upright and eased him into the front passenger seat. She looked perplexed and horrified as she swung the car onto the road. 'Where's everyone else? Wasn't there supposed to be a meeting?'

Elliot shook his head. 'I can't ... believe you came here.'

'Lucky for you I did.'

They said nothing else for several miles, finally joining

the A12. Elliot still didn't feel safe. He doubted he'd ever feel safe again.

'I found out who the Scissorman is,' Harri said in a subdued tone.

'I know who he is. A madman with a pair of shears.'

'That's not all.'

'Tonight, that was all that mattered.'

'You think so?'

Elliot shook his head, his face slack under its mask of dirt and blood. 'I saw it for myself. They tried to get the drop on us. It was sheer fucking madness. There was no reason for it. Ray Lonnegan ... he sussed them, I think.' Fleetingly, Elliot was unsure. Lonnegan had been correct to react the way he did; there'd been more Corporation assassins on the plot than they'd been led to expect, but his response to it had been so timely that it had verged on precognition.

'Turned into a shootout. Harri, people got killed.'

'Elliot ...' Her voice was almost a whisper. 'Please don't tell me *you* killed anyone.'

'Didn't have a gun, did I?'

'Thank God for that, at least.' She didn't say anything else until they'd pulled off the A14 onto the B1078 and were almost home. 'You've still not asked me what I learned about Jaq Marat.'

Elliot felt at his aching shoulder. 'How could you have learned anything?'

'I went online. It only took me fifteen minutes.'

'You went online?'

'I found a website,' she said. 'Unsolved Gangland Murders.'

'For Christ's sake!'

'Listen to me, Elliot. This is serious. The guy who runs it, Purple Gekko ...'

'Purple Gekko!'

'He's just a geek. But the info's out there in the public domain ... and he's gathered it all together for "true crime" enthusiasts.'

'And this is how you've found out all about the Scissorman?' He couldn't keep the scorn from his voice.

'Listen to me. That terrible murder of Sean Maloney back in 2009. I was thinking ... Why would they do something so awful to him? Slice his throat open, hack his tongue out?'

'Marat's a maniac. That's all we need to know.'

'But maybe there's more to it than that. Maybe it's symbolic.'

'Symbolic?'

'Think about it. They killed Sean for grassing. And after they tortured him, they cut his tongue out.'

Elliot pondered this. 'Speak no evil, you mean?'

'Of course.'

'But I thought this tongue-slashing lark was Marat's trademark anyway? That that's how he always does it?'

'Yes, but doesn't it add up?' She turned onto the narrow road leading to Ravenwood Cottage. 'Look, there was another victim. A London prostitute, an older girl who used to work south of the river. Sally Vye. Back in 2005, she was murdered and left in a derelict toilet. I never met her, but when I was working at the Honeypot, a couple of the other girls had. They mentioned her a few times, said she'd been killed for grassing.'

'So, you looked *her* up too?'

'Yeah, and it was the same thing. Elliot, she'd been tortured and then she'd had her throat sheared open and her tongue cut out.'

She slowed to a halt and applied the handbrake. The

cottage stood as she'd left it: frost coating its roof, but warm lamplight flooding from its windows. Neither said anything as Harri helped Elliot from the car. Inside the living room, she stripped his clothes off, turning pale at the sight of the bulletproof vest and the flattened slug half buried in it. Bundling his filthy, blood-stained rags into a plastic bag, she took it out through the kitchen and French windows and placed it in the non-recycling bin. Elliot, meanwhile, poured himself a large whiskey, which he gulped down in two mouthfuls. Harri then helped him upstairs, and ran a hot bath filled with salts and other balms. He'd been lying in it for five minutes, a compress over his eyes, his cold, twisted body gradually easing, when she reappeared, wearing a dressing gown and carrying an armful of fluffy towels.

'There was another one too,' she said. 'A couple of years before Sally Vye.'

Elliot uncovered his eyes, gazing at her wearily.

'This one was well before my time,' she added. 'His name was Bernie Bartelli. He died the same way. They found his body in a Wapping sewer in October 2001. Bartelli was sixty-six when he died, but he'd been everything. Pimp, dealer, loan shark. He was also suspected of being an informer, which is what Purple Gekko thought had led to his murder.'

'And he'd had his throat slashed open and his tongue ...?'

'Yes. Exactly the same.'

Elliot closed his eyes again. It wasn't that he disdained the work she'd done and the answers she thought she was providing. He was just too tired to fit it together.

'You've got three identical murders, Elliot. Probably more that we don't know about.'

'Look, the coppers are sensitive to these things.' He held

out a hand of reason. 'They'd have linked these three together and been all over them like a rash...'

'Get real!' Harri threw the towels down. 'These are gangland killings. The cops will never have got close to solving them because no one ever talks. But hey, I can see you're tired. I can see you've had a rough night. So why don't I just leave you to it, eh?'

She turned away and trod loudly downstairs.

Elliot groaned, before levering himself upright, towelling himself dry and pulling on a pair of shorts and a T-shirt from the airing cupboard. When he got back downstairs, Harri was standing by the drinks cabinet.

'So, what're you saying?' He leaned on the newel post. 'This guy, Marat...?'

'He's the punisher of informers.' She turned to face him. 'Surely it makes sense? The method he kills them by... taking out the tongue. When he's finished with them, they really *don't* speak any evil. That must be his role in the Corporation. Or one of them.'

Elliot lowered himself onto the couch. 'That's a lot of guesswork.'

'No.' She shook her head. 'More like *corroboration*.' She came up to him, her face ghostly white. 'Elliot, the police wanted me to give evidence against him.'

At first, he thought he'd misheard. 'What?'

'When I was at the Pink Elephant. That fracas I got into. You remember? A drunk attacked me on stage. I kicked him, and my heel went through his cheek.'

'Yeah, but...'

'They offered me a deal. Two local detectives. They were still looking into Sean's murder, and they knew I'd been at the Honeypot at the time it happened. They offered to drop the GBH if I could help them secure a conviction.'

'But you resisted?'

'Of course I resisted.' She almost laughed. 'What did you not understand when I said that no one ever talks?'

'Did they know you saw Marat lure Maloney to his death?'

'No, they were fishing. But good God, even if I hadn't seen him do that, you think I'd have told them anything? Inform against a guy like that? It would all have been unofficial of course, so there'd be no record of it, but the terror would still have been too much. It was too much anyway. Not only did I refuse and take my punishment on the chin, I determined to get out of the life. When you asked me out, said you'd take me away from it all... I wasn't going to refuse, was I?'

Elliot was stumped. 'This is all I was... an escape route?'

'Oh, for God's sake.' She dropped to her knees in front of him. 'I've been with you ten years since then. I went back to stripping for a brief time when we were short... in Felixstowe, of all places, somewhere I could conceivably have been recognised. How can you question whether or not I want to be part of your life?'

'All right, okay... I'm sorry.' Elliot was sullen, though. He hadn't wanted Harri to take the Felixstowe job at the time, but they'd been so strapped for cash.

Harri was still talking. 'The main thing is, I'll never forget those coppers' words: "Pick the Scissorman out of an ID parade, point him out in court... you'll be putting a creature away that should never have seen the light of day. You'll be stopping a piece of gangster filth in his tracks by doing the very thing he gets paid to put an end to." Those were their exact words, Elliot.' She gazed at him, squeezing his hands. 'I've never forgotten. "*The very thing he gets paid to put an end to!*"'

'Killing grasses?'

She nodded, tearful. 'This was the guy who'd come if you ever spilled the beans on the Corporation. Wherever you went, this man would hunt you down because that was his job.'

'And he keeps a red book to help him do it?' Elliot tried to sound sneery, but he didn't feel that way. It was all making a twisted kind of sense.

'Why not? What else was in that book? Why else was it in *his* possession? We know it's a list of entries ...'

'You're saying it's a list of people he has to kill?'

'Or maybe people he's already killed. Either way, you can see how important it would be to him. He'd have done anything to get it back. But even then, it wouldn't have been a straightforward case of handing cash over. Because once something like that is out in the world, it becomes useless to its owner – unless you and your guys were unaware what you'd got. And that's what he'd have needed to know.'

Elliot's thoughts ranged back to the barn, and the questions they'd fired at him.

'*Do you even know what that book is, bro?*'

'*I'd like to know that too. What is it you hold, uh?*'

'Elliot, he'd have grabbed you,' Harri said. 'He'd have had no choice. And then he'd have demanded you tell him what you knew, whether you'd deciphered the code or not. And the only way he could be sure you'd tell him the truth would be if he tortured it out of you. Don't you see ... you were literally walking into the lion's den.'

Elliot still wasn't convinced. 'And if he'd decided we didn't know anything, how could he have expected to get the book back? Why would Jim and Jo give it up? It'd be no deal all the way.'

'Good God, Elliot... do you really believe that?' She stood up, eyes bright with anger. 'Jim and Jo are so out of their depth it's untrue. I know you think they're wonderful, but they really don't have a clue what they're dealing with here.'

'But you apparently do,' someone said behind them.

They spun around in shock.

Just in time to see the Naboth siblings emerge from the darkened kitchen, Iago and a couple more of their thugs close behind. Jo was wearing a black double-caped overcoat and black leather gloves, and carrying the plastic bag full of filthy clothes, indicating that they'd entered through the open French windows. 'Which shows what a useful investment you and your hubby have been,' she said, her face an unnatural shade of white. 'Always assuming you haven't already sold us out.'

35

8 January (Wednesday)

'Excuse me,' Lynda said to the man. 'Is it Nick?'

He swung to face her, looking surprised. He was in his mid-thirties, about five foot ten and well built, with short fair hair and lived-in but attractive features. His clothing comprised a wool overcoat, worn over what looked like a crested blazer and a shirt and tie. She might not have batted an eyelid, except that he'd passed her on the path leading to the Neurosciences building in the grounds of Colchester General Hospital.

Lynda was alone at the time, Doctor Clarkwell having opted to use the Staff Parking.

'Detective Sergeant Hagen,' she said, flashing her warrant card. 'Collision Investigation Unit.'

'Erm, I …' He smiled. 'That's me, yes.'

'I understand you're a friend of Elliot Wade's?'

'Correct.'

'Apologies, I don't have your full name.'

'Scotzini.' He removed a kid glove to offer his hand. 'Nick Scotzini.'

Lynda shook it, and couldn't miss the expensive blue-faced Breitling watch on his wrist.

'Are you a local man, Mr Scotzini?' she asked.

'Hoddington,' he replied. 'It's just down the road. Look,

I hope you don't mind me keeping coming to the hospital like this. But so far I've had no joy seeing Elliot at all. I got in earlier today, but I wasn't supposed to be there, and he was fast asleep anyway. Can someone tell me what's happening?'

'We were wondering if there was anything *you* could tell *us*?' Lynda said.

His bewilderment deepened. 'Anything *I* can tell you?'

'It's just that, this morning at least, you seemed to be a little ahead of us. You came in here looking for Mr Wade before we even knew who the patient was.'

'Oh, I see.' He smiled again. 'It was a guess on my part. I heard on a local news bulletin this morning about a crash on the A12 last Sunday night and that you chaps were asking for witnesses. And well... Elliot and Harriet were due to visit me on Sunday, which would have taken them down the A12, but they never arrived. Neither answered their phones afterwards, so I was left clueless. When I rang around the hospitals after this morning's bulletin, I learned that the casualties had been taken to Colchester General.'

'That's interesting,' Lynda said, 'because this morning's press release named the female crash victim as Jill Brooks.'

'Yes, I realise that. But... well, there seemed to be an element of doubt.' He shrugged. 'I had to enquire. I recognised Elliot when I got onto the ward this afternoon, of course, but as I say, he was asleep, and then I got chased out by the nurses.'

Lynda was still intrigued. 'Just out of interest, why were they on their way to see you?'

'Actually they were coming for dinner.'

'Dinner?'

He shrugged again. 'I'm a bit of a chef. I like to cook.'

'Were you Elliot's friend, or Harriet's?'

'Both, I like to think. But I knew Elliot best. I was at school with him. Middlewich Boys, Suffolk.'

Lynda appraised the guy. In truth, he had private education written all over him. It wasn't just his looks and clothing; his manner was polite but confident, and he spoke perfect BBC English.

'And you've been friends ever since?' she asked.

'Well,' he smiled self-effacingly, 'there was a time when Elliot was tripping the light fantastic. When he was a Formula One guy. I didn't see much of him then.'

'But you didn't lose touch?'

'Oh no, and then, in 2013, he moved back to this part of the world. He'd inherited his father's house, you see. Ravenwood Cottage – I don't know if you know it?'

'I'm familiar with it, yes.'

'He moved in there with Harriet. She was his new wife. I'd never met her before then, but we don't live too far apart, so we sort of rekindled our relationship. Eventually, I got to know Harriet too. Smashing girl.'

'Is she?' Lynda phrased it as if she had doubts.

'Well, yes – smart, funny, good company ...'

Lynda considered. This didn't correspond with what Harriet's own sister had said, unless the younger woman had changed her ways in recent years. But then, if it was a lie, and Harriet was the narcissistic little jerk Susan Clarkwell had described, why would a sophisticated sort like Nick Scotzini have invited her to a dinner party?

'And you live in Hoddington?' she said.

'Yes, in Dedham Vale.'

Dedham Vale was the verdant countryside lying between Colchester and the B1068. It was accessible via the A12, so heading to Nick Scotzini's pad would have fitted with the direction of travel that the Wades had been taking on the night of the accident. It wasn't completely straightforward, though.

'Are you in the habit of holding dinner parties so late?' Lynda asked.

'I don't follow...'

'The crash happened sometime after nine o'clock.'

He shook his head. 'I can't explain that. I was expecting them at seven-thirty, and... well, they didn't show up.'

'Did Elliot have any problems that you knew about?'

The change of tack seemed to catch Scotzini by surprise. 'He didn't have a job, if that's what you mean. But he didn't really need one. He'd earned incredible money while he was racing, and he didn't just inherit the house. I understood there was cash too. Not a vast amount, but enough to live on for a while. Possibly, it had started to run out.' He looked glum. 'You think this incident was something to do with that?'

'I'm afraid we don't know. There's one rumour that he'd fallen in with a bad crowd.'

'I suppose he might've encountered a few bad eggs when he was in London.'

'This is after he finished racing, yeah?'

'Well, yes.' Scotzini sighed. 'His last Formula One season was a disaster. His response to that was to go drinking around the West End. I mean for months. After that, well, even though he had a good CV, it was over. I mean, he'd driven for McLaren, Brawn and Renault, but none of them wanted him back. He was done.'

'But nothing happened that might lead you to think someone might want to kill him?'

'Kill him?' Scotzini looked shocked. 'This is serious then?'

'I'll be honest with you, Mr Scotzini, we've reason to believe the crash on the A12 was an attempt on Elliot Wade's life. And it's not inconceivable that there could be another attempt.'

He blew out a long, vaporous breath. 'Good Lord ... Mind you, I suppose that would explain the armed guard. I tried to see Elliot again earlier this evening, and this time an armed officer was on duty, who wouldn't let me.'

'Yes, it's a protection detail. Can you tell me what Elliot's been doing in recent years?'

Scotzini scratched his jaw. 'Living quietly at Ravenwood Cottage. He bought a bar in Ipswich, but he wasn't much of a businessman. In the end, he sold it, but there was no drama. Seriously, I'm shocked. I had no idea we were talking attempted murder.'

'He definitely hadn't got involved with anyone he shouldn't have?'

'Nothing like that, no.'

'Okay, fair enough. Elliot doesn't seem to have any other living relatives?'

'No, that's right. They all died young. His mother in 2002, his stepmother around 2008. His father was the last to go in 2011. And he has no brothers or sisters.'

'Does he have any other friends?'

'None that I've met.'

Lynda glanced left and now saw Doctor Clarkwell approaching along a side path. 'I don't think I need anything else for now.' She offered a hand. 'Thanks for your help.'

He shook it, but from the look on his face, he wasn't satisfied.

'When will I be able to see Elliot?' he asked. 'I'm sure he'd welcome a friendly face.'

'I can't help with that.' She edged away. 'All I can suggest is that you keep ringing the ward.'

'Can you at least tell me if Harriet's okay? I tried to see her after the armed guard stopped me seeing Elliot, but there was a right old kerfuffle going on there too …'

Lynda looked back. 'Sorry … a kerfuffle?'

'Down at Intensive Care,' he said. 'People coming and going fast, doctors, nurses. Security staff. Real panic in the air.'

It took a second for Lynda to absorb this, before she started backing away. 'I'm sorry, Mr Scotzini. I have to go. It's quite urgent.'

She turned and strode hurriedly across the car park. Doctor Clarkwell, who'd been veering over the tarmac towards her, had to rush just to catch up.

'Is something wrong?' she asked.

'I don't know,' Lynda replied. 'I don't even like to think.'

36

3 January (Friday)

'My God!' Harri snapped, jumping up. 'You've got some nerve coming in here!'

'We've got serious stuff to discuss, darling,' Jo Naboth replied quietly, 'so my advice to you is keep your trap shut before we find some delinquent to shove his dick in it.'

'What the fuck, Jo?' Elliot protested, struggling to his feet.

'Who the hell do you think you are!' Harri shouted. 'You almost got Elliot killed tonight. Get out of here now! Get out of our bloody lives!'

Jo backhanded her across the face.

It was that simple. Without even looking, she dealt Harri a solid blow with the knuckles of her left hand. Harri tottered backwards against a wall of shelves, the ornaments there smashing to the floor. She went down onto her haunches, one hand clasping her mouth.

Elliot was not violent, and never had been. But his reaction to this was all instinct. He looked at Harri, looked at Jo, and looked at Harri again, the blood seeping between her fingers.

Then grabbed up a coffee table and lurched around the couch.

Jo didn't flinch, but before Elliot could get close, a sawn-off pump-action appeared from under Iago's anorak, the kid working the slide – *clunk/clack* – and aiming it at Elliot's face, bringing him to a dead stop.

It was Jim Naboth who moved next, taking the table from Elliot's raised hands, and throwing it across the room. The shotgun meanwhile remained trained on Elliot's head, Iago backing it up with that 'crazy kid' grin of his.

'What the fuck are you all doing?' Elliot retreated and hunkered down alongside Harri, who mumbled that she was okay. '*Jim!* What is this?'

Jim regarded him bleakly. 'That's what *we* want to know, Elliot? Weren't you supposed to contact us three hours ago, to let us know how you'd got on?'

Elliot helped Harri to her feet and then to the armchair, where she dabbed her bloodied top lip with a tissue extracted from her dressing gown pocket.

'How long've you been out there?' Elliot nodded at the darkened kitchen.

'What does that matter?' Jim said.

'Well, if you just heard me and Harri talking, you'll know what happened tonight. You'll know why I didn't get in touch with you.'

Their granite expressions gave nothing away. No one spoke.

So Elliot told them the whole story: about the encounter in the barn, about the flight to the derelict farmhouse, about the fire, about his solo escape across miles of difficult countryside.

'I've just got back,' he finished. 'I've not even had a chance to get on the blower.'

'No, but you had time to get yourself a bath,' Jo snarled. 'Look…'

Elliot's initial rage at what had happened to Harri was ebbing fast as the reality sank in.

The reality of having a loaded shotgun pointed at him. The reality that the whole gang were now spread around his downstairs, casually opening drawers, picking framed photographs up, dropping a large hint that there was nothing and nobody here they couldn't touch.

'Look ...' he said again, 'the negotiation didn't get anywhere. They didn't offer to buy the Red Book back. All they wanted to know was whether we knew what it was. As it happened, Harri had just tipped me off... I mean, you've heard her theory for yourselves. I obviously didn't want to mark their cards in case it changed the terms of the conversation. Maybe I wasn't thinking straight, but...'

'And then it all kicked off?' Jim said. 'Is that what you're saying? Just like that?'

'Exactly like that. They circled around the back of us and we had to fight our way out.' Elliot glanced at Harri, who still looked pale but glared at the Naboths defiantly. 'Christ, I can't believe you've done this. To my wife, in my own house!'

Jo ignored that. 'And somehow *you* were able to fight your way out, but Ray Lonnegan couldn't. Ray Lonnegan, the ex-para. Ray Lonnegan, the combat veteran.'

'Look ...' Elliot spread his hands. 'What did this character, Deano, tell you? This guy with the night-vision scope. The one who was supposed to have our backs.'

'He told the story pretty much as you have,' Jim said. 'Except he wondered why you two ran all the way through the barn to the other side, where you were out of sight. He didn't know why you didn't just turn around and run back to the car. He didn't see anyone behind you.'

'He didn't see *anyone*?' That was a mystery to Elliot. But

there were other mysteries here too. 'Why didn't he call you and tell you it had all gone shit-shaped?' He paused, watching their faces, and for the first time since they'd invaded the house, saw a flicker of unease. 'He *did*, didn't he?' Elliot said slowly. 'For Christ's sake, he *did* call you ... and you bastards didn't come.'

'From what Deano said, it was already over,' Jim replied.

'The fuck it was!' Elliot snorted. 'You were just shit-scared. You didn't want to face the Corporation yourselves, or at least you didn't want to risk them seeing you and one of their crew recognising you.' His anger bubbled into uncontrolled scorn. 'The Naboths! They've fucking shit themselves!'

Jo grabbed his throat. Elliot never saw it coming; the next he knew he was gagging as his windpipe was crushed by a claw of a hand that possessed genuine, tensile strength.

'You think we're playing a game here, racing driver man?' Jo growled into his ear. 'You think we're just going to shrug this off because you're good behind the wheel?'

'Get off him!' Harri shouted, jumping up, grabbing one of the broken ornaments and wielding it like a knife. 'I mean it, you fuckheads ...' She stumbled forward, offering the jagged shard. 'You might kill us, but I'll mark every one of you first!'

Jo almost looked amused as she released Elliot and pushed him away.

'I don't know what happened to Lonnegan,' Elliot stammered. 'Last I saw of him, he was in that burning house ...' He glanced at Jim, looking for a grain of rationality, anything he could reason with. 'You want the truth? It half crossed my mind that Ray *picked* that fight.'

Jim's face creased in bewilderment. 'What're you talking about?'

'Ray was the one who said there were people behind

us ...' Elliot shook his head. 'But like Deano, I didn't see anyone. It seemed odd.'

'You saying he made it up?' Jim looked sceptical.

Elliot shook his head. 'No, there were more of them than there was supposed to be. I'm sure this Jaq Marat's promises are about as reliable as a ten-year-old condom. But Ray was *ready* for that fight. I mean he *really* was. And he's the one who opened fire first ...'

'If you're trying to say that Ray Lonnegan, who's given us three years of loyal service, is playing for another side,' Jo advised him, 'I'd say you'd better be careful of the extremely thin fucking ice you're walking on.'

Harri scoffed. 'Three whole years, eh? Bet you know him inside out.'

Jo threw her a baleful glance. 'When I need the advice of a good-time girl, I'll ask for it.'

'Ray Lonnegan's participated in just about every job we've done in the last few years,' Jim said. 'He's one of *us*, don't you worry.'

'In that case, don't be concerned that he might've been taken alive,' Elliot said. 'Surely he's not the sort who'd talk?'

'Everyone talks, you fucking numbnut,' Jo retorted. But now she looked more concerned than angry. 'Even dead men talk.'

'You take any personals into that barn?' Jim asked.

'My phone,' Elliot replied. 'But I brought that back out with me. Don't know about Ray. They'll have his car, of course.'

'The Lexus was one of ours,' Jim said. 'It won't be traced.'

But Jo's frown deepened. 'All they'll need is his body. They'll have bent coppers on their payroll. They'll do his fingerprints, facial recognition ...'

'Not if he was burned,' Elliot suggested.

Jim looked at Jo again. 'That's something.'

'That's nothing. We've only got this dipshit's word he was in the fire. Even if it gets reported tomorrow that a charred body was found, we won't know it was Ray.' She swung back to Elliot. 'We've only got *your* fucking word for it that *you* didn't get caught and tell them everything straight away!'

'You think he'd still be in one piece?' Harri asked. 'Does logic not work for you?'

Jo glanced at her again. 'You seem to know an awful lot about this, for a fucking tom.'

'I only know what I found online,' Harri replied tightly.

'And what you saw all those years ago ... in that shithole brothel. And what those two coppers told you.'

'But doesn't it all make sense?' Elliot interrupted. 'About the Red Book?'

Jo locked eyes with him as if trying to probe Elliot once and for all. Before turning and glancing meaningfully at Jim.

'What?' Elliot asked. 'What have I not been told?'

When Jim responded, it was to Harri. 'You were bang on, darling. Over the last couple of days, we've got in touch with this rat-punk maths student who also happens to have a smack habit. As you can imagine, it wasn't difficult buying *him*. He's managed to translate the first couple of pages of the Red Book. All the way to the letter C, in fact. And yeah, it *does* seem to be a list of names and addresses in London. Your theory makes sense ...'

'Not that it's much consolation,' Jo interjected. 'Because as you can imagine, a comprehensive list of all the grasses in London would be fantastically valuable on the open market so it stands to reason that the Corporation themselves might, in the correct circumstances, pay big time to get it back. The trouble is that those circumstances now elude us. In fact, we've lost every bit of fucking leverage we ever had, because for reasons already stated, if the Corporation *have* got hold of Ray Lonnegan, even if he's a corpse, they'll work out who he is ... and trace him back to us without needing to pay a fucking penny.'

'Gee, that's tough,' Harri said. 'Imagine having to live with that worry.'

For the first time, Jo smiled.

'Not quite the worry you'd have to live with,' she said, 'if someone let it out that you'd seen the Scissorman in action. That you could pick him out of an ID parade.' She glanced at Elliot. 'How about that, superstar? You're already in trouble with the Corporation for being the other half of the team that shot up their outfit at Soaker's Farm. I mean, they might forgive that if everyone ends up getting what they want ... that was just business. But then the problem arises that you're also married to the one person who could witness against the Scissorman in court.'

'I told you, I'm not a grass,' Harri hissed.

Jo laughed. 'And do you think he'll take your word for it? Because let me tell you, if the Corporation come looking for us, they'll certainly find out about you.'

'Come on,' Elliot pleaded. 'Aren't we all on the same side here?'

'*We* are,' Jo replied. She nodded at Harri. 'Can't speak for *her*. Don't envy your future, Mr Wade. It's going to be like walking round with an unexploded bomb in your pocket.'

Elliot glanced at Harri agitatedly. She glared back, as if she couldn't believe that he'd harbour any doubt about her.

'Ultimately, it may have been a mistake bringing you into this,' Jo added, less threatening and more contemplative.

'Seems my little brother got a bit carried away after Christmas Eve. But whether he was wrong or not is irrelevant. This is how things are. We still hold the Red Book, but we can't sell it back to the Corporation. The best we can hope for is to buy ourselves a pardon ... by *giving* it back, perhaps with a little extra thrown in.'

Elliot glanced from one to the other. 'You want to give them my cut from the robbery? That works if it gets me off the hook. Most of it's still here.'

They pondered that.

'You earned that sixty-five grand, Elliot,' Jim finally said. 'You can keep it.'

'Sixty-five Gs wouldn't cover it anyway,' Jo added. 'No, you're going to do something else for us.'

'For God's sake!' Harri protested. 'Hasn't he done enough? Look at the mess we're in already because of you people.'

Jo's eyes bored into them both. 'You want out of this? You want to fix what you fucked up? Then listen to *me* very, very carefully.'

37

8 January (Wednesday)

'Now I see why you insisted on coming with me,' Susan Clarkwell said, hesitating at the sight of the police troop carrier halted near the entrance to the NICU, and the two armoured officers standing alongside it. With their heavy plating and visored helmets, and the pistols at their hips and MP5 submachine guns across their chests, they were more like human tanks.

'Nothing to worry about,' Lynda said. 'That's FSU, our firearms response team.'

'You didn't tell me there were guns involved.'

'We don't know yet whether there were or weren't.'

That wasn't entirely untrue. The bullet-like metallic objects that Lynda had found in the tree were still undergoing ballistics examination, which ought to tell them, firstly, whether they actually were bullets, and secondly, whether they were of a recent enough vintage to have been fired last Sunday night.

One of the menacing paramilitary figures now stepped out to block their passage. Lynda offered her warrant card, but he still shook his head.

'Sorry, sarge ... can't let you in.'

'It's my investigation that brought you here,' she replied.

'Fair enough, but they've asked us all to stay outside for the time being. There's some kind of crisis in there.'

Lynda glanced past his shoulder, but though she could see through the entrance into the IC waiting area, it wasn't possible to see further than that.

'What're we talking about?' she asked.

He shrugged. 'Dunno.'

Doctor Clarkwell flashed her NHS card. 'I take it you're not going to stop *me*? I work here.'

The firearms officer looked a little less certain.

'You're going to prevent a doctor going into a hospital?' Lynda said.

'No ...' The guy stepped aside. 'You're all right, miss.'

Doctor Clarkwell went through without looking back. At the very least, Lynda had hoped for something like 'I'll just see what's going on, and let you know,' but apparently that wasn't to be. Sensing that opting to wait would be futile, Lynda turned and headed around the hospital's exterior. En route, she called Clive, but there was no response, which didn't surprise her given that, officially, they were both now off duty.

On her arrival at Billington Ward, visiting time was ending, and members of the public were streaming out. She pushed past them and entered the ward itself. She was uneasy about marching straight up to Elliot Wade's bed. Despite any sudden developments that might have occurred, Kepler's instructions still rang in her ears, as did those of Mr Jaishankar – but somehow or other she had to find out what was going on. It therefore didn't help when she found Wade's bed empty.

Not just empty, but stripped, the cabinet beside it bare of any personal items.

Lynda went cold, a storm of crazy thoughts assailing her.

'We had no choice but to move him,' someone said.

Lynda turned and found a Nurse Zara Abimbola at her shoulder.

'Move him?'

'Into a private room. We can't have armed police officers on the wards. Oh … I assume you're a police officer too?'

'DS Hagen.' Relieved, Lynda flashed her warrant card. 'For a minute then, I thought he'd gone wandering.'

'He did, earlier. He left the unit. Ended up down in Neurological Intensive Care. It was Sister Margoyle who found him and brought him back.'

'What was he doing there?'

'Nothing. Just sitting and holding his wife's hand.'

'Holding her hand? I thought … well, there seems to be some kind of problem over there. I mean at Neurological IC.'

Abimbola looked puzzled, but then it struck. 'There was a bad accident on a building site this afternoon. Two men fell from a scaffold. Both suffered severe head injuries.'

'I see …'

That was awful news in itself, of course, but Lynda couldn't help the relief that again flooded through her.

'I'm afraid Mr Jaishankar still says that Mr Wade can't be interviewed until tomorrow afternoon,' Abimbola added, 'but if you want to check that everything's secure, I can show you where we put him.'

Lynda nodded.

The nurse led her down a side corridor. Lynda was disobeying direct orders, she realised. But the deeper she probed this case, the more mysteries were exposed and yet, in a short time, the whole thing would be taken off her.

This is high-level crime, DI Hollindrake had said. *And you're a Traffic officer.*

Her defiance was probably ill advised, but while she was here at the hospital on perfectly legitimate business, it made sense that she at least took note of Elliot Wade's new circumstances.

They passed a letterbox-type window on the right, positioned at shoulder height and filled with glass reinforced by wire mesh. Lynda glanced through and spotted the patient lying in bed, his bandaged head buried in a pillow.

'I see he's unconscious again – or is he sleeping?'

'Well . . .' Abimbola shrugged. 'I think it's a bit of an act personally.'

Lynda turned a quizzical look to her.

'I just think he doesn't want to talk to anyone,' Abimbola said. 'Earlier on, he was sitting reading the paper when this other police officer came in . . .'

Lynda was surprised. 'Which other police officer?'

'I didn't catch his name. Fair-haired, blazer and tie, nice coat, nice watch – big one with a blue face.'

'He didn't show you his warrant card?'

'I didn't think to ask because there were police everywhere by then.'

'And he definitely told you he was one of us?'

The nurse nodded. 'I told him the patient couldn't be interviewed, but he said he wouldn't be a minute. That he was just checking something. He came past this window, just where you're standing now, and headed around the corner to the door.'

Lynda moved to the next corner and glanced around. Five yards away, another of the firearms officers stood sentry by a closed bedroom door.

'That was when he seemed to change his mind and went back out,' Abimbola said.

'You mean when he saw the armed officer?'

'I suppose so. But it didn't make any difference. Mr Wade had seen him pass the window, and within half a second was miraculously asleep again.'

Lynda glanced back through the wire-mesh glass. The prone figure inside had not moved.

'You're saying he's putting this on?'

'Only for certain people.'

'Like the blond-haired man who said he was a police officer?'

'For him, definitely.' Almost as soon as she'd said that, Abimbola seemed to regret it. 'Well, that's what it looked like. At the end of the day Mr Wade's recovering from a basal skull fracture. Sleep is good. He's in here to get bedrest, and he's on tramadol. But in the time it took this man to get from the window to the door, he'd gone out like a light.'

Lynda considered this.

'So, is that blond-haired man not a police officer?' Abimbola asked.

'I'll be honest,' Lynda replied, 'I'm not sure who he is.'

38

5 January (Sunday)

Proceeding as agreed. The track tonight, 8 pm

The text had appeared on the throwaway phone that had arrived through the post that morning. And that was all it had said. But it was all that Elliot had needed.

Again, he drove alone along darkened, icy lanes. As he did, the jangle of an incoming call sounded. His eyes averted from the road to the number displayed on the hands-free. It looked familiar, but he didn't recognise it sufficiently to put a name to it, and as it was neither Harri nor Jim Naboth, he reached out and switched the phone off.

He passed the disused silage tower and swung along the unmade track, through the iron gate and into the same parking area where this whole thing had begun.

Switching the engine off, and disconnecting his phone from the hands-free, he saw that a voicemail had been recorded. Supposing that he'd better listen to it in case it was relevant to tonight, he played the message back.

'Hey, Elliot!' sang the unmistakably plummy voice of Nick Scotzini. *'Been away for a few days and just got in. I saw on the security camera that you were in Hoddington in the early hours on Friday morning. Whoa, fella ... you looked pretty banged up. Don't know what's going on, but I'm sorry I wasn't there to help.*

Listen ... I'll call you back tomorrow, see if I can catch you. But seriously, Elliot, I know your life gets complicated from time to time, but there's only me here at The Rookery, so there's always room for you and Harri if you need somewhere to lie low. Call me back, yeah. Seriously, mate. I'm sure we can sort something out.'

Elliot pondered it briefly before slipping the phone into his jacket pocket and climbing out.

The green door stood open. He sidled through, traversing the dank darkness towards the light shining from the hangar. When he entered it, several cars were waiting. As before, they were lined up in a row and covered by canvas. Jim and Jo Naboth stood there. Both wore everyday clothes, but both were gloved. Jim carried a small tan suitcase.

'You're early,' he said.

'I calculated that would be better than arriving late,' Elliot replied.

'Smartarse,' Jo said under her breath.

Elliot didn't respond to that. Whatever occurred, it seemed to be the case that he couldn't win over this woman. But even Jim was a cool, unsmiling presence now. Not that Elliot cared. With luck, tonight would be the end of his relationship with them.

Jim pushed the suitcase into Elliot's hands. It was heavy.

'There's two hundred grand in here, along with the Red Book,' Jim said. He produced a small key. 'This is the only key. So don't lose it.' Elliot shoved the key into his pocket. 'Follow these instructions and you won't have a problem. Veer from them, and who knows where it ends.'

'The last time I went to meet these guys, they were ready for us,' Elliot replied. 'I still think Ray jumped the gun, but they weren't going to play it straight...'

'You won't have to meet anyone if you shut your gob and listen,' Jo retorted.

Jim whipped the canvas off the nearest car. A beige Ford Mondeo sat underneath. 'This is another of our non-existent motors. And you're going to drive it into Central London. When you're there, take that suitcase to the left-luggage office at Charing Cross Station. Bear in mind it closes at eleven. So, don't fuck around. We want this done and dusted. If you end up having to do it tomorrow, we'll deal with it but no one's going to be happy. You understand?'

Elliot nodded.

'There'll be no hostiles anywhere near,' Jim added. 'The Corporation don't even know about this, so none of their soldiers are going to be hanging around. When you've stashed it at left luggage, you go into Covent Garden, to a pub on Rose Street called the Lamb and Flag. Do you know it?'

'Vaguely,' Elliot replied.

'Good. Go in, buy yourself a drink, act normal.'

'Listen,' Elliot said, 'I'm going to have Harri with me ...'

They regarded him in stiff silence.

He shrugged. 'If I'm doing it tonight, there's no option. She finishes her shift at nine, and I've got to pick her up.' He glanced from one to the other. 'Is that a problem?'

'Now you mention it, no,' Jim said. 'Because then you'll look extra normal. Go into the Lamb and Flag together, get drinks, have a natter, have a giggle. But before you leave, go into the toilets there, the third cubicle along. You use *this* ...' He produced a cardboard tube containing Blu-Tack. 'Stick the redemption ticket for the suitcase and the key to it behind the cistern. Are you listening to me?'

'Yeah.'

'Then head back here. Drop the Mondeo off and collect your own motor. Before you get here, though, you use that phone we sent to text us that the job's done. Then dispose of the phone. Properly.'

'And make sure you're well on your way before you do that,' Jo added.

'Correct,' Jim said. 'Because the moment you tip us off, we'll use back-channels to let the Corporation know where and how they can find their missing merchandise and a little something by way of restitution. In all probability, it'll be past eleven by then. So they won't be able to get it back till tomorrow, but that doesn't mean they won't send someone straight away. So like Jo says, make sure you're well on your way when you text us.'

'That's it?' Elliot asked.

'That's it,' Jim confirmed. 'Come back here, get your BMW.'

'You'll be searched, of course,' Jo said. 'Just in case you've been tempted to get light-fingered during the delivery.'

Elliot nodded. He'd expected that.

'Purely a precaution,' Jim said. 'And after that you can go home.'

'Until the next time,' Jo added.

Elliot glanced from one to the other. 'What do you mean "next time"?'

Jo frowned. 'What do you mean what do I mean?'

'Come on, Jo!' Elliot protested. 'Isn't this enough? I nearly got killed on Thursday.'

Jo's frown darkened. 'You're quoting Thursday like it's something we owe you for?'

'I did what you asked...'

She lurched forward, snatching Elliot by the collar. 'It's

because of Thursday that we're forking out two hundred
big ones!'

'What do you think we asked you here for, Elliot?' Jim
said. 'To do us a favour? This is part of what you owe us.'

Jo released Elliot, and he staggered back. '*Part* of it?'

'You're going to be doing jobs like this till that two hundred Gs is paid off,' Jo snarled. 'And if a *real* job comes along,
you'll be at the wheel again ... this time free of charge.'

'I didn't want to go to Soaker's Farm,' Elliot stammered.
'I told you I had no experience. Ray was supposed to make
the deal ...'

Jo lurched at Elliot again, but Jim stuck out an arm to
hold her back.

'If Ray was here now, *he'd* be the bagman,' Jim said. 'But
he isn't, is he?'

'Okay, okay ...' Elliot palmed the air.

A metallic clanking drew his attention to the hangar's
sliding doors. The white-haired guy from last time was
removing the heavy chain. With a creak and groan of oiled
timber, he pushed the doors open.

'The key's in the ignition,' Jim said, nodding at the
Mondeo. 'Go right when you get outside. There's a track
that leads behind the bleachers. The gate round there's open.'

Elliot nodded.

'Well?' Jo wondered. 'What the fuck are you waiting for?'

Elliot was on the A14, heading for the A12 junction, when
he realised that he'd picked up a tail. It was a Sunday night,
so there wasn't much traffic around, which made the blue
Vauxhall Corsa conspicuous, especially as it had emerged
from that maze of unlit rural roads shortly after he had. When
he swung onto the estate containing the Three Pigeons, and

the Corsa copied the manoeuvre, he felt certain. However, who could it be other than a Naboth man? He was carrying their £200,000; they'd want to be sure that it went to the right place. Almost certainly, this person would pull him over after he'd dropped the goods off, to search him. The Naboths had implied that he'd only be searched when he got back to Tunwood, but he hadn't believed that. They wouldn't want him to have time to stash anything he might have pilfered.

It didn't matter, though. All was good.

Harri emerged from the pub wearing her coat and scarf. He flashed his headlights, otherwise she wouldn't have recognised the Mondeo.

She hurried over and climbed in. 'Well?'

He told her everything, including Jo's revelation about the debt he owed them.

'It's what we feared,' he said. 'Or rather ... what *you* feared.' She made no comment. 'Just out of interest, meanwhile, I received this message earlier.' He held up his mobile and played Nick Scotzini's voicemail on the speaker.

After it had stopped, Harri gazed at him. 'You really want to bring Nick into this?'

Elliot shrugged. 'It's true what he says. He's got space. And it's not like the Naboths know him. We could hole up there for quite some time.'

She shook her head. 'Nick's a lovely guy, Elliot, but he's such an innocent. We do that, and his life would never be the same afterwards. Apart from anything else, this is crime. It's not just the Naboths he'd have to worry about. Do you want to do *that* to him?'

Elliot sighed. 'I only went there the other night because I had no option. But he sounds keen to help.'

'Because he's bored. Rich guys get bored. They think

things like this are an adventure. Remember when he tried to tackle that handbag thief a couple of years ago. He ended up breaking his collarbone. This time it could be a lot worse.'

'I know.'

'This is our mess, and it's down to us to fix it. So, we stick to the plan, yeah?'

'Sure.'

He drove them out of the car park.

They travelled in silence for some time, rejoining the A12, before Elliot checked the rear-view mirror and groaned. 'Shit ... they really don't trust us, do they?'

'What is it?' Harri asked.

'First there was a blue Corsa on our tail. Now it's a Citroën DS4.'

Harri turned, focusing on a pair of headlights travelling about forty yards behind them in the slow lane.

'You're certain he's following us?'

'He's been there a few minutes and he's made no effort to overtake. And we're only doing fifty.'

She looked to their front again. No other vehicles were visible ahead.

'Could just be someone who likes a slow, easy drive,' she ventured.

'Let's see *how* much they like it.' Gradually, Elliot decelerated.

Harri watched the needle circle backward from 50 mph to 45, from 45 to 40, from 40 to 35, 35 to 30. And all this on a national speed-limit road. She glanced around again. The DS4 remained about forty yards behind them, perhaps even a little further back.

'I don't understand,' she said. 'Why two different cars?'

He shrugged. 'Tailing someone is a lot harder than they

make it look in the movies. Usually you need two or three people in different motors. That probably won't be the last car we get suspicious of.'

Harri glanced back again, this time lowering her eyes to the back seat and the suitcase full of money. 'Couldn't be the police, could it?'

'I doubt it. The cops wouldn't make it so obvious.'

She turned frontward. 'So, the Naboths have put some guard dogs on us. If they're planning to shadow us all the way to Charing Cross, why didn't they just carry the cash themselves?'

'Because they're digging me deeper and deeper into their activities. The more I do for them, the harder it gets for me ever to grass on them, ever to even leave. They're tying me to them, Harri. It'll be like this from now on. Every piss-arse but illegal job that comes along. And every dangerous one too.'

'Right,' she said. 'Well, the restaurant's only ten miles from here. We do what we agreed, and everything'll be fine.'

'I hope you're right, darling. I bloody hope you're right.'

He accelerated again. Not racing, just easing his way back up from 30 to 40, to 50, to 60. The restaurant, which was a rather grandiose way to talk about the McDonald's drive-through near Colchester, was indeed only about ten miles ahead. However, they'd only travelled another mile when Elliot glanced into his rear-view mirror and saw that they appeared to have picked up another tail, a second pair of headlights now riding some sixty yards behind the DS4. He assumed that this would be the blue Corsa, and that it had caught up with them again. But then it pulled out into the overtaking lane and accelerated, bypassing them at speed. As it did, he saw that it was a green Nissan Juke. Elliot watched it veer back into the slow lane some fifty yards in front and promptly decelerate.

'What the actual fuck,' he muttered.

'I don't believe that,' Harri said.

'Tighten your safety belt.'

She stiffened. 'Elliot, what're you doing? We're almost there.'

'This is not good, Harri.'

Without signalling, he pulled out into the fast lane and hit the gas. They swiftly overtook the Juke, which made no initial move to follow but maintained a steady 50 mph, receding into the background again. However, now the DS4 also pulled into the fast lane and accelerated.

Elliot watched his mirror as he tromped the gas.

The needle rose from 70 to 80 and then on towards 90. But the DS4 was catching up. Elliot glided back into the slow lane, to allow it to overtake. It didn't, moving into the slow lane behind him, again about forty yards to their rear, though they were both still travelling at high speed.

'He doesn't mind us knowing that he's following us, does he?' Harri said.

'They wouldn't have expected us to expect anything else...' Elliot's words faltered as something in the nearside mirror caught his attention. 'Fuck!'

Harri glanced back and saw that the Nissan Juke was also coming up on the outside, seemingly in another effort to overtake them. Elliot pressed the accelerator, the Mondeo surging forward to 95, and then on towards 100.

Harri clutched at the dashboard. 'Elliot, I know this is half the speed you used to travel on the racetrack, but I'm really not happy.'

'It's only for a minute.'

His eyes flicked again to the mirror. The DS4 was also accelerating, but was being careful, or so it seemed, not to decrease the distance between them. However, the Juke was flying in its efforts to catch up.

Elliot watched the mirror. 'This is bloody ridiculous. What the hell is ...?'

Before he could say more, with the Juke on the cusp of overtaking the DS4, the DS4 swung out. Gears clashed and tyres screeched as the Juke took evasive action, hitting its brakes as it swerved back into the slow lane, and because it was travelling at 100 mph, losing all traction and pinwheeling off the carriageway onto an expanse of roadside grass. Elliot got his own foot down, but no further acceleration seemed possible. He glanced at the speed gauge. They were now travelling at 105 mph, and that, apparently, was this particular Mondeo's limit. Again, he checked the rear-view mirror. The DS4, having accounted for the Juke, had given up any pretence that it wasn't pursuing. It sped up from behind, hogging the fast lane. Elliot saw its front passenger window power down.

'Shit,' he said quietly, before shouting: '*Harri, duck!*'

The DS4 was less than twenty yards behind them. Elliot swung into the fast lane, to block its advance. The DS4's brakes squealed, and it fishtailed.

'The hell?' Harri wailed, hanging on for dear life.

'The bastard's not coming alongside us!'

'But if it's the Naboths!'

'That's not the Naboths!'

'Oh, dear God!'

Behind them, the DS4 manoeuvred back into the slow lane, where it hit the gas, surging up on their inside. Elliot swung back in front of it, and its brakes shrieked as it jerked back into the fast lane. Elliot swung in front of it a second time, but it was a feint, the DS4 then veering into the slow lane and bulleting forward.

Elliot checked the mirror. The DS4's driver's window was coming down as well.

'Who ... is it?' Harri stammered.

'I told you to get down!'

As the DS4 came neck-and-neck with them, Elliot risked a sideways glance. Harri still hadn't ducked, but he could see past her through the open driver's window into their opponent's darkened interior. He floored the brake – just as gunfire flashed.

The DS4 raced ahead as Elliot decelerated from 100 to 90, to 80, to 75. Dazzling red lights showed the DS4 was braking too. Elliot tromped the gas again, and tore up behind it, threatening to ram its rear-end. The DS4 accelerated to avoid impact.

'Hold on!' Elliot bellowed.

They were back up to 90 again, pressing towards 100, the darkened landscape whipping past in a blur. Ahead of them by ten yards, the DS4 began fishtailing. Tyres yowling, it swung over into the fast lane. Elliot swung over there too. They were less than five yards behind it. If it jammed on, there'd be the most monstrous collision this road had ever seen, but whoever this guy was, he clearly didn't want that. He swung left into the slow lane and braked, dropping back until he was alongside them again. Elliot hit the gas. The DS4 hit the gas too and veered straight at them. Elliot swerved away to evade impact. With a furious crashing and banging, he rode the barrier on the central reservation, before braking again and falling behind, swinging over into the slow lane.

The DS4 swung over and braked as well. Half a second

later, it was back alongside them, with another flash of gunfire. Harri screamed as Elliot's window imploded, the slug streaking past the ends of their noses, taking out the passenger window too.

Elliot tromped the gas, trying to gun the car forward, but again they were stuck at just above 100. It gained them maybe half a yard, when another shot was fired, demolishing both the backseat windows.

'My God, Elliot!' Harri wailed. 'Oh my God!'

'*I said, duck!*'

The DS4 surged up alongside them. Elliot glimpsed a pistol in a gloved hand. There was only one man in there, he was sure of that – the driver. And the bastard had to be leaning across his own front passenger seat to get to such close range.

Another flash, and another slug ripped through the interior.

Elliot glanced right again. The gloved hand was taking a more careful aim. As it did, the driver's face came into view. It was momentary, a flicker of ephemeral light illuminating his features: his oily tangle of hair and beard, his dark eyes, his hooked hose, his V-shaped, jack-o-lantern grin.

'Lonnegan!' Elliot shouted, as the DS4 veered across the line, closing the gap between them from inches to centimetres. By instinct more than design, Elliot spun the wheel left.

And hit a river of ice that had formed along the edge of the carriageway.

More gun flashes filled the rear-view mirror. Elliot shouted and fought the wheel, but with a clap of thunder, the crash barrier disintegrated and then they were plunging down through a nightmare jungle of black, twisted branches, the car jolting and smashing, filling with dirt and foliage, explosions of fibrous wood rending their ears, the bodywork caving in, metal squealing, buckling, the windshield raining on them as it detonated...

Part Three

39

8 January (Wednesday)

'Hi ... it's me,' Lynda said, when Don answered. 'Sorry I'm so late, but I'm on my way home.'

The A134 spooled endlessly out in her headlights.

'Chasing your tail again?' He sounded as tired as she felt.

'Feels like that,' she said.

'Me too.'

'Why? What's the matter?'

'Nothing,' he sighed. 'Just this writing lark. Not as straight-forward as I thought.'

'You said the new guy liked it.'

'He does. He reckons. But the amount of changes and corrections he's looking for, you could be forgiven for think-ing otherwise.'

'Isn't that the name of the game?'

'Suppose so.'

'Kids all right?'

'Yeah.'

'What did you cook for their tea?'

'Went and got some fish and chips. Got some for you too. Wasn't sure what time you'd be back, but they're in the oven. Low heat.'

In normal circumstances Lynda might've had a pop at him. They'd eaten out yesterday, and that had come to over a hundred quid. But a fish supper wasn't quite the same thing as the barbecue burgers and flat-iron steaks they'd had at Texas Tony's, plus she could hardly complain – Don sounded worn out.

'How long before you get in?' he asked.

'Half an hour.'

'Okay.'

At least he was being compliant, and a little less self-absorbed than usual. And that was something to be thankful for.

'You might be tired, darling,' she said. 'But you sound happier.'

'At last I know where I'm going,' he replied.

'Yeah. Wish I did.'

There was another brief pause.

'Case still not working out?' he asked.

'Oh, we've got plenty of leads. I just don't think I'm going to be on it for much longer. Rachel Hollindrake's decided it's getting a bit much for me.' She didn't bother to add: *And as this is the first real challenge I've had in years, it won't look good on the record.*

'Don't suppose there's anything *I* can do?' he replied.

'Not really.' She yawned. 'Unless you ever had dealings with someone called Nick Scotzini?'

'Scotzini?' He pondered. 'Distinctive name.'

'Yeah. I'm sure you'd remember it if you'd heard it before.'

'I think I *have* heard it before.'

Lynda straightened up. 'What do you mean?'

'This bloke lives around here, does he?'

'Just over the border.'

There was another brief silence.

'You know, I'm not sure why,' Don said, 'but I think we

did deal with someone whose name was Scotzini. What're we talking? A known villain?'

'Not exactly. Far from it.'

'I wonder ... might've been one of Sandy Rawlins' cases?' Sandy Rawlins had been a DS under Don's command back at Major Investigations. 'Think something happened in Colchester a couple of years ago.'

'I don't suppose you can find out, can you?' This was quite a request to make of someone who'd been out of the job two years. But Lynda was experienced enough to know that if you didn't ask, you generally didn't get. Not in law enforcement.

Don considered. 'I can give Sandy a call, I suppose. I've still got her personal number. What's this fella supposed to have done?'

'Well ...' This, Lynda realised, was the part where she might come unstuck. 'Impersonating a police officer for one thing.'

'What were the circs?'

She outlined them.

'Is that really naughty?' he asked. 'That he wanted to see his best mate, and the only way he could get into the hospital was by telling a little white lie?'

'It's not just that. He's not been straight with me, Don. He said that the shots on duty at Elliot Wade's bedside turned him away. In actual fact, he didn't even speak to them. Took one look at them and headed out under his own steam.'

'Makes sense if he'd been fibbing that he was a copper.'

'He also seemed to know all about Elliot Wade's background. I mean, he knew the dates of Wade's family's deaths, yet he didn't know that the guy has criminal connections in Ipswich.'

'Were these connections the sort of thing Wade was likely

to boast about? Could it be that no one else knew about them either?'

When Don put it that way, it seemed less suspicious.

'He's still not being truthful,' she said.

'Yeah, but it hardly adds up to a smoking gun. Have you checked his details?'

'He said he lives in Hoddington. I've checked with the electoral roll, and there's a Nicholas Scotzini living on Hillcroft Drive, smack in the middle of the village.'

'So, he *was* straight with you?'

'About that, yeah, but I'd still be interested to hear what Sandy knows about him, assuming it's the same fella.'

'Let me give her a call now. Ring you back in five.'

In actual fact it was more like fifteen, and Lynda was on the A137, past Ardleigh, when he rang back.

'Any joy?' she said.

'Well, I got through to Sandy, and she remembered the bloke. Nicholas Scotzini. Accountant from the Dedham area.'

'That sounds like him.'

'I hate to say it, love, but this is probably not what you're wanting to hear ...'

'Go on.'

'Basically, he's one of the good guys. Witnessed for Sandy back in 2016.'

'What happened?'

'Seems he's a bit of a have-a-go hero. It was a Saturday and he was in Colchester, shopping. Little old lady got her handbag snatched by a kid on a moped. It was looped around her wrist, and so he dragged her along the road, inflicting serious injuries. This guy, Scotzini, was about fifty yards ahead. Saw what happened, jumped out and tried to haul the kid off the bike. Ended up getting run down. Pretty badly chewed up himself.'

'How did this end up with Major Investigations?' Lynda asked.

'It was this moped thief. He'd been at it for weeks. Two or three people had got hurt, but none as badly as the old lady, or Nick Scotzini, as it turned out.'

'What did Sandy say about him?'

'She remembers him well. The case ended up not going to trial because the dipstick on the moped pleaded guilty. But she couldn't speak highly enough of Scotzini. Says he was more than ready to help. Real public-spirited bloke. And, well, Sandy being the maneater she is, a "blond bombshell".'

Lynda thought about that. There'd been something solid and competent about Nick Scotzini when she'd met him at the hospital. He was hardly film star material, but his looks weren't unpleasing. Without trying too hard, he'd given the impression that he was strong and capable.

'He's not just any old accountant, either,' Don added. 'He's senior accountant for a shipping line. He's minted.'

'Is he married?' she wondered. 'Does he have family?'

'Was married once, but not anymore. And no family. This is why Sandy fancied her chances. Apparently, he told her the only woman in his life was his housekeeper. Some old biddy who came in to cook and clean for him.'

Lynda said nothing to that.

'This any help?' he asked.

'Don, you're a bloody rock.'

'I am?'

'Dish those fish and chips up, will you. I've just got my appetite back.'

40

5 January (Sunday)

After the Mondeo plunged down the embankment, the grey Citroën DS4 proceeded south along the A12. Aware that there was a traffic camera on the Coles Oak Road bridge, about five miles ahead, Ray Lonnegan pulled off at the next slip lane. This took him up to the Stratford Road Bridge, where he crossed the A12 and rejoined it, heading north.

He drove back the way he'd come, bypassing the scene of the accident, noticeable now only as a gap in the crash barrier. A couple of minutes later, he reached the point where he'd veered the green Nissan Juke onto the verge.

There was nothing there.

Which was a problem.

He'd assumed that the Juke had been another of the Naboths' guard dogs. It had come from nowhere and he hadn't expected it, so he'd improvised by nudging it off the road. But increasingly, after he'd dealt with the Mondeo, he'd begun to suspect that he hadn't nudged the Juke hard enough. He gazed into his rear-view mirror at the empty stretch of roadside grass behind him. Not only had it not wrecked, it hadn't even suffered enough damage to be left marooned. It hadn't even left skid marks in the deep-frozen turf. Almost certainly, it had hit the road again, probably after he'd gone, but headed where?

'Shit,' he hissed.

It was even more vital now that he get on with things. Thanks to the lateness of the hour, the coast was clear. So, he pulled off at Stratford St Mary, crossed underneath the A12 and came straight back onto it, heading south again. Shortly after the crash site, a layby came up on the left, and he drove into it. This was particularly convenient, as aside from its entrance and exit, a row of straggling bushes masked it from the road. He pulled up and parked. During the daytime, there would be lorries here but at present it was deserted. He released his seatbelt and slid another magazine into the handgrip of his Glock 17, which he then inserted into the shoulder holster under his zip-up hoodie. He pulled the hood up and climbed out. Walking to the layby entrance, he glanced out. The A12 lay empty, so he set off, jogging north along its hard shoulder.

He'd travelled about a third of a mile, before he reached the point where the barrier had been flattened. He peered down the black tunnel torn through the embankment thickets.

It was possible that Wade and his missus had survived. He'd heard no explosion. There was no hint of smoke on the crisp winter air. They *could* have survived, yes, but travelling at that speed? And in a car which, in the usual fashion of the Naboths' private chop-shop, had had its air bags disabled?

He commenced his descent. It was impossible to be completely stealthy, so he kept stopping, leaning against trees to listen. Nothing moved in the void below. Even so, over the last few yards, he slid his gloved right hand under his hoodie, fingers resting on the grip of his Glock.

Now he could *see* it, the shapeless hulk of the Mondeo wedged against a tree that had almost fallen over with the impact. He could smell it too: the reek of an overheated engine; the stench of warped metal, melted rubber, and petrol. He continued down, gun drawn. With his other hand, he switched on a torch, but kept it to low intensity, its beam narrow so as to attract minimal attention. Despite that, the first thing it picked out was the Mondeo's nearside flank, which had crumpled like an accordion, its rear windows hanging with broken branches and tattered shrubbery.

His roving beam stopped on the girl, Harri.

Half thrown out through her door, she was still caught in her seatbelt and therefore upside down. The vehicle had struck the tree trunk with so massive a smash that its entire front section had canted upright by fifty degrees, the front seats tipped forward. The woman's seatbelt had held, so she likely hadn't hit the dash, though it was hard to be sure because the entire chassis had been hammered out of shape, the passenger door buckled from its moorings. From the extensive damage that she herself was showing, the branches and other woodland debris that had poured in through the windscreen had ripped past and over her with incredible force.

Lonnegan circled around the wreck, careful where he stepped. Black masking tape wrapped his boots to obliterate any imprints. The ground was iron-hard due to the cold but had been churned up by the crash, so the precaution was sensible.

At the car's other flank, it was the same story with Wade: his face, head and upper torso torn and filthy, his entire front caked in congealing blood. He hung there motionless, but whether dead or alive was of no consequence because lying on this side of the car was a tan suitcase. It had evidently been thrown out through the rear passenger door and had burst open, its contents scattered over twenty or so yards.

Lonnegan regarded it long and hard.

This was the pay-off for the Corporation. They weren't going to get it now, so he might as well find a more deserving home for it. But first, he squatted and leafed through the bundles of £20 notes rather than gathering them. The Red Book had to be here somewhere, but there was no immediate trace of it. He slashed his torch back and forth, rooting through the spilled cash, increasingly frantic, until finally settling back on his haunches.

'Okay,' he told himself. 'No time to fuck about. We get what we can.'

He shoved his pistol into his belt, grabbed the suitcase and began stuffing the bundles of money back into it. For the most part, these were intact, held together by rubber bands, but several had broken, casting their notes far and wide. He panted and sweated as he grubbed about on all fours. To make matters worse, the suitcase had originally been locked, but in the fury of the crash, the lock had torn itself open. He had to clamp it closed under his left arm, which was difficult if he wanted to hold the torch as well. At which point there was a twitching of foliage.

Lonnegan leapt up and spun around, dropping the case. Yanking the gun free, he pointed it straight-armed into the blackness.

There was no further sound. He stood stock still, ears pricked. And heard it again: a faint crackle of twigs and dead leafage, though now it was farther away. It could have been caused by an animal, but he held his position. When he heard the sound a third time, it was far off.

He didn't know what this signified. Most likely nothing,

but he could hardly take that chance. He tucked his gun away and retrieved the case. There was still plenty of cash strewn around, but it would take too long to gather it all. And yet, though it was time to go, he was still coldly furious about the Red Book. He shouldn't leave until he'd at least checked the car. He lurched back to the wreck, spearing his torchlight through its debris-filled interior, but at no stage seeing a glint of red leather.

The temptation was to dig around in there, yanking shredded branches aside, but that was no plan. Even his combat clothing could leave threads of fabric. It might even snag slivers of skin, and then he'd be finished.

'Fuck … *shit!*'

He approached the lifeless shape of Elliot Wade, and rifled the guy's ragged, bloody pockets. Wade groaned slightly. Lonnegan continued to search. He didn't hold out much hope that this would bring a result, but it was possible that Wade had opted not to put the Red Book in the case with the cash, and maybe to stash it on his own person. If so, there was no trace of it now. In fact, Lonnegan found only two items, both of them mobile phones: one of those throwaway devices, a burner, almost certainly provided by the Naboths, and Wade's iPhone.

The latter was a surprise and would be considered a security breach by the Naboths. If anything happened to Wade during his mission, this was the way they'd be traced. The bigger mystery, though, was still the whereabouts of the Red Book.

One possibility was that Wade hadn't even brought it, maybe holding it back for some reason, possibly as a bargaining chip. On its own, that wouldn't make sense, unless the crazy fool was working some angle of his own. Was that possible? Could he be trying it on with both the Naboths and the Corporation at the same time.

'Got to admire your balls, Elliot,' Lonnegan muttered. 'But they're no good to me.'

He thrust the burner back into Wade's jacket, but kept hold of the iPhone. At present, that was his only chance of making further progress. He tried to open it, but it was locked, its small VDU requiring a fingerprint impression.

That was no problem at least.

He squatted again, took Wade's left hand and pushed the pad of his thumb onto the screen. The device unlocked, and Lonnegan flipped through its contents as he grabbed the suitcase again and gambolled back up the embankment. He was near the top when a voice sounded from the tiny speaker.

'Hey, Elliot! Been away for a few days and just got in. I saw on the security camera that you were in Hoddington in the early hours on Friday morning. Whoa, fella ... you looked pretty banged up. Don't know what's going on, but I'm sorry I wasn't there to help. Listen, I'll call you back tomorrow, see if I can catch you. But seriously, Elliot, I know your life gets complicated from time to time, but there's only me here at The Rookery, so there's always room for you and Harri if you need somewhere to lie low. Call me back, yeah. Seriously, mate. I'm sure we can sort something out.'

When Lonnegan looked down, it had been sent from someone called Nick Scotzini.

'Well done, Mr Scotzini,' he said to no one in particular. 'Well done indeed. Your loyalty to your mate is commendable. It hasn't saved him, but it's certainly helped me.'

41

9 January (Thursday)

'Good job you're on your way in already,' Clive's doleful voice said from the hands-free. 'Because there's a briefing at eight. Kepler's called it.'

Lynda shook her head. Outside the car, the sun hadn't yet risen and the air was icy cold. 'Does he know we only start at nine?'

'Guess him and his Organised Crime monkeys start earlier,' Clive replied. 'They were already here when I got in. Three more of them. Setting up in our office.'

'What're you talking about? There isn't room in there to breathe as it is!'

'Why do you think I stepped out into the corridor to have this conversation?'

'Fuck's sake.'

'Rachel says it's temporary, but it doesn't look like that to me. They're just shoving our stuff out of the way.'

Lynda put her foot down to beat the next set of lights. 'How did *you* learn about the briefing?'

'Got a phone call at the crack of dawn. They told me to phone you.'

'So, *I* get the message second hand?'

'Then they told me they wanted three teas. Milk and two sugars in each.' If it was possible, Clive sounded even more despondent than he had when she'd first taken the call. 'Think they were taking the mick though because they all had a bloody good laugh about it.' He paused. 'So, what do we do?'

She chewed her bottom lip. Even though she'd anticipated this, she hadn't expected it so quickly. 'Well ... what *you* do is get them their tea.'

He took a second to respond. 'You serious?'

'Told you, Clivey ... From the moment Kepler showed up, we were hanging on to this thing any way we could. From here on, it's whatever it takes. I'll see you when I get in.'

She cut the call. She was now approaching the junction between Birchwood Road and the A12. But instead of heading south towards Chelmsford and the office, she swung north, bound for the Suffolk border.

This was naughty, but there was no choice in the matter. Besides, if there weren't already anomalies where Nick Scotzini was concerned, now something else had come up.

'I like to cook,' he'd told her. And yet the Nick Scotzini that DS Sandy Rawlins had been so impressed by had paid a housekeeper to come in and do that for him. Who knew what the truth was, but this had been one question mark too many.

She'd tried to contact him last night, first going via the phonebook. It had brought no result, so she'd then called Sandy Rawlins herself, learning that Scotzini worked in the British division of a US company, Culraven Merchant Marine. She'd managed to get through to Scotzini's office there, to hit a brick wall in the form of his secretary's answering machine. Googling hadn't progressed things much either. There'd been a single online newspaper reference to his act of bravery in Colchester in 2016, though the article hadn't said anything about his private life and the accompanying photo had only shown the high street where the incident had occurred. On top of that, Scotzini had no presence on Twitter, Facebook or Instagram, at least not under his own name. Lynda was sure there'd be something but hadn't spent the rest of the evening on it as she'd already given hours of unpaid overtime to this particular case. Anyway, the plan had been to bring the new line of enquiry to Kepler's desk this morning so that they could work on it together.

Now even that had changed.

Because she was damned if she was going to do all the digging and then sit back and perform paperwork while the Organised Crime Division pinched the credit.

She drove on through Dedham Vale. It had snowed during the night, not heavily, just putting down a thin layer, and now, with the sun rising and the sky blue, the fields and hedgerows sparkled white. Of course, Hoddington was the kind of place the Essex/Suffolk borderland did well at any time of year. Not that it was heaving on a Thursday morning in January. She saw little activity as she drove through, and when she ascended Hillcroft Drive and parked in front of number 18, also known as The Rookery, she was alone.

The house was a large, Jacobean-style residence, mostly hidden behind a high wall. At the front, a tall gate of latticed steel stood between two brick gateposts. There was a letterbox on the right-side post, but on the other a bell-push and an intercom. Lynda hit the button.

There was no response, so she tried again. And again. Without success.

She leaned against the gate to peer through to the top of the drive, where a Bentley Continental sat by the front door.

The gate opened.

Only a few inches, but with no pressure applied.

Lynda waited awkwardly, but no alarm sounded – none that she could hear.

The phone then jangled in her pocket, and she almost jumped out of her skin. She put it to her ear. 'DS Hagen.'

'Hello ...?' A nervous female voice. 'This is Maxine Molloy, Mr Scotzini's secretary. You left a message for me.'

'That's right,' Lynda replied. 'It's nothing to worry about, Maxine. I'm just trying to contact him, but he doesn't seem to be returning our calls.'

'Mr Scotzini's on sick leave at present.'

'Sick leave?'

'He emailed a note to me first thing on Monday morning. He thinks it's flu. Said he'll probably need the whole week.'

'Have you spoken to him personally?'

'Oh no,' the secretary said hastily. 'I wouldn't do that. He said that he really wasn't so good, and that we weren't to disturb him.'

'Okay, Maxine – thanks for your help.'

Lynda pocketed the phone. And pushed the gate again. It swung halfway open, and she stepped through onto the drive, staring up at the looming white and black-beamed house. She glanced back, and at the rear of the gate, noticed insulated electric cables connecting to a junction box near the top of the right-hand post, meaning that it had an electronic locking system, which now, somehow, had been deactivated.

If the fake news about Scotzini's illness didn't grant Lynda a right of entry here, *that* did.

Further down the gatepost was a Perspex door, behind which an interior compartment was half filled with mail. She walked over. Without opening the door, she couldn't be sure what it all was. Most likely the usual junk. But there was at least one edition of the *Courier*, a weekly freesheet that was delivered on Tuesdays, which meant that Nick Scotzini hadn't collected any of his mail for at least two days. And yet she'd seen him last night, at a hospital only nine miles away. The guy was here, he was home. And he wasn't ill.

Thanking Section 17 again, Lynda headed up the drive, edging around the Bentley, and approached the tall, yellow-painted door.

She hit a button and waited.

A bell chimed inside, but there was no response.

At the very top of the drive stood a wicket gate. Lynda pushed it and followed a passage along the side of the build-ing, which opened into an extensive rear garden: several interconnected lawns, all carpeted with unbroken snow, shrubberies around their perimeters. Following the building's exterior, she came to a smaller garden on the far side of it. Here there was a pair of French windows. They stood ajar.

That didn't just seem wrong, but *very* wrong. The lock on the front gate and now presumably the alarm system on the house had both been disengaged, the property standing insecure.

Under normal circumstances, she'd shout for support. But of course, she didn't have a radio. She had her phone, and could call CAD, but that would take time and there might be someone in here who needed her help.

She approached warily.

And saw damage down the windows' central joint, the varnished woodwork rent and split where a steel tool had been inserted.

Inside, she stopped short at the scene of destruction.

The dining room had been trashed. The central table had

been shoved aside and its chairs knocked over. Paintings hung askew on the walls, ornaments lay broken.

'Hello!' Lynda called, moving into a passage. 'Police officer ... anyone need assistance?'

Silence greeted this.

She pressed on.

The Rookery's downstairs was laid with parquet flooring and filled with antique fixtures and fittings. But there was evidence of disturbance everywhere: pictures knocked from their mounts, shards of glass and porcelain littering the carpets. In the lounge, the rug had been rolled up and pushed aside, a heavy couch turned over. In the middle stood a carved wooden chair, which seemed to have been brought from the dining room, with lengths of what looked like washing line tied in loops around its arms.

She approached this with growing unease, only to spot something on the mantelpiece that had survived the destruction. Pulling on a disposable latex glove, she took it down. It was a framed photograph depicting a man and a woman. The latter was in an evening gown and full make-up, with silver-blonde hair done up high, while the former wore an evening suit and black bow tie and looked to be in the process of receiving some kind of award: an engraved glass plaque framed with gold. Lynda had already seen that same award lying in this very wreckage. She turned and spotted it again, near the door. When she picked it up, the engraving indicated that Employee of the Year, 2015 had been awarded to Senior Accountant, Nicholas Scotzini. She moved back to the mantel and took the picture down.

It did not portray the Nick Scotzini that Lynda knew.

His face was leaner and gentler. Boyish in fact, with a wide mouth, generous eyes and a mop of curly fair hair. At which point, the image was obliterated as a crimson droplet splashed down on it. Lynda jumped backward and looked up.

A wet, red patch blotted the ceiling overhead, from which more drops were now falling.

She located the main staircase on the far side of the kitchen. The upstairs comprised a single, wood-floored corridor with bedrooms leading off it. Lynda navigated to a point corresponding with the blood patch, in what she assumed was the master bedroom, where a trail of blood droplets led across the beige pile carpet to a recessed wardrobe.

The parquet floor downstairs, and the wooden staircase and landing would not easily have shown blood, but this bedroom carpet was different. Cautiously, she tried the wardrobe handle. The door clicked open – and as it did, there was a clatter from downstairs.

Lynda turned sharply.

Another clatter followed. And then the full weight of a man landed on her.

She squawked and staggered, and the weight slid off to strike the bedroom floor.

The breath caught in her throat as she backed away from a pale, bony shape wearing only a vest and a pair of underpants, both of which were liberally stained with blood. His arms and legs were horribly bruised, his wrists and ankles scored by rope burns, his face battered to pulpy, unrecognisable ruin.

Lynda felt sweat on her brow, felt her head swimming. Even so, she had to get down on her knees to check for basic life signs. There was no pulse; only a single eye remained intact, its pupil fixed on her with glassy lifelessness.

She got back to her feet, and movement caught the corner of her eye. She spun to face the bedroom window, which looked out over the extensive lawns, where a figure wearing dark clothing, including a hoodie with the hood pulled up, was sprinting towards the nearest wall of shrubs.

As she dashed to the top of the stairs, she grabbed the phone from her pocket.

'Lynda?' Clive answered. 'Where are you? The conflab with Kep—'

'Bollocks to the conflab,' she retorted, heading down. 'I'm at The Rookery on Hillcroft Drive, Hoddington.'

'What?' He sounded shocked. 'That's not even our—'

'Listen, I'm no doctor, but there's a murder victim on these premises.'

She bolted across the ground floor, aiming for the French windows. Now that she was focusing, she could see the blood trail on the woodwork, and understood why the rug in the lounge had been rolled up in the corner – a cleaning process had commenced, and then *she'd* arrived.

'Lynda, I don't understand ...'

'I think the victim is Nick Scotzini.'

'The guy at the hospital?'

'No, that guy was an imposter. And a murderer. Listen, Clive, we need supervision and CID down here. We also need someone at the hospital to speak to Elliot Wade. Mr Jaishankar's orders have held things up long enough ...'

'Lynda ...' He sounded dazed. 'What're *you* doing?'

'What do you think?' She burst into the garden. 'I'm pursuing the suspect.'

42

9 January (Thursday)

As Lynda hurried down the lengthy, snow-covered garden, she called CAD direct. The call was answered by Sergeant Tom Willit.

The Computer-Aided Despatch office was mostly manned by civilians these days. But Willit, who was in his late fifties and still working because he wanted the full pension, was a permanent supervisory fixture on day shifts.

'Lynda?' He sounded confused. 'Just had an odd call from Clive Atkins...'

'That's correct, Tom,' she interrupted. 'I'm chasing a murder suspect, currently heading across the back garden of 18 Hillcroft Drive, Hoddington. If you can let Suffolk know... they need to attend that address pronto, the scene's insecure. Tell them the French windows at the back of the house have been forced. That's how the offender achieved entry... that's the only way they're going to get in.'

She heard him pass the details on. 'Lynda, have you got a description for us?'

'Only the basics. Male, I suspect. Height... roughly five foot ten. Dark clothing, including a hoodie top. The victim is the occupant of 18 Hillcroft Drive. A certain Nicholas Scotzini. Least, that's who I *think* he is. He looks to have been severely beaten. Tom, the assailant was still on the premises when I entered. He must've been hiding because he legged it while I was upstairs discovering the body.'

'Okay, I've got all that. We have a couple of Essex patrols en route in lieu of Suffolk getting in on the act. ETA five minutes.'

'That's fine, I'll keep calling you back.'

'Received, Lynda … just keep tabs on the suspect, yeah? Don't tackle him on your own.'

She shoved the phone into her pocket as she forced her way through a wall of privets. On the other side, she found herself in a narrow lane running between the backs of other large village houses. In neither direction was there any sign of him. She went left and within fifty yards, a passage appeared on her right. It was a footpath hemmed in on either side by hedges. At the far end, she glimpsed a dark-clad figure turning left. She scrambled in pursuit, and entered another village road: gated drives, extensive gardens and picture-postcard houses, pristine snow covering everything. There was no one around until she glanced left and squinted. The road descended a shallow gradient, and about sixty yards down, a figure was walking away along the opposite pavement. A figure in dark clothes, with a hood pulled up. Lynda strode in pursuit, not crossing the road. She passed a signpost telling her that she was on Hobart Way, and called CAD.

'That's on the northern outskirts of the village,' Willit said. 'Any indication where the suspect's headed?'

'Dunno,' she replied quietly. 'He could have a car round here. That's my concern.'

'You're still not confronting him on your own.'

'You don't need to keep telling me that, Tom. I saw what this bastard did to Nick Scotzini. But it would help if I had some support.'

'Units are en route. Closest is three minutes away.'

She cut the call.

At the bottom of the hill, Hobart Way intersected with another road, Carling Lane, though there were only one or two houses on this one, both on the right. On the left, an open gateway led through onto the flat, snowy expanse of a playing field. The hooded figure was already halfway across it. Lynda didn't go straight after him but ducked behind the hedge, watching him through its leafless twigs. A belt of trees occupied the far side of the playing field, and the figure was approaching it. She chewed her lip. If he vanished into that, she'd lose him. She was going to have to go after him, which meant that she too would be out in the open and very visible if he happened to glance back. But what choice was there?

She rounded onto the playing field and set off across it as quickly as possible without actually running. The solitary shape ahead still didn't look round. He reached the outer wall of trees but turned right and walked along the front of them. Lynda hugged the left side of the field, scurrying faster and faster. Her target was now approaching the wood's distant edge, where it ended at what looked like ploughland. He turned the corner and disappeared.

She broke into a run. When she reached the treeline, she kept on running. The ground was firm despite the thin snow, enabling good footing, but she was feeling the effort, the heart thudding in her chest as she approached the corner of the wood. She slowed down and cut through the trees, which at this point were widely spread, finding herself on a well-trampled footpath heading north between the wood and the ploughed field.

The figure was again some seventy yards ahead, climbing

through a stile. Still, he didn't look back. Once over the stile, he diminished from view as if descending a slope. Lynda called Tom Willit as she ran, doing her best to explain where she was.

'I think I know where he'll come out,' Willit said. 'Woodcock Road's on slightly lower ground than Milton's Wood and the Carling Lane playing fields...'

'Fine, Tom... just get someone there.'

'Trouble is, Lynda, they're all now on Hobart Way, wondering where you are.'

'Get them *here*.'

She reached the stile. It was a ladder ascending several rungs to a cleft in a dry-stone wall and then descending on the other side. Breathless, she clambered up.

Beyond it, frosty grass swept downhill to a narrow country lane – Woodcock Road, she presumed. There, a timber footbridge lay across the River Stour, its surface partly sheathed with ice. Her quarry had already crossed and was halfway up another path, which led through a clutch of bare trees towards the outline of a church.

Lynda jumped down the other side of the stile, descending the slope, and raced across the road and bridge. The path up to the church was stony and slippery, but she only halted when she'd passed between the trees and was confronted by the church itself.

From a distance, it had looked typical of the many English country churches that dotted this pastoral landscape. But this one was mossy and dingy, its central arched window filled with plywood. Alongside the path stood a noticeboard, but it had warped and twisted with age, the gold-leaf lettering on the front no longer readable.

She continued forward until she spotted her prey again.

He was still walking away, this time along the east side of the church, vanishing around its next corner. Lynda called CAD as she stumbled in pursuit.

'Just stand by, yeah?' Willit said. 'Support units are only three minutes away.'

'Three minutes is a long time, Tom,' she panted. 'I haven't got eyes on him, and he's a murder suspect. How's it going to look if I lose him?'

'You have a duty to yourself and your family ...'

'I also have a duty to the public.' She hurried forward.

The decayed edifice of the church loomed on the left as she followed the path. Already she was among tombstones, most just leaning, eroded shapes in straggling, snow-covered grass. On the other side of the church, it was more of the same.

A lot more.

Literally a forest of headstones and obelisks.

And suddenly, nothing moved out there.

Lynda halted. He could easily be close by, a dark upright figure, but she wouldn't notice him among so many others. Eyes straining, she focused on two shapes in particular. One, about thirty yards in front of her, turned out to be a stone angel. The other, which was further back, she had to scrutinise more carefully, but it gradually resolved itself into a stone plant pot atop a plinth. Both wore coats of snow, which had made it more difficult to identify them. In fact, the graveyard was more deeply blanketed than any of the roads and gardens she'd seen that day, because as no one ever came here now, the snow of mid/late December had not been trampled away, meaning that last night's fall had settled on top of it.

Which worked out well, because when Lynda looked

down, she saw footprints trailing away, curving along a path between the sepulchres.

She followed, her breath smoking white.

Other paths diverted off at regular intervals, but the footprints always led on – until abruptly, they turned right along a narrow side path. Lynda halted again. To the left of the side path stood what looked like a mausoleum: a small, roofed building built from heavy black stone. Before she even got there, she saw that the footprints turned into it. She followed them warily. The trail led through the front entrance, a shelf of snow hanging over an arch of engraved Latin characters, and below that a doorway, though there was no door, just a barred gate hanging open.

Behind the gate, a steep flight of steps descended into a lower vault, the narrow dimensions of which she could only just identify because, though light seeped down into it through at least one more aperture, possibly an entrance on the other side, it looked horribly cramped.

With a soft *crunch*, a foot trod behind her.

She stiffened. There *was* another entrance, and her quarry had come back out through it. Before she could turn, a blow struck the back of her neck. The world cavorted as she sagged to her knees and fell face-first. She wasn't entirely knocked out, but initially was so stunned that she had no clue where she was. All she knew was that someone had grabbed her by one of her ankles. Only when she was hauled around in a circle, slush slithering into her clothes, did a sense of helpless fear flood through her.

'N ... no,' she muttered, clawing out.

Her fingers scrabbled through snow and gravel, and then an iron gate creaked, and she was being lugged down into the depths, one tread after another striking the back of her skull. When this finished, she was on flat ground in stagnant darkness: the vault, she realised – a tight, claustrophobic hole that had never been intended for the living. Her vision adjusted, but she could only sense her captor's dark outline as he stood over her. She tried to move, but the messages transferred to her limbs were dull and sluggish.

Then there was a grating of stonework. Lynda heard the guy grunt as he pushed at something. It grated again, after which he turned, leaned down and rummaged through her pockets, eventually taking something away. Her phone. He slipped it into his own pocket, and then slid his arms underneath her. She tried to struggle, tried to hit him. Again, it was useless. With a single, muscular effort, he heaved her up and over his shoulder, before pivoting around and lowering her again. But not onto the floor... into a box.

A stone box, Lynda realised. On top of a dais.

A sarcophagus.

A new horror speared through her.

She sensed the solid stone walls on either side of her. Then he pushed her backward onto a bed of mould and filth. Broken fragments stabbed into her, reminding her that someone else had lain here once. It was only when she heard that grating sound again, and saw that monstrous black lid sliding over the top of her, that she was jolted into motion. She thrust her gloved hands upward, but the last sliver of light winked out, and two inches above her face they encountered unyielding stone.

Lynda screamed.

She'd been in here less than a second, but already the air was turning stuffy. Sweat broke out all over her body. When she tried to turn over, the confines of her prison were too tight. Terrified, she scrabbled at her anorak pocket before remembering that it was empty.

'Oh my God,' she choked.

No one knew she was here. No one ever came to this place. No one would find her.

'*Ohhh my God!*'

Adrenaline pumped through her as she braced her back against the foulness underneath and pushed forward flat-handed on the underside of the lid.

It didn't budge. And why would it – it was a granite slab, inches thick.

She screamed again in the opaque blackness. Wildly, hysterically.

And suddenly, there was another sound.

At first Lynda thought she'd imagined it. But then she heard it again: another voice, muffled. She couldn't tell what it was saying, but it wasn't the guy who'd put her here because it sounded concerned.

'Where are you?' it called. 'Sergeant Hagen – where are you?'

'In here!' she shrieked, lungs almost bursting.

She banged on the lid, turning part-way over, trying to ram it upward with her shoulder. Throwing herself at it again and again, until at last it began to shift, though mainly, it transpired, because someone on the other side was assisting. The grating sound was wonderful, light falling over her, fresh air pouring in.

'Yes, yes,' she panted, applying her hands to the lid's edge, which another pair of hands already gripped and were hauling backward.

A wedge-shaped gap appeared, and she squirmed out through it, wriggling free like a squirrel, before dropping over the coffin rim and falling to the ground, back and shoulders heaving as she lay nose to the dirt.

'Christ!' a voice gasped. 'I saw you at the far side of the playing field. You were miles off, though. I kept calling but you didn't hear.'

Lynda glanced up, still wringing with sweat.

He was a young cop, no more than twenty-one, wearing the divisional kit of the Suffolk Constabulary. He looked ashen in the half-light.

'I left the car on Carling Lane, had to follow you on foot,' he stammered. 'You were so far ahead I couldn't get your attention ... thank God I kept going. I saw you come into this graveyard, saw him drag you underground ...'

Lynda could barely speak. Partly because a new sense of terror now gripped her.

'Where is he?' she hissed. 'In God's name, where did he go?'

The question caught the young officer off guard but was answered in short order as a hooded shape stepped out of the shadows behind him. Two karate blows fell, and the lad dropped, a puppet with its strings cut. Lynda cowered away, expecting a barrage of blows to rain down on her as well. But, to her surprise, it never came. Instead, she heard a heavy thudding of feet as he vacated the vault by the nearest of its two stairways.

Immediately, she understood why. More sounds of the upper world were reaching her: gruff male voices shouting, the crackle of static on police radios.

'We're down here,' she cried, scampering over to where the young cop lay, checking his carotid artery. He was alive but unconscious. 'We've got a casualty down here!' She got up dazedly. 'Officer needs medical assistance ...'

She swayed to the top of a stairway, tottering out into the bright, cold daylight, and making her way to the main path as though drunk. As she reached it, she saw a figure running towards her, heavy feet clumping.

It was *him*, the guy in the black hoodie top. He'd been trying to flee the graveyard, only to find several police officers barring his path. They were close behind him, but damn it, they weren't getting *this* collar – not after everything Lynda had just been through.

She launched herself as he passed, a full-on dive, grappling with his legs, wrapping her arms around them just like they did in rugby matches on the telly. The fugitive went sprawling, face-planting on the path, the wind rushing out of him.

'Got you, you bastard!' Lynda crawled over him, grabbing one of his arms and twisting it behind his back.

He was rock-solid with muscle, but half a second later male colleagues were around her, equally brawny, equally brutal, descending on him knees-first, applying the handcuffs as roughly as they liked.

Lynda yanked his hood back and saw, as she'd suspected, the same guy from the hospital who'd identified himself as Nick Scotzini, only now his face was strained and dirty and he was bleeding from a cut over his left eye.

She patted him down, pulling her phone from his pocket and finding a wallet. She stepped back as they lugged him to his feet, flipping through his documents. They contained various forms of ID, often with different names attached, and photographs, most of which only partly resembled the sweaty, bloodstained mug in front of her, though on further scrutiny, she saw the similarities. He was a bit of a chameleon, this character, and he'd affected a particularly big change to make himself look like Scotzini.

'I don't know what your game is,' she told him. 'But you're under arrest on suspicion of murder. You don't have to say anything, but it may harm your defence if you do not mention when questioned something you later rely on in court. Anything you do say may be given in evidence … you little shit!'

43

9 January (Thursday)

When Clive Atkins arrived at the hospital, he was still dazed. How they'd gone from an unexplained road accident to guns, gangsters and now a home-invasion homicide, he couldn't quite fathom.

He crossed the car park to the Billington Ward. It was only midday, so the waiting area was empty when he passed through. A nurse he didn't know occupied the nursing station; he identified himself and showed his warrant card.

'We were told we couldn't disturb Mr Wade until this afternoon at the earliest,' he said. 'But seeing as it's now lunchtime, perhaps I can go through?'

She indicated the side corridor. 'You know the way, I'm guessing.'

He didn't intend to interview the patient yet. Whatever Lynda said, and whether or not Mr Jaishankar's isolation order had expired, DSU Kepler had not yet rescinded his own instructions. And at present, he was out somewhere with his team, and couldn't be consulted. But at least Clive would be here, ready to jump in.

He flashed his warrant card to the firearms officer on the bedroom door, which stood open. Inside, the bed was empty but a nurse, gloved up, was bundling blood-stained bandages into a plastic sack. It was Zara Abimbola, whom he'd met before. She recognised him and smiled.

'I understand we can speak to our patient at last?' he said.

'I've just changed his dressings and he's gone to the loo.' She nodded to a door with a red light over the top. 'He's much improved. You shouldn't have a problem.'

As she bustled out, Clive's phone rang. He saw Lynda's number and moved back down the passage to take it.

Lynda didn't bother with a preamble. 'Where are you?'

'Billington Ward.'

'What's Wade had to say for himself?'

'Nothing yet. He's taking a leak.'

'Clive!' She sounded exasperated. 'We need to know what this guy's been up to.'

'Relax. I'm standing outside his room. But I'm not going in there till Kepler says it's okay.'

She sighed. 'Where is Kepler?'

'Dunno. I've left him a message.'

'What about Rachel?'

'She says we have to go through him, but I think she's on her way down here. Where are you, anyway?'

'A&E.'

'You okay?'

'It's not me. It's the suspect. He clouted his head on the floor when I was locking him up. Now he's claiming he's dizzy and can't see properly.'

'Shit.'

'It's an act, Clive. For whatever reason, he's trying to buy time. Anyway, it doesn't matter. The main thing is we've got him. As soon as he's been checked by one of the doctors, he's going to Colchester nick. At that point, I'll come over and join you, just to see what this Wade fella's excuses are like.'

Clive wasn't comfortable with that. 'Kepler...'

'Kepler can get his arse down here or miss out on the fun.'

'So long as it's you who tells him that, and not me. Does our suspect have a name?'

'Several, as I understand,' she said. 'But we've run his prints now, and the info coming back to us is that he's Raymond Lonnegan. From Manchester originally. Ex-special forces. He's got a good sheet, though. Juicy stuff and lots of it.'

'This is our guy then?'

'This is our guy, there's nothing surer. Keep Wade on ice for me.'

The call ended and Clive turned back towards the private room. As he passed its narrow letterbox window, the bed was still empty, which seemed odd. When he rounded the corner, the firearms officer on the door yawned and rubbed at his jaw.

'He still having a piss?' Clive asked.

The shot looked surprised. 'Sorry... what?'

'Wade.' Clive pushed the door open and indicated that there was no one in the room.

The shot seemed puzzled, but then focused on the red light. 'Looks like it.'

'Bloody long piss.' Clive entered the room, moving to the door and listening. There was no sound on the other side.

'Everything okay?' a voice intruded.

Nurse Abimbola had come back in, carrying a tray with a cup on it, containing what looked like pills.

'Our friend's still in here.'

'Still?' Placing the tray on a sideboard, she crossed the room and knocked. 'Mr Wade... you okay in there?' She knocked again. 'Mr Wade?'

There was no reply.

'This area's secure, isn't it?' Clive said. 'I mean, there's no other way in?'

'There's a fire door accessible from inside the toilet,' Abimbola said.

'In *there*?'

'Basic fire regulations.'

'Bloody hell!' Clive knocked on the door again, full-fisted.

'You can't open the fire door from outside,' the nurse said. 'No one can get in that way.'

'No, but they can get *out*.'

Her mouth dropped open as it dawned on her what this might mean.

'Is there an override for this lock?' Clive asked.

Abimbola dug into her smock and pulled out a plastic keyring with several magnetic cards attached. She selected one and pressed it to a control panel alongside the door, which clicked open.

'Mr Wade?' she said, entering and stopping dead.

The bathroom was empty, but the fire door stood open. Clive pushed through and stepped outside into an annexe to one of the hospital's staff-parking areas. There were a few vehicles around, but there was no sign of anyone on foot. The only movement came from the snowflakes spiralling down. He went back inside. 'Shouldn't this door be alarmed?'

'Yes,' she said, 'but look.'

He glanced up, to where an insulated cable running up the doorjamb to a borehole in the ceiling had been cleanly severed.

44

9 January (Thursday)

'Lynda!' Kepler said. 'What is it you don't understand about me being new SIO on this enquiry?'

Lynda had taken the call out in the hospital car park, where fresh snow was now falling.

'There's nothing I don't understand about it, sir.'

'In which case, can you explain why this morning alone you've now disobeyed me twice? First of all, failing to turn up at a briefing that I explicitly requested you attend. And secondly, going down to Colchester General and getting involved with our two casualties.'

'Sir, come on,' she said. 'Things have moved on a bit since yesterday.'

'Yes, and they've moved on without me knowing much about it.'

She could understand why he was miffed. He'd come into this thing direct from the Organised Crime Division at Scotland Yard, all puffed up and preening himself, only to find the rug ripped from under his feet on his first morning. He'd no sooner installed himself at his new desk than the case had been solved by a bunch of woodentops.

'Sorry I didn't have time to copy you in, sir,' she said. 'I didn't even have a radio with me, but I got a sniff of something and I *had* to go for it. Isn't that the proper way?'

There was a long silence.

'I'll tell you what,' he eventually replied. 'We'll discuss any disciplinary matters that may spin off from this later. But we *will* discuss them, trust me. Now, what's the situation with the prisoner?'

'Mild concussion and a cut on his eyebrow. Nothing serious. Didn't require anything other than superficial treatment.'

'What's your first impression of him?'

Lynda thought about it. Other than to proclaim that he felt ill and didn't know where he was, which hadn't fooled the Casualty staff, who'd despatched him back into police custody with an Elastoplast on his eyebrow, Ray Lonnegan had said nothing else, neither confirming nor denying his identity and refusing to offer an explanation for why he was running from the crime scene. He hadn't resisted when, three minutes ago, they'd bundled him into the back of a police vehicle and driven him out of the hospital car park. It was a Traffic car rather than an official prisoner transport, one officer to drive, one in the backseat with the suspect, which hadn't been ideal, but all the transport vans had been otherwise engaged, and Lynda hadn't wanted Lonnegan at the hospital any longer than was necessary.

'He's compliant now,' she said. 'But I'm not totally buying it.'

'How so?'

'Well, we've already done a bit of digging on his past, and I got some preliminary results texted to me just now. Quite a background, Lonnegan's got. Ex-squaddie. Five years with the Parachute Regiment, three in Pathfinder Squadron ... that's like an elite search–and–destroy unit. Saw action in Afghanistan and Iraq and was decorated with the

Conspicuous Gallantry Cross during Operation Shader. Made two attempts to join the Special Air Service. Failed on both occasions, though only because of his psyche evaluation. The shrink concluded that he was an effective combat soldier, well suited to the stresses and rigours of close-quarter battle, but that when it came to more subtle matters, he, quote, "lacked judgement". It's perhaps no surprise that since then he's been working enforcement for various low-level crime syndicates. I've been sent a couple of pix from the database. His most recent look on Civvie Street was a beard and straggly dark hair. He obviously changed all that in his efforts to impersonate this poor guy, Nick Scotzini, I suspect so that he could get closer to Elliot Wade. He's no ordinary hoodlum, that's for sure.'

Kepler pondered that.

'How's the crime scene?' she asked.

'I'm down there now with Suffolk CID. Their lab rats are due here any time. Just for your interest, it was a gunshot that killed Scotzini.'

That surprised her. 'I didn't see anything that looked like a bullet wound.'

'That's because he was shot in the back.'

'Execution?'

'Hard to say. We'll know more shortly. I assume Lonnegan's on his way to the custody suite at Colchester?'

'That's correct.'

'Good. I'll meet you there in half an hour.'

Lynda walked towards the recovery wards. 'Any chance I can have a bit longer, sir? I'd like to interview Elliot Wade. I know you wanted to speak to some informants first, but the whole thing's happening now, and the longer we give him, the longer he's got to make up stories. He's already feigned unconsciousness a couple of times to try and keep us at arm's length. He especially didn't want to talk to Nick Scotzini. In my opinion, he'd pegged him for this Lonnegan character straight away. And that could give us an opening.'

'I don't want him arresting yet. Or cautioning.'

'I'm with you there, sir.'

'Okay. It's now twelve minutes past one. I'll see you at Colchester at half past two.'

Kepler cut the call. Lynda slipped the phone back into her pocket, only for another voice to assail her. She turned and saw Clive huddling through the increasingly heavy snowfall.

'Lynda ... *Lynda!*'

Lynda was still covered with filth and grave-dirt, her left knee visibly bandaged through a hole ripped in her slacks – and yet Clive didn't even notice.

'Wade's gone,' he stammered.

'*What?*'

He blurted out everything that had happened.

'Wasn't the bloody fire door alarmed?' she said.

'Yeah, but he bypassed it using a surgical scalpel. This guy's a special case, isn't he?'

'Gee, do you think? First thing, we need to double the guard on the woman ...'

'She's gone too!'

Lynda skidded to a halt, hitting him with a look of total disbelief. 'She's seriously ill!'

'I went over there soon as I saw that Wade was missing. She's gone.'

Lynda swung around and ran. When they arrived at the internal door to Neurological IC, it was so chaotic on the other side, staff members darting back and forth, that it was several seconds before anybody buzzed them through, and then Lynda only needed to glance into the room where Harriet Wade was being treated to see the bed skew-whiff and a pillow on the floor, the cables and tubes hanging loose.

45

9 January (Thursday)

Traffic officers were well trained to drive in snow. The trouble was that no one else was.

It was just under three miles from Colchester General Hospital to Colchester Police Station, and the vehicle in which Ray Lonnegan was being transported, a standard Essex Roads Policing Volvo V70 with a bar of blue lights across its roof, would normally have had no problem making the journey. Unfortunately, there were lots of other road users about, and as the snow was still falling, they were driving ultra-cautiously, which gradually created a gridlock. In next to no time, no one was getting anywhere – and the snow was still coming down in a feathery cascade. The Volvo's windscreen wipers thudded frantically.

'Think we could use some of this global warming I keep hearing about,' Ray Lonnegan commented from the back seat.

'Shut up,' retorted PC Tim Philbin, the big, bespectacled Traffic officer seated next to him.

Lonnegan, who was dirty and bedraggled, with a plaster on his left eyebrow and streaks of blood down that side of his face, smiled to himself. His hands were cuffed behind his back, but he seemed amused.

'You think it's funny?' Philbin said. 'What you did to those two police officers?'

'Didn't do anything to anyone.'

'And that won't cut it either. Denying the bare-faced obvious tends not to work when you're dealing with intelligent people. But dickheads like you never seem to learn that!'

'Tim!' Gina Tubbs warned from behind the Volvo's wheel.

'Twenty years ago, you'd have been made to run a fucking gauntlet for what you did back there. If Larry Pupper turns out to be badly hurt, you still may.'

'Tim – give it a rest!'

Philbin had been three years in Traffic, but only six years in the job overall, and so was still inexperienced enough to get angry in tense situations. In contrast, Tubbs, a fourteen-year vet, was jumpier about the fact they had a well-connected offender in their midst. And now, of course, they had the blessed snow to contend with.

With a screech and *clunk*, the two vehicles in front – a red Toyota Yaris and a blue Nissan Micra – shunted together. Tubbs watched, exasperated, as the two drivers got out. The one in front was a guy in his late twenties with a mop of carroty red hair, wearing a waistcoat over his shirt and tie, while the one behind was a young woman in a Parka. Heated words were exchanged in the middle of the road, and then the carrot-top spotted the police car. He pointed, and the twosome sidled around their vehicles.

Tubbs powered her window down.

'Did you see what happened?' the guy asked, leaning in, shivering. His orange wire-wool hair was rapidly filling with snowflakes.

'Yes,' Tubbs replied. 'But I can't deal with this now. I'm otherwise engaged.'

'She ran straight into the back of me. Doesn't that mean it's her fault?'

'Are either of you two hurt?'

They shrugged.

'Exchange your contact details, okay?' Tubbs said. 'Let your insurance companies sort it out. And you need to move these vehicles. I'm sure they're both still drivable.'

Disgruntled but ready to comply, as horns were tooting to the rear, they returned to their cars.

Relieved, Tubbs drove on. But it was laborious going, heavy snow blanketing the vehicles and the road surface and the hooded pedestrians hurrying along either pavement. She could have activated her beacons, but what difference would it have made? It wasn't the volume of traffic; it was the weather.

'Isn't that a dereliction of duty?' Lonnegan asked.

Tubbs didn't dignify him with a response.

'Those people wanted help and you didn't give it,' he persisted. 'Are modern coppers not able to do two things at once, then?'

'You think you're one of these clever little shit-rags, don't you?' Philbin said. 'Think you're going to push us into giving you a good hiding? Is that how you expect to walk?'

'Tim!' Tubbs warned him.

'In the old days, they'd leather you because there'd be no consequence. These days, the job's run by virtue-signalling bastards who are more concerned about how they look to the politicians than in fighting crime. Doesn't mean we don't *want* to do it, though. So, I'd watch my mouth, if I was ...'

'*This'll do us!*' Tubbs interrupted, happier.

A helmeted constable, wearing a hi-vis slicker, had

emerged from the swirling flakes on the left-hand pavement. He waved and shone a torch to catch their attention.

Tubbs steered to the kerb. The constable retreated along the pavement, giving hand signals to show that they should go left. She spied a double-sized gap between two shopfronts, where a gate had been opened. If memory served, this passage connected with a maze of minor service roads behind the shops. The constable had now backed to the other side of it, but continually swung his torch to indicate that they should enter.

She swung the Volvo left, travelling thirty yards along a roofed passage, before coming out into an alleyway, along which they could only go right. Sheer brick walls reared up on either side, and snow was now hammering down, almost rendering the windscreen wipers ineffective. Tubbs slowed again. But then, about fifty yards on, saw the twinkle of a revolving blue light. Encouraged, she got her foot down.

The blue light winked out.

Confused, she braked. They skated for yards before stopping.

Just in time, in fact, as a few feet in front of them, a vehicle materialised from the left. A heavy vehicle, a wagon, reversing into their path with such speed that its wheels also locked, its rear bumper striking the brick wall on the right.

Tubbs reached for her radio, only for the window alongside her to explode inward. She squawked, shielding her eyes and face, and freezing rigid as the muzzle of a pistol was pressed into her cheek. Philbin struggled to get to his own radio, when *his* window detonated too, a gun barrel jamming itself into his left ear.

'Get out!' they were told. 'Hands where we can see them!'

The person who hauled Gina Tubbs out into the snow

was considerably taller and broader than she was. He wore a black leather jacket over a black sweat-top, while a black knitted balaclava covered his face except for his eyes. He turned her roughly around, took her own cuffs from her pouch and locked her hands together behind her back. When he kicked her legs from under her, she fell face-down. On the other side of the Volvo, it was the same with Philbin.

Wild thoughts assailed the male cop as he was pressed against the side of the car, a sibilant voice hissing orders. A gloved hand attempted to twist his left arm behind his back, no doubt to try and pinion him with his own cuffs – at which point the prisoner, the precious prisoner, would be gone, and he and Gina Tubbs would be laughed at for the rest of their careers.

Philbin thrust his heavy form backward, barrelling his captor against the nearest wall, body-slamming him into it. The would-be abductor grunted, his hand spasming open and his pistol going flying. Philbin threw himself back again and again, crushing the bastard even as he stood upright, slamming a meaty elbow around, crunching it against the ski-masked head – and then taking a shudder-inducing blow in his own groin. A cannonball of nausea exploded in his abdomen. He gagged and tottered, his glasses slipping halfway down his nose. When he looked up, it was into the grinning face of Ray Lonnegan, who'd slipped out of the police car, and though his hands were still fastened behind his back, had proved useful with his right knee. Philbin's legs buckled and he sagged to the ground, but not before Lonnegan swung his knee up again, smashing it into his face, breaking his glasses, flattening his nose to pulp. The next thing Tim Philbin knew, he too was face-down, the snow in front of his dazed eyes turning red.

'If it's any consolation,' a voice said into his ear, 'you were right and all them modern coppers were wrong. You *should* have given me a kicking… it would have saved you getting one.'

46

9 January (Thursday)

'I don't bloody believe this!' Lynda said. 'How can someone just walk a critical care patient out of hospital without being challenged?'

She and Clive were in the hospital security office, in the company of Security Chief Sophie Hallorhan, a short, squat woman with iron-grey hair and black epaulettes on the shoulders of her white shirt. One of Hallorhan's underlings, a young Asian guy, whose breast-pocket tab said that he was Ranveer Rana, was seated in front of several screens, his fingers bouncing across a keyboard as he attempted to enhance various black and white images.

They'd already singled out one snippet of footage. It depicted Elliot Wade leaving the Neurosciences Building by a rear door, pushing a figure swaddled in blankets in a wheelchair, and carrying an intravenous drip feed over his shoulder. He'd removed his neck brace and the bandage around his head, and was wearing hospital scrubs, along with a pair of white trainers and a white coat. The back of his head was still shaved and covered with a large plaster, but he could, at a casual glance, have been taken for a member of staff. In any case, the snow had just started falling. Anyone else out there would have had other things on their minds.

Lynda and Clive watched carefully, but though the footage

illustrated how Wade had left the hospital buildings, it didn't show where he'd gone to from there, because he pushed the wheelchair out of frame. They scanned via other cameras, rolling the footage back and forth to try and close in on the time period between 12.45 and 13.15.

The search was fruitless.

'We've tried all the main entrances and exits,' Hallorhan said. 'Is it possible he could have stayed in the hospital grounds?'

'I can't see what bloody sense there'd be in that,' Lynda replied tersely.

Clive mouthed an apology. Hallorhan nodded in acknow-ledgement. She too had noted DS Hagen's flustered and bedraggled state.

'There's a trade entrance at the back of the hospital,' Rana said. 'It's not open to the public. We bring in supplies that way and send out items for disposal.'

'Let's have a look,' Lynda said. 'Let's stop messing around!'

'Lynda,' Clive whispered.

'I'm sorry, guys!' She scrubbed a hand through her matted hair. 'But I can't tell you how serious this is.'

Rana's fingers danced across the keys, images flickering by on the screens, interiors as well as exteriors: a garden with benches, a taxi rank, a covered area where ambulances had lined up.

'Come on, come on,' Lynda chuntered.

'Here,' Rana said.

The screen portrayed a boundary hedge with a slip road leading up to it, though this one was controlled by a striped barrier. Grassy areas lay to either side, fast disappearing under a mantle of snow. Rana hit another control and the footage ran backward, the snowfall easing, the ground cover dissipating, the barrier rising and falling as the occasional vehicle reversed in or out. He stopped it dead when the clock in the corner read 12.57, a familiar figure having laboured backward into view, dragging a shrouded form in a wheelchair.

'Damn it,' Lynda said. 'This was over half an hour ago.'

Rana ran the footage forward – the figure of Elliot Wade, who looked to be tiring, trudging behind the chair. The barrier didn't lift, but there was space for him to get around it, which he duly did, turning right onto the pavement. At that moment, a vehicle passed the gateway from left to right, clearly braking. Unfortunately, when it stopped, it was out of sight behind the hedge, but Wade reacted to it, kicking the wheelchair's brakes into action, and then, though it was a struggle for him, lifting both the bundled shape and the drip, and carrying them around the corner.

'Someone picked them up?' Lynda said. 'What road is that?'

'Turner Road,' Hallorhan replied.

Lynda glanced at her. 'That's residential, isn't it?'

'Mainly.'

'So, at least we can do a door-to-door.'

Rana ran the footage back and forth, but whatever car it was, it remained a grey blob.

'I think there's a bus stop on Turner Road,' Clive said. 'Not too far from that exit. It's possible there'll be a local authority camera covering it. If there is, we might get a VRN.'

Before he could say more, his mobile rang. He stepped out of the office to deal with it. Lynda turned back to Rana. 'Can you run that film one more time, Ranveer? See if you can do it in slo-mo.'

Rana complied, but it was the same result.

'Sod it,' Lynda snapped. She swung around to Clive, who now came stiffly back in. Immediately, she spotted his change of body language, 'What now?' she asked.

He shook his head in shock. 'You're not going to believe this. You are *not* going to bloody believe it!'

'How's Tim?' Gina Tubbs asked, still dabbing a red-blotted tissue at her nose, which had broken on contact with the snowy ground and been bleeding profusely ever since.

'He's having minor surgery,' Lynda said, 'but he'll be okay. How are *you* feeling?'

'I don't know.' Tubbs had blanched with shock, which was the main thing the nurse now bustling around in the A&E booth was treating her for. Fresh tears came into the Traffic sergeant's eyes. 'Jesus, Lynda, I thought we were going to be killed.'

'But you weren't. So, it could've been worse.'

'We lost the prisoner, though, didn't we?'

'Gina, having a gun in your face is the ultimate don't-argue. No one'll blame you.'

Tubbs sniffled. 'Are you going to take a statement? I might as well give you everything while it's fresh in the memory.'

'I don't think I'll be the one copping for that job. I suspect Organised Crime will take over now. Officially they're already in charge.'

'I'm sorry, Lynda. Everything you went through ... grabbing hold of the bastard, getting stuck in that box. *You're* lucky to be alive as well.'

Lynda glanced around at the sound of male voices. Two men with dark suits and serious faces had come in, and stood in conflab with DI Hollindrake, who'd also just arrived.

'In fact,' Lynda said, 'I believe they're here now.'

'Lynda!' Hollindrake crossed the room. 'I need to speak to you. You all right, Sergeant Tubbs?'

'As well as can be expected, thank you, ma'am.'

Hollindrake acknowledged that with a curt nod, and then stepped away, beckoning Lynda with a long index finger. Lynda followed her into an adjoining passage, at which point the DI confronted her with a face of fury.

'What the devil do you think you're playing at?'

Even though she'd been expecting a reprimand, Lynda was surprised. 'Excuse me?'

'Look at the state of you.' Hollindrake indicated her grubby sweater and anorak, her torn, blood-stained slacks. 'You're seriously on duty in that condition?'

Lynda bristled. 'Rachel, everything's been happening at a hundred miles an hour. You're saying I should have toddled off home to get changed?'

'You could have freshened up a little.'

'I couldn't just abandon the fort. Someone had to try and hold this thing together.'

'You couldn't even wash your hands and face?'

'Rachel, you *do* understand what's happened? Apart from the attack on the prisoner transport, we've got another serious offence here in the hospital. Harriet Wade had no capacity to consent to withdrawal of medical treatment. So, we're now looking at a kidnapping.'

'I'm well aware of the seriousness of the situation, sergeant. But for that reason alone, you need to be on top of your game and from what I'm hearing, and now seeing, you clearly aren't. For God's sake, you put Lonnegan in a Traffic car, not a secure transport...'

'They'd still have bushwhacked it. Every time guns appear, we lose — you *know* that.'

'Look ...' The DI made an effort to calm herself. 'You did a good job this morning, even if you flouted the direct orders of a senior supervisor. But it's also the case that you were nearly killed, and as a result of that now seem to be running around this hospital like some wild-eyed Stig of the Dump. Am I not supposed to question your judgement?'

Lynda understood this thinking. She also understood that it would make things worse if she continued to argue. All along it had been Hollindrake's concern that she was too inexperienced to handle so demanding a case. Blindly insisting that she should be allowed to carry on, when she patently needed a rest, would confirm those suspicions.

'Where's Clive Atkins?' Hollindrake asked.

'Collecting footage from a local authority camera covering a bus stop on the east side of the hospital. A vehicle stopped there, and we're pretty sure the Wades got into it. With any luck, the camera will show us a VRN.'

'Okay.' Hollindrake nodded. 'That sounds like a plan.'

Lynda shrugged, sheepish now that tempers were cooling. 'I was supposed to be meeting Kepler with the prisoner, but that's obviously off. So I'll head to the office and get my paperwork in. Don't worry, I'll go home and have a shower first.'

'You can go home, have a shower and spend the rest of the day with your family.'

'But—'

'You need to get yourself together. And that's not going to happen in the middle of all this.'

'Rachel, I'm not off-duty for another three hours.'

'I don't care. Go now while no one's looking. I'll fix the roster.'

Lynda turned despondently away. Only to swing back. 'One question. When I come in tomorrow, what am I going to find? Me and Clive back on routine enquiries?'

Hollindrake sighed. 'Lynda, do you seriously think you can make the running on this? We've got one murder and at least three attempted murders, we've got clear links to high-level criminality, and a professional assassin on the loose. Don't you think we're just a little bit out of our league? And when I say "we", I mean me as well. In contrast, Andy Kepler handles enquiries like this all the time.'

'Can't we be part of it?' Lynda pleaded. '*We* started this ball rolling, and I was the one who collared that bastard, Lonnegan – no one else did.'

'That decision will be taken above my head. But if I'm asked, I'm going to make a case for "no" because I need you and Clive doing your actual jobs. By this time tomorrow, we'll have another RTC in the vicinity that's going to need more than roadside scrutiny. I'm sorry, Lynda – I know it won't be as exciting as all this. But real life goes on. Now go home, get cleaned up and have a nice evening with your kids. Back in tomorrow as normal for what's certain to be a full diary.'

And a deskload of boring crap, Lynda said to herself, trudging out.

As she headed home, her mood was not helped by the excess of cars on the road and the difficult driving conditions, though at least the snowfall was easing. She still had a radio; Clive had checked one out for her that morning and given it to her in the hospital. Officially, she ought to have returned it to the office, but that would have been a lot of trouble when she could do it the following day. In addition, it gave her a chance to keep tabs on the enquiry, though she was too disconsolate to pay it more than passing attention. She was back in Manningtree before she caught something that made her sit up.

A description had been issued for Gina Tubbs' assailant.

'*IC1 male, wearing dark clothing and a ski mask*,' the CAD operator said as Lynda pulled into Westcombe Close.

'*No facial description possible, but approx six foot four inches tall. Strong, athletic build. Spoke with a local accent. One distinguishing feature ... subject had a small, X-shaped scar on the right side of his neck. All units received?*'

An X-shaped scar.

It took several seconds for that to sink in.

A vehicle Lynda didn't recognise, a maroon Jaguar, was parked outside her house, but initially she was too distracted to pay it attention. There might be lots of men in the world with X-shaped scars on their necks. But there was only one Lynda knew.

She switched the radio off and walked up the drive.

Terry Sullivan had been a good mate of Don's back in Major Investigations, as Don was always boasting. He'd even boasted how Sullivan had been a big guy, six foot four, and how that day at Tilbury, a Stanley knife had left an X-like scar on his neck.

She'd normally have considered it a coincidence – if that had been the whole of the story. But it wasn't. Because, after he left the Major Investigation Team, Terry Sullivan had transferred to the National Crime Group at Scotland Yard. In particular, the Organised Crime Division.

She was still so lost in these thoughts that she'd walked straight through into the living room without even popping into the downstairs lavatory to wash her hands and face. It wasn't a smart move; if the kids had been in the lounge, they might have been upset to see their mother in a dishevelled state. But as it was, they weren't.

Don was looking smarter than usual in plaid shirt and jeans. He got up from the sofa with what looked like a large whiskey in hand. But he wasn't drunk and was smiling.

'Look who it is,' he said. 'Got yourself into a bit of a scrape, I understand?'

'How do you understand that?' she asked.

'Because we've got a guest. A mate of a mate has just popped in to say hello.'

Lynda realised that someone was sitting in the armchair with his back to her. He now stood up and turned. He too had a drink in hand.

Somehow it was no surprise to see Detective Superintendent Andy Kepler.

Of the Organised Crime Division.

47

9 January (Thursday)

'Hello, sir,' Lynda said. 'This is unexpected.'

Kepler smiled. 'You must've known I'd pop in to discuss mutual friends at some point?'

Lynda became aware of her torn, dirty clothes. 'Oh ... sorry. Tough shift, I'm afraid.'

'Don't worry about it,' Kepler said.

She glanced at Don, who seemed amused that she'd got into some roughhouse.

'Kids okay?' she asked.

He nodded. 'Sent them to play upstairs.'

'Okay. I'll just go and get cleaned up.'

She hurried upstairs into the en suite, where she stripped, sticking all her clothes into a plastic bag just in case there was a request from the SCIs at the Nick Scotzini murder scene, and then hopped into the shower. A few minutes later, she pulled on some old jeans and a sweat-top, popped in to say hello to the children and then headed back downstairs. She was halfway when she heard Kepler's voice through the open living room door.

'Things have changed a lot even since your day. This knife-crime thing is the big issue. Street gangs are now more involved in widescale distribution than ever before. They're all affiliated to different firms, and there are no peace treaties at street level.'

'Should be glad you're not still in, my love,' Lynda said, entering. 'Should be *very* glad.'

Don, back on the sofa, nodded sagely. 'I must admit it's easier writing about it than doing it. At least, it *would* be if I was earning a crust.'

Kepler broke off from his appraisal of Lynda. 'The writing career's not coming on then?'

Don sipped his scotch. 'Let's just say that when I started, I had a bit more to learn about the craft than I thought.'

Kepler mused. 'That applies to everything, doesn't it? But, I mean, if there's anything *I* can do ...'

Lynda moved to the drinks cabinet. 'National Crime Group has influence with the publishing world, has it? Wonders never cease.'

'You know the Yard, Lynda,' Kepler replied. 'Everyone knows someone who knows someone.'

'Hear that, love?' Don laughed. 'We wasted our time in Counties. We should have been in the smoke, where it's all happening.'

'Oh, you'd be amazed where it's happening, Don.' Lynda turned to Kepler, offering the bottle of Highland Park that Don had already treated him to. 'Top-up, sir?'

'Wouldn't say no.' He leaned forward. 'Now that we're both off duty.'

'You're off duty already?' She added a couple of fingers to his glass. 'After the way the case went nuclear this afternoon?'

'Call it a privilege of rank, then.' He grinned at Don. 'I'll be going back to the office after, but if I have a slight whiff about me, no one's going to query it.'

Don grinned. '*Some* things about the good old days haven't changed then, eh?'

Lynda gave him a wan smile. 'Once again, my love ... I think you'd be surprised how many things about the good old days haven't changed.'

Don frowned at her, and then at Kepler. 'I wasn't born yesterday, you know. All this cryptic stuff ... Is this something you can't discuss as long as I'm sitting here?'

Kepler shrugged. 'Not so much things you shouldn't hear, as things you wouldn't *want* to.'

'Intriguing.'

'But this is *your* house,' Kepler said, 'and your scotch, which is damn good, by the way. So, who am I to lay the law down?'

There was a sudden barrage of high-pitched voices from upstairs as the children commenced arguing about something. Don drained his glass and stood up. 'Seems like now's a good time for me to get up there and reacquaint Charlie with his castle.' He lumbered to the door, turning to Kepler before leaving. 'Just remember what you said, Mr Kepler ... this is *my* house and *my* scotch. If Lynda's due a bollocking for something, and *I* decide it's a bit too much, both can instantly be denied you.'

His wink only thinly veiled how serious he was.

'Don't worry,' Kepler said airily. 'No one's going to get a bollocking. And this won't take long anyway.'

As Don's heavy feet thumped upstairs, Lynda sat on the sofa's armrest.

'That was a big promise,' she said.

'What was?'

'That it won't take long. You think I'll be so easily won over?'

Kepler smiled again. 'Come on, Lynda, you've been married fourteen years to a poster-child for the way *real* police work sometimes needs to be done.'

'That's one way to admit that this afternoon your men illegally sprang a murder suspect out of Essex Police custody. And used violence in the process.'

Just to the back and side of his chair, next to the radiator, there was a small, leather-topped table. He placed his glass on it. 'Sadly, when in Rome you do as the Romans do.'

'You mean that when you want people to think you're gangsters, it's best if you act like them? So, in other words, Terry Sullivan was just pretending to be dumb when he failed to conceal his one distinguishing feature?'

'It's true,' Kepler admitted. 'Sully should've worn a rollneck sweater. Soon as that description got out, I knew we were going to have a problem.'

'"We" as in me and you?' she said.

He gave her a sad smile. 'Who else has had Terry Sullivan round for tea?'

'It was no pleasure, I can assure you.'

'None of this has been a pleasure, Lynda. But you have to look at the bigger picture. Do you want to know what the object of the gun attack on the A12 actually was?'

'You've worked it out already?'

'I knew before I arrived in Essex.'

'And I guess you were just dying to tell me?'

'Far from it, but when there's no actual choice . . .' He picked his whiskey up and sipped it. 'Have you heard of the Red Book?'

She shook her head.

He shook his too. 'Such a pity today had to happen. You guys really were miles off. For your info, the Red Book is an innocuous-looking volume that was inadvertently stolen during an armed robbery at Harwich.'

'That nasty one last Christmas Eve?' Lynda said. 'You've got the skinny on that too? That was heavy stuff!'

'Like I say, there's a bigger picture here. Much bigger.' He leaned forward. 'The Red Book – and I'm trusting you with sensitive intel here, so you'd better respect this – the Red Book contains a comprehensive list of all the official informants currently working with the Metropolitan Police.'

At first, Lynda didn't know how to respond. The concept alone was hard to grapple with.

'*All* of them?' she asked rather lamely.

He nodded. 'It was compiled by a bent officer somewhere in the hierarchy of the Met, providing an all-in-one database of info vital to the underworld. Obviously, it was in code, but it was also handwritten and scruffy rather than typed into a computer file, so that it could never easily be copied, which made it very valuable indeed. The bent cop responsible, who has never been caught, then acquired himself a huge retirement fund by selling it to the Corporation.'

'The Corporation?' she said. 'London's premier syndicate, or something to that effect?'

'In a nutshell, yes. Now, this lot are clever lads, and soon realised what they had. Being men of ambition and thinking they could make better use of it than crucifying a few grasses and setting them afloat off Execution Dock, they got in touch with *us*.'

'"Us" as in the Organised Crime Division?'

'Who else?'

'Like minds, eh?'

'The deal they offered was simple. None of those names on the list would be harmed, and the list itself would never be shown to anyone else ... in return for the Organised Crime Division going easy on all Corporation activities.'

'That would have been easy enough. That's what you do, anyway, isn't it?'

'Don't be a bitch, Lynda,' he said quietly. 'It's not just *your* future at stake here.'

'Oh yeah, you were going to help Don out. Pardon me if I snigger.'

'I *seriously* advise you not to.'

'Go on,' she said. 'Let's hear the rest.'

'The deal was that the data would be put in the safekeeping of one Jacques "Scissorman" Marat, the Corporation's grass-hunter in chief.'

'Sounds like quite a guy.'

'Just hope you never have to lock him up. But despite that, the data would never be used so long as the truce held.'

'The Corporation had Scotland Yard over a barrel, basically?'

'That's one way of looking at it.'

'You mean that's the *correct* way to look at it ... until the Red Book got stolen during the Harwich blag?'

Kepler shrugged. 'The truce was certainly threatened when the Red Book got lifted. But it sounds as if it was in the process of being delivered back when the incident on the A12 occurred.'

She arched a quizzical eyebrow. 'I can categorically assure you that no such book was found at the crash scene.'

'I know.' He shrugged again. 'And that's a mystery. The A12 gunman, who, as you've already twigged, is the same person who killed Nick Scotzini, is very keen to retrieve the book – and apparently, he hasn't succeeded yet.'

'Who is this lunatic, this Ray Lonnegan?'

'Exactly who you suspect. He's an ex-para turned enforcer for a small-time firm in Ipswich. Heard of the Naboths? A brother and sister outfit. Jim and Jo.'

'I know *of* them.'

'Most likely, they're the team that pulled the Harwich job.'

'You've got proof of that?'

He laughed. 'Gimme a break, Lynda. None of this is provable but that doesn't mean we don't know it to be true.'

'It's no wonder you and Don got on so well.'

'And then Lonnegan turned. Seven days ago, just over a week after the robbery, he got into a fracas with the Corporation at a place called Soaker's Farm, probably while negotiating the return of the Red Book, and he either killed or wounded a couple of their guys. Afterwards, when he'd gone to ground, he started weighing up the pros and cons and realised that he'd offended the more dangerous faction. His solution was therefore to steal the Red Book from the Naboths and deliver it back to its rightful owners.'

'But if the Red Book was on its way back to the Corporation anyway, why bother?'

'Because the Corporation didn't know the book was on its way back, and if Lonnegan gave it to them *himself*, it would make up for Soaker's Farm. That was the deal he made with them.'

'And presumably he made a deal with you too, to allow all this to happen?'

'It would have been perfect for us. Even you must admit that.'

'Only if you believe Lonnegan,' she said. 'How do you know he isn't looking to steal the Red Book so that he can sell it on to the highest bidder?'

Kepler laughed. 'Because one way or another he's going to

get hunted. Better that it's the Naboths than the Corporation. And much better the Naboths than both of them.'

'And where's Lonnegan now?'

'Still following his only lead, I guess. Elliot Wade, the guy who had the book in the first place, and presumably, the only one who knows where it is at present.'

Lynda considered this. 'Which is why Wade fled from the hospital and took his wife with him? Because he'd seen Lonnegan sniffing about, pretending to be his mate ... and knew that their only chance was to get the hell away?'

'With someone like Lonnegan after you, who wouldn't have run?'

'You realise that Lonnegan will kill those two idiots? Like he killed Nick Scotzini. Like he nearly killed me.'

'That's possible, yes.' To his credit, Kepler looked uncomfortable when he said this.

'But still you unleashed him?'

'There was nothing else we could do.'

'If you're still in contact with Lonnegan,' she said, 'you can call him off.'

'It doesn't make sense to do that. Look, Lynda, the Red Book can't just vanish into the wind. How can we possibly risk the details of all the CIs in London – many of them vital to ongoing high-level investigations – becoming the subject of a black-market auction? Surely even you can see what a disaster that would be?'

She stood up. 'Call him off and go after Elliot Wade yourself.'

'And if we get him, why would he help us? Why admit that he had any connection to that armed robbery when it could see him go to jail for twenty years? Be sensible, Lynda. The Corporation have already possessed the Red

Book once. They could have photocopied it ... they could have committed it to memory for all we know, and we can't change any of that. So, the only solution is that the status quo must persist. They've *got* to get the Red Book back and the truce *must* hold.'

Lynda's phone pinged in her pocket, signifying a text. She glanced at it casually.

And glanced at it again.

It was several seconds before she could take it in.

Kepler drank down to the bottom of his glass. 'I'd like to get you on side here, Lynda, by appealing to your sense of duty, by appealing to your experience.' He placed his glass on the table again. 'You're sixteen years a copper. You know it's not all cakes and ale ... that sometimes we have to do dark stuff for the greater good. It's not desirable, but it's the way things are.'

Lynda pocketed her phone and picked up the bottle of Highland Park.

'Believe me, I don't want to do it by getting tough,' Kepler intoned. 'Now that you know what's at stake here, you surely believe we'll do that if we must.'

'Having seen the way you got tough with Gina Tubbs and Tim Philbin,' she replied, 'I've no doubt it's not just mine and Don's careers that might get chucked in the dumpster.'

'We'll do what we must. But that's up to you.'

She approached him, offering the bottle. 'Another?'

'One for the road?' He held his glass out. 'Why not?'

She reached down to pour the Scotch. He didn't notice that she hadn't removed the cork until she dropped the bottle on the floor and in the same movement snapped a handcuff to his wrist, pushing his arm back to the radiator, where she snapped the other cuff to its feeder pipe.

Kepler sat there blinking. He yanked at his hand, but the cuffs held firm.

'What ... what's this?' he stuttered. 'Have you gone stark staring mad?'

'Don't talk. Just get your phone out.'

'My phone?' His cheeks tinged red as he glared at her.

'Hand it over,' she said, palm outstretched. 'Then we can get this thing moving.'

His scowl cracked into a nasty grin. 'You're serious, aren't you?'

'Gimme your phone now!'

'Or what?' He smirked. 'You'll torture me? I can't see that, somehow.'

'No. I'll call Don down and tell him you tried to touch me up.'

Kepler's expression changed, feral rage giving way to uncertainty, to alarm even.

'Yeah.' She nodded. 'Then *you'll* know what it's like to be on the wrong end of the good old days.'

He still made no effort to comply, a sheen of sweat on his brow as he tried to think this thing through. It probably wasn't the fear that Don would beat him up, but that Don would get involved at all. The fewer people who knew about a 'black bag' operation like this, the better. She stepped forward and he made no resistance as she rummaged through his jacket pockets and pulled out his phone. He watched her as she moved out of his reach and opened it. None of the contacts listed corresponded in any obvious way with Ray Lonnegan. She supposed that she ought to have expected that. Irritated, she shoved the phone into her own pocket and searched him again, turning his pockets inside-out.

He watched her with wry amusement.

'You realise how fucking ridiculous this is?' he said.

'I can bend with the breeze like the best of us,' she replied. 'You're right; sometimes there's no other option ... but I cannot countenance murder. So, you have to contact Ray Lonnegan ... Give me the number and I'll ring it on our landline. Then you can tell him to stand down.'

He laughed again. 'I couldn't do that even if I wanted to. Lonnegan's bent on fixing things with the Corporation.' His laughter faded. 'He'll do anything – do you understand? *Anything* to get the Red Book back to them.'

48

9 January (Thursday)

When two girls came out for a smoke, Lonnegan made his move.

He'd been watching the back of the club for half an hour. It was only what he'd have expected in this quarter of Felixstowe, a squalid alley and a single wooden door with a bare bulb hanging over it. The two girls were likely between acts because, though they still wore their glittery make-up, their hair hanging full and lush as if blow-dried and sprayed, they were dressed in tracksuits and slippers. They huddled face-to-face, giggling at each other's quips as they shivered and pulled hard on their cigs. The club's back door, meanwhile, stood open, issuing a lurid red light.

Lonnegan walked forward in blokish fashion, gloved hands deep in his black combat-jacket pockets. The women turned startled looks towards him.

'Evening, ladies,' he said. 'Hope you don't mind, but I'm popping in.'

Both stepped aside as he passed, but though the brunette remained quiet, the blonde jabbered something. Lonnegan turned and looked at her.

'Polish?' he said. 'Or Russian?'

She looked frightened by that. He decided that it was Russian and moved into the interior.

The heat was cloying in there, the atmosphere muggy, pungent with the smells of sweat and perfume. Lonnegan could already hear the bump-and-grind music from the front of house and the muffled, riotous shouting. Halfway along the corridor, a security man in a monkey suit, a massive guy with the saggy, paunchy look of a heavyweight gone to seed, was leaning against a wall.

'It's okay, mate,' Lonnegan said. 'Just need to speak to someone. Won't take long.'

The security man stepped out, shaking his head. He might have been out of shape, but he still filled the corridor. This counted for nothing, though, when a spanner appeared in Lonnegan's right hand. The first blow was a lightning backhander to the left side of the jaw. With a crack of bone, the bouncer's head spun part-way around. Though his knees buckled, he didn't go down straight away, and it took a second blow, this one to his right cheek, and a third across his left temple, before consciousness left him.

Doors came up to left and right. Lonnegan kicked them open. Mostly, they were small, damp dressing rooms filled with worm-eaten furniture and draped with lingerie and other sparse, sparkly garments. Sometimes there were half-dressed girls in there. Usually they were fixing their make-up or reading magazines. One was snorting coke from the back of her hand.

At the end of the corridor, a flight of dirty wooden steps led upward, but another employee of the club was on his way down: a drag artist, wearing heavy make-up, huge lashes, and a floor-length sequined dress split to the thigh. But it was clear that this was a man rather than a trans-woman because he'd already taken his platinum wig off, revealing a shaven bonce, and was carrying his high heels.

Lonnegan had been at the Pussycat Bar in the audience – this was where he'd first seen Wade's sexy wife with her Polish friend, it was where he'd first seen her with Wade – and he clearly remembered that this character, Charmaine, was the compere who introduced the individual acts.

Charmaine stopped dead, staring at the intruder, and then heard a rising commotion further back. Before he could react, Lonnegan lurched forward, ramming the spanner crosswise against his throat, pushing him back into the nearest wall.

'Just the person,' Lonnegan said.

'Who the…?'

'Shut up and listen because I haven't got much time.'

'You can't come in here…'

Lonnegan slapped the side of his head. A hefty, echoing *whap*, it wrought instant compliance.

'That's better,' Lonnegan said. 'The bird I'm looking for is Polish. Her name's Anja. Used to do a double act with this blonde chick called Harri.'

Charmaine said nothing.

Lonnegan pressed the spanner against his Adam's apple, causing him to gulp painfully. Behind them, the clamour rose.

'Don't think about not answering,' Lonnegan said, leaning forward until his eyes were like luminous moons. 'Because you have no idea how much I want these ladies. I know the blondie's gone. But Anja will do. You tell me where I can find her, and it'll be a small price to pay for me not stress-testing your skull till it cracks open like an egg.'

49

9 January (Thursday)

Don glanced from Lynda to Kepler and back again.

It was inevitable that he'd come down once he'd heard the raised voices. But even so, he hadn't expected to enter his lounge and find an Organised Crime Division superintendent handcuffed to a radiator. Lynda's explanation had left him even more stupefied.

'I mean, whatever you think about letting villains take each other out, you must admit that this is going a bit far?' she said. 'The Organised Crime Division could at least make an effort to rein Lonnegan in ... but this specimen isn't even going to try. Because he's happy to let two people, namely Elliot and Harriet Wade, get killed rather than see the Red Book fall into the wrong hands.'

'Lynda,' Kepler said tiredly. 'What don't you get about Lonnegan being the perfect mechanism for retrieval and disposal of the Red Book? I mean, for Christ's sake — if he goes unpunished afterwards, it's surely a price worth paying? Look ...' He turned to Don. '*You* of all people must see what's happening here? We can't *do* this thing officially. Because that would mean letting it out that the Corporation possesses knowledge of all the Met's informers. And we certainly can't make it public knowledge that the Organised

Crime Division was doing a deal with a syndicate like that. How would it look?'

Don pondered the predicament.

'As long as Ray Lonnegan's out there, the Red Book will make its way home,' Kepler argued. 'And we don't even need to get our hands dirty.'

'Apart from springing a prisoner from custody, you mean?' Lynda retorted. 'And injuring two Essex police officers in the process?'

'That was minor stuff compared to what I'm talking about.'

She turned to Don. 'Are you hearing this?'

'Elliot and Harriet Wade are scallies,' Kepler interjected. 'Fucking lowlifes. Why do you care, Lynda? That blag in Harwich was pretty bad news!'

'How involved were they?' she asked.

'Wade's a bit player, but he was involved enough to make sure they won't play ball with us.'

'Offer them immunity if Wade cooperates.'

'Why would he agree?' Kepler scoffed. 'He's less likely to be prosecuted if he keeps his mouth shut.'

'So, the solution is for us to kill them?' she said. 'Are you serious?'

'Not *us*, no.'

'It won't necessarily come to that, will it?' Don interrupted. 'If this guy Lonnegan wants the Red Book, maybe those losers'll give it up as soon as he shows?'

'They haven't done so far,' Kepler replied.

'Even if he spares *their* lives, he's already killed one person,' Lynda reminded them. 'As far as I know, this Nick Scotzini wasn't involved in anything.'

Again, Kepler looked discomforted. 'I don't know what

happened there. But I'll tell you now, Lynda, there'll be many more deaths, *many* more, if the Red Book ends up in the wrong hands.' He looked at Don again. 'Surely *you* can see that this conscience coppering is an absolute joke. You were old-school, a former Major Investigations man ...'

Don glanced at Lynda, who watched him warily.

'Never expected you'd get yourself into a pickle like this,' he said.

'I'm not sure it's a pickle, is it?' she replied. 'Surely there's only one solution?'

'Course there bloody is,' Kepler agreed. 'Get me out of these cuffs, and I can go back to the office. You two meanwhile, can enjoy the rest of your evening. The main thing is you don't gob off. This meeting never happened. And you, Sergeant Hagen, have no clue about the identity of the guy with the X-shaped scar. It doesn't get easier than that, Lynda ... I'm not asking you to lie, just say nothing. If Lonnegan kills the Wades – and it *is* an if, I agree with Don – the bodies won't even be found, and the likelihood is they won't be missed. And then lots of clandestine police ops all over the south of England can proceed as they were, with no one any the wiser.'

'And the Corporation continue to get a free pass,' she said.

'That's the downside of it. But we are where we are.'

'Which is the wrong place.' She shook her head.

'Seriously? After everything I've just told you?' He looked at Don. 'Can you credit this? Did this woman of yours learn nothing from your career?'

'My career ended in shit,' Don said.

'You were injured out. Honourably.'

'That's what you call it?'

'Everyone knows you were a good detective, Don.

Look…' Kepler yanked on the bracelet holding him to the radiator pipe. 'At least get me out of these fucking cuffs.'

Don shrugged. 'They're Lynda's cuffs. I haven't got the key.'

'Get Lynda's then.'

Another shrug. 'We don't have that kind of marriage. I can't force her to do something she doesn't want to.'

Lynda had edged away but regarded her husband with surprise when he said this.

Kepler glowered. 'For Christ's sake, Hagen! This is your wife's career we're talking about! Save her from herself! If she won't give up the key, get a fucking hacksaw!'

'Just wait a sec.' Don waved a hand for calm. 'If you can break Lynda's career, maybe you can also *make* it, eh? Let's say she plays ball. What're we talking that's reasonable? DI within six weeks? DCI within six months? Detective Super within a year…'

'Have you gone mental?' Kepler blurted.

Don shook his head. 'Funny how you guys never have as much power when it comes to doing someone a favour.'

'Get the hacksaw, for fuck's sake!'

'Hold your horses.' Don headed into the kitchen and started rummaging in drawers.

'And you?' Kepler turned his gaze on Lynda. 'Jesus Christ…'

'I don't care what deal you've got going with the Corporation,' she said. 'I just want to make sure no one else gets killed. And if *you* won't stop Ray Lonnegan, I'll have to.'

'You're a Traffic officer, love. Okay? Plod with wheels. You're so out of your depth that it would be laughable if it wasn't so sad.'

'No luck with the hacksaw,' Don said, coming back in. 'But I found these.'

He crossed the room to Kepler, who pulled his chain taut, expecting to see it somehow severed. What he wasn't expecting was Don to grab him by his free wrist, slam it against the other one and, using a second pair of handcuffs – these older and somewhat rustier – clamp that one to the radiator too.

When he realised what had happened, Kepler looked dazed. 'What the bloody ...?'

'Pair of *my* old cuffs,' Don said. 'And guess what – I haven't got a key to those either.'

'You fucking idiot,' Kepler hissed.

'There is this, though.' Don produced another object from behind his back.

A roll of silver duct tape. Before Kepler could object, he'd stretched it out, torn off a strip, and plastered it across the captive's mouth.

'Can't have you keeping swearing in the house when the kids are upstairs, can we?' Don said. 'I get reprimanded for it, so you should too.'

Kepler mumbled something inaudible, but his eyes spoke murder.

'Sit nice and tight, Mr Kepler,' Don said. 'If you can do that, I'll go and look in the shed for a hacksaw. But seriously, mate, that's going to depend on how quiet you can be while me and the missus go for a quick conflab.'

50

9 January (Thursday)

'Okay, Anja ... this isn't hard,' Lonnegan said, admiring the statuesque Polish girl, even though she lay on the small, rickety divan where he'd just thrown her. 'You used to get up on the stage here with an English bird called Harri. You used to do a schoolgirl act together.'

A couple of years had passed, but she was recognisable as the sultry, sulky redhead that Lonnegan remembered. At present, she wore only a thigh-length dressing gown, but hugged it around herself as he stood over her. Charmaine, meanwhile, was crouched in a corner, eyes darting fearfully between them.

'All you need to do,' Lonnegan said, slapping the spanner into his left palm, 'if you want to retain your status as happy dancer, and not get downgraded to plug-ugly cripple sweeping up the used condoms out back, is tell me where I can find this Harri?'

The Polish girl shook her head. 'I don't know ...'

'That's *so* not what I wanted to hear.'

'How could she possibly know?' Charmaine protested.

'Shut it, Danny La Rue. You've done your bit by bringing me in here. No sense making things hard for yourself again.'

'No one keeps tabs on ex-employees,' the compere insisted. 'Once they've gone, they've gone.'

Lonnegan pondered that. 'I don't think that applies to *you*, does it, Anja? I seem to remember that you and Harri were pretty matey. And don't bother telling me she's living the dream in some country cottage near Stowmarket. I know about that already. I want to know where she might go in a crisis.'

Anja shook her head again. 'I not know where you find her.'

Lonnegan grabbed her left ankle and lifted her long, shapely leg. She gasped with fright, whimpering at the sight of his raised spanner.

'Lovely pin you've got here,' he said. 'But not for long...'

Before he could land the first smashing blow, a shoulder was thrown at the dressing-room door, once, twice, three times, and the chair Lonnegan had used to brace it fell away.

Another huge security man stooped through, this one with a shaggy beard and hair.

Again, he was the size of a wardrobe.

Again, that didn't save him.

The spanner cracked first across his right knee, which left him hopping, and then rattled across the front of his face, breaking his teeth and his nose. The bouncer tottered, still on one leg, blood drooling through his beard. Lonnegan struck again, a wide, sweeping blow, delivered to his left elbow, and then again to his right cheekbone. The guy toppled forward, lifeless as timber.

Anja and Charmaine stared at the body aghast.

'Okay, I'm obviously running out of time.' Lonnegan kicked the door closed. 'So, let's get things moving.' Shoving the spanner into his belt, he leaned down, grabbed the in-sensate bouncer by his lank, bloodied hair and yanked his head up. With his free hand, he pulled the Glock from the holster under his jacket, fired a single deafening shot into the ceiling, and jammed its barrel against the side of the bouncer's head. 'Tell me what I want to know, or I decorate this shithole with the few brains this fucking mule was born with.'

'She has sister,' Anja said quickly, eyes goggling with terror.

'Keep talking,' he instructed.

'We call her "Doctor Susan".'

Lonnegan chuckled. 'She's a doctor? You ripping the piss?'

'No, no, I swear.'

'Where does she live?'

'I not know.'

Lonnegan tutted and took aim at Charmaine, who shrank backwards in horror.

'Colchester,' Anja half screamed.

He scrutinised her. 'She lives in Colchester?'

'*Tak*.' She nodded. 'Sometimes, Harri take girls to her ... to private treatment room. For STD.'

Lonnegan laughed. 'She must've seen you lot coming. Would've been a lot cheaper on the NHS. Unless you're all illegals, of course. Which wouldn't surprise me in the fucking least.'

'She no charge.'

'She no charge?' His laughter faded. 'She did it from the goodness of her soul? Well, there's something you don't hear every day. Where is this fucking saint?'

The girl hesitated.

'I'm sure you've *all* been to this treatment room.' He switched his aim from Charmaine to Anja, herself, and cocked the pistol again. 'So, tell me all about it, including the address ... and we'll make like none of this ever happened.'

*

372

'I don't know what you're planning here, darling,' Don whispered as he and Lynda stood in the hall. 'But I hope you've made the right decision. My police career's over. Yours might be too.'

'I don't think so,' she said. 'This Red Book thing has got to be one of the biggest foul-ups in British police history. You reckon they'll want that story to get out?'

'And what if Sully goes to prison?'

Lynda sighed. This was a genuine concern. Don and Terry Sullivan had been big buddies.

'I'm not planning to whistle-blow,' she said, unsure whether or not that was true, but still so appreciative of her husband's unexpected support that this at least was her ambition. 'I'm not naming names unless I absolutely have to. But Lonnegan was *my* case and *I'm* going to be the one who brings him in.'

'Lonnegan, eh? Sounds like a handful.'

'He is. And he has to be stopped.'

Don nodded. 'Well, just remember to get that message to the right people when the whole weight of the top brass threatens to come down on you.' He glanced into the lounge. 'You'd better get on with it ... there's only so long I can keep Kepler here.'

'I can't believe you're okay with this,' she said, as she handed him Kepler's phone.

'I'm the old-schooler, remember?'

'You don't want me to be better than that, a more modern officer?'

'Modern isn't always better, as maybe you're now realising. Anyway, I *do* have an ulterior motive. When this is all over, I get to write the book.'

She kissed him, and it was a proper kiss, the first they'd

shared in several years. But now was not the time, and she broke away – before kissing him again, a quick peck on the cheek, and dashing out of the house.

Once in the Qashqai, she checked the text she'd received while in mid-conversation with Kepler; the message from Clive Atkins that had precipitated this whole reckless action.

Bus stop camera came through
VRN of car that took the Wades identifiable
Belongs to a green Nissan Juke.
Registered to . . .
You won't believe this . . .
Doctor Susan Clarkwell

51

9 January (Thursday)

As they approached the coast, the snow covering the ground lessened until eventually it lay thin as tissue. The temperature outside had risen to about two degrees above zero.

The house finally came into view, located off an otherwise empty lane, the trees and bushes to either side of it naked skeletons. It was built from whitewashed brick with blue-painted woodwork. No doubt in summer it possessed holiday charm, especially with the sea a couple of hundred yards beyond it, but the building itself, while not exactly dilapidated, looked shabby. When Elliot parked in front of it, he saw that its paintwork was peeling and dingy, the rest of its façade cruddy with moss.

'I acquired this place several years ago as part of my divorce settlement with Gerald,' Susan Clarkwell said from the back seat, where she was cradling the unconscious form of her sister. 'I've not used it much since then. Haven't had the heart to.'

Elliot switched off the engine.

They'd left the main road network perhaps eight minutes ago and hadn't seen another vehicle or habitation since. He had to admit that he felt safer now than he had at the hospital. But he didn't feel totally secure. He took a long, searching look at the deep, dank shrubbery encircling the property. Not that he could blame Susan for bringing them here. It had been Harri's idea to use this place as a hideout once they'd hatched their plan to steal the Red Book. If anything, Susan had been nervous about it.

He opened the back door of the car to assist with Harri. The patient was still swaddled in blankets, her head wrapped in bandages and gauze. Of course, Susan had taken all kinds of additional precautions so that she could bring her here, putting together an emergency bag that had included blood pressure-monitoring equipment, an ophthalmoscope, additional dextrose/saline bags and giving sets, a plastic airway and different types of emergency medication. She'd fitted the patient with fentanyl patches for pain management during the journey, and had made continual observations while they were travelling, which included checking for deoxygenation, fitting, tremors or what she referred to as 'thrombolytic episodes'.

'You sure you're going to be able to look after her here?' Elliot asked, carrying Harri the short distance to the large front door.

'Well, she's not out of the woods yet,' Susan replied, unlocking it.

'I don't know what that means.'

'It means that she ought to live so long as she gets lots of rest and the correct medication.'

'*Ought to?*'

'We're doing what we can. Just, please, get her out of this cold.'

While Susan got her bags, Elliot entered the building, half tripping over a couple of brown-paper parcels. Beyond those lay an extra-large lounge with a stone-flagged floor. Susan pushed past him and bustled around turning lamps on, though any light they issued was weak and yellow. For all its spaciousness, the air in there was musty, while the furniture, of which there was plenty – a couch and three armchairs, a dark, heavy sideboard, an even darker, heavier Welsh dresser – added to the air of gloom.

'Over here.' Susan threw the cushions off the couch.

Elliot laid Harri down gently. The doctor then eased him out of the way so that she could attend her patient. He stood and watched.

Susan Clarkwell had been very frightened about participating in this thing, and when she'd learned that to pull the plan off, they would need to lie low afterwards in one of her own properties, she'd been especially alarmed. Of course, they were past the point of no return now, so her demeanour appeared to have changed back to one of brisk efficiency.

Harri had first contacted her about it the Saturday after the Soaker's Farm disaster, by which time she and Elliot knew roughly what the Naboths were expecting of them. They hadn't had the specifics at that point, but they'd known the plan would be enacted imminently, and when Elliot was summoned to the Tunwood Raceway the following day, Harri had called her sister again, telling her to be waiting with her car in the vicinity of the Three Pigeons. Susan had been so scared by this point that they'd feared she'd want to pull out, but surprisingly, she hadn't. Elliot hadn't wanted to involve Susan at all, but Harri had insisted that she was the ideal person for the job – and to a degree at least, she'd been proved right.

'There's a kettle in the kitchen,' Susan said, pulling on a pair of disposable gloves. 'Fill it with clean water and bring it to the boil. There's an airing cupboard under the stairs. There should be some clean, dry towels in there. You'll also find a central heating master switch … if you could turn that on, please. And can you bring me some bin liners?'

Elliot did as he was asked, checking the place out in the process.

It was more modern than it had looked. He noticed a widescreen TV in one corner, a wi-fi modem and walkabout telephones. In the kitchen, along with all the usual accoutrements, there was a dishwasher, a microwave oven and an electric can opener. However, the basic structure of the building was more venerable, its interior layout almost baronial, the lounge enormous and overhung on two sides by an upstairs landing balcony with darkened doorways leading off it.

'Those'll be your packages,' Susan said when he returned with the things she'd asked for.

Elliot went to the front door and picked up the two parcels, one of which was addressed to him, the other to Harri. He tore them open, finding their personal documents, driving licences, credit cards and so forth, plus Harri's mobile. He'd posted them all to this address on the day before the crash, and it was a relief to find that they'd arrived. The idea behind this had been twofold: firstly, so that there'd be no ID on either of them if anything went wrong on the A12 (the only exception being Elliot's own phone, which he'd kept with him in case of emergency); and secondly, so that they could try to live as normal a life as possible after selling the Red Book without having to go back to Ravenwood.

Of course, in their wildest dreams they'd never been expecting a serious car crash and for the police to get involved.

He placed the items on the sideboard and wandered back to the couch. Susan had changed Harri's dressing, confining the bandaging to the girl's shaved cranium, laying bare her face, which was still puffy, bruised and dotted all over with sutures. The doctor had also made use of the bulky brass lampstand on a nearby table by hooking the drip-feed over the top of its shade.

Elliot hugged himself as he watched.

He had a man's Parka and tracksuit on, which Susan had brought for him in the Juke, but underneath that, having binned the hospital scrubs, he wore nothing. It wasn't the cold that cut him, though; it was the sight of Harri lying torn, broken and insensible.

'Level with me,' he said. 'Is she going to be okay?'

Susan took her pulse. 'It'll be a long haul.'

'Why's she still unconscious?'

'Because she's sedated, but it'll wear off soon.'

'I hated taking her out of the hospital. But once I saw Lonnegan there, I knew I had no choice.'

'So you told me.'

'He's also the one who did this to us.'

'You told me that too.'

'Sorry...' Elliot found his temper fraying. 'Didn't mean to bore you.'

The doctor didn't look up.

'I've got some questions for *you*,' he said, 'if I've a mind to ask them.'

She continued tending her sister, checking her blood pressure.

'For example,' he said, 'what happened after the crash?'

She still refused to look around. 'I'd remind you, before you start making accusations, that *I* rescued you from the hospital and that you're in *my* house.'

'I appreciate that, but you need to understand...'

'No, *you* need to understand, Elliot...' she glanced up,

her face tense and pale, 'that nothing happened as you said it would.'

'I told you there could be variables...'

'No one said I was going to get driven off the road.'

Elliot understood that this would have frightened and disoriented her, even though she'd brought it on herself. Not that unexpected things hadn't happened.

Supposedly, he and Harri had headed down the A12 to London, to leave the Red Book and the suitcase of money at the Charing Cross drop-off. What the Naboths had not known, of course, was that Susan Clarkwell would drive after them, though not making contact with them because it was likely they'd be tailed by a Naboth spotter – which in the event they were, the blue Corsa. Their intent had been to trick the spotter by stopping near Colchester at a roadside diner, where Harri would get herself and Wade a take-out burger and chips, which they'd eat in the car. After eating, they'd drive off again, but only after depositing their rubbish in a car park bin, said rubbish secretly containing the Red Book. With luck, the tail would ignore this and follow them back onto the A12, and then to London, where he would see them stow the case at Charing Cross left luggage, and once they were on their way back, pull them over and search them. While this was happening, Susan had the straightforward job of remaining at the A12 diner and when the coast was clear, rummaging in the bin and retrieving the Red Book. They would then make their separate ways to this place.

The first thing that went wrong, of course, was that after Wade had picked Harri up from the Three Pigeons, from where Susan had also commenced to follow them in her Juke, the blue Corsa had dropped out of sight, apparently replaced by a silver-grey Citroën. At the time, Elliot hadn't known what this had signified, but he understood why the Citroën had swerved at Susan's car, sending her careering onto the verge.

'The idea was to follow us, not hug us,' he said. 'I know that by driving in front of us, you thought that would look less suspicious. But it didn't. You were so close to us by then that he thought you were riding shotgun. That's why he attacked you. He was clearing the way to get at us. It's not your fault, though. I know you've never done this before.'

Susan got to her feet, bundling bandages into one of the bin liners.

'I was terrified, okay?' Her eyes glinted, and Elliot was surprised to see that she was on the verge of tears. 'I tried to get going straight away, to get back on the road and follow you ... but my hands were shaking so much I could hardly hold the wheel. Eventually I caught up enough to see you and that other car, the silver one. And then I saw flashes of light. When I realised they were gun flashes, I dropped back. Of course I did. How could I possibly intervene? I'm a doctor, okay? I've never even seen anything like that before!'

'No one would have expected you to intervene ...'

She glared at him. 'When I saw you go off the road, I was so horrified I just hit the brakes. Made a U-turn. But I hadn't got far when my conscience kicked in. This was my little sister, after all. The first turn I came to, it took me down to a village called Stratford St Mary. Halfway through it, there's a country lane, a farm track running parallel to the A12. It finally stops at a farm gate. On the other side of the gate, there's a field that joins Little Crickledon Wood. I climbed over it ... didn't take long. From the moment you left the road to me finding you, it was ten minutes tops. You were both alive, of course. It was a miracle. But you were in such a bad way ...'

Her words petered out, eyes glazing. Elliot knew from his race days that even doctors could be shaken by the gory carnage resulting from high-velocity impacts.

'What about the Red Book?' he asked.

'I looked, but there was no sign of it. There was money lying around. The case had burst open. But no Red Book. Then I heard someone coming down the slope. I had no clue who it was, but I felt certain it was going to be the person who'd shot at you. So I hid in the trees. Not too far off ... I could see him searching around the vehicle. He even searched you as you hung out the driver's door. That was when I *knew* it was him. He had a torch, and he kept shining it towards me, as if he'd heard me creeping around.' Tears now dripped. 'Good Lord, I thought at one point he'd seen me, I thought I was going to be killed ... so I just kept moving away, quietly as I could. Until ... well, until I was heading back to my car.'

'And that was it?' a voice whispered. Surprised, they turned to Harri. Her bloodshot eyes were open, fixed on her sister. 'You left us there to die?'

52

9 January (Thursday)

Woodfleet Row lay deserted.

There was a faint, bluish glow, the moon reflecting from the unbroken snow, but many nooks and crannies had been plunged into blackness. Noticeably, there were no electric lights in any windows and no cars in any of the bays.

Lynda drew up in front of Doctor Clarkwell's office block and sat wondering what her next step ought to be.

The doctor's home address had again been deserted, so this had been the next place to check. Not that it felt like an obvious hideout. It seemed ridiculous to try the front door. Even if the doctor was in there with the two escapees, she would hardly have left it unlocked. Lynda's thoughts strayed again to the 'back door', that fire door on the first floor, from which the alarm had been disconnected. She contemplated the doctor's last words after they'd left the building together.

'*My car's at the back. That's why we didn't run into each other earlier.*'

Lynda rolled her Qashqai forward, and the alley entrance materialised from the shadows on her left. She turned down it, wheels crunching. By the looks of it, someone had been here since the snowfall – tyre marks were visible. That might indicate that Doctor Clarkwell was on site now, parked in her private yard at the building's rear. However, when Lynda emerged into the yard, which was surrounded on all sides by high, faceless buildings, with a fire escape on the left, there were no other vehicles present.

She got out of the car, looking up to the top of the fire escape – and saw that the fire door was ajar. She focused her torch on the steps. On each one, footprints indented the snow.

She ascended ultra-cautiously, the old metal structure reverberating even though she trod softly. On the top platform, she observed that the fire door had been forced. Its rim and the wooden jamb were splintered top and middle, as if someone of considerable strength had jemmied it.

She thought again about the broken-open French window at The Rookery. A shiver passed through her, but there was nothing to be done about it now. She had a radio in the car, but it would be out of juice. She had her phone in her pocket, but who was she going to call?

She pushed the door open and listened.

There was no sound. When she stabbed her torch in, it exposed the corridor all the way to the first turn. There was nothing out of the ordinary. She crept along the passage towards the unmarked door. As she'd anticipated, that too stood open, also damaged at its edges where a brace and bit had rent the wood. Lynda flicked her torch off. Again, she listened hard. There was something about the quietness overhead that she really didn't like. Maybe it was her police sixth sense kicking in, but there was nothing worse than *knowing* there was someone there and not being able to see or hear them.

At the top of the stairs, a faint glimmer of moonlight denoted the open doorway to Doctor Clarkwell's private rooms. It gave her no comfort, exchanging the anonymity of total blackness for this faint icy gloom. Nevertheless, she pushed the door. It opened silently. She leaned forward into the open space, certain that if a figure was standing in there, she'd see it. But she saw nothing, except, to her right, the pale blue rectangle of the archway leading into the consulting room.

She sidled towards it, holding her breath, and something crackled beneath her feet.

Glancing down, she saw strewn paperwork. She remembered that various documents had lain on a shelf nearby. No doubt, whoever had come in before had knocked it askew. She edged to the side and proceeded to the arch. At any second, she expected someone to come leaping out of it. There was no other way for them to vacate the place.

She halted in front of it, a dew of sweat on her clammy brow.

Then, something rustled to her rear. She went rigid. Muscles taut as wire, she turned to look.

Her vision had adjusted, and she could see those sheets of paper on the floor moving slightly, nudged by a gentle breeze seeping up from below. She almost laughed at the cliché of it, but in all the time on the job, she didn't think she'd ever been this frightened. Holding her breath, she stepped through the arch into the main area. This larger room, being the section with the window, was brighter than the antechamber. Even then, nothing appeared to be out of place – until she noticed that the row of cabinets on the wall were all open, their doors hanging awkwardly, as if they'd been broken. Slowly, Lynda exhaled.

And the light came on.

She was dazzled – and yelped with the terror of it, dropping to a crouch as she swung around.

The light was on in the antechamber as well. But nobody came at her.

She held her defensive posture, ears pinned back. Pinprick silence.

She rose to her feet. And ventured to the arch.

There was nobody in the antechamber either.

'They're on timers,' Doctor Clarkwell had said. 'It's a complicated arrangement, but they switch on and off all night.'

Lynda turned back to the consulting room. The cabinets had been ransacked, along with the cupboard. The few items on the doctor's desk were now on the floor, scattered. She glanced into the corner of the room where an examination curtain stood open – there was no one behind it.

Feeling as if the bird had flown, Lynda circled the desk, seeing that all its drawers had been pulled out, the locks shattered by heavy, brutal blows.

It was standard stuff, but she'd already concluded that this was not a routine burglary. How would the intruder have known to find his way up into this half-hidden attic? How would he have known which entry door was not alarmed? And how would he have known all that and yet *not* known that the place contained nothing worth stealing?

Unless, of course, he'd found what he was looking for and had taken it away.

Lynda swung back to the open drawers, the scattered personals. Had they once contained a diary or address book?

'Damn!' She hurried back through the antechamber. '*Damn it to sodding hell!*'

But as she crossed that smaller room, one of the loose papers on the floor caught her eye. She swept down and scooped it up. At first glance, it was mundane documentation. But as she scanned it, pieces fell into place.

It was a council tax bill. Addressed to *Susan Clarkwell* of *Bay View House, 14 Bay View Road, Aldeburgh, Suffolk.*

Doctor Clarkwell had a second home.

Possibly the intruder hadn't noticed this, had simply rushed in and out.

'Yeah, right,' Lynda said.

53

9 January (Thursday)

'How could I have called someone, Harriet?' Susan demanded. 'I didn't know how safe that would have been.'

If it was possible for as brutalised a face as Harri's to look shocked, it did so now. 'Safe? We were lying in a ... mangled car.'

'I mean safe for me. The police can trace calls these days.'

'You could've gone to a ...' Harri was awake but only just, and struggling to form full sentences. 'To a ... phone box ...'

'Would you have known where the nearest one was? I don't remember the last time I saw a public phone. Even then they might have traced me.'

'Glad ... you had your priorities right ...'

Elliot sat at the foot of the stairs and listened tiredly; his head was starting to ache. Harri was weak but holding the moral high ground appeared to have energised her a little.

'You're obviously feeling better,' Susan said, reaching down.

'Don't touch me,' Harri snapped, only to cringe.

'Harri!' Elliot interjected. 'Susan's nursed you like a baby. Without her, I wouldn't have been able to get you here.'

'Where ... are we?' she asked.

'Bay View,' he said.

'Thought it was ... too posh ... for the NHS.'

'Look, I'm sorry,' Susan said, sounding stressed again. 'I can't say more than that. I wish I'd never agreed to participate in this. Especially when I had to lie to the police, pretending I didn't know anything about the accident ... pretending that I was a heartless sister who didn't care whether you lived or died.'

'Let's forget the recriminations, eh?' Elliot said. 'The main thing is that the Red Book's missing.'

Harri gave him an agonised stare. 'H ... how?'

'I wish I knew,' he said. 'And I bet Ray Lonnegan wishes he knew. If he'd found it after he shot us off the road, I doubt he'd have come to the hospital. What's also worrying about that is why he was pretending to be Nick Scotzini.'

Harri looked confused. 'Nick?'

'Lonnegan came to the hospital in Nick's clothes. He told the staff that he was Nick.'

'Is Nick okay?'

'How do I know?'

'You haven't ... called him?'

Elliot spread his hands. 'First of all, I haven't got a phone. That vanished in the crash too, the burner the Naboths gave me had just enough juice left for me to ring Susan from the hospital, but it's dead now, and if we use the landline here, or Susan's phone ... and something *has* happened to Nick, the cops'll be all over us.'

Harri's eyes fluttered closed. She struggled to swallow. Susan checked her temperature and made adjustments to the drip. 'I'm going to give you some antiemetics, okay? That'll reduce the nausea. I might start you on warfarin too. We can't risk a blood clot.'

'Could the police ... have found the Red Book?' Harri asked.

'They could,' Elliot said. 'Except that Susan got there first.'

'I looked for the damn thing, but it wasn't there, okay?' Susan said over her shoulder. 'And when that man came, I'm sorry but I panicked... I mean for God's sake, Harriet!' Susan finally allowed herself to get cross. 'When you rang me on January 4 and asked if I wanted in on this, you never mentioned that people would be shooting at us.'

'We weren't expecting that ourselves,' Elliot said.

'Why did you even ask me?' Susan demanded. 'I've no experience of this sort of thing.'

He shrugged. 'You ticked all the boxes. Firstly, you didn't know what the Red Book was, and so could hardly spill the beans if it went pear-shaped. Secondly, no one else knew you, so you were unlikely to come under suspicion. And thirdly,' he looked awkward, 'Harri said you'd do it because you needed the money.'

Susan threw a reproachful glance at her sister.

'I know your private practice is... in trouble,' Harri mumbled. 'You were never a businesswoman... Suze. But there was another reason... if you want the truth.'

'And what was that?' Susan asked tersely.

'I owed you.'

'You owed me?'

'It would've... paid us, Suze. Really... well.'

That would have been true, Elliot thought. He pondered how it might have turned out had they been able to put the final part of their plan in motion, offering the Red Book for auction from the safety of this hideout. When it was over, he and Harri would have had enough cash to disappear forever, and Susan, who no one even knew about, could have done whatever she wanted.

Harri tried to sit up, but with no more strength than a ragdoll, she failed.

'None of that.' Susan sat down next to her, taking her in her arms, cradling her.

'Sorry, Suze,' Harri slurred. 'All those years ... when I was ... running wild, and you were ... busy. I ... *I* was the one being selfish.'

This was a new one on Elliot. As far as he'd always been told, the rift between the two sisters had stemmed from Susan's snootiness about Harri's lifestyle. Which was why he'd been surprised when Harri had suggested bringing the older woman into their plan.

'Sorry ... Gerry was such a ... rat,' Harri said. 'Should've ... supported you. You needed ... me.'

Elliot edged away. He and Harri went back a decade. But as he'd already discovered, he hadn't been privy to any of her personal life before then. It now seemed intrusive to be here. Besides, he had to get the lay of this land.

He went back into the kitchen. It smelled dank, a fine film of dust lying across the worktops and the tiled floor.

'After ... the split,' he heard Harri say in a noticeably weaker voice, 'you even ... treated ... my friends. Gave them ... their own door at the back. Never charged them ...'

'You guys needed help,' Susan replied. 'And that was *my* field. Besides I was trying to make amends.'

Elliot couldn't see anything beyond the kitchen window, only darkness. But he waited anyway, affording them a little privacy, fascinated by the free treatment revelation. Presumably, that had meant free treatment for Harri's sex worker pals. From the instant he'd met Susan Clarkwell, she'd been stand-offish, but she hadn't struck him as the cold fish that Harri had often described. She'd been frightened when he'd first got Harri into the Juke outside the hospital, but in addition to that, she'd also been concerned for her sister, and worried that what they were doing would worsen her condition – even to the point where, on the outskirts of town, she'd insisted that they swap over, Elliot taking the wheel. On top of that, to learn that she'd run a free-of-charge clinic for strippers and prostitutes ... Well, she couldn't be a bad sort. It also seemed to imply that the two sisters had tried to make up in the past – at least to an extent.

His thoughts were disrupted by an intensifying of his headache, which had localised at the lower back of his skull. He rummaged in a few cupboards to see if he could find some Anadin or paracetamol, though they'd be a poor follow-up to the co-proxamol he'd been on in hospital.

Inevitably, there was nothing. Eventually, he went back into the lounge.

Harri still leaned in her sister's arms but seemed to have gone quiet. Her eyes had closed.

'Everything okay?' he asked.

Susan nodded. 'She made a big effort talking to us just then. She's passed out.'

'Is that bad?'

'Not atypical of the condition.' Susan glanced up at him. 'She should be in hospital, Elliot.'

'I agree. But at present we need to hide. Speaking of which, this is probably the right time to remind you that when we first made this plan, you said you had access to a firearm.'

'Gerald's shotgun.' Susan looked worried. 'You seriously think we're going to need it?'

'You saw them open fire on us.'

She gently disentangled herself from the patient and stood up. 'I'll go and get it.'

'How come your ex owned a shotgun, anyway?'

'There's a clay-pigeon range about five miles away. Gerald was a member. He left the gun here when we split up. I'm sure that at some point he'll want it back.'

She went up the stairs. Elliot listened for half a minute as she opened and closed drawers, and then trotted back down, carrying a gun-shaped leather case. She placed it on the coffee table, unfastened several buckles, and unzipped it. Inside, lay a break-action double-barrel shotgun. On picking it up, Elliot noted the 'Beretta' signature engraved on its steel side-plates; a mark of genuine quality.

'It's a lovely piece of work.' He broke it open. 'But it's unloaded.' He turned to Susan. 'Any cartridges?'

She looked unsure. 'Let me check in the kitchen.'

Elliot continued to examine the weapon as if he knew what he was doing. He'd fired guns before, but only in the controlled environment of a private range. Harri muttered something, and he glanced up, but she was still asleep. She looked so weak and vulnerable, and of course so terribly hurt, that tears welled into his eyes. *He'd* brought her to this. It had been all *his* doing.

'I've found this,' Susan said, coming back in with a small box. 'But there are only two cartridges left.'

Elliot took them. Ensuring the safety was on, he inserted the cartridges, and snapped the weapon closed. 'Maybe you can see what supplies we've got, make a list of what we'll need ... and I'll watch the road. Is there somewhere I can perch?'

She led him up to the first floor, and told him that he could take his pick of the rooms facing the front of the house. There were four of these. One was a bathroom, and its windows were frosted, so that was no use. The other three were guest bedrooms; small, poky spaces containing the kind of shabby, shoddy furniture you picked up at thrift stores.

Their windows were sash-windows for the most part, but though they all gave reasonable vantage, none was especially better than the others. Bay View House stood parallel to the road, so, although there were several trees between them, most were bare, giving him a broader view than he'd have had in summer. But even then, the road curved past the property rather than led up to it and was only visible for a hundred yards on the left and maybe forty on the right. It also seemed improbable that anyone encroaching on this place with criminal intent would approach so openly.

With that in mind, Elliot walked along the landing balcony to the north end of the house, where there was a box room. This also had a window, but it looked out on woodland, which was heavily overgrown and thick with shadow. To the right of it, a flat greyness denoted the sea.

'Is there any way I can check the east side of the house?' he asked.

Susan led him onto the landing and pointed across the interior to the far balcony where there was only one door leading to the master bedroom.

A protracted moan sounded downstairs. It was subdued, but the strain was noticeable.

'The fentanyl's wearing off,' Susan said. 'And I've got no more patches. I'll give her a pethidine jab.'

'Whatever you think,' Elliot replied.

Before she went, she glanced one last time at the loaded firearm.

'Surely these men won't come here?' she said. 'How can they possibly know about this place? How can they know about me?'

Elliot shrugged. 'You were treating hookers for free. How long do you think that lot can keep their mouths shut?'

'None of them knew I was Harri's sister. We didn't even have the same name.'

'There's one who might have known. A Polish girl called Anja.'

'Anja ...?' Susan tried to remember.

'The problem started at this Honeypot dive in Earl's Court,' he said. 'Seems like Harri witnessed a gangland murder while she was there.'

'God ...' Susan looked shocked. 'Was it these same people?'

'Near enough. It frightened her so much that she left, went upmarket to the Pink Elephant in Knightsbridge. That's where she met this Anja. They got friendly, started doing a routine together. They'd come on stage wearing school uniforms, and start stripping each other off for the appreciative crowd ...'

'Jesus ...'

'Then one night, Harri got into a scrape. Some drunk tried to get up, and she injured him badly. The cops offered her a deal if she'd identify the Honeypot murderer. She refused, but she was terrified of word getting back to this crew that she knew something. The only person she could confide in was Anja ... and, well, sounds as if Anja had had similar problems back in Poland. To be frank, this was the last thing she needed. When Harri left the Pink Elephant on my arm, it wasn't long before Anja left too, not just the club but London itself. A few years later, when we were struggling, she got Harri a short contract at the new place she was working, the Pussycat Bar in Felixstowe. But things weren't the same. They were still buddies, still performed the same act together, but Anja was on tenterhooks. She was petrified that at some point this trouble would come to her door too. Either the police, who'd send her back to whatever awful fate awaited her in Poland, or even worse, whoever was looking for Harri.'

'I *do* remember Anja,' Susan said. 'Beautiful, busty redhead?'

'They all look beautiful and busty on stage.'

'But it was so long ago, and she was pretty drug-addled.'

'So how can you trust someone like that not to talk?'

'I can't imagine she'd remember very much.'

'Even if there's only a one per cent chance someone'll come here, I'll need *this*.' Elliot patted the shotgun. 'And I need to stay awake.'

Susan nodded. 'I'll make some coffee.'

She went back downstairs, while he walked around to the other balcony, entering the master bedroom. This one boasted a four-poster bed, but it smelled no less musty than everywhere else.

He looked from the window. Below, the lawn was expansive and thinly sheeted with snow. Beyond that there was a rockery and then a tumbledown stone wall. From there, bracken rolled down to a narrow beach. There was just enough moonlight to illuminate the lines of surf coming in on the easterly wind. Nothing else moved.

Outside, by the north-west corner of the house, a deep clutch of rhododendron bushes gave Ray Lonnegan the perfect cover, and a clear visual of the building's upper tier, and the dark figure hefting the firearm, who moved in silhouette from one window to the next.

'Brave man, Elliot,' the ex-para muttered. 'Never gave you a hope of making it this far. But sadly,' he slid a fresh magazine into his Heckler & Koch UMP, 'this is as far as it goes.'

Elliot finally lodged himself in the middle room, on the side of the house facing the road. There, he waited and watched, and wondered how long he could keep this up for; his head increasingly felt like a lump of lead.

And then, abruptly, he straightened up. Had he just spied movement?

He leaned against the window. Down to the right, a large evergreen bush was quivering. That could be in response to the sea breeze, but for half a second he fancied there was a human figure moving amid its full, heavy leaves.

He hurried along to the next room, where he pressed his nose against the pane, eyes straining. It was a tricky angle, the bush about ten yards to the right – but now not moving.

Had the wind dropped? Just like that?

He thumbed the safety catch off the shotgun – and saw it again.

This time he was certain.

A figure had sidled out of the bush, stepping behind a sycamore to the left of it.

'Fuck!' he breathed, his whole skin crawling.

The problem was what to do next. He could probably open this sash window to about half its height by lifting the panel with his fingers. But that would be noisy. And what kind of field of fire would it grant him?

As if anticipating this difficulty, the figure stepped out into full view. Elliot threw himself aside, just as the stroboscopic flashing commenced, the window exploding in a billion fragments.

He lay breathless on the glass-strewn carpet.

Outside, the swift, short burst ended, and he heard the *clunk* of a car's bodywork. The bastard had fired that opening salvo to buy himself some cover. He'd seen that an opponent was watching from the window.

Elliot lurched back to his knees, peeking out. But he couldn't see properly as the car was almost directly below. He took a chance and stood up. There was another strobe-like flash, this time from behind the parked Juke. The window frame erupted inward, black holes punching into the wall on the other side of the bedroom.

Elliot jumped aside, triggering the shotgun. It bucked in his grasp; the *boom* in the confined space was deafening, but his aim wasn't far off.

When he risked looking again, he'd hit the Juke's nearside flank, pockmarking it with shot. The problem was that the submachine gun man had been sheltering on the offside. And he wasn't there now anyway; he was scuttling the remaining few yards to the house, unleashing automatic fire as he did. Downstairs, Susan's cries of alarm were drowned in the thunder of shooting but rose in intensity as slugs blasted through the front door.

Wafting at smoke and dust, Elliot blundered out onto the landing balcony. Downstairs, the gunfire ceased, and the silence was ear-shattering.

He staggered to the balustrade and looked down.

The front door still stood in its frame, but he could see where its locks and hinges had been shot through. Susan, meanwhile, was approaching it from the side, with the coffee table in her hands. Clearly, she intended to try and shore it up.

'Susan, get away from there!' he shouted.

White-faced with terror, the doctor glanced up at him – just as a heavy boot impacted on the door. It swung against her with maximum force, slamming into her head, dropping her in a lifeless heap.

Elliot raced to the top of the stairs.

But it was too late.

Before he was halfway down, both women lay unconscious and at the mercy of a figure in black combat fatigues, hefting a submachine gun.

'How you doing, Elliot?' Ray Lonnegan called up to him. 'Come on down and join the party.'

54

9 January (Thursday)

'Don't think about pulling that trigger, Ray,' Elliot said, descending the stairs, his shotgun levelled, its stock braced in the crook of his arm.

The intruder trained his weapon on Harri from near point-blank range. A grin split his sweaty face in two. 'Why's that, mate – you going to shoot me?'

'Only if you force me to.'

'Not supporting that twelve-bore the way you are. You'll shatter your humerus.'

Elliot halted on the bottom step. 'And blow your head off in the process.'

Lonnegan grinned all the more. 'You sure about that?' He still spoke with a northern accent, but it wasn't as harsh as previously. 'If that first shot was anything to go by, you'll more likely hit the fireplace.'

'From this range, even I can't miss.'

'And how about me? This is an H&K UMP .45 calibre. It fires six hundred rounds per minute. This lady'll be dead meat, and you know it. You all will.'

'That's going to happen anyway,' Elliot said. 'You can't afford to let us live. So why not drop it, eh? Before I get you first.'

Lonnegan tutted. 'You know, I was starting to like you,

Elliot. But now you're being dumb. All I want is the Red Book. So why not give it up? You're not going to sell it on yourself. You haven't got the contacts. So, hand it over, then we can all go home.'

'No chance.'

'Me and you were comrades, weren't we?'

'Hardly that.'

'Well, if nothing else we've got some talking to do – and this is no way. One of us slips, trips, gun goes off. I'll tell you what, mate, I'll go first.'

To Elliot's astonishment, Lonnegan lowered his sub-machine gun, bent down and placed it on the floor. When he straightened up again, his hands were empty.

Elliot stepped off the staircase and approached until he stood by the end of the couch. The shotgun remained level. 'I could blow you away so easily right now.'

'Why would you do that?'

'You tried to murder us on the A12.'

Lonnegan shrugged. 'I had no choice. I thought you had guard dogs. I took care of the first one – that fucking idiot, Iago, making it blatantly obvious he was following you in that blue Corsa. Do you know he almost got caught by a cop yesterday, when he was supposed to be watching your place?' He shook his head with disgust. 'Anyway, I slashed two of his tyres while he was waiting for you at the Three Pigeons. But the next thing I know, we're back on the road and now you've got a green Nissan Juke shadowing you. It wasn't as easy then. If you were going to have the Juke for company all the way to the drop-off, where was I going to bushwhack you? It had to be there and then, on the empty road.' He stuck a thumb towards Susan. 'I didn't realise it belonged to this lady here, of course. The main thing is none of this is personal.' He expanded his empty hands. 'I never kill anyone I don't need to. Come on, pal – at least lower the shotgun, take your finger off the trigger. One slip is all it takes.'

Reluctantly, Elliot lowered the shotgun. Lonnegan nodded and smiled. And in a blur of movement, reached behind his back and produced a Glock, levelling it one-handed. 'You total pillock, Elliot. Now let that cannon go.'

Elliot was staggered that he'd been duped so easily, but that speed of hand would have put Wyatt Earp to shame.

'I mean it,' Lonnegan advised. 'Just let it go. Don't try anything.'

The damp, pale face in front of Elliot was absolutely firm. The gloved fist pointing the pistol had done so many times. Elliot's hand flexed open and the shotgun fell to the floor.

'I still can't give you the Red Book,' he said. 'It got lost in the crash.'

Lonnegan looked at him long and hard, before backing across the room, reaching down and taking Susan by her left wrist, hauling her back over towards Elliot and Harri. When he released her, she lay close to the couch. He retreated again, pistol pointed.

'Is Susan okay?' Elliot asked. 'She took a hell of a whack.'

'That's the least of your problems.' Lonnegan glanced from Harri to her sister and back again. 'Which of these sleeping beauties gets it first, Elliot? Which is of least value to you?'

'For Christ's sake, Ray ...'

'No, for *your* sake, Elliot!' Lonnegan's voice was suddenly a whipcrack. 'For *your* fucking sake! Because you're about to lose the two most important people in your life ... and the order it happens in is your choice.'

'If I had the damn book, I'd give it to you willingly!'

'Is it possible you don't believe I'm going to do this? Think back to Soaker's Farm.'

'How could I forget that?'

'Who started the fight, Elliot?'

'*You* did. Who the fuck else?'

'Exactly. For no reason at all.'

'You said they were trying to outflank us. Not that I saw any sign of that.'

'You know why?' Lonnegan gave a crazy, fluting chuckle. 'Because I made it up.'

'You made it ...' Elliot was baffled. He'd assumed that Lonnegan had started that incident simply because he was a firecracker, a bad-tempered lunatic who couldn't handle confrontation. Now, a different story was unfolding. 'You wanted the Red Book so much?' he said slowly. 'So much ... that you *deliberately* picked a fight with the Scissorman?'

'Well, duh!' Lonnegan chuckled again. 'Soon as I learned what the book contained – courtesy of you, I have to say – there was no other option. We might well have had trouble anyway, but from that moment on I knew I had to engineer it, just to be sure there was no deal. I had to leave the Scissorman's teammates dead so that the Naboths, who talk big but are essentially a pair of small-time tosspots, would go back to the Corporation simpering, offering the book for free.'

'How did you know I'd be the delivery boy?' Elliot asked.

'I didn't. But I knew that whoever it was, he'd receive his orders and collect the package at the Raceway because he'd also need an untraceable car.'

'You were hidden at the Raceway?'

'Why would I need to be, Elliot? You know I have a

history in clandestine ops. You know I have weapons, kit, tech…'

'You bugged the place?' Elliot didn't know whether to be impressed or appalled. 'You went to all that trouble, used all that expertise… just to pinch a list of London grasses?'

'That list is worth a shitload of money.'

'What if the Corporation had made a copy of it?'

'Even if they did, which I doubt,' Lonnegan said, 'it's in hand-scribbled hieroglyphics, which it'd take a genius several years to decipher in full. The main value of the Red Book to the Corporation is that as long as it sits in their vault, their treaty with the Organised Crime Division stands and their businesses go on. The coppers want the treaty intact too, because while it is, their legion of informers doesn't get wiped out.'

'But surely they won't pay you so much that it'd be worth you turning both the Naboths *and* the Corporation against you? No amount of money is worth that.'

'Truly spoken like someone who's never been short of cash.'

'Hang on, whoa…' Elliot still didn't buy this. Particularly as a new idea was now emerging from left field. An idea so outrageous that at first, he feared he'd make a fool of himself just voicing it. But he now looked at Lonnegan with new fascination. 'Is someone close to you on that list, Ray? Shit – are *you* on that list?'

Lonnegan's smile turned crooked.

'Christ almighty, you *are*, aren't you?'

'I'd stop right there, if I were you.'

'All this time I thought you were some hardcase enforcer… and yet you're just a grass.'

'Who do you think grasses are, Elliot? You think they're

all Ron Moody "Fagin" figures who can't abide being bad. We're as hard-nosed as they get, pal.'

'I should've seen it.' Oddly, Elliot felt angry as well as bemused. 'All that mouthy, hairy madman crap when we first met. That wasn't you at all, was it? That was a show for Jim and Jo. Deep down, you were way too sophisticated for them.'

Lonnegan shrugged. 'You need to be if you want to get paid from both ends. The Harwich blag – that was big money. So I kept that one to myself. But other, lesser jobs … easy enough to drop the miscreants in the shit and rake it in from the official reward or the grass fund. Sometimes I set the jobs up – found myself a bunch of fall guys who couldn't have organised a piss-up in a brewery on their own. The Organised Crime Division didn't mind. They still got the arrests. At some point I'd have given them Jim and Jo – when they were no longer any use to me.'

'And then the Red Book business came up?'

'Tell me where it is, Elliot, and you'll all survive this night.'

'Even with what I now know about you?'

'You certainly won't survive if you don't.'

'I honestly don't have it.'

Lonnegan was looking tired. 'Elliot, you know how much of a pro I am. Which means I'll do what it takes, even if it's something I'm not keen on. For example, I wasn't keen on killing your buddy, Nick.'

'You killed Nick?' Elliot hadn't wanted to hear his suspicion confirmed.

'It was *your* phone that led me to him.' Lonnegan's tone implied that this made it Elliot's fault. 'I overheard that message he left. Then there was that mysterious green Juke. His house wasn't too far away. Seemed like you'd been cooking something up with him.'

'But you know that isn't true.'

'I do now, but I didn't last Sunday night. So, I paid him a visit in the early hours of Monday. Nice pad, eh? Perfect spot for me to lie low in for a couple of days. Plus, Nick ... well, he held out under questioning. Looked like it was going to take me a bit of time anyway.'

'You fucking maniac!' Elliot's voice trembled with rage.

'Cut me some slack,' Lonnegan said. 'It soon clicked that I wasn't getting anywhere. So, then I had to go back to the hospital to find you two ...'

'You didn't need to kill him.'

'Didn't plan to. But he tried to escape.' Lonnegan mused on this. 'Didn't like having to keep leaving him tied up while I was at the hospital. I mean, he was in a bad way by then, but there was always a chance he might get loose ...'

'*You fucking psycho!*' Elliot shouted.

Lonnegan shrugged. 'Turns out that was *exactly* what he was planning. Idiot thing to do really. I was ready to leave. I'd been there three days by then. We kept getting calls. I'd made him email a sick note to work the first day, delete his social media – all that, but other folk kept ringing up. Friends, I guess. Wanting to know this, that and the other. I knew I couldn't ignore those calls forever. Someone'd get worried. Then I ran into the coppers, and I could tell they were suspicious. It was time to cut out, but that very morning he tried to do a runner ... I had no choice but to pop him.'

'Is that what you'll be telling yourself the rest of your life?' Elliot wondered. 'That you couldn't have taken down a guy who was so hurt that he probably couldn't walk straight without using lethal force?'

Lonnegan gazed at him. 'Truth is, Elliot, I can act all tough about it. But you never get used to killing.' His smile had evaporated. 'It haunts a man, tortures him. So I've tried, whenever possible, not to kill. And yet twice now, *you've* lured me into situations where I had to do it ... so, you see, there are all sorts of reasons why I should pull the trigger on you and your loved ones. But you can still change that ... by handing over the Red fucking Book.'

Elliot said nothing else, merely glared.

'Seriously?' Lonnegan looked amazed. 'After everything I've just told you?'

He shook his head again, and without further warning, moved his aim away from Elliot, down to Harri, cocking the pistol. And with a scream, Susan catapulted herself up from where she lay, trying to grapple with him, trying to wrench the weapon away.

How long she'd been playing dead was anyone's guess. Probably not long; all she'd needed was sufficient time to hear his threat and see what he intended to do. For his part, an attack from below was the one thing Lonnegan had not been expecting. Even so, the woman was directly in front of him as they wrestled, the muzzle of his Glock jammed against her breastbone when it detonated.

The thundering gunshot was almost entirely absorbed by her body even though she was flung back with jackhammer force. But the determination with which she'd attacked him had taken him by surprise. He tottered, off-balance.

Elliot flung himself forward. The two of them collided, and though Elliot was the less athletic, he was larger and heavier, his sheer weight slamming Lonnegan down onto the stone-flagged floor, driving the wind from his lungs. Two things then happened simultaneously: as Elliot rolled to get away, he kicked the UMP, and it clattered off into the tight black recess beneath the Welsh dresser; at the same time, the Glock was knocked from Lonnegan's grasp.

For a couple of seconds, neither was armed.

Elliot scrambled on all fours towards the shotgun. He grabbed it and spun around on his knees. But everything was happening so quickly. He still expected the winded Lonnegan to be on the floor. Instead, the ex-para was already up. He'd retrieved his pistol, and now dived behind one of the armchairs.

Elliot fired. The *BOOM* was ear-pummelling, and it blew out a wad of springs and stuffing from the chair's backrest, though he couldn't see if Lonnegan had been hit. Frantic, Elliot slung the gun over his shoulder by its strap, and jumped up, grabbing Harri in both arms.

She'd shrunken to skin and bones over the last week but was still an awkward bundle in her blankets and padding. With the strength of the desperate, he turned first towards the half-open front door – only to realise that this wouldn't work. He'd have to cross the room to get to it, having to pass the armchair behind which Lonnegan was still concealed. Instead, he thudded his way up the staircase, the lampstand flying free behind him, the intravenous drip yanking loose from Harri's arm.

He was three-quarters of the way up when a pistol shot sounded, and a spindle was blown out just behind him. He made it onto the landing, dizzied by sheer effort. Another shot was fired, and a chunk was kicked out of the balustrade. The first room they came to was the one where Elliot had been shot at before. He blundered back in, backheeling the door closed behind them. Dumping Harri on the bed, he twirled around, looking for anything he could use as a barricade. Another shot rang out, and a fist-sized gap exploded in the door's top right corner.

Elliot grabbed a sideboard and tried to heft it away from the wall. It was hellishly heavy, its feet dragging along a dusty carpet into which they'd all but buried themselves. Again, his reserves were boosted by the strength of terror, and he managed to jam it end-on against the door, before ducking down – just as another couple of shots punched through. He glanced around. Even in the darkness, he could see Harri moving, moaning softly. He scrambled upright again, scooped her in both arms and lowered her down on the other side of the bed. Panting, dripping sweat, he crouched alongside her, trying to tear a strip from her own blankets so that he could bind her wrist, which was pumping out blood from where the drip had been freed.

Beyond the bedroom door, boots clumped up the stairs.

Elliot froze.

They continued along the landing, but now slowed from a run to a walk. Lonnegan was being cautious. He clearly didn't know how much ammo Elliot had left.

When they were very close, the footfalls fell silent.

'Nice move, Elliot.' Lonnegan's voice carried through the punctured woodwork. 'But this lass downstairs ... she's dying a slow death. You want to leave her, while you two hide up here? For an ex-Grand Prix superstar, it's not a good look.'

Elliot's brow was spangled with sweat, the breath wheezing from his aching chest, his head pounding. He was a long way from fitness. But it was true; he hadn't thought about Susan.

'Hey listen,' Lonnegan said. 'If you don't give a shit about her, perhaps you're more concerned about yourself. You think you're safe? You think that door'll keep me out? Good joke, Elliot. You see, I'm going to go downstairs now, and somehow or other I'm going to move that big chunk of furniture and I'll fetch my UMP up here, and then there'll be nothing left of this door but splinters, do you hear me? And nothing left of the room behind it either.'

'Approach this door, Ray, and I'll blow you in half.'

'You really think you're going to sell the Red Book? You haven't got a fucking clue, pal. The Corporation'll suss you, and then they won't just kill you and Harri – they'll kill everyone you love, everyone you like, everyone you fucking know. And it won't be the Scissorman this time ... oh no. That was the easy way out. That was just for grasses. With you, it's going to be worse. Because you've not just stolen from them, you've stolen from them *twice*. Telling you, pal ... it's going to be nutcrackers, meat-grinders, blowtorches.'

All through this monologue, Elliot had been tying off the linen strip around Harri's arm. Now, he loosened the empty shotgun from his shoulder. Loudly as he could, he cracked it open and snapped it closed again.

'Ah well,' Lonnegan said. 'You try to give a guy fair warning...'

Four shots were fired in rapid succession from an angle alongside the door rather than in front of it. The first double-tap smashed through the upper hinge on the top-left corner, and though Elliot couldn't see because the sideboard was in the way, the second one doubtless took care of the lower hinge.

'That thing'll come down now if I blow on it,' Lonnegan laughed.

Elliot raised the shotgun, useless though it was.

'So, imagine what's going to happen,' Lonnegan said, 'when I come back up here with...'

An engine rumbled, tyres crunching grit.

All noise and movement out on the landing ceased.

A pair of headlights travelled across the front of the cottage, briefly flooding each room.

The silence on the other side of the door was breathless, stunned.

Elliot then heard feet retreating along the landing towards the stairs.

He leapt up and staggered over to the shattered window, leaning out through it.

55

9 January (Thursday)

It was only as she parked in front of Bay View House that Lynda wished she'd managed to speak to Andy Kepler when she'd called him twenty minutes ago rather than leaving a voicemail.

She'd explained what she was doing and where she was going and had said that it was up to him whether or not he provided back-up. Though she'd expected that it would bring him here, to the outskirts of Aldeburgh, it wouldn't perhaps have done so at astonishing speed. And there lay the problem. Because now that she was here alone, it didn't seem like a good idea. Not least because although the front door to the house stood ajar, it also hung lopsided as if damaged, and as she approached it, distinct patterns of bullet holes became visible in its surface.

When she halted, she was five yards short of it, every nerve jangling.

'Detective!' cried a frantic voice overhead. Lynda glanced up and, to her bemusement, saw Elliot Wade leaning out through a broken window. 'Lonnegan's coming down!' he shouted. Even as Lynda heard this, a rumble of feet descended a stairway inside. 'He's armed and he's going to kill you! Take this!'

Wade lowered some lengthy object towards her, which

she was astonished to see was a shotgun. He held it by the tips of its barrels, so that when he released it, it only dropped four or five feet before she caught it.

As she did, a figure appeared in the entrance.

Lynda levelled the weapon, finger hooked on the trigger.

Lonnegan skidded to a standstill, astounded. He had a pistol in his right hand, but it was up by his shoulder, as if he'd literally been about to swing it onto a target. Now it froze there.

'*Police officer!*' Lynda shouted. '*Drop it!*'

Lonnegan's eyes protruded in angry disbelief. Then his mouth twisted into a strange little smile. 'You again.'

'I said, drop it!'

'You know, you girls really need to get back in the kitchen.'

'I'm back in the kitchen every sodding night, thank you very much ... after I've done a hard day's work chasing scumbags like you.'

His smile became a sneer. 'You think that *saying* you're a copper means you actually are?'

'Yeah, I'm such a fake that I've only managed to catch you twice in one day.'

'You're not going to shoot me. You know why, darling, and no disrespect intended, this is a simple statement of fact – you haven't got the balls.'

'*Drop – the – gun!*'

'Why should I?' he laughed, and still he hadn't relinquished his weapon.

'Because you're under arrest for the murder of Nick Scotzini, escaping from lawful custody and assaulting police officers – and that's just for starters.'

With infinitesimal slowness, he began to bring his weapon around.

'Don't you do it.' She raised the shotgun so that it was trained on his face.

'No – don't *you* do it.' His gun was still coming around.

'You move that gun one more inch, I'll shoot.'

'Oh, dear … it's still moving.'

'*Don't make me do it, Lonnegan!*'

But now she saw the black hole of his muzzle. What could she do? She'd rarely handled a firearm, let alone shot anyone before.

Lonnegan laughed again, wildly, crazily …

56

9 January (Thursday)

It was the most satisfying thing Elliot had done since finishing ahead of Lewis Hamilton in Shanghai in 2009, the heavy brass lampstand whistling down in an arc, impacting on Ray Lonnegan's cranium with such force that it bent clean over. The guy went out like a candle, collapsed into a crumpled heap of meat and bone, his pistol clattering away.

The police detective outside was a Sergeant Hagen, or so Elliot thought; he remembered watching her from the corner of his eye in hospital, and Nurse Abimbola telling him her name afterwards. She currently stood hefting the shotgun, wide-eyed, shaking. Elliot stepped out of the house and over the body.

'Sorry, but I had to do that.' He kicked the pistol across the drive. 'That shotgun's no use. It's not even loaded.'

She gazed dumbly at the weapon. 'I thought...'

'This is Ray Lonnegan.' Elliot dropped the lampstand and squatted alongside the fallen figure. 'He's a gangster and a murderer.'

'I...' The policewoman was still tongue-tied, fuddled by the whirlwind of events. 'I... I know that.'

'We need some handcuffs. Do you have any?'

'Handcuffs?'

Blood seeped through Lonnegan's close-cropped, dyed-blond hair, but when Elliot put his fingers to the guy's neck, the pulse was strong. 'Quickly! He's only stunned!'

'Yeah, handcuffs.' Coming jerkily to life, Hagen turned, laying the shotgun down first. 'I have some spares in my car.'

She blundered to the Qashqai, leaning in and fumbling in the glove compartment.

'We've got to get this thing moving!' Elliot shouted after her. 'We've got a gunshot victim inside.'

Hagen was already on her way back with cuffs in hand. She looked worried by that. 'Who's been shot?'

'My wife's sister. Her name's Susan Clarkwell. You'll have to hurry. I think it's bad.'

Hagen hunkered down, crossed Lonnegan's wrists behind his back and cuffed them together. After that, Elliot led her indoors. They were both rushing, but the policewoman came to a halt at the sight of the partially wrecked room, and in the middle of it, Susan Clarkwell lying motionless, a visible hole torn through her middle, a crimson pool underneath her.

'Where's the other girl?' Hagen said tightly.

'She's upstairs. I'll get her.'

As the detective attended the prone figure, Elliot mounted the stairs three treads at a time. He'd fleetingly felt empowered by his defeat of Ray Lonnegan, though now the cost of that win was coming home to him. At least it looked as if Susan was alive, the policewoman kneeling next to her, her ear to the doctor's mouth.

He turned into the bedroom, edging past the sideboard.

Harri was still curled in her swaddle of blankets. Her lids fluttered on eyeballs now glazed and red-rimmed. She was beaded with sweat and mumbled something incoherent as he leaned down and scooped her up. As he descended the stairs, he glanced over the bullet-scarred banister, and saw Sergeant Hagen sitting on the couch. Her jeans and anorak were smeared with blood.

Grey-faced, she looked up at him and shook her head. 'I'm very sorry.'

Elliot stumbled to a halt. 'She's dead?'

A slight incline of the policewoman's head served as a nod.

He stared incredulously at the body. Susan's eyes were closed. She'd have looked serene, as if sleeping, had all colour not drained out of her.

'Did... did she say anything?' he asked.

Hagen stood up stiffly. 'She named Ray Lonnegan as her murderer.'

'Anything else?' Elliot asked; he'd have probably cried had he not been so fraught. 'Nothing for Harri?'

'She said to tell Harriet that she loved her and that she was very sorry for everything.'

Elliot stood rigid. His own pain, which had withdrawn to the back of his skull during these frantic proceedings, flooded his head again, making him feel weak, giddy.

'I'll tell... I'll tell her that,' he said. 'But we need to get her to a hospital first.'

'We will,' the policewoman replied. 'But also, you need to tell me what happened here.'

He told her as they walked, quickly and in no particular order, trying to cram in every detail of the events that had occurred since he'd taken Harri from the hospital.

Outside, Hagen nudged Lonnegan with her toe, and he moaned.

'This lunatic's almost back with us.' Now that the shock

was fading, she was regaining control, turning into a cop again. She glanced around, spotted his pistol and went to pick it up. Pointing it at the ground, she examined it, locating the safety catch and switching it on. 'Put Harriet in the Juke,' she said. '*You'll* need to take her to hospital. Before you go, I need some help with this fella.'

Elliot stumbled to the Juke, which was showing damage, though as it was mainly bodywork, ought to be driveable. Heaving Harri to his shoulder, he opened the front passenger door, brushed the fragmented glass from its seat, and lowered her into it, belting her into place. When he got back over to Hagen, she'd half lifted Lonnegan to his feet. He'd come around, but was woozy, his dyed hair matted with gore, blood drying down the middle of his face.

'We put this guy in the front passenger seat too,' Hagen said. 'My car.'

Together, they manhandled Lonnegan to the Qashqai and pushed him inside bottom-first. With his hands cuffed behind his back, he didn't sit comfortably.

Hagen didn't care. 'Here.' She offered Elliot the pistol, knocking the safety off.

Puzzled, he took its handgrip, but she didn't initially release it. She locked eyes with him. 'Don't think about trying anything stupid, Wade. There's been enough stupidity here to last us a lifetime.'

'Okay, but what do you want me to do with it?'

'Point it at Lonnegan so that he doesn't misbehave.'

Elliot trained the weapon on the prisoner with both his hands. 'And if he does?'

'Blow his brains out.' She leaned in through the open door. 'You hear that, Ray? I've given this man permission to shoot if you try anything.'

Lonnegan slurred something incomprehensible.

Hagen opened the glove box again, dug inside and produced a small key. 'Lean forward.'

Groggy as hell, Lonnegan complied, the wound on top of his scalp glistening red.

Now Elliot understood. The detective had to reach around to the back of the prisoner and unfasten the left-hand cuff. It would be the perfect time for the bastard to try something, in which case he'd buy a bullet – there was no question about that in Elliot's mind. He even closed in until the Glock's muzzle was less than an inch from the guy's temple.

But Lonnegan was in no condition to make things happen.

Dazedly, he allowed Hagen to lift his hand to the handle fixture in the ceiling, loop the spare cuff through it, and then lift his right hand, locking his wrists back together. It wouldn't be the ideal way to transport a prisoner, or the most humane, but Hagen was going to be alone with him, so it would have to serve.

'I'll take that,' she now said.

Elliot restored the safety and placed the Glock in her palm. She slid it into her anorak.

'Be careful anyway,' Elliot said. 'He's one of the names in that Red Book, so he's not going to give this thing up easily.'

Hagen glanced around, startled. 'Lonnegan's in the Red Book?'

Elliot nodded. 'He told me that, himself. He's a grass for the Organised Crime Division.'

'I'll be a ...' At first, she looked startled by this, but it didn't last for long. 'Okay. In that case it's even more important that we get him locked up. The nearest police station with a holding facility is Martlesham. So, that's where *I'm* headed. You get Harriet to hospital as planned.'

'And what if I don't? What if I just take off?'

She shrugged. 'To where? Who've you got left to protect you, Elliot, if not us?'

Elliot was intrigued. 'Are we talking some kind of witness protection deal?'

She gave him a frank stare. 'That's up to you.'

His head sagged down as he tried to think it through. Hagen was right. There was nowhere they could go where they'd be safe. The original plan they'd put together with Susan would only have worked if they'd had possession of the Red Book, and even then, it would have been high risk. They didn't even have any money.

Right now, a life of suburban anonymity under assumed names seemed well worth the small price of having to help this police officer with her enquiries.

There was one problem, however.

He shook his head. 'We've nothing to trade. The Red Book's gone astray, and we've nothing else to offer you.'

Hagen eyed him sceptically. 'How about a certain armed robbery in Harwich last Christmas Eve?'

'I ... erm, I don't ...'

'Let's start this thing the way we mean to go on, Elliot,' she said, 'by being truthful. Now, I suspect you only had a peripheral involvement, but that'll still be enough to send you down for years, on top of any offences you've committed during all this palaver. So, my question to you is simple: can you give us the team who pulled the blag?'

Elliot didn't have to ponder this question for long. It wouldn't be pleasant standing up in court, naming names while the owners of those names sat in the dock and watched him. But how much lower could his standing in the underworld be than it was right now?

'Yeah ... I can give you the team,' he said. 'Or the main ones.'

'Good enough.'

'But you've got the power to make this deal on your own – a detective sergeant?'

'No. Initially, you're going to have to trust me. Which hospital are you taking Harriet to?'

'I don't know if there's any unit around here that can deal with her injuries. So probably back to Colchester. It's only forty miles.'

'Okay. Take her straight to Neurological Sciences, and then wait. Okay, Elliot? *You wait!* I'm going to arrange for other police officers to meet you there. In the first instance, it's going to be a Detective Inspector Rachel Hollindrake. You understand me so far?'

'Hollindrake, okay.'

'Tell her *everything*.' She peered at him. 'Do you understand, Elliot? Not just about the Harwich blag, but everything else that's happened since. You follow me? *Everything*.'

'Yeah, I get you.'

'Okay, now go. Your wife's ill.'

57

9 January (Thursday)

'I'll say this for you, Lynda ... you don't do things by halves.'

It was a surprisingly affable response from Rachel Hollindrake given that it was after ten o'clock at night when Lynda Hagen had rung her, and that she'd now spent fifteen minutes sitting through an account of what sounded like the most outlandish police shift in law-enforcement history.

'You sure this is all kosher?' the DI asked.

Lynda traipsed back across the downstairs at Bay View House, halting by the body of Susan Clarkwell. It was never a pleasant aspect of crime-scene management, but that was where the victim must remain. Necessary procedures would commence as soon as practicable, and once it was no longer needed here, the body would be removed with all due reverence.

'It's kosher,' Lynda confirmed, 'but it isn't going to count for anything if we don't get someone down to that hospital to take charge of Elliot Wade.'

There was a long, pensive silence. 'I'll make some phone calls. You really think he's going to talk, because we'll be going out on a limb if we make this happen?'

'He'll talk, Rachel. He hasn't got any other choice.'

'Okay ... and Lonnegan is a clean arrest?'

'No problem whatsoever with that; we've got him banged

to rights,' Lynda replied, walking out to the Qashqai, inside of which the prisoner's hands were still shackled above his head.

'Okay, well, I'll get things moving while I'm on my way to Colchester General.' Hollindrake yawned as she said this. Lynda knew that the DI often turned in early on weeknights and could picture her lanky figure stumping up the stairs of her house to change out of her pyjamas. 'Just out of interest, where's Kepler at the moment?'

'If he got my message from earlier, he should be on his way now. In case he contacts you, there were two firearms here that I was aware of. But I've had to remove them both for safety reasons. I can't hang around, Rachel … I've got to get this suspect to Martlesham nick.'

'Okay, right. I'd say good work, but this sounds like one hell of a mess and an absolute shedload of paper.' Hollindrake cut the call.

'You don't know the half of it,' Lynda told the empty airwaves.

Pocketing her phone, she turned back to the front entrance. The door hung sideways and was riddled with bullet holes. There was no way to bar it. She headed to the car. It went against every inch of her training to leave a crime scene insecure, especially with a body lying in situ, but the longer she dallied here, the more Lonnegan would regain his strength and the more determined he'd be to get loose. On top of that, Kepler ought to be here soon, and she didn't want to meet him. Lonnegan was *his* grass, so how he'd react to seeing the guy in custody was anyone's guess.

She drew the Glock from her pocket as she climbed in on the driver's side. Lonnegan was fully conscious now, but slumped, his wrists still firmly manacled. He eyed her inscrutably from between streaks of dried blood.

'You see this?' She showed him the weapon. 'You'll note that I'm still wearing my gloves. So, whatever happens while we're driving, the only prints on it are going to be yours.'

He said nothing.

'You mess around while we're on the road, Ray – try to kick me, try to get free, and I won't hesitate to plug you. You know why? Because I'm not going the same way as all these others who've fallen into your path. My kids are going to see their mum again.'

He bared his teeth in a bloodstained half-smile, but it didn't reach his eyes, which he averted to the front. Lynda kept the pistol in her right hand, flat against her belly, while she used her left to pull her seatbelt into place, turn the engine on and put the car in gear. It rumbled to life, and she turned the wheel 180 degrees, spinning them off the lot.

They drove along the silent, tree-lined road. There was no further conversation between them, but it worried Lynda that Lonnegan seemed to be relaxing. It wasn't difficult to understand why. Elliot Wade might have had little to trade, but that was not the case with Ray Lonnegan. His word could see a lot of people out of a job.

But then his eyes widened, and he jerked upright as bright light flooded over them.

She jammed her brakes on so abruptly that they skidded for several yards.

The route ahead was blocked by a wall of glaring lights, a barricade of vehicles with their headlamps on full beam, to the immediate rear of which a blue beacon was swirling.

Lynda swore under her breath. 'Don't move, okay? Don't

even blink – I might just be able to persuade them that those bobbies you injured in Colchester were accidents.'

She flipped the Glock's safety catch on and slipped it into her anorak pocket. She could already make out the vague shapes behind the lights and had no doubt that a number of high-powered weapons were pointing their way. She also knew how jittery a police firearms team could be when called out late at night.

'Would've been a waste if you hadn't managed to get out of that stone box,' Lonnegan suddenly said, his voice croaky. 'You seem like one of the good ones.'

She turned to look at him. 'There are actually quite a lot of us.'

His smile half returned. 'Keep saying that. You might even start believing it.'

'Take my advice, Lonnegan – for your own good, keep it zipped from now on.'

He shrugged and slumped back into his shackles.

Cautious and steady, Lynda opened the driver's door and climbed into view, hands raised.

'I'm a police officer!' she shouted. There was no response from behind the bank of spotlights. 'I said I'm a police officer!' She approached warily, arms held aloft and wide apart, her open wallet dangling from her left hand to show her warrant card. 'Detective Sergeant Lynda Hagen, Essex Police. I have one prisoner in transit. Raymond Lonnegan. He's under arrest on suspicion of murder and is immobilised with handcuffs in the front passenger seat. We have two firearms. One, a shotgun, is unloaded and in the boot. The other, a Glock pistol, is in my coat pocket. It's loaded but it's been used in at least one murder and I've seized it as evidence.'

She continued to advance until she was about fifteen yards

from them, at which point she halted, not so much curious as bewildered. They hadn't issued a single command, ordering her neither to stand still, nor kneel nor lie on the ground.

She squinted to see through the intense glow. Car headlights for the most part, though perhaps a couple of handheld flashlights too, dark figures behind them, pointing rifles at her. She squinted harder, seeing no obvious sign of ballistics helmets or shields, chequer-banded caps or police insignia. Except for the single swirling light.

A steely *click* sounded in the night.

Lynda ran pell-mell for the foliage at the side of the road. She dived headlong into it, plunging through frosted, clawing twigs, icy snow exploding as she hit the ground, rolled and scrambled back to her knees. Panting, she gazed back through the leafless mesh, and was jolted with shock as a monumental barrage of gunfire opened up, drilling her Qashqai every which way, taking out the windshield, hammering the bonnet so that it flipped open and flew off, ripping up chunks of alloy and upholstery throughout the interior. Ray Lonnegan's dim form jerked and danced in his bonds as round after round struck his head and torso.

Lynda watched aghast, mind awhirl with thoughts that this couldn't be happening, that she was flashing back to a movie of some sort, but reality kicked in and she scurried forward on all fours, struggling through the last of the bushes before getting to her feet and running on into the deep-frozen woodland.

And not before time, as gunfire raked the coppice behind her.

She risked a wild glance back as she dashed. Saw gunflashes aimed in her direction, saw winter undergrowth shredded, shrubbery chopped, tree trunks smashing and splintering.

She threw herself down and rolled again. It knocked the wind from her, the frigid ground as hard as iron, bullets whistling above her. When she got up and ran a second time, now weaving between the heavier trees, slugs still rained after her, ploughing up divots of soil, tearing the bark from the larger trunks.

She took refuge behind an immense oak, crushing herself against it, her body drenched with sweat. The gunfire ceased, but initially she couldn't get her breath. Her thoughts spun. Any moment, she expected to hear crunching footfalls, to see the slashing spears of handheld torches, to hear more metallic *clicks*.

But it didn't happen.

The seconds became minutes.

Lynda tried to steady herself so that she could hear something beyond the juddering of her own heart. But the night lay silent.

After what seemed the longest time, she risked a peek backward.

Darkness had returned, reducing the wood to a shadowy realm of monolithic uprights and leafless bushes. She couldn't even see the headlights on the road, which was no more than a hundred yards away.

Numbed and nauseated, she slumped onto the ground.

From somewhere in the near distance, sirens approached.

58

9 January (Thursday)

Several unmarked police cars had arrived, all of them showing blue lights and blaring out sirens. On sighting Lynda's
gunfire-riddled Qashqai, they slowed to a halt one behind
the other, their sirens deactivating. Almost certainly, they
belonged to the Organised Crime Division. The foremost
of them, a maroon Jaguar that Lynda had last seen on
Westcombe Close, braked and halted a couple of yards from
the wreck. A number of Scotland Yard detectives spilled
out and approached, though none passed the Jag, out of
which DSU Kepler now emerged. There was no air of panic
considering that a vehicle certified for use in police operations was sitting in front of them blown apart from stem to
stern, or that a vague human outline, drenched ruby-red, was
slumped in the front passenger seat.

But then Lynda was on full view at the side of the road.
Safe. Arms tightly folded.

Kepler came to her first, buttoning his overcoat, pulling
on his gloves. To his credit, he looked a little shocked by the
condition of the Qashqai.

'Thank God you're all right,' he said.

She arched an eyebrow. 'Well, it's no thanks to *you*, that's
for sure.'

He feigned bewilderment. 'I don't know what you're talking about.'

'Don't worry, sir. The main target got taken down.'

Kepler walked to the Qashqai's passenger door but didn't need to lean in too far.

'Nasty, eh?' she said.

He straightened up again. 'It's never advisable to mess with the Corporation.'

'You knew they'd send a team here, didn't you?' she said accusingly. 'You knew that full well – which is why you facilitated it.'

Again, he feigned puzzlement. 'I didn't facilitate anything.'

'Just like you knew Lonnegan had no choice but to recover the Red Book. Just like you knew the Corporation couldn't possibly allow him to keep it because you'd told them he'd destroy it rather than return it to them. Which is why you tipped them off about where he was going to be.'

He snorted, as though amused. 'Me? Tip off some gangster vermin? You've lost the plot, darling.'

'You *must* have,' Lynda insisted. 'No one else knew he'd come down here. And you only knew because I left you a message.'

'The Corporation could have found out by other means.'

'Either way, it's solved one of your problems. Dead men telling no tales and all that.'

He shrugged, as if this was an unlooked-for bonus.

'Why didn't you identify Lonnegan as an Organised Crime Division grass?' she asked.

'Maybe because the relationship was confidential.'

'Oh, so he *was* a grass?' She chuckled. 'I was told that second-hand, but thanks for confirming it.'

Kepler looked irritated by his misstep but maintained an

air of calm. One glance over his shoulder was sufficient to reassure him that no one else was in earshot.

'Make that accusation all you want, Lynda,' he said quietly, 'but you'll never find proof.'

'I've no doubt of that. You won't want it getting out that you've been using informers who were also blaggers and murderers.'

'On the subject of the Harwich blag,' he said, 'I understand that you've initiated some action via DI Hollindrake?'

'That's correct, sir. One of *my* informers is going to deliver the team that did it.'

'I see.' He looked away, his gaze distant. 'And while you were putting DI Hollindrake in the picture, did you happen to mention what you think you know about Organised Crime Division personnel aiding Lonnegan's escape from Essex Police custody?'

'What I *think* I know?' She laughed. 'You mean we're now pretending it didn't happen?'

'Because, you see, I've been in touch with DS Terry Sullivan to get his take. Seems he was at the other end of the country when that custody break happened.'

'And I assume he's got lots of witnesses to corroborate that story?'

'Of course. We like to be thorough.'

'The subject may still come up,' Lynda said, hating herself for this but hardened enough by the events of the last few days to know when *not* to push her luck. 'Those two officers who got hurt know what they saw. But Lonnegan's not going to say anything. My informant doesn't know anything about that escape. And, well, Terry Sullivan and I have mutual friends, so let's just say that no one's going to hear it from me.'

Still looking away, Kepler nodded.

'In return for which...' Lynda said, in a voice only half dripping with sarcasm, 'I'll have at least a couple of those promotions that you said you couldn't organise. And those masonic connections who you hinted might impede my husband's writing career can now ensure that it soars.'

Kepler smiled thinly.

'There's one other problem,' she said. 'And this one is out of my hands. No one may ever learn that you guys engineered Ray Lonnegan's escape, but it may still emerge that he was your grass because the Red Book has yet to surface.'

For the first time, Kepler looked shocked. 'I thought...'

'Elliot Wade doesn't have it. He lost it during the crash. So Lonnegan didn't manage to retrieve it, despite his very best efforts.'

Kepler's shock turned quickly to anger. 'Wade's lying. No one else had access to it.'

'If he is, he stood there and let Lonnegan shoot his sister-in-law and still didn't hand it over.'

'*Fuck!*' Kepler said, his eyes wide with alarm. He walked back and forth. '*Wade! It must be Wade ... he has to have it ...*'

'Sir, Elliot Wade is not some hard-boiled tough guy. And he knew Lonnegan was the real deal. He'd have given the book up once his wife was threatened. Besides, by now he'll be in protective custody. He's giving us the Harwich blaggers. You going to go blundering into that with your size twelves?'

He turned and barked frantic orders to his Organised Crime Division men, who leaped into their cars and gunned them to life, swerving around the Qashqai in their haste to get to Bay View before Suffolk turned up and treated it like a real crime scene.

'I trust you've taught them not to leave their prints everywhere?' Lynda said.

'Don't try to be clever, DS Hagen.' He signalled his Jaguar, which eased forward, the front passenger door swinging open. 'As long as that Red Book's astray, we're in limbo.'

'Why?' she asked. 'It means the Corporation can't kill any of your informers. It also means you won't have to keep bowing and scraping to the bastards.'

'And like you said, when it resurfaces – what happens then?'

She shrugged. 'I guess you're going to have a stressful time wondering about that.'

He scowled at her, before climbing into the car and slamming the door.

59

10 January (Friday)

Lynda went into the lounge that morning expecting to find the usual state of disorder, but it was tidy, tidier that it had been the previous night when she'd left Kepler handcuffed to the radiator pipe. Hearing movement, and smelling something pleasant, she ventured through to the kitchen, and was amazed to see Don cooking bacon and scrambled eggs, and slurping from a large mug of coffee.

This was a first in quite a while, given that it wasn't seven o'clock yet.

'You're up early,' she said.

He half jumped. 'Whoa, sorry, babe. Didn't see you there. Erm, yeah. Thought I'd try and get back to the world. Got an email from Abby last night. Those changes I made have hit paydirt. Barry Harvey's made me an offer. Fortress are going to take *Nick 'Em*.'

Not atypically, he hadn't enquired how things had gone for her, even though he'd known that she'd been chasing a dangerous lead. The fact that she'd cleaned up before there was any chance her kids saw her, showering and donning a tracksuit, a clean pair of trainers and a fresh anorak, was probably partly responsible.

'That's wonderful,' she said. 'Congratulations.'

'It's only a two-grand advance. But it's a start.' He shovelled his eggs onto a slice of toast and laid several strips of streaky bacon over the top. 'Oh sorry, I've not made *you* anything. I wasn't sure what time you'd be in.' He walked into the lounge, adding rather reluctantly, 'You can have this, if you want? I can make another.'

'It's okay,' she said, following him. 'I'll get something after I've sorted the kids out.'

'I had a phone call this morning,' he said, sitting down.

'Yeah?'

'From Dave Mackeson.'

'Your old super at Major Investigations?'

'Correct.' He smiled. 'Sounds like the entire machine was put in motion last night because of you.'

She shook her head. 'I was in the right place at the right time.'

'That's not what I was told. Dave says he won't be surprised if you get a commendation.'

'Even *I* haven't heard that yet.'

'All these years I've been giving you a hard time for not being the real McCoy, and then look. Last night in here, for example. That was a right caper. Never knew you had it in you.'

'I wouldn't have been able to pull that off without you,' she said. She could have said 'without your constant provocation', but didn't. It would have been true, but then it was also true that Don had helped her, at no small risk to himself. 'I only hope there's no comeback for you after that.'

'I can't imagine your man Kepler wants it proclaimed from the rooftops that he's been springing murder suspects out of custody.'

'No, that's certainly true.'

'Plus, I *did* try to help him get out of his cuffs. It just took ages to find the right tools in the shed.'

'Sorry I dropped you in it last night, Don.'

'Nice to still have a role to play.'

Lynda couldn't help loving that. Only someone like Don would have viewed a 'black op' like that in such terms. A more straitlaced copper would've had a problem from the start. Clive Atkins would have run a mile.

'Not that everything's resolved,' she said. 'But we've solved the A12 mystery, not to mention the murder of Nick Scotzini – and a woman called Susan Clarkwell, I'm sorry to say. The real bonus though, at least as far as Major Investigations are concerned, is that we've been locking up several suspects for that Christmas Eve heist in Harwich.'

Don laid his fork down. 'You're joking!'

'Jim and Josephine Naboth. Those names ring a bell?'

'*Bloody right!* Someone's finally banged Les Naboth's old firm up, eh? And *you* were involved?'

'I provided the intel.'

He hooted with laughter.

'They were arrested an hour ago at Dover,' she said. 'Minutes before they had a chance to skip the country.'

Don laughed again. 'I hope you were telling the truth when you said I'd get first dibs on writing all this up.'

'We'll have to wait till it's been dealt with by the courts. And that's going to be a ball-acher. There're lots of loose ends to tie.' She eyed him sideways. 'A lot of stuff we'll have to bury.'

He shrugged. 'So goes it. Lots has changed about the job, Lynda, but not that. You can't always fight these enemies of society on fair and even terms.'

Lynda didn't know what to think about that. So often at

functions, she'd cringed at Don's drunken stories of corners cut and rules bent. But no one could argue that on this occasion at least, results hadn't been achieved.

When Don went to wake Charlie and Daniella, Lynda stepped out into the back garden.

It was a beautiful morning, the silver eye of the sun winking over the frosted rooftops, the sky a pale, washed-out blue. It was bitterly cold, of course, the grass white and stiff, clumps of frozen snow dotting the rockery.

Next to the shed, there was a rusty wire-mesh basket on a tripod, the ashes in the bottom from last November, when they'd burned some autumn leaves. She brought it onto the grass and opened the shed. Its musty interior was floor-to-ceiling with junk, but there was also a stack of logs and kindling, a few sheets of dried-out newspaper, a bottle of lighter fluid and a box of stay-light matches.

She took them all outside, where she crammed the logs and kindling into the basket, scrunched some paper into balls, tucking them in at appropriate points, and doused the whole thing in accelerant. Suddenly self-conscious, she glanced back at the house. The children's bedroom curtains were still drawn, and she could hear muffled moaning as Don got them up.

Relaxing, she applied a match. The first chunk of ethanol-soaked newspaper caught immediately, and soon the kindling was alight, cracking and spitting.

Lynda warmed her hands.

There were certain events yesterday that she knew she'd never get over, even though she'd put on a brave face for Don. There was no question that from this point she'd have nightmares about stone sarcophagi, but even that had dwindled to near irrelevance compared to the events at Bay View House.

Lynda had crouched alongside dying people before, but fatal injuries incurred in road accidents were somehow less personal than those wilfully inflicted. Of course, as a police officer you had a duty not to let this kind of thing affect you, not while you were working; if *you* fell apart in the face of tragedy, who was there to take care of it? You had to be strong, you had to gird yourself for moments like that. And after a while, because you did it so often, it became second nature. If it screwed your head up later, that was your problem – and there was no point complaining because, shit, you chose this career.

Susan Clarkwell had been sufficiently compos mentis when Lynda knelt next to her to mutter that there was no hope, that she'd been wounded next to the heart; to also tell her, though only in a broken, feeble whisper, in a voice so faint that Lynda had needed to place her ear directly next to the grey, froth-slathered lips: '*This shooting ... killing. Too bad ... too dangerous ...*' Though her eyes were unfocused, though she'd flinched with every word, she'd pressed on, blood foaming from her mouth. '*Harri. She's not ... not wicked. She can't ... she can't blackmail ... these people ...*'

Her final words had not been as Lynda had reported them, namely that Susan loved her sister and was sorry for everything. That had been Lynda's own interpretation of the message. Instead, the doctor's ultimate dying words had referred to a stone on the blackened hearth. A stone that didn't appear to be loose until Lynda probed at it with her fingers. A stone she was able to waggle free, and then push back again afterwards.

The logs in the wire basket had now caught, a healthy blaze flaring up.

Lynda reached inside her anorak. It had been a nervy thing carrying the Red Book around all night, especially when she'd had to transfer it from the bloodstained anorak to a clean one, which had taken place in the locker room at the SCIU, where someone could easily have walked in. She opened it and flicked a few pages into it, amused by the unintelligible scribble. Not only was it in cipher, it was the worst handwriting she'd ever seen. Good luck to anyone who fancied trying to translate it. For all that, it was a good two hundred pages thick.

Who knew the Met had so many confidential informants? She shrugged, yawned. And dropped it into the flames.

One thing Lynda had been firm about as soon as she'd taken possession of the Red Book. The Organised Crime Division was not getting it back. But that was okay, because though they'd be sweating for a while, particularly Andy Kepler, now that it had gone for good they'd have full deniability that it had ever existed, and their blushes would ultimately be spared. On top of that, the Corporation wouldn't have it either and it was almost certain that they didn't have a copy. Otherwise why had they tried so hard to get the damn thing back? They'd be hurting for sure. They'd be furious that they'd lost such a great piece of leverage.

'Good,' Lynda said aloud.

Epilogue

'"A body found inside a barrel dumped in Deptford Creek, South London, has been identified as 43-year-old French-Canadian national, Jacques Marat, well known in underworld circles and believed to have connections to several gangland murders."'

Harri glanced up from the newspaper article she'd just quoted.

Elliot, in the armchair next to her, had been engrossed in a paperback. He looked around.

The private hospital room was the last word in cosiness: lemon-scented, wood-panelled and shag-pile carpeted, with its own en suite and vases full of daffodils on every flat surface. A floor-to-ceiling window gave a stunning view down a sweeping, sun-drenched lawn to a belt of pine trees running along the shore of Loch Tummel. Beyond them, the April breeze drove its sky-blue waters in line after line of advancing whitecaps.

But just for the moment, their attention was elsewhere.

Elliot sipped at his Diet Coke. Harri, who still wore a headscarf to cover her shaved scalp and the extensive scarring, but whose facial wounds were largely healed, sat back against the pile of pillows and skimmed the rest of the article.

'Sounds like his hands had been tied behind his back,' she

said. 'Cause of death was "a single, execution-style gunshot to the back of the skull".'

Elliot was thoughtful. 'Being reliable has its perks. You don't fail the Horsemen. But he'd done them good service previously. Guess that's why he got off lightly…'

Credits

Paul Finch and Orion Fiction would like to thank everyone at Orion who worked on the publication of *One Eye Open* in the UK.

Editorial
Emad Akhtar
Tom Witcomb
Lucy Frederick

Copy editor
Clare Wallis

Proof reader
Jon Appleton

Audio
Paul Stark
Amber Bates

Contracts
Anne Goddard
Paul Bulos
Jake Alderson

Design
Debbie Holmes
Joanna Ridley
Nick May

Editorial Management
Charlie Panayiotou
Jane Hughes
Alice Davis

Operations
Jo Jacobs
Sharon Willis
Lisa Pryde
Lucy Brem

Finance
Jasdip Nandra
Afeera Ahmed
Elizabeth Beaumont
Sue Baker

Production
Ruth Sharvell

Marketing
Helena Fouracre

Publicity
Francesca Pearce

Sales
Laura Fletcher
Jennifer Wilson
Esther Waters
Victoria Laws
Rachael Hum
Ellie Kyrke-Smith
Frances Doyle
Georgina Cutler

Rights
Susan Howe
Krystyna Kujawinska
Jessica Purdue
Richard King
Louise Henderson

Operations
Jo Jacobs
Sharon Willis
Lisa Pryde
Lucy Brem